Also by
SUZANNE ENOCH

A Devil in Scotland

SUZANNE ENOCH

St. Martin's Paperback

A DEVIL IN SCOTLAND

Copyright © 2018 by Suzanne Enoch.

All rights reserved.

For information address St. Martin's Press, 175 Fifth Avenue, New York, NY 10010.

ISBN: 978-1-250-09545-9

Our books may be purchased in bulk for promotional, educational, or business use. Please contact your local bookseller or the Macmillan Corporate and Premium Sales Department at 1-800-221-7945, ext. 5442, or by e-mail at MacmillanSpecialMarkets@macmillan.com.

Printed in the United States of America

St. Martin's Paperbacks edition / February 2018

St. Martin's Paperbacks are published by St. Martin's Press, 175 Fifth Avenue, New York, NY 10010.

10 9 8 7 6 5 4 3 2 1

For Karen Hawkins, Stephanie Laurens,
Victoria Alexander, Linda Needham,
and Susan Andersen—

I'm honored and humbled to be your friend,
if a little worried about your standards.
You guys are the best!!

Prologue

Inverness, Scotland, 1806

Becca would be in the morning room, most likely, because she didn't like fights. Callum MacCreath slammed the drawing room door in his brother's face and stomped down the straight-angled stairs to go find the one sane guest—and the one female—in MacCreath House tonight. Let the quartet of devils upstairs make their bargains and plan how to spend their riches. He wanted no part of it. None. Not when it involved choosing blunt over damned common sense.

Just the idea that his older brother Ian, Earl Geiry, would let himself be pulled into a scheme with someone as greedy and self-serving as the Duke of Dunncraigh surprised him. Horrified him, rather. Of course he felt like he'd been shot between the eyes, because he hadn't had the faintest idea about any of it. Aye, he could see some of the twenty-six-year-old's reasoning—the Mac-Creaths had intermarried with clan Maxwell for centuries, and Dunncraigh was *the* Maxwell, the clan's chief. Power sought power. Whether the MacCreaths *should* be standing so close to the duke was another question entirely. He knew the answer, drunk or sober. But Ian's sobriety hadn't kept him from being entangled in this disaster-in-the-making.

As for Callum, he had begun to wish several minutes ago that he hadn't come home tonight by way of the local tavern. Or that he hadn't come home at all.

But Rebecca Sanderson had been here all evening, apparently pulled into the middle of this nonsense without an ally in sight. That, he regretted. And if they'd pushed her into something she didn't want, he would see to it that it didn't happen. Period. Growling that pledge to himself, he stopped outside the closed morning room door. "Becca?" he called, trying to keep his voice level. He thudded his knuckles against the old, well-polished oak door. "Are ye hiding?"

"I do not hide," came from inside the room, in her cultured English accent. "You were all being loud and ridiculous, and so I left."

Callum didn't think *he* had been ridiculous, but that was neither here nor there. "I'm coming in, lass."

He pushed down on the door handle and stepped into the room. Rebecca Sanderson, the very English daughter of the very English George Sanderson who was still upstairs in the quartet of would-be business titans, stood close by the fireplace, her arms crossed over the deep blue silk gown that dripped with beads from the waist to the floor, her eyes of the same sapphire narrowed beneath a very artful tangle of blond hair as she looked up to gaze at him.

"I'm sorry I missed dinner," he said, shutting the door behind him again and turning the lock. He and Becca had known each other for ten years, since she'd been eight and he, ten, but tonight she looked far more . . . adult than he could previously recall. It unsettled him. The whole damned evening unsettled him, and the amount of whisky he'd consumed did nothing to help with that.

"I'm sorry you missed it, too," she said. "And I'm sorry you went out drinking, and I'm sorry you decided to stumble into the middle of this and accuse everyone of conspiring behind your back." She lifted her chin a little. "We—your brother—attempted to include you on several occasions, but you couldn't be bothered."

So now she was speaking on Ian's behalf. He wanted to grab hold of her bare shoulders, and clenched his hands to keep from doing so. "I'm fairly certain nae a one of ye mentioned that ye and my dull-as-dirt brother were contemplating getting married," he ground out, the words sticking in his throat. "I would have recalled that."

"Ian—Lord Geiry—was supposed to tell you a week ago. Evidently"—and she sent a pointed look at his rumpled black jacket and trousers—"you haven't been home in that long."

He looked down at his attire. Aye, Jamie Campbell had tossed up his accounts on the Hessian boots, and he might have spilled a bit of this or that on his sleeves, but the Seven Fathoms hardly had the strictest of dress codes. "I've been about," he hedged. "And why am I the villain here? I'm nae the one who's tried to drag ye into buying a marriage with a dowry of ships."

"No one's dragging me into anything," she said stiffly. "I would hope you know me better than that."

He did. And it comforted him a little. Perhaps it had all been talk and speculation, and nothing was settled. Nothing had been agreed to, and she remained no one's pawn. "Then I dunnae need to remind ye that ye've agreed with me fer years that the Duke of Dunncraigh cannae be trusted any farther than he can be thrown. Or that ye laughed when I said that if Ian had one more dinner with Dunncraigh, the duke would think him a pimple on his backside."

"It doesn't matter what we said before. You shouldn't jest about either of them, Callum. It's not seemly."

Callum edged closer to her, his jaw brushing the coiled blond hair at the top of her head as he leaned in. "What say we go down to the tavern, Becca, and leave the dusty brigade to rattle papers and pound their chests all on their own? I reckon they'll nae miss us."

Her cheeks darkened a shade. "You know I cannot," she commented, the proper English tones still sounding out of place this far north in the Highlands. "Ladies do not spend their evenings in taverns, especially in the company of young men with questionable reputations. And especially not under the circumstances."

"I dunnae care about the damned circumstances."

He spoke more fiercely than he meant to, and she backed away half a step. "They are what they are," she countered. "Profanity won't alter anything."

"I thought ye liked going down to the Seven Fathoms. If ye . . . Ye ken Ian will nae take ye down there. He's likely got cobwebs growing on him." And she most certainly did not, which was one of thousands of reasons Rebecca Sanderson and Ian MacCreath shouldn't even be talking about marriage. Now she and he—that made much more sense, now that it occurred to him. If he hadn't spent most of the past week—or year, really—at the Seven Fathoms, it might have occurred to him much earlier.

Blue eyes met his, then glanced away. "You shouldn't say such things," she insisted. "Your brother has a great deal of responsibility on his shoulders, and he carries it well for a man of only six-and-twenty."

"And he'll carry it just the same way when he's six-

and-sixty," Callum said dismissively. "Ye're nae but eighteen, and I'm nae but twenty, and I say we should spend the evening dancing reels in the Seven Fathoms, where the patrons at least have beating hearts and nae dust and rust settling in their bones. If the old men upstairs want to make poor business deals together, let 'em."

"Lord Geiry—Ian—isn't dull, Callum. Or old. And you shouldn't say such things about your own brother," she repeated, her voice sharp despite its low volume.

"Why the devil should I nae?" he returned, frowning. "We've both been saying the very same thing about him since yer da' moved ye up into the Highlands. The only thing Ian's ever done with us was go swimming in the loch, I reckon because that's the only thing he could ever beat me at."

"Callum, d—"

"Ye do recall on that first day we met when I dared ye to climb that oak tree, and Ian said ye'd break yer neck?" He flicked a finger along her throat, realizing with an odd . . . thud in his gut that he liked touching her. And not in the same way he'd boosted her into a saddle or helped haul her atop a stone wall to find bird's eggs. Why had he been spending so much time at the tavern, anyway? It had been weeks, or perhaps even months, since he'd last gone fishing—or dancing, or riding—with her. "Yer neck's nae broken."

She grimaced as she looked up at him. "I did scrape my knee. You shouldn't have dared me, and I certainly shouldn't have accepted. Your brother was correct. That doesn't make him dull. He's been trying very hard to ensure your family's safety and well-being into the future. You, on the other hand, smell of whisky and cheap perfume."

He ignored the last bit. That first part sounded far too . . . ordinary for the Becca he knew. "Ye've been in on these talks, then, have ye?" he asked. "Ye knew Ian wanted into the shipping company with yer da', and ye knew they meant to lease the docks from Dunncraigh, and ye nae said a word about it to me."

"You haven't been about, Callum," she retorted. "If you hadn't spent so much time half drowned in whisky and lightskirts you might have noticed. You're drunk now. Don't try to deny it."

Oh, he was drunk. Definitely. He could call it his armor to defend against his brother's nonsense, but it was becoming clear that he'd missed some fairly significant happenings. His heart abruptly twisted. Had he been too slow, too dismissive of what he perceived as nonsense? Had he waited too long? "It's true, isnae?" he prompted, bile rising in his throat with the words he didn't want to speak. "Ye've done it. They didnae try to force ye, because ye agreed to marry him. Ian, fer God's sake." He swallowed, willing the words away and not succeeding. "Why?"

Her shoulders lifted a little. "The silly things I did back when we were children embarrass me now. *You* embarrass me now. I was eight years old when I climbed that tree. I am not eight any longer." She eyed him. "And you're not ten." Rebecca took a breath. "You're not respectable, either, and you don't want to be. Your brother is. And I've known him forever, and he and my father have similar business interests. It makes sense."

"Aye, Ian's respectable," he agreed, still trying to grasp all of the nonsense that had come flying at him tonight. He half expected Ian to be foolish about this new opportunity; his brother practically lived in Dunncraigh's pocket these days. Clan politics, business, all fascinated Lord Geiry—and thanks to Becca's father a fleet of ships and a new, thriving business came with her, or would eventually.

But Rebecca climbed trees and liked to learn the lyrics of bawdy tavern songs. Ian would bore her to death inside a month. Everyone could see that. Everyone could see that *he* would have been a much better choice for Becca. At the least he wouldn't tangle her into business with the clan Maxwell chief.

But she'd known about the dock and the fleet even though he hadn't had a whiff of the goings-on, and she'd agreed to all of it. He stirred that around in his head for a bit. That was why she hadn't wanted him to make fun of Ian earlier. Because she'd agreed to be his wife. She *wanted* to be Lady Geiry.

Well, he hadn't agreed to any of it. He wasn't some cotter cowering in fear and hoping his lord and master hadn't decided to replace him with sheep. And the first one to say he was too young to understand was going to get punched in the head. Becca was two years younger than he was, for Lucifer's sake. And until—unless—she and damned Ian had a son, he remained the bloody Geiry heir.

The idea of Ian and Becca having children together made him abruptly want to be ill all over again, which sensation made him wish he'd stayed at the Seven Fathoms tonight. By tomorrow, though, all of this might well be beyond repair. "When did he ask ye?" he forced out. "Or romantic that he is, did Ian send ye a note saying how mutually beneficial a union between ye and him could be, especially with Dunncraigh taking an interest?"

"Callum, don't be like that."

"Be like what?" he countered, moving between her and the door when she glanced in that direction. She didn't get to flee until he'd had his say, until he'd made sense of all this. "Be annoyed that the lot of ye decided on our entire lives and didnae bother to mention it to me?"

"Perhaps if you possessed the ability to hold your tongue and listen without insulting everyone with whom you disagree, your brother might have made the effort to include you in the decision," she retorted, her words clipped and blue eyes narrowed.

That snapped his mouth shut. "But they did include *ye*," he countered, stalking closer again. "Ye truly had nae an objection to any of this?"

"Your brother is a kind, honorable man. To what would I object?"

He poked a finger into her shoulder. " 'Kind and honorable,' " he repeated, sneering the words. "He's to be yer husband, Becca. Cannae ye say he's passionate? That he adores ye, and ye, him? All ye can say is that he doesnae kick dogs?"

"That is not—"

"Do ye reckon he'll take ye dancing? Or go with ye to look for shells by the seashore? Or teach ye how to drink whisky? Ye should be marrying me, not that musty old stuffed shirt." As he spoke, he realized that while she hadn't considered who would be her perfect match, he'd figured it all out.

He and Becca got on well, and she was a damned sight better at conversation than Una down at the tavern. He couldn't speak to her other parts, but if they were akin to what he *could* see, he would be more than satisfied. And she had given him a look, from time to time, that made him think she wouldn't object if he kissed her. Now he wished he hadn't resisted the temptation.

"Ye ken ye dunnae want *him*," he pursued, cupping her cheeks in his hands. "Marry *me*, Becca."

She blinked. "Marry *you*?"

"Aye. We'll go on a grand adventure, never lay our heads in the same place twice. We'll—"

"And why would I want that?" she countered, pushing his hands away. The fair cast of her skin lost all its color. "Aside from the fact that you never thought of marrying me until this minute, you couldn't afford to take me any farther than Glasgow. Why would I choose a drunk . . . boy who has no future but what his older brother deigns to give him? Do you truly think looking for shells and fleeing from place to place ahead of creditors is a solid foundation for a marriage? And that is beside the fact that you've done nothing but insult the man to whom you owe every ounce of your future. You've also insulted me, and the duke, and everyone else here tonight who's decided on a course different than the one you prefer. You're a loud child, Callum, and I see nothing at all marriageable in that."

If he looked down at himself, he was fairly certain he'd find his skin flayed off. It felt that way, anyway. "So I'm nae a catch?" he bit back. "Because I'm nae a first-born earl? Because I ken how to have a wee bit of fun? If all ye require is money and a title, and a husband so dull I'm near to being convinced he's nae laid with a lass ever, then by God ye've chosen well. If ye feel the need for some excitement, for the touch of a real man, I reckon ye know where to find me. Choose quickly, though; after he's had ye, I'm nae certain whether I'll still want ye or nae."

"Callum!"

Hiding his abrupt flinch, Callum turned to face his brother's bellow—only to be knocked back onto his arse by a hard fist to his jaw. Of course the earl would have a key to the morning room. *Damnation*. Moving with less grace than usual, he scrambled to his feet. "Ian, ye ken—"

"Nae another word," the earl growled, and hit him again.

This time Callum moved away from his brother as he stumbled upright. He and Ian had tussled before, but not for years, and not . . . not like this. "Bastard," he grumbled, tasting blood.

His brother's face had gone white, his jaw clenched so hard Callum could practically hear it creaking. "I've excused yer damned drinking and whoring and wagering and yer absences because I reckoned ye a lad who needs to dance with his demons before he sets them aside. This . . . This is . . ."

"Unforgivable," the Duke of Dunncraigh supplied, entering the room behind Ian. "Trying to steal another man's wife. Yer own brother's wife. That's nae a man to have beneath yer roof, Geiry."

Ian clenched his fist, then opened his fingers again as Callum braced for another blow. "I cannae believe ye would . . . But there ye stand, and I heard every damned word of it." He gestured sharply at Rebecca, his hand shaking. "She called ye a drunk boy. That's too kind, by far." He drew in a hard breath. "I want ye gone. Oot of my house, and oot of our lives. Ye're nae my brother, because a brother wouldnae do what ye just tried to do to me."

A block of solid ice dropped onto Callum, cold and hard and suffocating. The foggy sense of nightmare broke into crystal-clear shards as his brother spoke. He felt frozen, and stunned. And empty. And he had no argument, drunk or sober, because he knew damned well he'd said all those things. "Ian," he rasped anyway, spitting blood. They didn't understand. Aye, he'd stepped too far, but so had Dunncraigh with all his sudden interest in docks and shipping. The duke had merely intruded more subtly, and with money in his hands. And Rebecca . . . It was all too sudden. Too swift. "Dunnae make—"

"Go away, Callum. I dunnae care to know where. And dunnae come back. Ever."

His spine stiff, Callum managed a nod. Aye, he'd been drunk, but he couldn't be certain he wouldn't have said all those things anyway. "Ye've the right of it. Ye might have told me what ye planned, and I'd have argued against it, but I suppose ye didnae want to hear what I had to say. But ye listen now, Ian MacCreath. This is a mistake. *He's* a mistake. Our own da' called him a cannibal, eating a man alive and taking all that he has, then leaving the bones to bleach in the sun." Callum jabbed a finger in the duke's direction. "But ye and Rebecca have yer marriage and yer fleet of ships and yer litter of bairns, and ye keep tangling yerself in with Dunncraigh until ye realize ye're the fly and he's the spider. I hope I never have cause to say I told ye so, Ian. I truly do. And now the lot of ye, go to hell."

Turning, he stalked to the door, his gut churning. A nightmare. What the devil had happened? And why couldn't he wake up?

"Well done, Geiry," Dunncraigh commented smoothly. "Ye've seen the worst impediment to the future ye desire, and ye've dealt with it like a man."

Callum stopped in his tracks and whipped around, stalking back up to the duke, to his clan chief. "And ye, ye rat-faced villain," he snarled, "if I *ever* hear of anything ill happening to my brother or to his wife, I will come and find ye. Even if I have to claw my way oot of hell to do it. And I'll end ye. I swear to God."

Sending a last look back at his gray-faced brother, Callum turned once more to Becca. She wanted this. She deserved it, then. And he hoped she regretted every damned second of it. Then he turned around again and walked out the door. And he didn't look back.

Chapter One

Kentucky, 1816

The bushes on the far side of the ravine rustled again. Sinking lower into his crouch, Callum MacCreath slowly unslung the rifle from his shoulder. A light breeze touched his face, moving his scent behind him, away from the steep, crumbling bank. Readying the rifle, he put his fingers to his mouth and gave a low, two-toned whistle.

A heartbeat later a huge, bristle-backed gray boar ripped out of the tangle of vines and deadfall, squealing as it plunged down the steep wall and into the shallow creek at the bottom. The large, jet-black figure behind it stayed right on the boar's heels, growling and nipping at the pig's backside.

The boar scrambled up the near side of the ravine, screeching as it caught sight of Callum, its mouth agape and impressive tusks dripping water and saliva as it charged. Ignoring the earsplitting noise, Callum lifted the rifle, narrowed one eye, and squeezed the trigger. The boar pitched forward onto its tusks and rolled to a stop in a cloud of dirt. Then it began sliding back down the slope behind it. A second later it splashed into the shallow creek.

The black wolf, though, skidded to a halt on the near bank and followed the pig's descent with unblinking yellow eyes. Then it turned, licked its jowls, and gazed at Callum as he stood upright.

"Ye could go fetch it for me," he commented, propping the rifle against the bear-clawed trunk of the nearest blue ash.

When in response to that the wolf only sank onto her haunches, he brushed the tips of his fingers across the coarse jet fur running down her spine, then hopped down to the creek bed himself. Crouching again, he pulled the knife from his boot and swiftly dressed the boar before he rinsed his hands and the blade in the slow-moving trickle of water. Even without its guts the beast likely weighed close to a hundred fifty pounds, but then the big bastard had been eating things that didn't belong to it.

With a grunt he hefted the animal across his shoulders and straightened, using a small dogwood to haul himself back up the side of the ravine. Retrieving his rifle, he set off north through the forested tangle until he reached the ridge beyond and its slightly easier terrain.

Twenty minutes later the wolf appeared at his side. From the red of her muzzle she'd detoured to enjoy the boar innards he'd left behind. The top of her head just reached his hip, her long legs with the large padded paws easily matching his pace over the uneven ground, black death on four feet.

"I reckon ye ken I like a challenge, Waya," he noted, angling toward the rising sun as the trees began to thin around them, "but next time ye might look for a boar that doesnae weigh near twice what ye do."

With a low whumph Waya sped into a smooth trot, entering the large clearing ahead of him. A dozen wood-and-stone buildings stood scattered in a loose circle surrounded by a twenty-foot-tall split-rail wall. Inside, amid the clatter and thump of industry, a half-dozen workers left a pile of boards and approached him.

"That's the boar what's been tearing into the silo?" one of them asked, giving the wolf a wide berth.

"Waya thought so," Callum returned, handing the animal over to a pair of lads from the cookhouse, who half dragged the beast indoors. "One of them, anyway. We tracked him for three miles, but he didnae go visiting any of his smaller pig friends. He's dinner now, regardless."

"Aye, Mr. MacCreath, and thank the devil for that. At least the smaller ones dunnae eat as much."

"Callum," Rory Boyd called, trotting up to him. "Young Geoffrey Winter came up here before dawn with word from his da' that the damned Thomas boys are making offers for the rye crop all up and down the river."

Callum shrugged. "We pay better, Rory. Always have, always will."

"Aye, but *we* dunnae suggest what a dangerous territory Kentucky is or mention how easy it is for folks' cabins to catch fire," the shorter man returned. "That's some good incentive there."

"I'll nae have that." With a scowl, Callum whistled Waya to his side, and she trotted back down the outside stairs leading from the second-floor rooms they shared. "Send MacDougall and the twins down with a reminder to the Thomas lads that they're the third set of Irish lunatics to try to take my business, and that if they dunnae move downriver by June they'll find me a bit annoyed."

Boyd grinned. "That should do. The last time ye were a bit annoyed with a lad, he ended with a broken jaw and passage back to Bristol."

"He should've known better than to try passing his whisky off as mine. How's Arnold dealing with the new lads?"

"Och, ye ken how gentle Arnold is. Even with that broken wing of his he's still working them down to scarecrows. That was after he had to swear to them that ye're nae some witch or a demon, of course."

That was nothing new. Aside from his hard-earned reputation for directness, he supposed it was that like most male MacCreaths he boasted a green left eye and a blue right eye. Ian had the same oddity, as had their father. Not so long ago several of his ancestors had been burned as both witches *and* demons because of precisely that peculiarity. These days, though, lasses seemed to find his two-colored eyes attractive, thank Lucifer. He much preferred a roll in the bedsheets to a stake-burning. As far as his men were concerned, if they thought him a bit of a demon, and if that ensured their loyalty, he'd no objection. "If a man's scared to work for me, he's nae a man I *want* working for me."

"They're still here." Boyd cleared his throat. "Young Winter also brought up the mail from town. Ye've another letter."

He would have preferred to continue debating whether or not he was a devil. At least the letters came less frequently these days. "Put it with the others," he said dismissively, heading for the large, canopy-covered slab of flat earth they'd set aside for barrel making.

"I ken ye dunnae wish to read them, Callum," Boyd said, lowering his voice as he hurried his shorter stride to catch up, "but burning them's a bit permanent, aye?"

"Aye. That being the point. Have the new mules and wagons made it up here yet?"

"Deveraux says by the end of the week. But about the let—"

"That's what comes of trusting a Frenchman," Callum interrupted. He could practically feel the disapproval coming off his foreman, and with a scowl he slowed. "The letter's from Scotland, aye?"

"Aye. Aye, it is."

"Is it from Crosby and Hallifax?" he asked, naming the firm that managed his business on the far side of the Atlantic.

"Nae. It's from a Mr. B—"

"If it's nae business, *my* business, I've nae use for it," Callum broke in again, annoyed that he'd actually rushed his response to keep from hearing the name. But anyone in the whisky business knew to contact the Kentucky Hills distillery through Crosby and Hallifax. And anyone from Scotland who wished to contact *him,* personally, could go to the devil. "Burn it, Rory."

The foreman sighed. "As ye wish, Mr. MacCreath."

"I'll lend a hand with Arnold," Callum decided. "We'll need another dozen barrels by Wednesday." Anything to keep his thoughts away from the letters that had begun arriving about four years ago and what they contained, as if he had any desire to know that Ian MacCreath and Rebecca Sanderson-MacCreath had a basket of bairns and their ludicrous business with Dunncraigh had netted them all the money in the Highlands. That wasn't his life, and they weren't his family. They'd made that damned clear, and if they deigned to offer him some sort of forgiveness, well, he fucking well didn't want it. And if they'd written to send him more insults, he didn't want those, either.

"Aye," Rory said, obviously not reading his thoughts. "I can smell how nicely she's coming along."

Ah, the whisky. Callum could smell it, too. Corn and rye, boiled down for three days before it was combined with wheat and buckwheat mash in just the right proportion—the scent reminded him of Scotland at the oddest of times, even more so than the mix of fading Highlands and Lowlands accents of most of his men. The air at the moment smelled more like a bakery than a distillery, but after three or five or seven years, depending on the size of the barrels and the maturity of the brew, it would be some of the finest whisky in the world.

He glanced toward the large barnlike building at the center of the clearing. Hell, some of the barrels had been lying there in the dark for nearly eight years now, and he would leave them for another three or four. For the rest, though, smaller barrels meant less time to mature, which meant faster turnaround times, faster profits, and faster growth for the place he'd named Kentucky Hills. *His* place.

While initially he'd begun the venture mainly because it required sweat and muscle, with the bonus that it allowed him to move as far from civilization as he could get, he did appreciate the irony of it, as well. Whisky and its pursuit had ruined his life that night, so it seemed only fitting that he use it now to make himself a living. A very good living. The reputation Kentucky Hills had earned along the way for a fine, smooth brew with a unique taste had been unexpected but welcome byproducts, as was the reputation *he'd* earned for being a man with whom others did not trifle.

As for the Highlands, he'd relegated it to a faraway place where he'd once lived for a time. The sooner it faded completely from his memory, the better. All he needed to remember about the damned Highlands was that folk there liked their whisky.

Shaking himself, he stooped beneath a roof of canvas to enter what they'd deemed the barrel room. A wiry, white-haired imp of unknown age stalked among the uncured casks spaced out on the dirt, muttering to himself as he made certain they stood round and open at the bottoms like Indian teepees. Firewood lay stacked on the ground at the center of each unfinished barrel, while two younger men fitted iron ribs around another group that were already being fired.

"Arnold," he said, handing his rifle off to Boyd, "I hear we'll have more whisky than barrels to hold it, come Wednesday."

The imp's face went scarlet, his good arm flapping. If the other hadn't been in a sling, he likely would have lifted into the air to join the flock of ducks heading north toward the south fork of Red River. "Ye gave me but two new lads, MacCreath, both scrawny as scarecrows. Ye cannae expect miracles when ye give me shite."

"If ye'll stop yer bellyaching," Callum replied, shedding his bloodstained hunting coat, "I figure I'll lend ye my two hands."

Waya snorted at one of the fires, then padded off in the direction of the cookhouse—no doubt in hope of handouts. Callum, though, rolled up his shirtsleeves and began dragging the remainder of the barrel frames into place for firing and sealing.

Arnold stepped back, lifting an eyebrow. "Ye ken most of us need some assistance to do that," he observed.

"He's a damned demon," one of the striplings muttered, though Callum pretended not to hear.

The barrelmaker didn't pretend any such thing. "A devil? Nae. What yer employer is, lads, is a bloody grizzly bear. Dunnae expect me to coddle ye."

Chuckling, Callum heaved over another half-finished barrel. "Dunnae be so hard on 'em, Arnold. We cannae all be as big as mountains or as handsome as the devil."

The cooper guffawed, slapping a knee with his good hand. "Ye hear that, lads? I can give ye work to make ye stronger, but ye'll have to curse yer mamas for yer looks."

Still grinning, Callum gathered up an armload of cedar logs. A few years ago he wouldn't have been able to heave the barrels alone. But a few inches of height, together with some well-honed muscles and the anger which drove him to use them, had turned him from a stupid drunken pup into a man other men favored with a healthy respect. And that suited him exceedingly well.

"Mr. MacKenzie," the other lad said, grunting as the two of them hammered another iron rib into place, "if we finish these barrels today, will ye finally tell me who can read me the letter from my ma? I reckon she had Father Michael write it out for her, because the father's the only man in Carach-duan who can read or write, but—"

"That's enough, lad," Arnold snapped, sending Callum a grim look. "I'll read it to ye myself tonight, if ye'll stop yammering about it." The old man straightened. "He doesnae ken the rules here yet, MacCreath."

Callum narrowed an eye as he looked at the two lads all over again. Neither of them looked even as old as he'd been when he'd fled Scotland. At least one of them had attachments back home, which meant the boy had come here searching for a better life rather than simply escaping from something unpleasant. He preferred when men came looking for a new start, a clean break from whatever former misery their lives had been.

Even so, he hadn't made it a rule that no one was allowed to speak about family or friends back in the Highlands. He'd merely requested—on several occasions—that they do their reminiscing and letter-reading out of his presence. "It's more a guideline," he said, as he returned to stacking wood for charring the inside of the barrels. "But aye, ye've work to do. Without these barrels, by Wednesday we'll risk fouling the balance of the whisky before it even has time to settle."

The chatty lad—Rob or Raymond, as he recalled—bobbed his head. "I ken, Mr. MacCreath. It willnae happen again."

"Good."

Once they'd finished overturning the half-finished casks, Arnold began stuffing pine needles and old newspapers into the bases of the wood piles, then lit them one by one. With two remaining though, he paused, looking down at the worn, torn newspaper page in his good hand. He looked at it for a good minute, in fact, his expression as frozen as the rest of him.

"Arnold MacKenzie," Callum commented, grabbing a handful of tinder to prime the next fire over, "if ye're nae dead, ye might consider blinking."

The old cooper did blink, looking up to stare at Callum with an expression of . . . dread? "Lads," he said, "go get someaught to eat."

"We cannae leave the barrels untended," Rob or Raymond countered.

"I've been seeing to charring casks since before ye da' was a twinkle in yer *seanair*'s eye," Arnold retorted. "Now git with ye!" The entire time he spoke, his gaze remained on his employer.

An uneasy shiver went down Callum's spine. Arnold MacKenzie had all the grace and subtlety of a newborn moose, and something clearly troubled him. Newspapers, news, never brought an ounce of good. That was why he hadn't read one in ten years. He glanced at the lads running off to the kitchen, wishing for a moment he could join them.

It had been a very long time since he'd run from anything, however. "What's got yer tongue tied, then?" Callum asked brusquely. "We've work to do."

"I, uh . . . I happened to glance doon here, and I might've—I think I did, that is—spy the word 'Geiry.'"

"And I should never have told ye or Rory a thing about it," Callum retorted. "Throw it in the fire. We've casks to ready." If his . . . If Ian MacCreath and his lovely wife had ten strapping bairns and had donated funds for a statue or a library or something, he didn't want to know about it.

Arnold rocked from one foot to the other, but kept the paper clenched in his one good ash-stained hand. "I cannae toss it away, lad," he finally said. "It's but a few words left here. I can read it to ye or ye can read it for yerself, but ye need to know what it says."

The cold settled deeper, pinching at his lungs. "Tell me, then," he snapped. "And make it quick. I'm beginning to find ye annoying."

The old man looked down at the paper again. "Aye," he said, lowering his voice still further, and cleared his throat. "This paper's from New York, dated last December, though I cannae make oot the precise date. It's—"

"I dunnae care where or when it's from," Callum interrupted. "What does the fucking thing say?"

"It's a headline. Part of one, anyway. '—*rd Geiry, Drowned in Loch Brenan, Mourned b . . . ,*'" the cooper read, sounding out the letters of the partial words as he went. "And there're two words below I can make oot—'accident' and either 'weather' or 'heather.'" He took a breath. "Lad, I'm sorr—"

"Stop," Callum interrupted. Sound roared around him, filling his abruptly hollow chest. Men talking, the ring and snap of chopping wood, birds, the wind in the trees up the hillside. He wanted to cover his ears, but his limbs had frozen. And through it all, one thought pierced him, cold as winter, and sharp as a knife.

The news didn't surprise him. Aye, he'd thought he'd be avoiding news of family and friends and acquisitions, of Ian further entangling the family business with Dunncraigh and clan Maxwell. But the second Arnold MacKenzie had looked at him, that paper in his one good hand, Callum had known.

Making himself pull in a breath, he put the firewood back in its stack and straightened. "See to the casks," he ordered, and turned on his heel.

Boyd sat in the office, bills of lading, orders, invoices, and shipping schedules spread out before him on the desk. "The two new lads fled past the window a moment ago. They werenae on fire, though, so I reckoned . . ." The Kentucky Hills foreman trailed off as he looked up. As his gaze found Callum the half smile dropped from his face, and he stood. "What the devil's happened?"

Did he look different? He felt different. He couldn't even put a name to the thoughts rumbling through his mind, except that he wanted to hit something. Badly. "That letter from *B* something. Did ye burn it?"

"Nae. I'll do it now if ye want, b—"

"Give it to me."

Without another word Boyd dug it out from the desk and handed it over. His jaw clenched so hard he was surprised the bones didn't crack, Callum looked down at it. Addressed to him, aye, from one Bartholomew Harvey, Esq. A solicitor. A very English one, from the name.

Slicing his finger through the wax seal, he unfolded it. "Dear sir," he read to himself. "This is my fourth attempt at reaching you. As I noted in my previous correspondence, I have been charged with informing you of the unfortunate death of Ian MacCreath, Earl Geiry. I will not discuss matters of inheritance, etc., herein, but request that you contact me immediately so we may conclude this business. I shall make one more attempt hereafter, but be aware that if unsuccessful, I will be forced to report to the Crown that you also are deceased, and the Geiry title will pass to your cousin, James Sturgeon. Respectfully, Bartholomew Harvey, Esq."

Every word pounded like a hammer into his soul. " 'Conclude this business,' " he growled. "Aye, we bloody well will."

"Callum?" Boyd asked, his brow furrowed.

"Ye'll see to the business, Rory," he said, moving to shove the missive into his coat pocket and then remembering he'd left the garment in the barrel tent. He would need it, and a few other things he could throw into his saddlebags. A trunk or two could follow.

"Aye, of course I will. What's afoot?"

"I'm going back to Scotland," he returned, striding out of the room with Rory on his heels. "I swore an oath to kill a man. Time for me to see to it." He'd known ten years ago, damn it all, and he'd fled. He'd followed his brother's orders rather than stay put and keep an eye on damned Dunncraigh. And now somehow the duke had removed Ian from the equation. And so now the duke and anyone else involved would pay in blood, if he had to burn down the bloody Highlands to do it.

Chapter Two

"Ye," Callum barked, jabbing a finger at the thin young man with the crisply starched cravat who stood on the dock. "Crosby and Hallifax?"

"I said to put another rope on that net!" the lad yelled up at the sailors who loaded heavy barrels into a net. "Nae a soul gets to drink any of that fine whisky if it spills all over the docks!" That dealt with, he faced Callum. "Can I help ye? I'm in the middle of some-aught. These barrels need to get racked at the warehouse before they all turn to vinegar."

"Are ye Crosby and Hallifax?"

The fellow frowned. "I am their representative, aye," he replied, then took an abrupt step backward, nearly falling over a pile of buckets, as Waya loped down the gangplank to join them on the dock. "Sweet Mary! Is that a—"

"A wolf," Callum interrupted. "Aye. Take me to yer offices."

"I . . ." He cleared his throat. "I can point ye in the correct direction, but I'm to count whisky barrels and oversee their unloading. Kentucky Hills Distillery is our largest client, and I willnae—"

"Fuck the whisky," Callum retorted, pushing against four damned weeks of nothing to do but pace the deck of *The Rooster* and decide whether a rifle ball or a knife would be better suited to end Dunncraigh. As eager as he was to bury the man, though, and as sure as he was that Ian MacCreath hadn't drowned, he needed to be even more certain who, exactly, had murdered his brother. He could name at least four additional suspects even without having been in Britain for ten years. All of which meant that he needed information. Quickly and accurately. "Crosby and Hallifax. Now."

The younger man blinked. "I've a duty, sir. Inventory figures, profits, and losses dunnae record themselves. I've nae missed an ounce in a shipment in two years, and I willnae do so now. So allow me to point ye on yer way, or go find the offices yer own self."

Callum tilted his head. Most of his profits came from America these days, but the Highlands couldn't get enough of his used barrels for him to keep them stocked. All that, however, remained beside the point. He had a task to see to. Nothing else mattered, up to and including Kentucky Hills Distillery and its shipment of whisky.

"Perhaps we need an introduction," he said, taking a step closer and offering his hand. "Callum MacCreath. The man who pays a large portion of yer salary."

"I . . . Oh. Oh, sweet Mary and Joseph." The fellow fumbled and dropped his clipboard, bent to pick it up, then thought twice about that and straightened again to grab Callum's hand and attempt to shake it off his arm. "Mr. MacCreath. I had nae idea ye were on yer way here."

"I didnae expect to be," Callum returned, retrieving his hand and whistling Waya back to heel when she began stalking a crowd of seagulls after a fish head. Beyond the wolf a woman screeched and fell into the arms of her companion. No one had seen a wolf in the High-lands for over half a century. He meant to make good use of that particular fact. "Now walk."

"Of . . . of course. This way." Handing the clipboard to *The Rooster*'s first mate, the young man headed off the crowded dock, weaving through the hordes of people and crates and animals that congregated at the harbor. "I'm Kimes. Dennis Kimes," he said, looking back over his shoulder.

As they continued up the street a light rain began, the deepening mist obscuring the far side of the harbor and the tops of the masts behind them. *Ah, Scotland.* Icy pricks dug into his skin through his coat, but Callum refused to acknowledge the cold. Every Highlander knew the weather was as it was, and even after ten years away his blood hadn't thinned enough for him to give in to the shivers.

"What brings ye back here, Mr. MacCreath, if ye dunnae mind me asking?" Kimes ventured, turning a corner to move directly away from the harbor and up the slight hill. A selection of houses and shops, but mostly shipping offices, lined either side of the street. Men hurrying about with shoulders hunched against the rain gave first Waya and then him second looks. A few of them crossed themselves. Good. He knew damned well the impression a big man with two-colored eyes and a black wolf at his heels would make here. Let them notice, and let them wonder if he was the devil him-self. They'd all know soon enough who he was.

"Death brings me here," he returned. "Death and mayhem."

Silence. "I . . . I dunnae ken what to say to that," Kimes stammered, nearly tripping over a small dog that took one look at the wolf and fled into an alley.

"There's naught to say. Tell me about Crosby and Hallifax. Which do ye trust more?"

"They're my employers, sir. I trust them both, as I wouldnae work for thieves or liars."

Callum refrained from countering that everyone was a thief or a liar, or more likely, both. "Who's kinder to widows and orphans, then?"

"That's an odd question."

"It's my question. Answer it, if ye please."

"Mr. Hallifax then, I suppose. He once gave his coat over to a shivering old lass, and he nearly always has pennies for beggars." Kimes stopped before a door like every other door on the street, if perhaps slightly cleaner. The shutters of the windows just past it were open, but the curtains inside stood half drawn. "This is it, Mr. MacCreath. Shall I show ye in?"

"Aye. And introduce me to Crosby."

The lad pushed open the door. "Aye. But—"

"Dennis, what are ye doing here?" a loud voice interrupted. "Ye're to be counting Kentucky Hills barrels. The ship came into harbor this morning. Did it nae dock?"

Callum stepped inside to take in the sight of a short, rotund man with long wisps of hair above either ear, both sides trying to meet at the top of his otherwise bald head. A half-dozen other men sat at scattered desks or carried stacks of paper about, while two open doors at the back showed slightly better kept desks and lanterns.

These were the men he'd written after he'd acquired the property in Kentucky, the ones who'd answered him in the manner he cared to hear. They'd helped to make him a wealthy man in his own right, and he'd made them wealthy in return. And he'd never thought to set eyes on them.

"Aye, the ship docked, Mr. Crosby. With a passenger on board. He's asked to see ye, so I've brought him."

The fat man straightened from looking at rows of numbers over the shoulder of one of his clerks. "A passenger? Do I look like I have time to be gawked at by visitors on holiday? And . . . what in God's name is that?"

He pointed a plump finger at Waya, who yawned, giving everyone in the office a very fine view of her canines.

"That would be a wolf," Callum supplied. "*Canis lupus*, to be exact. And I'm nae a visitor."

"Mr. Crosby, this is Callum MacCreath," Kimes supplied.

"To be exact," Callum followed.

The accountant smoothed the hair running up one side of his head, his pink face going a mottled red. "Mr. MacCreath! I had nae idea ye were set for a visit. Please! Come in and sit doon." He walked forward, holding out his hand.

Waya growled, and he jerked it away again. "Down, girl," Callum cautioned, and stuck out his own hand. "Crosby. We've some things to discuss in private."

"Of course. This way." He indicated the left room.

With a nod Callum and Waya moved past him. "And Mr. Kimes," he added. "I reckon I'll have some use for him."

Kimes hesitated, but from his glance at Waya it was more about being closed in with a wolf than anything else. Then he edged inside the office with them and closed the door behind him. Michael Crosby sank into the wide, sagging chair behind the desk and steepled his hands, elbows resting on his gut. "What can we do for ye then, Mr. MacCreath? If ye've a yen to look at our books, I'm more than happy to have Mr. Kimes fetch them for ye. I assure ye, we've made every effort to—"

"What do ye know about the death of Lord Geiry?" Callum interrupted. The words continued to stick in his throat, even after he'd gone through them in his head a thousand times in the five weeks since he'd left the distillery. Murder, suicide, accident, mistake—all the possibilities ended with the same result. His brother was dead. And that couldn't be allowed to lie. Not without him knowing every damned detail.

"Lord Geiry?" Crosby sat back. "He drowned a year or so ago, didn't he? Someaught about driving a carriage in the rain and he slid down the bank of the loch. Why does . . ." His small eyes widened. "Ye're *that* Callum MacCreath? Geiry's brother?"

"That very same one."

"But lad—ye need to see the magistrate. Now. Ye've an inheritance, and a title, and—"

"And first I want to know exactly what happened. Exactly." Callum dipped his hand into the thick, rough fur of Waya's back. *Steady.* He could be furious, aye, but action could wait until he knew where to aim it. "Old newspapers, witnesses, any rumors of what might have been afoot at the time. I want them all. And then ye can bring the magistrate here to see me."

"It may take us a few hours, m'laird."

"Then get to it. I've arranged to have my luggage brought here." He narrowed his eyes, hesitating now to ask the question that had dragged at him the most. "The house here in Inverness. MacCreath House. Is it occupied still?"

"Aye," Dennis supplied. "Lady Geiry spent her whole year of mourning here in town. I saw her just last week, finally put off her black crêpe. Poor lass, she's had a bad patch, first with Geiry, then her own da' pass—"

"Her da'?" Callum broke in. "George Sanderson is dead?"

A muscle in Crosby's plump cheek jumped. "Lad, ye've been gone a time, aye? Ye might prefer asking these questions of yer own. Dennis said that Lady Geiry's in town. She'll have the answers ye want, I reck—"

"Nae," Callum growled. He'd given up hoping this all might be a nightmare, but every additional bit of information he heard made things worse. And then there were the things he hadn't wanted to consider, the question that if his brother's death hadn't been some idiotic accident, who else had been involved?

And Becca. The last time he'd set eyes on her she'd flayed him to the bone. Aye, he would go see her. After he'd acquired every bit of information available about her, his brother, Dunncraigh, and their business enterprise. Something tickled at his mind, and he edged forward again. "Ian—Lord Geiry—died before George Sanderson, ye said?"

"Aye," Kimes supplied, jumping when Waya swiveled her head around to look at him. "Barely two weeks apart, it was. The talk was that Mr. Sanderson's heart couldnae take the loss of his beloved son-in-law." Keeping his hand close against his chest, he pointed one finger at the wolf. "She looks hungry."

"She's always hungry," Callum said absently, scratching behind her ears. "If Ian died before George, then Rebecca's the one holding the reins to the fleet." If it had been the other way around, whatever she inherited would have belonged to Ian . . . and now, to him. But in this circumstance, her father's holdings couldn't go to a dead man. That happened to be very . . . coincidentally handy for her. Unless it hadn't been a coincidence.

That thought dogged him, chewed at him, for the next

three hours as he read through old newspapers Dennis
Kimes had begged or borrowed or stolen from sources
the lad wouldn't even reveal. At least one of them
smelled like lemon verbena, though, so he suspected the
lad's mother to be involved.

What he read didn't leave him feeling any easier.
Just the opposite. Ian had been driving a phaeton from
the Geiry estate a few short miles from Inverness, past
Loch Brenan and into town. He'd done it for no uncov-
erable reason, in the middle of a rainstorm and at night,
according to his wife of nine years. The next morning
a pair of shepherds found the unhitched phaeton ten
yards into the loch, the harnessed horses grazing
nearby with a broken tress hanging off them, and then
they'd spied Ian floating facedown a foot or two beyond
that.

He'd imagined it. For the week it took him to get to
Boston, then for the duration of the four weeks across
the Atlantic, he'd imagined what might have happened
to his brother. Reading the account there in slightly
melodramatic black-and-white, though, was worse. This
wasn't his imagination. This wasn't one of the scenar-
ios he'd had nightmares about back when he'd first sailed
away from Scotland. Back then those possibilities for
disaster had come with a sense of . . . smugness. He'd
warned Ian, and he'd been right. But now Ian—his older
brother, his friend, his conscience—was dead. And he
didn't feel smug or righteous. He felt fury.

When he'd gleaned everything he could from newspapers and rumors, he had Kimes go fetch both the
magistrate and this Bartholomew Harvey, Esquire, fellow. For another hour he signed papers, learned Ian's
financial status, and handed all pertinent papers over to
Crosby and Hallifax. Mr. Harvey, Esquire, looked like
he'd swallowed a bug, but Callum wasn't about to trust

his new—and old—holdings to someone who hadn't already proven themselves to him.

"You should be aware, sir—my lord, that is," Mr. Harvey said, his voice as pinched and annoyed as his expression, "that I am exceedingly proud of the work I did for your predecessor."

Callum lifted his gaze from signing yet another batch of papers. "And for the Duke of Dunncraigh, aye?"

"Of course. And for Mr. Sanderson. The fleet, the docks, it's all very complicated." The solicitor flicked his fingers toward Mr. Crosby. "Too much so to risk handing it all over to a glorified clerk, in my opinion."

"I have the same letters after my name as ye do, Mr. Harvey," the rotund accountant stated. "I simply choose nae to brag about them."

"Well, I'm pleased then, Mr. Harvey," Callum took up, "that ye managed to send off a letter in my direction, given how busy ye must have been with dividing up all those profits."

"I sent you *four* letters, my lord. The last two over the objections of Lady Geiry, I might add."

Every time one of the men here mentioned poor Lady Geiry the dear, unfortunate countess, Callum's jaw clenched. He'd been there, that night. And he remembered every damned word they'd exchanged. Rebecca Sanderson had married for an empire, and now with the death of her husband and her father most of it had landed right in her lap. For the moment, anyway.

Of course she wouldn't want him found. All the Mac-Creath properties, the MacCreath investments and money, and everything that her father had owned, were at this moment in her custody and care. The second Callum appeared, though, everything—all but her father's share of the business—went straight to him.

"Why wouldn't the lass want his lordship found?"

Kimes piped up, his arms full of contracts and papers. "Someone would take the title, even if it didn't happen to be Callum MacCreath. Ye've a handful of cousins, do ye nae, m'laird?"

"Three male cousins," Callum supplied. If they all still lived. Odds were that at least one of them survived. The Sassenach solicitor had mentioned James Sturgeon in his last letter, anyway. "I'm curious to know her objections to me being found, Mr. Harvey. Indulge me, if ye would."

The solicitor opened his mouth, arrogance and affront practically dripping from him, only to snap it shut again as Callum set aside the pen and straightened to send him a level-eyed gaze. Men did as he asked these days. Men who lived a much rougher life than did the solicitor.

"Lady Geiry said her late husband had written you several times over the years," he offered stiffly, "and that you'd never responded. She considered you either uninterested, or more likely, dead. And in all honesty I would have acquiesced to her wishes, except I did not want to risk my reputation should my findings be challenged later in court."

"Then I applaud yer diligence, Harvey. How fares the widow, these days?" He had every reason to ask, Callum reminded himself. The head of the family had the right—the obligation—to know the situation of those under his protection. Even if he suspected one of them might have aided another's demise. Especially then.

"The past fourteen months have been quite trying for her, of course," Bartholomew Harvey returned after a slight hesitation. Evidently he realized he had no claim of confidentiality when faced with the new earl. "First her husband, then her father passing on, the uncertainty of her own future, all that in addition to being an

English lady surrounded by Scotsmen—and far away from the land of her birth . . . She's quite admirable, really."

"Dunnae be dramatic, Harvey," Crosby took up. "The land of her birth is but three days to the south. *I* reckon she's stayed on here because she's a yen to be the future Duchess of Dunncraigh."

And there it was. Callum used every ounce of his considerable self-control to remain seated, though he couldn't have hidden his flinch even if he'd known the words were coming. Only a handful of questions remained, then. "Dunncraigh has a wife. Or he did, a decade ago. Mousy little thing, with a cunning gleam in her eyes."

"He still does have a wife. I was referring to the present Marquis of Stapp. Dunncraigh's oldest son."

Callum swallowed back a curse, shoving it down into his chest. Donnach Maxwell. Of course. The self-centered pig had been drooling over Rebecca ten years ago. Evidently she'd given in to his charms—or more likely his wealth and title. He stood, pulling on his heavy buckskin gloves. Now he had but two questions. Had she helped murder Ian for money? Or to gain herself the loftiest title in the Highlands?

"Gentlemen," he said evenly, "ye'll find me at Mac-Creath House. Kimes, call on me tomorrow at ten o'clock. I reckon I'll have some instructions for ye."

"Aye, m'laird."

Now he meant to claim what belonged to him—and to end anyone and everyone who'd had anything to do with gaining him this inheritance. Even if Rebecca Sanderson-MacCreath happened to be one of those any-ones. Especially then.

Chapter Three

"M'lady," Pogue the butler said, "ye've another bouquet of posies. I took the liberty of having 'em put in water." He indicated the tall vase on the foyer table. The sprays of roses and long-stemmed lilies in yellows and reds looked like Hogmanay fireworks.

Rebecca MacCreath, Countess Geiry, paused at the bottom of the main staircase to smell the sweet spice of the flowers. A card accompanied them, of course, but she already knew who'd sent them. Donnach Maxwell had been sending flowers at least twice a week for the past two months.

She unfolded the card anyway. "May the pain of your grief be eased by the salve of my kind regards. Donnach."

It wasn't the most poetical thing she'd ever read, but then after nearly twenty notes in the same vein the Marquis of Stapp must have been running low on platitudes. "Put it in the morning room please, Pogue," she said, and preceded him into the east-facing room at the front of the house as her Skye terrier, Reginald, sped down the straight staircase to join her. With his long white hair reaching to the floor , the snowy silk broken only by his dark ears, nose, and beard, he looked rather like a mobile footrest—not that she would ever tell him such a thing. "And let Agnes know I'll be taking Maggie with me to the milliner's in half an hour."

The silver-haired Scot nodded. "I'll see to it at once, m'lady." Dipping his head again, he left the room, shutting the door behind him.

Rebecca picked up her calendar from the desk and walked to the window to read through it as Reginald sniffed at her, then jumped onto the nearest sunlit chair and curled up to begin snoring. Today remained hers except for finding a new chapeau. Tomorrow, though, she had Lady Polk's luncheon, and then both an afternoon recital and an evening at the theater as Donnach's guest.

She wrinkled her nose. That seemed too much; she'd been out of mourning for Ian for three months, and her father for two, and her life had never been a whirlwind of social engagements, anyway. Three events in one day might be unseemly. What, though, to cancel? Certainly the recital would be more trying, with a dozen mamas hovering about, anxious to see that their marriageable daughters showed well, and the rest of the guests being dissected for any telling yawn or muscle twitch. That sort of scrutiny would be nothing new, but over the past year her composure had developed more than a few cracks that hadn't entirely healed.

With a sigh she sat at the small desk to write out her regrets to Mrs. Adair—Latharna was more likely to understand her absence than Donnach would be, anyway. At least the theatrical performance was *A Midsummer Night's Dream* this time. Last month when the Marquis of Stapp had invited her to share his private

box at the theater, it had been to see *Everyman*. At least
he'd apologized afterward, though he'd lost a handkerchief to her weeping.

Everyone had been deferential to her, in fact. She
knew why, of course; widowed and orphaned within a
fortnight, she'd been the favorite tragedy of Inverness's
noble circle for the past year. Completely aside from her
present position as the Countess Geiry she was worth
well over twenty thousand a year thanks to her father's
estate, which made her the wealthiest widow in Scotland. Perhaps in all of Britain.

As she dusted sand over the fresh ink of her note, she
caught sight of the half-dozen letters from Ian's cousins. They hadn't been quite as deferential, but then once
the courts declared Callum unreachable or dead, James
Sturgeon would take the Geiry title and the one-third
ownership of Sanderson's—and the entirety of this
house—for himself and his family. Even so, they'd been
mostly pleasant, suggesting they come visit, not so they
could measure the curtains, but so she would have the
familial support for which she no doubt yearned.

At the moment she mostly yearned not to be whispered about and stared at every time she ventured out
of doors, for people to simply wish her good morning
and chat about the weather or fashion as they used to
do. She would undoubtedly find more anonymity in
London, but Inverness had been her home for twenty
years now. Her father's business—her business, rather—
had its headquarters here. She would garner suitors in
both towns, but she knew the ones here.

She would have to leave MacCreath House sooner or
later, but she liked the big, rambling house and the view
from the front windows that overlooked a pretty stretch
of the river Ness. Likewise her days of spending sum-
mers at Geiry Hall in the middle of the Highland coun-

tryside were numbered, as well. Thankfully her father had left her their old home closer by, but she preferred it here. She had since she'd set eyes on the house at age eight—but part of the attraction then might have been its two residents. Ian and Callum MacCreath, the two most handsome young men she'd ever seen, and they'd all become fast friends before she could even think that perhaps she should have been looking for companions of her own sex, that she should have been practicing her embroidery instead of learning to shoot a gun. The perils of being raised by an indulgent father, she supposed.

Well, she'd learned to embroider since then. She even played a fair pianoforte, if she said so herself. Ian had enjoyed culture, and so, she'd discovered, had she. Rebecca tucked the missives back into the rack where she kept them. Ian had wanted a proper, discerning, upward-reaching life for them, and he'd achieved it. She remained thankful for it every day.

As for his brother . . . She couldn't even imagine her life if she'd allowed herself to be tied to that wild, ramshackle drunk of a boy. Disgraced, laughed at, pitied, poor—it would have been horrible. If once in a while she'd imagined it as anything else, well, that could be forgiven, she supposed. It was natural to be occasionally curious about the other paths of her life, the ones she hadn't taken. The moment she began to wander too far down them, though, it meant she needed to find something else with which to occupy herself. Especially these days, when some of the paths had fallen out of sunlight's reach.

Rebecca pushed to her feet as Pogue opened the front door to accept the day's mail. "Pogue, hold the boy a moment," she called. "I've a note to be delivered, if he'd care to make an extra shill . . ."

She rounded the door and stepped into the foyer. The

butler stood there, but it wasn't the mail boy at whom he stared. The man filling the entry stood a good three or four inches taller than Pogue, who was six feet himself. The brown caped greatcoat and black jacket beneath it with its wide lapel and silver buttons looked of fair quality but well-worn, as did the black leather calf-high boots and the buckskin breeches stuffed into them. The huge black dog standing at his heels, yellow, unblinking gaze on her, could have been some child's nightmarish dream of a hellhound.

All that, though, she noted in passing, on the way up to the face she could only see in shadowed profile as he spoke to the butler. He wore his straight brown hair a little long but neatly trimmed, the windblown mahogany resting against a high cheekbone and a lean, tanned face with a faint scruff of beard, as if he hadn't shaved today. Straight nose, a hard chin that set off his firm mouth, a handsome profile to be sure.

Then he turned his head, fixing her with his direct gaze. Beneath a double slash of dark eyebrows, his right eye was a cool blue, the left a grassy green. Rebecca's fingers felt abruptly cold. Distantly she heard the tap and swoosh as the letter she'd held hit the floor and slid beneath the table beside her, noting the sound as the cold rushed from her hands and feet up her spine to her skull, freezing everything in between.

"Did ye think me dead as well, lass?" he asked in a low voice.

"Callum," she said, and everything went white.

Callum snapped his mouth shut over the remainder of the cutting remark he'd been about to make. Instead he looked down at the twisted pile of pretty lavender silk and arms and legs and golden-blond hair that made up his sister-in-law. She'd never fainted in the entire ten years he'd known her, but then she wouldn't have expected to be confronted by the brother of the man she'd likely helped murder.

"My lady!" Pogue said, sinking to his knees beside her prone body. The butler took her hand and began patting it urgently. "Lady Geiry!"

"Leave be," Callum ordered, and stepped over Rebecca. A vase of posies sat by the window in the morning room, and he picked it up, tossed the flowers into the waste basket, then returned to the foyer and dumped the water over his sister-in-law's head.

She sputtered, waving her arms over her face, and jerked upright. The perfect coil of thick blond hair atop her head sank to one side, dripping past her ear, but she didn't seem to notice it as she caught sight of him again. "What—"

"Ye fainted," he supplied, handing the glass vase to the butler.

"I do not faint!" she protested, running a hand across her face and then belatedly pushing at the stack of her hair.

"I dunnae care what ye do," he returned, facing her again. "Stand up. I'll nae speak to ye while ye're on the floor."

For one thing, it made her look vulnerable, and he didn't like that. And he didn't like the twist he'd felt in his gut when he'd heard her voice, or that he'd had to take a breath before he looked at her. She'd had Ian in her life for nine years that he hadn't, and she had the spleen to look . . . regal when she'd walked into the foyer. Regal. Not at all broken or torn by grief.

She reached up a hand, and with a sideways glance at him Pogue stepped in to take it when Callum didn't move. Callum didn't want to touch her. This woman had flayed him alive the last time they'd conversed. And aside from everything else, he could blame the last ten years on her. He'd *been* blaming her for them, rather, and what he'd learned earlier today hadn't given him any cause to change his mind.

A white mop with black ears tore around the corner of the morning room door in a frenzy of high-pitched yowling and barking, launching directly at him. In the same instant black flashed in front of him. Waya lifted the wee thing up in her jaws, and Rebecca shrieked as it began squealing.

"Release, Waya," he ordered. "Put it down. It's nae yers."

Turning her yellow eyes on him, the wolf opened her jaws, and the now disheveled mop thudded to the floor. It rolled upright, then with another screech tore up the stairs and vanished.

Evidently the wee beast wasn't alone, though, because as it fled another form hurtled down the stairs at him. Shrieking in some sort of childlike fury it jumped at him, and he reflexively caught it by the waist in midair. "You leave my mama and my dog alone!" it yelled, pummeling him with two wee fists.

It was female, judging from the dress and the long, dark-colored hair twisting out of a half-finished braid. Callum lifted it higher, to look it in the eyes—and his heart wrenched with a sensation he couldn't even put to words. One green and one blue eye looked back at him, fierceness in every line of her scrunched-up, angry face. God, she looked like Ian, even down to the dimples in her cheeks.

"Who are ye?" he asked, surprised at the effort it took to keep his voice steady. He tilted his head, still holding her at eye level.

"I am Lady Margaret," she stated in a very proper English tone as she abruptly stopped trying to hit him, though she continued gazing at him suspiciously. "Who are you, sir?"

Rebecca stirred. "Maggie, this is y—"

"I'm Callum," he broke in. For God's sake, he'd just found the one soul he knew to be innocent of . . . everything. No one else would do the introductions, put her own prejudices into the mix. "Yer uncle, I reckon."

Her face eased a little, though she kept her blue eye narrowed. "You have eyes like me."

"Aye. How old are ye?"

"I turned six nearly four weeks ago. I'm almost six and a half," she returned. "How old are you?"

"I turned thirty about ten weeks ago," he returned, though he honestly couldn't remember how long ago it had been. A lifetime had passed in the space of the past few weeks.

She nodded, her braid unraveling further. "Did you hurt my dog?"

"Nae. He came at me, and Waya pointed oot that that wasnae a good idea."

"Who is Waya?"

He angled her slim torso so she could see the wolf below her. Sweet Saint Michael, she felt as delicate and light as blown glass. How did such creatures manage to come into the world at all, much less survive it? "That's Waya," he said aloud.

"Oh, my heavens. What is it?"

"It's a wolf. A she-wolf."

Her two-colored eyes widened. "A wolf? Is she yours?"

"Nae. We're partners."

She studied the wolf for another moment, then looked back at him. "Will she eat me? I don't wish to be eaten."

Callum shook his head, conscious that he wanted to wrap this wee lass in his arms and flee with her back to

Kentucky, where he knew he could keep her safe. Until
Ian had justice and he had his revenge, though, neither
of them was going anywhere. "Waya will protect ye,
lass. She'd nae—never—hurt ye. Both of us are here to
protect ye." That might not have been so ten minutes
ago, but now, and from now on, it was the truth.

"Well, I'm very brave all on my own, but thank you.
May I pet her?"

"Maggie, I don't think—"

"Aye. Just dunnae ever do it when she's asleep. Call
her name first so ye dunnae startle her."

With surprising reluctance he let her go, setting her
feet onto the floor, then squatted down beside her to
wrap an arm about Waya's shoulders. The wolf had
likely scented the bairn and his relationship to her before he'd even been aware of Margaret's existence, but
he wanted to be certain the wolf understood. "Waya,
this is Margaret," he said, taking the lass's absurdly wee
hand in his free one and guiding her fingers down to
brush along the wolf's throat, her most vulnerable place.

"Hello, Waya," the lass said softly, then unexpectedly
hugged the wolf full around the neck. "You're so lovely!"

Callum tensed his arm, ready to intervene. The big
wolf, though, edged her head around and licked Margaret solidly on the ear, then gave a happy *whumph*
sound.

That had been simple. Hiding his deep breath, he
straightened again to find another pair of eyes glaring
at him. These were a light blue, and it didn't take much
effort to interpret their expression. Becca didn't want
him there—which gave him yet another reason to stay.

"When did you return to Scotland?" she asked, making another effort to straighten her wet hair and then
giving up.

"This morning," he returned, not bothering to ask

how she'd known he had been away from Scotland. Ian, at least, had sent letters to Kentucky, and she'd urged the solicitor not to send the last one. This wasn't the conversation he wanted to have—intended to have—with her, but with the bairn present it would have to do. He would get his answers from her, just not at this moment. The past ten years had taught him patience. Patience and how to apply just enough force to get what he wanted or needed for his business.

"Ian thought you in Kentucky," she went on, her voice hesitating a little over her husband's name as she confirmed his suspicions. Or perhaps he'd just wanted to hear it do so. He couldn't be certain. "Were you?"

"Aye." If she wanted to have a civil conversation, she could carry it.

"How did—"

"That prissy solicitor of yers. Bartholomew Harvey. He said ye didnae want me found, but I reckon he values his reputation over yer . . . whatever it is ye wanted. Me *not* being here, I assume."

She nodded tightly. Even with ten years being gone from here, he still would have recognized her in a crowd. Her face had rounded a little, adding a softness to her countenance that she hadn't had at eighteen. Given the amount of time he'd spent studying her bosom when he'd been twenty, now at thirty he would have been prepared to swear on a stack of Bibles that she'd made some improvements there, as well.

"Where will you be staying?" she continued.

"Here."

Her eyebrows dove together, her soft-looking lips compressed tightly. "You most certainly cannot think to reside here with me and Maggie."

"I most certainly can," he returned.

"Waya should stay with us," the bairn put in, giving

the black wolf a vigorous scratch between the ears. "Her fur is very rough."

Rebecca's fair skin paled further. "I am not—"

"Office?" He pointed toward the room where Ian had once kept his books and correspondence.

"Yes, b—"

"In there," he cut in. "Pogue, my bags will be arriving shortly. I'll take the master bedchamber and connecting rooms." Deliberately he glanced back at Rebecca, very much doubting that she'd moved out of those rooms in the past year.

"I . . . Of course, Master Call—I mean, Lord Geiry."

"Hold a moment, Pogue," Rebecca countered, and with a damp swoosh of her lavender skirts led the way into the office.

"Waya. Guard," Callum murmured, and the wolf extricated herself from the bairn's clutches to go sit staring at the front door. He'd been reining in his temper, his words, his desire to lash out so tightly that his muscles practically groaned as he followed her. If she still thought of him as the short-tempered, adventurous boy she'd once known, she'd just made a very large mistake. He looked forward to pointing that out to her.

The office had always been neat, and as he walked inside all the books were still lined up precisely on the shelves, while an open ledger lay parallel to the edge of the desk, a pencil perpendicular to that atop the pages. It almost seemed as if Ian was still there, and had only left the room a moment ago. He shook off the sensation. Rebecca seated herself behind the desk as he closed the door, shutting them in. So she wanted the position of power; she could take it, as far as he was concerned. He had *the* power.

"You cannot stay here," she said abruptly, slamming the ledger closed. "It's not proper."

Callum leaned back against the door. "That's how ye greet a dear friend ye havenae seen in ten years?" He gazed at her until she glanced away. "Ye look proper, still dressed in half-mourning colors even, but I'm beginning to have my doubts about yer sincerity."

"You may have been my dearest friend a decade ago. You are not any longer. And don't you dare blame me for that." She smacked the flat of her hand against the desk, likely wishing it was his face. "I have no greeting for you. Leave, Callum. No one wants you here."

"I want me here, and I reckon that's what matters. I'm the Earl Geiry now, lass, whatever ye thought might happen."

"Whatever I thought might happen?" she echoed. "I thought it would be your cousin James and his family taking the house, but I would hope they would have given more than two minutes' notice before they threw my things out of the bedchamber where I've been laying my head for the past ten years."

He folded his arms across his chest, lowering his head to gaze at her directly. "I'd suggest ye nae go complaining to me about being thrown out of a *room* without notice. I left the fucking country with what I bore on my back and naught else."

"Language, sir!"

Aye, he'd have to mind his language, and his temper. Kentucky had been a bit more rugged than Inverness. Aside from that, he had a task to accomplish, and he'd do well to remember that bellowing and punching might not be the best way to accomplish it. Not at the beginning, anyway. Not until he knew the name of every man—and woman—who'd had a hand in killing Ian.

"Do ye have any more children?" he asked brusquely. Margaret had changed things, in ways he couldn't even begin yet to foresee. The angel of death he'd meant to become had someone to protect, now.

"No, we—I—don't have any more children. Ian sent you letters. Did you not receive them? He spent a great deal of money to track you down."

"I dunnae ken why he would, being that he issued an order and I followed it. But aye, I received his letters. I didnae read them. I used 'em for kindling." The first letter had been a shock when it had arrived, a little better than five years ago. As far was Callum was concerned, he'd moved himself as far across the world as he possibly could from the Highlands, and once there, as deep into the woods and hills as the terrain and the natives would allow. And then Ian had somehow found him. Now he wondered if his brother had written to announce the birth of his daughter. It didn't matter, of course; until five minutes ago he hadn't wanted anything to do with bairns from his brother's happy marriage. Until he'd set eyes on the delicate, defenseless sprite.

"You never read any of them? *Any* of them?"

She looked at him, her gaze traveling from his worn boots and breeches up to his jacket with one button missing, before she met his gaze again. He knew the appearance he presented, and he didn't much care what she might think of him. This wasn't about him, and it was only about her if she'd had something to do with Ian's death.

Callum narrowed his eyes. "I dunnae reckon what I did out in Kentucky has any bearing on anything. Though I did miss seeing any letters *ye* might have written me. I had a yen to burn some of those, as well, but they nae did arrive."

"I never wrote you."

If he hadn't hated her for ten years, that might have wounded him. As it was, he shrugged. "Just as well. I've more interest in what ye might be up to today, anyway. A wee bird told me, for example, that ye've had Donnach Maxwell calling on ye. The Duke of Dunncraigh's firstborn, no less."

"Who is this wee bird?" she demanded, clearly exasperated. Good; that made two of them. "You said you only returned to Inverness this morning."

"Aye, I did. Dunnae dodge the question, Lady Geiry. Do ye mean to wed the Marquis of Stapp? Has he been whispering to ye about how easy it'll make managing yer fleet if he marries ye, since ye've had all yer businesses entwined for ten years now?"

She lifted her chin, which would have been haughty if she didn't still have hair and water running down one side of her head. "I am a widow. I believe whom I choose to see is my own business, and none of yours."

He nodded. "So it is. Unless he's been having that conversation with ye for longer than a year."

"You go too far, sir," she snapped, her fingers beginning to shake before she folded them into her lap. "Your brother and I were perfectly happy. I will not lower myself to answer your asinine, ill-meant accusations."

She hadn't forgotten how to hold her own in a conversation, for damned certain. He refused to admire her spleen. "Then dunnae. But Donnach Maxwell willnae be calling on ye here. Nae any longer. I'll nae have him in this house."

"You cannot—"

"My house," he interrupted. "My rules."

"Then you may have this house," she snapped, pushing to her feet. "I have Edgley House by the harbor, and *that* belongs to me. You stomp about this house as long as you wish. You'll do it alone."

She strode up to him, clearly expecting him to move out of her way. Callum remained where he was, wondering if she had any idea how very patient he was being. He could *make* her tell him what she knew about Ian's death, and just how close she'd become to Donnach Maxwell; of that he was certain. But blunt didn't suit him. Not today, anyway, when his memories were nearly thick enough to walk upon. And not after meeting the little one. And the wee lass had changed more than that. He couldn't sit alone in his fortress and plot his vengeance against the world while Margaret MacCreath and her two-colored eyes smiled innocently at him.

"Go if ye like," he said, keeping his voice low and level. "Lady Margaret stays here."

All the color left her face. *"What?"*

"I'm Lord Geiry. She is my brother's daughter, and therefore my ward. She goes where I say. And I say she stays with me."

"You devil!" Rebecca swung her open hand at him.

He knew it was coming, and lifted his arm to block the blow. Then he caught her wrist in his fingers. "I'm being very kind at the moment," he said, releasing her the second she pulled away. The touch seared him, and not with the anger and disgust he'd expected. "I'm allowing ye to stay if ye wish. Ye might consider that before ye begin slapping and kicking." The Rebecca he remembered had never been much for slapping, but she'd had a hell of a kick. That likely wasn't proper enough for her any longer, but he didn't care to find out for certain.

She tromped to the desk and back again. "Why did you come back?" she finally snapped, pacing again. "Why? Because with Ian gone you would finally have his money? Because you would do anything to make a stand against Dunncraigh? It's been ten years, Callum.

The duke has been nothing but kind for all that time, and especially since Ian died. I don't know how I would have managed to sort through my father's business or keep Ian's going without his or Donnach's expertise on the matter. So keep your stupid, petty grudges to yourself, and do not ruin my life, or Maggie's, because of them. Take the title, take the money, take the house, but leave us alone."

He tilted his head. Was that the man he'd been? It sounded familiar, in an uncomfortable, far-off way. "I'm nae here for any damned money," he stated, grinding out the last word. "And in Kentucky we've nae use for earls or dukes. I own a business that I began, one that I reckon earns me more income than Geiry ever could."

She looked him up and down again, color returning to her cheeks. "You don't look it."

"I didnae dress to impress ye, Rebecca."

Lady Geiry sniffed. "If you have your own money, then why are you here? You'll ruin everything!"

Callum had become accustomed to keeping his own counsel, to knowing the hows and whys of a thing and simply expecting his employees to do as he ordered. He hunted alone but for Waya, and after his exit from Scotland ten years earlier, he'd found that he preferred it that way. And he fully meant to ask his own questions in his own time to discover what, exactly, had happened to his brother. Still, all he had now was a vast, smooth surface of unknowns. If he stirred the pot, however, a morsel or two might emerge.

"I was stacking kindling," he began, pushing away from the door and walking to the window when the memory made him restless, "and found a bit of newspaper that said Lord Geiry was dead. Then I found the last letter I'd received before anyone could burn it, and read it. Half an hour later I was on my way back to

Scotland. As for the why, it was one word I read. One word I keep hearing. Do ye ken what the word was?"

She'd pivoted to keep him in view. "I'm . . . I'm sorry you had to learn about Ian's death that way, Callum. I truly am. But this has been difficult enough. Please go away, and don't muck about in what we're just managing to get straightened out. We're trying to move forward again."

" 'Drowned,' " he said, ignoring her protest. Well, not ignoring, but memorizing every word for future study and reference. "Ian drove off the bank of Loch Brenan and *drowned*. Didn't break his neck, didn't get crushed beneath the wheels, but *drowned*. Ian. The lad who caught fish with a spear from under the water. The lad who'd go swimming with us, but wouldnae go shooting or riding because he couldnae bear to look the fool."

"What? I . . ." She took a deep breath. "Accidents happen, Callum. He took the phaeton out in a storm, and a terrible thing happened. Don't try to make it worse than it was."

"Ye'll have to excuse me if I choose nae to take yer word for anything, lass. Especially when ye're being courted by Donnach Maxwell and practically calling Dunncraigh yer da' a year after losing yer true papa." Returning to the door, he pulled it open. "I'll be sleeping in the master bedchamber. Unless ye and I are sharing it, ye'd best have yer things out by midnight."

She stalked past him. "Don't you dare speak a word about this drowning nonsense to Margaret," she hissed. "I think sometimes she still expects her papa to come walking back through the front door." Her voice caught. "If you've come only to look for conspiracies, look well. You won't find any. And then go away. Or at the least, let me leave with my daughter."

Callum watched her return to the foyer to collect

young Margaret and then head upstairs, calling for servants to help her move her things to the yellow room, wherever the devil that was. He wanted to walk the house, to familiarize himself with it all over again, but he would do that tonight, after everyone else had gone to bed.

As for Rebecca, when he'd gone over this plan in his mind, he'd forced her out of the house. He didn't trust her; she'd stood against him once, and so she could go to the devil with the rest of clan Maxwell. Margaret's existence had altered that. The one person he knew to be innocent in Ian's demise was going nowhere. The closer she remained, the better he could protect her. If that meant Rebecca had to remain beneath his roof as well, then so be it. The truth, as Shakespeare had written, would out. And God help Becca if she was involved.

Chapter Four

Rebecca paced the morning room floor, her gaze angling to the mantel clock every time she reached the farthest point from the window. Someone was punishing her. That was the only reason for this disaster that made any sense. And whoever it was had the ability to slow down the progression of time, as well.

Finally the front door opened, and she gripped the back of the couch to keep from rushing into the hallway. When Pogue knocked on the half-open door, she gestured him forward. "Get him in here, and shut the door," she whispered. "And please let me know if Lord Geiry stirs from his bedchamber."

The butler nodded. "Of course, my lady." Turning, he practically grabbed the young man by the scruff and shoved him into the morning room. "In ye go, lad."

Bartholomew Harvey, Esquire, tugged down at the front of his jacket as he regained his footing. "I'm here, my lady. You said it was urgent."

"I sent for you an hour ago," she returned, keeping her voice low.

"It's only six o'clock, Lady Geiry. I was dead asleep,

I'm afraid, and the office had to send someone to my apartment to wake m—"

"Did you know Callum MacCreath was on his way back to Scotland?" she interrupted.

He blinked. "No. I most assuredly did not. The first I knew of it was yesterday when he summoned me to that accounting office of his. Bloody Highlanders." He flushed. "I beg your pardon, my lady."

"I told you not to send any more letters seeking him," she returned, ignoring his atypical profanity. Callum MacCreath could make a saint curse. "You've ruined everything."

"The law is the law, my lady, as I explained before. The title requires an heir. And he is the heir." He frowned, his thin brows furrowing. "If it wasn't him, it would have been James Sturgeon. Or someone else, if not him. Things must be settled by the book. You are aware of that."

"Of course I am. I just . . . I just didn't want it to be *him*." For years she'd tried to forget that last night, until she'd finally realized she would be much better off remembering how angry and hurt and insulted she'd been, rather than how fond she'd been of the stupid man—boy—for the ten years previous to that.

When she'd first caught sight of him yesterday, she'd barely recognized him. Taller and broader across the shoulders, he looked like he'd spent the last ten years doing hard labor. The worn clothes certainly supported that, despite what he'd said about not needing Ian's money. He looked even more handsome, the hard masculinity of him firmly defined. But that dark, cynical glint in his two-colored eyes—that was new. As was the way he'd trod over her plans as if they, and she, didn't even exist.

"May I ask, my lady," Mr. Harvey said, making her jump, "what it is you require of me? It is quite early."

She clenched her hands together. "Yes. How do I get rid of him?"

"'Get rid of'? In what way, my lady? Because if we're discussing something . . . nefarious, I cannot—will not—be a part of—"

"Stuff and nonsense," she snapped. "He walked in here and claimed my daughter as his ward, and refuses to allow her to leave his care. Surely I have a higher claim on my own offspring."

"Ah. No, I'm afraid you do not. Lady Margaret is Lord Geiry's niece, and in the absence of her father—his brother—he is her guardian."

That panic she'd felt yesterday when he'd announced that she could go wherever she pleased, but Margaret would stay, hit her all over again. Maggie, Lady Mags as the Highlanders called her, was all she had. Her only claim on what her life had been like prior to last year, the only bit of home and hearth and warmth she had remaining to her. The only part of Ian she could see, other than the portrait hanging in the library.

"But there must be something I can do," she protested. Being in the same house with Callum, even for one night, had upended ten years of calm and peace, ten years of her being the lady she knew she could be beneath the scraped knees and stupid mad adventures. For heaven's sake, she'd tried to hit him, when nothing in ten years had ever stirred her to such violence. Even Ian's death, while it had brought her to tears and grief, hadn't filled her with such . . . fury.

"I'm not certain how to advise you, my lady. Or whether it's proper for me to do so."

She faced the solicitor. "Why not? Or does he have your loyalty?"

"He let my entire firm go from his employment yesterday, Lady Geiry, so I owe him nothing." He paused, tugging at his jacket again. "In fact, while I still work with some of Dunncraigh's properties, I have no dealings with anyone connected to this household, unless you'd care to secure my services. You do still have several holdings, thanks to your father's will, I believe, and they remain yours until marriage. Some of them, even after th—"

"Yes, I'd like to secure your services," she interrupted. Men and their deals. She'd tired of them ages ago. "Draft whatever papers you need me to sign. Your first priority is to extricate my daughter and me from the clutches of that man."

He bowed. "I shall return shortly, then. Good morning, my lady."

"Yes, yes." She waved a hand at him. "Without delay."

Once he'd gone she sank onto the couch and gazed out the window, laying her head along her outstretched arm. All night she'd tossed and turned, dreaming of being attacked by wolves and of Ian swimming about Loch Brenan, except that his face was blue and mottled as it had been when they'd found him, but another man had been standing on the far side of his grave, looking at her with two-colored eyes.

A soft tap sounded by the door, and she looked up. The black wolf gazed at her, large yellow eyes unblinking. She gasped, straightening. After a moment the animal swung its head toward the stairs, and then turned toward the front door as Callum reached the foyer. He paused in the morning room doorway to eye her much as the wolf had.

"Pogue," he said, still looking at her, "I'll be out for an hour or so. If Lady Margaret isnae here when I return, ye can expect the lot of the household staff to be handed their papers."

"She'll be here, m'laird," the butler returned from somewhere beyond her view. "Ye have my word."

"And where are you going?" Rebecca asked, annoyed that he'd stifled a plan she hadn't even had time to consider. Blast it all, they should have fled last night—though the wolf no doubt prowling the halls would have made that nearly impossible.

"Pogue says there's a horse in the stable hasn't been ridden for over a year," he returned, pulling on his gloves. "Thought I'd put him through his paces."

"No one rides Jupiter," she retorted, before she could stop herself. For heaven's sake, if he wanted to go riding and then broke his neck, that would be his own fault. It would certainly remove several of her worries.

He grinned, the expression making her breath catch just a little and doing something she didn't like to her chest. "I'll risk it. I dunnae reckon ye'll weep tears for me if I'm killed."

"Not a single one."

"Dunnae worry yerself, lass. I've nae forgotten how to ride."

"I don't care."

She did remember how he used to ride, utterly fearless and taking far too many chances. He'd been mesmerizing. He still was, apparently, since she stood up to watch through the window as Malcolm the groom led the big bay stallion around to the front of the house. Donnach had urged her to sell the brute, but Jupiter had been Ian's one indulgence, his one dangerous thing. She thought it was silly and sentimental, but now if it took Callum down a peg or two, perhaps some good could come of her reluctance to part with the animal.

The bay stomped, then backed up, blowing, as the

wolf trotted onto the front drive. As the two beasts stared at each other, Callum walked up, took the reins from Malcolm, and swung up into the saddle. Jupiter whinnied, starting to rear, but Callum didn't tighten his grip, instead kicking the stallion in the ribs and leaning in to say something she couldn't make out. The bay bucked, then set off down the short drive at a dead run, the wolf loping behind them.

"That man can ride," Malcolm commented to Pogue as the two men stood by the front steps, their words carrying to Rebecca through the open front door.

"I reckon he'll have half of Inverness claiming the devil and his hellhound are about," the old butler returned.

The groom spat. "Aye. And I'm nae certain they'd be wrong about that."

Rebecca wasn't so certain about that, either. The Callum MacCreath with whom she'd grown up invented nonsensical rhymes, drank more than he should have at places where he should not have ventured, and had clearly idolized his older brother even while he constantly argued with and teased him. As he'd reached his twentieth year the drinking had gotten worse and the humor lessened, until she'd begun to think he would never mature into anything other than a loudmouthed buffoon. Adding Lord Stapp and the Duke of Dunncraigh into the mix had only made him as combustible as black powder and as dangerous as an unaimed shot.

That man, though, the one at this moment likely spreading panic through the outskirts of Inverness, didn't much resemble the Callum she'd known. He'd come in like the winter wind, shoving all resistance aside, and it had happened so fast she still hadn't found her feet. And she needed to find her blasted feet. The sooner the better.

"Mama," Margaret said, dancing into the morning room, "Agnes says I must stay up in the nursery, but she's afraid of Waya, and I want to see her."

Waya? The wolf, Rebecca remembered belatedly. "The wolf and your uncle went for a ride," she said. "And yes, you should remain up in the nursery until we can find another place to stay."

The six-year-old stopped spinning her circles. "We have to leave? Why won't Uncle Callum let us stay? He seemed very nice to me. I'll ask him, if you like."

No, she didn't like. "He will permit us to stay," Rebecca said slowly, deciding against informing the sprite that she'd essentially become a captive. "I'm not certain we should, though. He's an unmarried man, after all."

She stopped. He *was* unmarried, wasn't he? She hadn't asked, but she'd assumed . . . No, he must be single. Otherwise he would have informed her that she was now the Dowager Countess of Geiry or something equally old and finished sounding. And the way he'd looked at Margaret, as if she was both precious and alien at the same time—he was not a man who'd spent any time with children.

None of that mattered, though. What mattered was that Callum seemed to be set once again on making trouble, and she wanted Margaret nowhere near it. Or him. "Don't fret though, butterfly," she said, moving to take her daughter's hand so they could spin together. "We have your grandpapa's home closer to the harbor. I simply need to make some arrangements before we can officially move in."

Margaret flapped her free arm up and down. "I'm glad Uncle Callum is here," she stated. "Everyone's been going to heaven and leaving us here alone."

Yes, they had been. Rebecca sighed. "We're not

alone," she returned. "We still have Lord Stapp and the Duke of Dunncraigh. And your friends, and mine."

"Well, I do like Sarah MacKenzie quite a lot, but she's afraid of dogs, and I have a wolf now."

"You do not have a wolf. Your uncle has a wolf. And we won't be sharing a house for long." The sooner they could both remove themselves from the complications he represented, the better. If Mr. Harvey couldn't discover something, she would find someone who could. Money certainly wouldn't be an issue. Rebecca tugged her daughter toward the hallway. "Now let's go have some breakfast before it gets cold."

"Very well. I intend to save all my ham for Waya, though."

"As you wish. I would imagine a wolf prefers uncooked meat, though."

"Oh. I hadn't thought of that," Margaret returned. "Excuse me, then. I have to go see Mrs. Kirkland and tell her I would like some raw ham for breakfast."

Oh, dear. "Just don't eat any of it, yourself, Maggie."

The six-year-old giggled. "I'm not a wolf, Mama."

No, Margaret wasn't. But there were two wolves residing at MacCreath House now. Waya, and Callum. A man who'd been a puppy ten years ago had matured into something else entirely—a hunter, a predator. One who seemed to be looking for prey. And she had the disturbing feeling that he might be looking at her.

Half an hour later as she sat shaking her head at her daughter, presently seated at the breakfast table with Reginald on her young lap, she could almost pretend that Callum MacCreath's arrival had been a nightmare, that he'd vanished with the morning mists as a warning for her to be more grateful for what she had remaining.

"I do hope you'll remember that in polite company we do not feed Reginald on the tabletop," she commented, resting her chin in her hand and trying not to smile at the sight of the white Skye terrier sticking his long tongue out as far as he could manage to reach the scraps of meat Margaret had placed on the smooth mahogany surface.

"I'll remember," the six-year-old said, giggling. She nudged a scrap of meat closer to the dog, and Reginald gobbled it happily.

Someone rapped on the front door, and a moment later Pogue stepped into the room. "My lady, Lord Stapp wish—"

The Marquis of Stapp brushed past the butler. "Callum MacCreath?" he snapped, scowling as he looked about the breakfast room. "Is it true?"

Her beau generally showed more decorum and civility upon his entrance than that, but she imagined Callum had a poor effect on everyone. "Is what true?" she asked, mainly to hear what impression her brother-in-law had made since his arrival.

"Belleck came calling this morning, said his valet was huddled below stairs with the rest of his servants and swearing that the devil and his hound had ridden past the house this morning. And the dock's buzzing about Callum MacCreath and a monstrous black wolf. Have ye seen him?"

"Uncle Callum's living here," Margaret announced, feeding Reginald the remainder of his scraps. "And so is Waya."

Donnach Maxwell pinned the girl with his gaze. " 'Living here,' " he repeated, eyes narrowing. "And who is Waya?"

"His wolf," Rebecca supplied. "He appeared yesterday afternoon. I had no idea he—"

"Ye told me he was dead, Rebecca." Shoving a chair back, he dropped into it.

"I said I *thought* he was dead. As did you. How else do you explain why a man who's had a sizable inheritance and a title waiting for him would refrain from collecting it for better than a year?"

He looked down for a moment, then slammed his hand onto the table. "Damnation."

"If you please, my lord," she protested, moving around to place her hands over an impressed-looking Margaret's ears.

"What? Oh. My apologies, Lady Margaret."

Rebecca kissed her daughter on the top of her dark hair. "Go upstairs to Agnes," she instructed. "Take Reginald with you, if you wish."

Margaret sighed. "Yes, Mama. Please tell me when Uncle Callum returns. I want to play with Waya."

Good heavens, what had happened over the past day? Her daughter wanted to play with a wolf, *she'd* been removed from her own bedchamber, and she and Margaret had become prisoners in the home where she'd lived for the past ten years. She sat in her daughter's vacated chair. "Yes, he's here. I had nothing to do with it."

With a deep breath, Donnach nodded, his light brown hair short and precise as his dark green jacket and gray trousers. "Of course." He sat forward, reaching across the table for her hand. "Then gather yer things. Ye and Margaret will come stay at Samhradh House."

She blinked, surprised. "With you?"

"Aye. With me. We'll be wed by the end of summer anyway, and I'll have my mother come stay as well, if ye like, so there willnae be any scandal."

"I . . . Thank you, Donnach. That's very generous of you. It's not necessary, however. You know my father left me Edgley House."

"Aye. I'll help ye move yer things there, then." He straightened. "Pogue!"

"No, Donnach. I don't—"

"I'll nae have ye in the same house as that drunk," the marquis interrupted, standing again as Pogue entered the room. "And that's final."

"Aye, m'laird?" the butler asked.

"Arrange to have Lady Geiry's and Lady Margaret's necessities packed. They are leaving the house."

"I cannae do that, m'laird," the butler intoned, lowering his head.

"The devil ye say," Donnach returned, glowering. "It wasnae a request, man. Now!"

Did he honestly think she hadn't already considered leaving? "Donnach, I c—"

"Donnach Maxwell," Callum's low voice came, and Rebecca turned, startled, toward the doorway. "The first rat to come scratching at my cellar door."

Callum stood there, his broad shoulders nearly brushing the doorjamb on either side. She didn't see the wolf, but no doubt the beast was somewhere close by, ready to eat anyone who disagreed with him. She put an involuntary hand over her chest. He'd always been trouble. Now, though, he seemed . . . lethal.

The marquis stood, facing the door, his hands clenched. "The prodigal son," Donnach said, making a small movement that might have been him having second thoughts about approaching the new Lord Geiry. "Who dug ye up?"

Rebecca couldn't blame him for hesitating; Callum had to be two or three inches above six feet now. And where before he'd been whip-thin, somewhere over the past ten years he'd put on solid muscle. She doubted he carried an ounce of fat on him, and he looked strong enough to lift a mountain over his head.

She'd noticed all that yesterday, but he seemed even more . . . striking with Donnach standing there and hesitating to approach him. She'd always thought of the marquis as tall and capable, but Callum MacCreath was the devil himself.

"I distinctly remember telling ye, Lady Geiry," Callum noted, his gaze moving to her, "that Stapp isnae welcome in this house. Did I nae make myself clear?"

"He just arrived," she hedged. "I haven't had a chance to tell him anything. And he was only attempting to decipher the rumors about you."

"Dunnae make excuses for me, Rebecca," Donnach said. "If this boy thinks he can intimidate me, he's welcome to try it."

Callum tilted his head. "A boy, am I? If it comforts ye to think so, dunnae let me stop ye. I've only one bit of advice for ye today. Get out. Now."

"We were just leaving. Rebecca, we'll send for yer things later. Go fetch Margaret."

"If ye've a yen to take the lady with ye, I've nae objection," the new Lord Geiry commented smoothly. "The bairn stays here."

Donnach lowered his head a fraction. "So be it. Rebecca, let's be off."

Startled by his matter-of-fact response to the idea of her leaving Maggie behind, Rebecca looked at the man who'd been her confidant for much of the past year, and her friend for considerably longer than that. "I am not leaving my daughter, Donnach. I hope you know me well enough to realize that."

Finally the marquis looked back at her. "Ye cannae wish to remain beneath the same roof as this monster," he stated, his tone an odd mix of disdain and pleading. "I was there that night, if ye'll recall. He insulted ye and yer dear husband to the point that his own brother drove him away."

"I recall." Deliberately she seated herself again. "Find a way to remove my daughter from his protection and I'll happily join you at Samhradh House. Until that happens, I will remain here."

"Ye heard the lass, Stapp. And if ye dunnae leave through my front door now, I'll set ye outside through the window."

People didn't talk to Donnach Maxwell that way. And they certainly didn't threaten him. For heaven's sake, he was the heir to the chief of clan Maxwell. Donnach certainly didn't seem to know how to take it, either. He bristled, his hands curling into fists. "Ye still need to learn some respect, b—"

Callum moved. Before Rebecca could do more than gasp, he had Donnach by the back of the shirt and the rear of his trousers. Hauling the shorter man around like one of those giant men in the Highlands games, he heaved. First the vases and plates that sat on the table beneath the window crashed to the floor. Then the wood-framed glass panels shattered into splintered shards that caught sunlight as they spun—and Donnach disappeared through the window.

"Mayhap ye'll recall now that I mean what I say. So ye go run to Dunncraigh," Callum growled in a carrying voice, as the curtain rod fell onto the side table. "Ye tell him I know what he did to Ian, and that I'm a man of my word. I'll be seeing both of ye. Soon."

With that he turned on his heel and left the room. For a moment Rebecca sat there, stunned. No one, even in the Highlands, did what he'd just done. Not to the Duke of Dunncraigh's firstborn son and heir. Callum Mac-Creath had just declared war on his own clan.

He'd thrown her—and Maggie—into the middle of

his battle as surely as he'd tossed Donnach through that window. That infuriated her. But just as troubling was the abrupt realization of how certain he was. Not even Callum, at least the one she'd known ten years ago, declared war without good reason. He thought Ian had been murdered. And he thought the Maxwells had done it.

As certain as she'd been that Ian had made a rare mistake and paid for it with his life . . . No. It had been an accident. Because if it hadn't been, everything in the past year had been a lie. And the idea that Callum had hold of the truth, the thought of what he might do with it, troubled her even more.

Chapter Five

Callum sat back in the library chair, half a glass of whisky by his elbow and a wolf sprawled out at his feet. Half of him regretted shutting Waya in his office before he'd gone to confront Stapp; seeing him with an arm chewed off would have been damned satisfying. On the other hand, throwing him through the window had uncoiled the rage that had been racketing about in his chest for the past five weeks. For the past ten years, if he wanted to be honest with himself.

The deep breath he took felt like the first one he'd managed in all that time. He'd plotted and set a course, aye, and run up his colors when he'd taken Waya out for a ride this morning, but finally he'd been able to fire that first shot. Now it would get interesting.

"You knew he would come calling, didn't you?"

Callum slanted his eyes toward the glass of whisky, but left it where it sat. "I'd a hunch, aye."

Rebecca crossed in front of him and made a wide detour around the wolf to seat herself daintily on the chair opposite. "And what if you're wrong? What if Ian did simply slide off the road and drown?"

"I'm nae wrong." He lifted his head to look at her.

She had her golden-blond hair pinned up properly again, a halo about her face with the morning sun behind her. Somewhere in the past decade she'd gone from being pretty to truly beautiful. In the back of his mind the thought scratched at him again that he'd never kissed her. Half the lasses about Geiry Hall had been in his bed by his twentieth year, but he'd never touched the one with whom he shared his adventures.

"But if you are?" she persisted. "Because I have no reason to think that night was anything but a horrible accident. Ian was angry about something, decided he needed to drive into Inverness without waiting for morning or for the weather to clear, and off he went over my objections. You know he was never rash or impulsive, but he did get impatient. And that night he was impatient."

"What made him angry and impatient, then?" If she'd had a hand in this, every word she uttered needed to be looked at from two sides, but that didn't mean what she said couldn't be useful.

"I don't know. He didn't tell me. He rarely told me anything." She shifted a little. "Your hand's bleeding."

He lifted his left hand, hanging over the arm of the chair. Blood dripped from where a small piece of glass dug into his knuckle. "Hm."

"That's all you have to say? You threw a marquis through a window. I suppose I should be thankful we were on the ground floor."

Callum lowered his hand again. "Donnach should be, ye mean."

She rose again, walking to the door and saying something to a maid outside the library before she returned to her seat. "So you had a hunch he would come calling, but that's not all of it. You *wanted* him to make an appearance. You always delighted in needling him."

"I reckon ye've got that backward. He nae missed a chance to jab at me, and I couldnae resist snapping back. But this isnae about who caught the bigger fish. And nae, I'm nae making a secret of being here," he returned. "Did I expect him to come by and ask about me? Aye. He killed my brother. Of course he wants to know what my plans here might be."

"So your ride this morning wasn't about fresh air or Jupiter. It was about being seen."

Rebecca Sanderson had always been a clever lass. As poised and ladylike as she'd become, she hadn't lost her wits. How had that been, he wondered, with her in the company of his methodical, unimaginative brother? But then she'd chosen Ian. He needed to remind himself of that. "Dunnae fret. Ye and I've both made it clear that ye and Margaret arenae here willingly."

"But you don't care if I'm here at all."

"Ye made yer bed, lass. Ye lie in it. The only question I have about ye at this moment is whether or nae ye had someaught to do with Ian's 'horrible accident,' as ye called it."

A maid slipped into the room, handed Rebecca some cloth and gauze and a bowl of water, and departed again. Approaching him, Rebecca knelt at his feet beside Waya and gestured for his hand. "You know me. Do you honestly think I would ever hurt Ian?"

He lifted his head. "I dunnae know ye. I *knew* ye. But then ye did someaught I couldnae even have imagined, so there's a good chance I've always had ye figured wrong."

Glancing up at him, she took his hand. "Then I'll tell you directly. I mourned for Ian," she said quietly, putting her fingers around the shard of glass. "This will hurt."

"I'm nae likely to cry," he stated, and refused to

flinch as she pulled it from his knuckle. "And saying ye mourned a man doesnae mean you didnae first harm him."

She put the cloth over the cut and pressed down, lifting her face again to look him in the eye. "I didn't harm him," she returned. "I had no reason in the world to do so. He and I always got along well, and we had a good marriage. We were well respected by our peers, and he was always kind to me. And he gave me Margaret. I know you think I married for a title and for wealth, and that's partly true. I also married Ian because he was . . . safe. He wouldn't gamble away our future, or take up with a mistress, or get drunk and do something impulsive that would come back to haunt us later."

"But ye willnae say ye loved him?" She'd made the omission of the word fairly obvious, but he was petty enough that he wanted to hear her say it.

"I loved him," she countered. "He provided me with a good, comfortable, happy life."

His jaw clenched. "And I wouldnae have?"

The second he spoke he regretted the question. He didn't care what she thought of him; that time had passed ten years ago. At the same time, he knew he'd fashioned a great portion of the last ten years in order to refute exactly that of which Rebecca and Ian had accused him. He wasn't that idiotic, spoiled, drunken boy any longer. But even that idiotic boy had been correct about something. He'd blustered about everything, though, and so he'd been unable to make them listen to the one most important thing. That would never happen again.

"You don't want me to answer that, Callum," she responded, removing the cloth and setting it aside to wrap gauze about his hand.

"I asked the question; answer it."

"Aside from the fact that you didn't ask for my hand

until after your brother had already secured it, you continually argued with and belittled everyone around you. Especially those who outranked you. If I'd chosen you, your . . . disobliging behavior would have seen us ostracized and ridiculed, until the point that Ian finally cut you off and we were forced to live with my father—or flee somewhere where we could attempt to begin again. You might have thought that an exciting adventure, but I wanted a family. Children. That required stability and safety."

She'd damned well thought it through. As he had. And he couldn't even pretend to be surprised that they'd come to the same conclusion. She hadn't forgotten his mistakes, and neither had he. But her knowledge about his character lagged ten years behind his. "And now that ye've been widowed, ye've set yer sights on Donnach Maxwell for yer safety and stability? Because I dunnae give his continued survival very high odds."

"Stop saying such things," she countered, a bit of exasperation touching her voice. "Whatever your useless 'investigations' conclude, I can be compelled to testify against you if something happens to either him or the duke."

"'Investigations'? Ye reckon I'm that civilized? But ye didnae answer my question. Do ye think to marry Stapp?"

"I'm considering it, yes."

Callum held her gaze as he let her words sink into his bones, her cloudless blue eyes a shade deeper than he remembered. Could it be sorrow? Or regret? He shook those thoughts out of his head. They weren't useful. "I'll nae allow that, lass."

Her eyes narrowed. "I'm an heiress in my own right, Callum. Because of the . . . circumstances, I don't rely on the Geiry title or income. And you cannot stop me from doing as I think best for myself and my daughter."

"I can stop ye from doing any damned thing I dunnae agree to where Margaret's concerned."

She practically growled at him. "If—when—I remarry, my husband will . . . have a say."

"I doubt it," he retorted. "If that's yer plan, though, I can stop it, too. Ye've lived in the Highlands for more than half yer life, Rebecca. Surely ye've heard of levirate marriage?"

She released his injured hand as swiftly as if he'd burned her. "You must be joking," she snapped, her voice quavering. "You'd try to force me to marry *you*?" She shook her head, backing away. "You'd never succeed. Levirate marriage was designed to keep wealth within the clan's bloodline. Donnach Maxwell *is* clan Maxwell. He'll be *the* Maxwell, after his father's passing."

"I'll admit," he returned, standing and stalking after her, "that I'd find a complication or two. Being that the law was specifically created to enable a man to marry his brother's widow, I do have a leg to stand on, I reckon."

"Dunncraigh would never approve it."

"I've enough money to put that into question with the courts," he commented. "And ye're assuming Dunncraigh would be alive to disapprove." He stopped his pursuit as her back came up against the window, and instead placed his hands on her shoulders. He didn't want to touch her, but he needed to know. "Swear someaught to me, lass. Swear ye had nothing to do with Ian's death, and look me in the eyes when ye do it."

He'd given her that challenge before, over the years, and she'd always risen to the occasion. This time, for the first time, he wasn't so certain. But she lifted her chin to gaze straight at him. "I had nothing to do with Ian's death. I swear it." Rebecca swallowed. "And I'll do you one better, Callum. If you're able to convince me that he didn't drown by accident, I will help you prove it in court."

That, he hadn't expected at all. Tilting his head, he studied her face, her expression, the straight, tense line of her shoulders. She might have a secret or two after all this time, and questionable taste in men, but she wasn't lying.

Yesterday he'd sailed into the harbor at Inverness ready to burn to the ground anything and everyone who stood in his path. Then he'd discovered Margaret and altered his plans accordingly. And now it seemed he might—*might*—need to alter them again. Removing Rebecca from his enemies list wouldn't make her an ally, but it could change some things. And since he had no intention of waiting for a court to decide anything before he acted, she could be useful.

"Do you agree?" she prompted after a moment.

"Aye. I agree."

Her shoulders rose and fell. "Splendid. Then let me go."

"And if I dunnae let ye go?" His gaze lowered to her mouth. As they'd grown out of childhood together he'd had a few good chances to kiss her and had missed every opportunity to do so, and then ten years to think about what he hadn't done, why he hadn't even seen it until it was too late. But she didn't belong to Ian now. She didn't belong to anyone.

"Then I'll accuse you of being drunk and irresponsible again," she muttered, her voice still not quite steady.

For the devil's sake, he'd meant to hate her. He'd fairly well managed to do that for ten years. But for most of the ten years previous, they'd been friends and companions, nearly inseparable until he'd discovered sex and whisky. Callum bent his head, brushing his lips against hers. Liking the sensation, he took her mouth in a warm, slow kiss. She tasted of tea and annoyance, and something else that he couldn't quite name, but that made his cock sit up and take notice. This, her, was something he'd wondered about for a very long time. She put her palms against his chest, but before she could decide to push him away he took her wrists and drew them behind her back.

Could he trust her? He had no idea. All he knew at the moment was that after ten years of waiting and speculating and imagining something he'd never thought would come to pass, he felt that damned kiss all the way down his spine and everywhere in between.

Callum straightened, releasing her hands at the same time. "I'm nae drunk," he murmured, and with a short whistle calling Waya to his side, left the room.

"My lady, shouldn't you be dressing?" Mary asked, as the maid swooped into the wardrobe to place some freshly laundered clothes.

Rebecca started, lifting her head from the book she hadn't been reading. "Hm?"

"You're to go to the theater tonight, aren't you?" the maid returned, her cheeks darkening. "Unless Lord Stapp has canceled. I . . . Well, it's none of my business, I'm certain."

The theater. She'd completely forgotten. Judging by the condition of Callum's hand after it had gone through the window, she didn't imagine Donnach would be willing—or able—to show himself in public tonight. Heavens, she hadn't even leaned out the window to inquire after him, though her concern likely wouldn't have been well received.

"I have no idea," she said, setting the book aside. Robert Burns had never sat well with her; he felt far too many wild emotions for her taste, and felt far too comfortable discussing them. But this afternoon she'd been drawn to the poetry despite not being able to concentrate enough to make any sense of it.

"I suppose you couldn't send over a note to inquire, either?" Mary suggested, a trace of humor in her voice.

"No, I don't suppose I could," she returned.

She should be appalled, horrified, or at the least furious at what had happened this morning. Aside from her beau being thrown through a window, her brother-in-law had kissed her—and not in a friendly, brotherly manner. He'd always been a disruptive force, and that had clearly not changed. That didn't explain, however, why she hadn't been more outraged at his treatment of Donnach, or at his attempts to command who she wouldn't be allowed to see.

Lord Stapp had always been kind to her, from the moment Ian had announced their engagement. He'd always had a friendly word or two for her whenever he and his father met with her husband or her father for business, and after Ian's death he'd been the first one to appear and assure her that she wasn't alone. When her father had passed away, he'd helped her make the funeral arrangements and had brought Maggie a doll. Only gradually had his friendship become more romantic, and he hadn't begun pressing the issue at all until her official year of mourning ended two months ago.

And while lately he'd begun to make mention of a future that assumed they would be married, she'd made the same assumptions herself. Today at the breakfast table he'd seemed somewhat . . . intense, but then he'd just learned that the position Ian had held in their mutual business had been taken over by Callum—a man with whom he'd never dealt well.

"My lady?"

Rebecca took a breath. "I seem to have drifted away for a moment, Mary. What is it?"

"What do you wish to do about this evening?"

"Ah. Well, I'd hate to dress and not have him call, but I'd dislike even more if he called and I wasn't dressed."

"I thought Lord Geiry forbade him to call here," Mary noted, selecting a pretty red silk and lace gown from the wardrobe and lifting it.

Yes, there was that. If she had been more certain of her footing where Callum was concerned, the way he'd taken over her life would be very annoying. It *was* still annoying, since now people—certain people—couldn't even call on her at the house where she was being forced to stay.

And he'd only kissed her to shock her, to demonstrate how little power or control she had. As if she wasn't already aware of precisely that. It didn't matter, then, that he knew how to kiss, that he'd for a moment reminded her of what young girls had dreamed of when they imagined princes and heroes coming to call. No, not princes and heroes. Rogues and pirates. Even more delicious, those.

Before he'd reappeared—good heavens, had it only been a day ago?—she'd been happy. Happier, at least, each day a little better than the day before. She'd begun to look forward again. Donnach knew her father's and her late husband's business, had a large stake in it, even, and she could think of no one better to take over her portion of it upon their marriage. It should have gone to Ian, except that he'd perished before her father. If the reverse had happened, literally everything she owned except for Edgley House would now be in Callum's possession.

She shivered. "You know I can't wear such things yet," she said, moving to the dressing table. "The violet one with the black lace will do." A night out would be welcome; any distraction to keep her from dwelling on might-have-beens and should-have-beens and should-never-bes, all when she'd thought to spend the next week balancing invitations and broaching the topic of Donnach and marriage to Margaret.

"I haven't seen much here in the Highlands to convince me that they adhere to proper traditions of mourning," the maid commented, but replaced the scarlet gown in the wardrobe. "It's been well over a year now, regardless."

"Yes, but I've been in double mourning actually, haven't I?" Rebecca returned without heat. "I've already tempted censure by wearing colors at home." She sighed. "Yes, I could wear the red. It just doesn't feel . . . correct."

"I don't think a soul could find a single fault in how you've carried yourself, my lady, if I may say so. And thank goodness you're permitted to return to Society; you have some color in your cheeks again, finally."

Despite having lived in Scotland for over half her life, Rebecca had decided that upon becoming Lady Geiry she required some assistance with propriety and decorum. Hiring an English maid from a well-respected southern household had raised some local eyebrows initially, but she'd never regretted it. Mary would never believe that her mistress had once climbed trees and gone swimming in the loch while only half clothed. And as she'd tried to forget everything she'd ever done in Callum's questionable company, Rebecca found that very appealing.

In the violet and black at least she felt pretty again, and she remained convinced that the most significant improvement in her earlier doldrums had been when after six months she'd been able to stop wearing that awful, scratchy crêpe and heavy bombazine. Perhaps next month she would attempt something brighter, depending on the occasion.

Once Mary had finished weaving black and violet ribbons through her light hair and pinning the lot into a rather artistic tangle at the top of her head, she went to find Margaret so they could sit for an early dinner. As for Callum, well, he was on his blasted own. He couldn't be allowed to disrupt her life any more than he already had.

"Then what's Cherokee for 'bear'?" Margaret's young voice came through the open door of the nursery, and Rebecca slowed her approach.

"Yona," Callum's deeper voice returned.

" *'Yona,'* " Maggie repeated, mimicking his slightly faded Highlands accent. "Do you have a *yona* for a pet, as well?"

"Nae. They sleep through the winter. I couldnae abide all the snoring."

Margaret laughed. "But you've seen a bear?"

"Oh, aye. I have the skin of one decorating my floor back in Kentucky. But ye ken Waya's nae my pet. We're a pack of wolves, she and I. I look after her, and she looks after me."

"Can I be in your pack?"

Rebecca stirred, stepping into the room. "It's *may* I be in your pack," she corrected, hesitating again at the sight of Callum sitting cross-legged on the floor opposite her daughter, Waya in between them squirming about on her back while Reginald hid behind Agnes the nanny and peeked around her skirts to sniff and whimper. "And the answer is no."

Chaos. The man personified chaos. Always had, always would. At the same time, she was abruptly thankful that other than their unusual eyes, he and Ian didn't look much alike. Especially now. Ian had been slender and compact, but Callum had become sinew and muscle and grace—a hard life, she realized. Whatever the past ten years had been for her, they'd been hard for him. He'd worked hard. No one looked like that from lounging about writing poetry. Even sitting there on the floor he looked deadly.

"Why can't I be in Uncle Callum's pack?" the six-year-old queried, rubbing her hand along the wolf's belly as if the beast was someone's pet poodle.

"Because proper young ladies aren't wolves."

"She has ye there, lass," Callum unexpectedly agreed. "I reckon if only those of us in this room know it, though, ye can be in my pack."

She rose up on her knees, leaning over the she-wolf to hug her uncle. Her small arms couldn't meet around his broad shoulders. "Thank you, Uncle Callum. I'll be a very good wolf."

With a chuckle he hugged her back, lifting her over the wolf to perch on one of his thighs. Then he looked up at Rebecca over the girl's head. "It appears yer mama thinks she's going somewhere this evening," he commented. "Should we ask her where?"

"I heard Agnes and Mary talking about it this morning," Margaret replied, pulling an old watch out of her uncle's pocket and flipping it open. "They were wondering how she would go to the theater if Lord Stapp couldn't come calling to escort her." She turned over the watch. "This has Mama in it."

For the first time since his return, Rebecca saw Callum flinch. Gently he put his big hands over Margaret's small ones and retrieved the timepiece. "It's an old watch," he returned, clicking it shut again.

"I have no idea whether I'm going out tonight or not," Rebecca said, following the watch with her eyes as he returned it to his pocket. She'd never sat for a miniature portrait that she recalled. Where had he gotten a picture? "I thought it would be rude not to be ready if he sent word for me to meet him."

Setting Margaret aside, Callum easily rolled to his feet. "Mags, stay here with Waya for a moment, will ye? We need to get her accustomed to staying by yer side, being that ye're part of the pack now."

"Oh, of course!"

Moving forward, he took Rebecca by the elbow in a firm grip that didn't hurt, but that she couldn't have escaped if she'd wanted to. Together they walked to the head of the stairs, where he drew her to a halt. "Ye mean to stand by Stapp?" he asked in a low voice. "After what I told ye about Ian nae drowning? After Stapp tried to get ye to leave this house without Mags?"

"I've known Donnach for better than ten years," she returned in the same tone. "He's been my friend. The last thing I remember *you* doing is breaking your brother's heart."

His two-colored eyes narrowed. "If ye—"

"I said I would aid you if you convinced me. I'm not convinced of anything but the fact that you're willing to throw people who outrank you through windows and that you think a kiss can mend all the insults and misery you handed me that night. Now let me go."

He released her elbow. "I told ye before I'd nae stop ye from leaving the house," he rumbled. "Mind yer venom, woman, or I will stop ye from coming back inside."

"*My* venom?" she snapped, and jabbed a finger into his chest, hard even through his jacket and waistcoat and the thin shirt beneath that. *Concentrate,* she ordered herself, and poked him again. "I have not done a damned thing wrong, Callum. *I* didn't run away. I didn't—"

"I didnae run away, either," he retorted, his jaw clenched and the words tight.

"Very well. I didn't act so poorly that I was forced to leave my home," she revised. "I did everything I was supposed to, and as I've said, I had nothing to do with Ian's . . . demise. So be a little nicer to me, or don't expect me to be any nicer to you." Rebecca took a step closer to him, even though she had to lift her chin to hold his gaze. "For all I know, you've come here with the express purpose of creating destruction and chaos, simply because you blame Donnach and Dunncraigh and Ian and my father and me for your behavior that night and you want revenge on the lot of us."

There. It likely wasn't the wisest accusation to make, especially considering he literally could toss her from the house the same way he'd done with Donnach, but he didn't seem to realize that he was the only one carrying doubts about other people's motives.

"Dunnae mistake me," he returned, his voice still hard and low. "I do mean to have my revenge. But not for that night. I remember quite well what happened, lass. I remember that if I hadnae gone to the tavern—again—I might have been here to keep Ian alive." He closed his mouth, taking a deep breath. "If ye had naught to do with Ian, then ye've naught to fear from me. As long as ye dunnae side with those who did him harm."

Which meant Donnach, of course, and his father—the two people who'd aided and guided her through the turmoil, who'd taken on some of Ian's and then her father's responsibilities when she'd felt completely overwhelmed. "As long as you convince me that they're guilty."

He gazed at her for a long moment. "I want to trust ye, lass. We were friends once. Good friends. Or at least I reckoned we were."

She wasn't certain friends ever kissed the way he'd kissed her earlier. But in all honesty that was the first time he'd ever touched her like that. And he'd only brought up marriage that night because Ian had done so first. "We were," she agreed. "As for now, I hope you've noticed that your niece has no preconceived notions about you, because I never attempted to carry tales about you."

"Ye nae thought to set eyes on me again, so what would the point be?"

With a slow breath she lowered her hand again. "About six weeks before he died, Ian mentioned you in Maggie's hearing. She adored the idea of having an uncle in the Colonies and demanded to know everything possible about you—not that either of us knew very much. Or even if you were still alive." Rebecca sighed. "The fact that you've suddenly appeared, and with a wolf of all things, is simply the extra gravy on the goose, if you must know."

"At least one lass in the house is happy to see me, then," he mused, looking her up and down again in a way that made her blush. "Ye look very fine, Rebecca. It'd be a shame for ye to stay at home tonight. It'd be a greater shame for ye to be seen going about with Donnach Maxwell, especially considering what I mean to do to him. But I reckon I'll leave that up to ye to decide."

His gaze lowered to her mouth, and stayed there. Her breath hitched; if he kissed her again now she might do something mad like remember that she'd once imagined a life with him. That she'd once wished he would see her as more than a slightly unconventional friend.

When he turned around and started down the stairs, she realized she'd begun to lean toward him a little. Scowling, Rebecca straightened, her fists clenching. This would not do.

Halfway down to the landing he turned around to look up and face her again. "If ye do see Donnach, feel free to tell him I said that. I'd nae have ye keeping my secrets when ye dunnae trust me."

No, she didn't trust him. But that didn't seem to be the problem. He didn't care if she trusted him or not. He didn't care if the men he'd declared to be his enemies knew his plans or not. Did he care, though, if he was wrong?

A small shiver went down her spine at an even more troubling thought: what if he was right?

Chapter Six

"Enter," Callum said, keeping his gaze and his attention on his brother's accounts books. He'd spent nearly a decade working on his own books, but his had been concentrated on one entity: the Kentucky Hills Distillery. Ian's fingers were in dozens of ventures, businesses, properties, banks, and of course a good third of Sanderson's, George's fleet.

Pogue opened the office door and slipped inside. "As ye requested, m'laird," he whispered, looking over his shoulder like a bairn expecting to be caught with his hand deep inside the biscuit jar. He handed over a folded note.

Callum opened it. The note, written in Lord Stapp's too pretty hand, was surprisingly brief; he'd thought for certain that the marquis's venom would take at least an additional page. No doubt both Stapp and Dunncraigh considered him beneath their notice these days, though, a drunk fit for nothing but bellowing. Good. It would make them easier to drag to hell if they weren't even looking. That would make his revenge less satisfying, though. He damned well wanted them to know what was coming.

"Dearest Rebecca," he read to himself, "I had anticipated arriving at your doorstep to escort you to the theater this evening. For your own safety, however, I think it best I not darken your halls tonight."

"For her safety," Callum repeated aloud, snorting. The coward. It wasn't Rebecca's safety that concerned Stapp.

He looked down again. "I request instead that you will concede to meet me and my father for breakfast at Maxwell Hall at nine o'clock tomorrow morning. If we are to hold to our plans for betrothal and matrimony, we must anticipate that your brother-in-law will attempt to interfere, and we must strategize accordingly. Yours, Donnach."

So Donnach's primary concern was that he wouldn't be able to marry Rebecca. That made sense, when his family had a considerable amount of money wrapped up in her father's shipping enterprise—her share and control of the company would go to whomever she wed. Of course Donnach wanted that. Had he wanted it badly enough to kill Ian for it, though?

Callum could answer that in his own mind, but now he evidently needed to convince Rebecca, as well. He had no real reason for doing that, except that at this moment he wanted her to believe him. To believe that ten years ago he'd been correct. And perhaps, to believe *in* him. He didn't expect to survive this, after all, and if the legal records could show that he'd been justified, he supposed his soul and his pride would rest easier.

"What do ye mean to do with that, m'laird?" Pogue prompted after a moment, gesturing at the note.

He wanted to burn it. That would only delay all parties, though, rather than resolve any issues among them. Folding it again, Callum handed it back to the butler. "Give it to Lady Geiry," he instructed.

"Aye." With a bow, Pogue headed from the room.

"Wait."

"M'laird?"

"Where's a respectable place for a lad to go have a meal?" he asked, scowling at his own weakness. "Where a respectable lass could also show her face without causing a scandal?"

"Ah. I would say MacCulloch's Tea House just across Black Bridge. They say the Madeira's fine there, but the brandy's watered down. Or I could name a handful of taverns where ye'll find a number of handsome lasses and much better drink, m'laird. The Seven Fathoms still stands."

A tavern would be easier, he told himself, even as he shook his head. Not the Seven Fathoms, though. Not there. "Tell Rebecca I'll be taking myself to MacCulloch's Tea House at eight o'clock, if she'd care to join me."

"Aye." The butler hesitated. "Isnae that asking for trouble, lad? If I may say so?"

"I reckon it is," Callum returned, going back to the ledgers. "I'm nae one to shy away from trouble."

The butler nodded and pulled the door closed behind him. Rebecca had provided no proof that she hadn't had a hand in Ian's death except for her word, but Callum tended to believe her innocence, regardless. Innocent didn't equal trustworthy, however.

When he'd first heard the news, he'd wanted her to be guilty. He'd wanted an excuse to punish her—not because of Ian, but because of the way she'd insulted and dismissed him ten years ago. Now, in part because of young Margaret and in part because he'd nearly kissed Rebecca for the second time in a day, he'd begun debating what he truly did want her role in all this to be.

"Stop," he muttered at himself, flipping another page. He had a task. One task. Nothing else mattered.

Callum closed his eyes. No, he needed to amend that statement now. Margaret MacCreath mattered. His brother's daughter. His niece. Whatever he did, she needed to be and would be protected. Mags was innocent in all this, and she was his blood. Two months ago—and for the ten years before that—he hadn't wanted to know anything about his brother's life, his happiness, his wife, or his hypothetical offspring. He'd met the bairn a day ago, and now he couldn't name anything more precious to him in his entire life. Before he took his revenge, before he put a target on his own back from both the rest of clan Maxwell and the law, he needed to see that she was safe and protected.

Finally he closed the ledger and shoved it away from him. He couldn't decipher all of it, no matter how long he spent staring at the figures. Not without knowing more about Ian's holdings and who else had a share in them. Pulling a sheet of paper from the desk, he scribbled a note to Michael Crosby. His accountants might not have managed Ian's accounts, but they knew numbers. And they would have more familiarity with other Scottish businesses than he did.

The office door rattled and swung open. "You might've asked me yourself," Rebecca said, stopping in the doorway.

He pushed to his feet, ignoring the speeding of his pulse. "Ye dunnae have to join me. Ye did get all dressed up, but ye can stay at home if ye like."

"I'm not certain I wish to be seen with you," she returned, not moving despite his approach.

Callum stopped, the . . . anticipation in his chest shifting into renewed anger. "Because I'm trouble? Because I'm a drunken boy or someaught?"

Blinking, she did take a step back. "Because you're dressed like a drover fresh from driving a herd of cows to market," she retorted. "MacCulloch's Tea House is a respectable establishment."

"Och. Give me a damned minute, then, and I'll change my clothes."

"Do you have any other clothes? Ian's are in the attic, but I'm afraid you're taller than he was."

"My trunk's arrived from the ship. Wait for me."

Tromping up the stairs, he dug into the trunk where he'd had Boyd throw whatever he might need while he rode off to Boston and secured passage on *The Rooster*. A handful of clean shirts, a black coat he didn't remember purchasing, an extra pair of trousers, and a kilt in the Maxwell red, green, and black. Lifting it, he shook it out. Little as he wanted to be draped in Maxwell colors, it could serve a purpose, he supposed. As he'd pointed out, he wasn't trying to hide. Just the opposite. Earl Geiry was dead. Long live Earl Geiry. And death to all his enemies.

It was perfectly acceptable, Rebecca reminded herself, for a widow to dine with her brother-in-law. No one would think anything of it. In this instance they wouldn't, anyway, because any observers would be too occupied with gossiping about when Callum MacCreath had returned, whether he was as wild as he'd once been, and whether that had actually been a wolf in his company this morning, or a hellhound. She doubted anyone would even notice her, which would be very pleasant for a change.

As for whether Callum had been tamed, she couldn't answer it herself. He definitely seemed more . . . controlled, but whereas before she would have described him as a wildfire causing destruction in every direction, now he burned on the inside. When he finally did explode, she didn't want to be anywhere nearby.

"Will this do, then?" he asked, trotting down the stairs with the wolf on his heels.

Rebecca opened her mouth to answer, then shut it again. She saw men in kilts all the time; this was the heart of the Highlands, after all. But most of those men didn't look like Callum MacCreath. All he needed was a claymore in his hands, and he would have been the image of Scotland, itself—or at least the one the English ladies whispered longingly about when they ventured this far north.

"Yes," she said belatedly, when he cocked his head at her. "Very acceptable." She cleared her throat. "You cannot mean for the wolf to join us, though. You'll frighten everyone senseless."

"She's been seen once today," he returned, squatting in front of the beast. "That's enough for now. Waya, guard the bairn. Guard Margaret."

With a soft *whumph* the wolf turned and padded silently back upstairs, and Callum straightened again. While his attention was elsewhere for once, Rebecca drank him in. Good heavens, he was striking. And her head barely came to the top of his shoulder, she couldn't help noting once again. "Are you certain my daughter is safe with that beast?" she made herself ask.

"Aye. Nae a soul Waya hasnae met had best enter the house, though, until I return."

"What would she do?"

"Rip their throat out, I reckon," he said coolly, in the same tone another man might use to discuss the weather. He took his greatcoat from Pogue and shrugged into it as the butler helped her on with her full-length black redingote with its puffed sleeves and ivory buttons.

"Are ye permitted to wear colors now?" Callum asked, gazing at her as she turned to face him.

"Yes. I'm wearing color. Violet."

"Violet's a half-mourning color. Ye're nae still in mourning."

"Not officially. Are you going to dictate what I'm wearing now?"

"Nae. I'm just wondering whether ye're still mourning, or ye're just aiming to look like ye are. To discourage anyone from pursuing ye, for example."

She began unbuttoning the redingote again and un-knotted the ribbon about her waist. "I'm not going to dinner with you if you're going to lambaste me every second."

Callum took the black silk ribbons out of her hands and knotted them back around her, the tug and twist of it far too intimate for her peace of mind. "I'll wager ye five quid that I can keep up a polite conversation longer than ye, Rebecca. How's that?"

God, she hated already when he gazed at her like that, as if he could see straight through her skin and into her soul. Of course if he actually *could* do that, she wouldn't have to keep defending herself about Ian's death. "I'll take that wager, sir. On one condition."

"Aye?"

"That you won't simply throw five pounds at me the moment we leave the house so you can continue berating and questioning everything I do or say."

"Agreed," he said promptly, in his deep brogue.

Since she stood there in her theater gown and coat, he'd left her with no other excuse not to join him. She was somewhat relieved, though, when the barouche appeared at the front of the house. He didn't mean to drive them himself, and he hadn't chosen a closed coach. Of course that might well be because he wanted to be seen again going about Inverness, rather than because he cared for her sensibilities.

Outside he handed her into the barouche himself, then took the rear-facing seat opposite her. Hopefully her relief didn't show on her face, but she would much rather be able to keep both eyes on him than have him seated directly beside her.

"Are ye warm enough?" he asked abruptly, gesturing at the folded blanket on the seat next to her.

"Yes, thank you. Are you?"

"My knees are a wee bit chilly, but I'll manage," he returned. "There're more lights along the river Ness than there used to be. It's pretty."

"The population in Inverness grows every year. They may not call it the Clearances any longer, but villages in the countryside continue to shrink or vanish as their chiefs try to hold on to their lands."

"I see it in America," he agreed, his mild tone a continuing and pleasant surprise. Perhaps he desperately needed the five pounds he'd wagered. "Half of Kentucky claims one clan or another. There isnae so much rivalry there, though. Mostly it's Highlanders against the rest of the world trying to call the place home."

"So you . . . work with men from other clans?" she ventured. Ian had said something about a distillery, but Dunncraigh had been present and had turned it into some jest about how much liquor Callum must be consuming there, and she hadn't brought it up again.

"I employ about a hundred men from about a dozen clans, I'd reckon. At Kentucky Hills I've space for forty or so, but then I've the warehouse in Boston and the one we're building now in Charleston for better distribution, plus the nearly finished one here in Inverness. I've discovered if I lease a warehouse from someone else, they tend to sample the wares."

"Then Kentucky Hills is yours alone?"

He narrowed one eye, shifting a little as they bumped over the wooden, hollow-sounding Black Bridge. "How much did ye and Ian ken about where I was?"

"As I said, Ian went to great expense to track you down. He told me a little, but . . ."

"But ye didnae want to know any more than that," he finished.

"No, I didn't. You broke Ian's heart. You . . ." She hesitated. Where hearts were involved this was a tricky business, and telling him anything of her feelings, even more so. "You broke my heart, as well." He opened his mouth to respond to that, but she lifted her hand. "Not the way you're going to imply, I'm certain. You were my friend. My dearest friend."

"If I was all that, I dunnae think ye would have kept yer engagement a secret from me."

"Of course I would have. I did. I know you."

He shook his head. "Ye knew me," he amended. "Ye dunnae know me."

That would seem to be accurate. She had no idea what to make of him now. "Very well. I *knew* you. I knew you would take it badly, which you did, so I didn't want to broach the subject. Are you going to yell now and deny any of that?"

"Nae, since we both saw what happened." He blew out his breath. "I told ye I got letters I imagine were from Ian. I had my foreman toss them in the fire. Honestly, I didnae even want to touch them. I spent a time being spiteful. After that, I . . . I suppose I just didnae want to know. I left the lot of ye behind. I figured reading about yer life, how happy ye were, how many bairns ye had . . ." He rolled his shoulders, clearly

uncomfortable with the conversation. "I didnae want
to know I'd been wrong about ye getting tangled with
Dunncraigh, and I didnae want to know I'd been
correct."

"But you came back."

"Once that newspaper caught my attention, I couldnae
pretend it hadnae. And I swore an oath."

"You didn't swear anything to Ian," she pressed, wondering if she wanted to be a part of this conversation,
after all.

"Nae. I swore to Dunncraigh." He gave her a grim
smile that sent a shiver down her spine. "I mean to keep
my word."

"But what if you're wrong?"

"Then ye'll have what *ye* wished for, Rebecca. Me,
out of yer life. Permanently, this time."

He might have been referring to leaving again for
Kentucky, but from his tone he seemed to mean something even more final. Rebecca shivered again. For
heaven's sake, before he'd returned she'd been finding
her footing again. Everyone, even with the overly dramatic expressions of pity and behind-her-back murmur-
ings, had been kind. She'd begun learning something
about her father's business. She had a suitor who seemed
only to want the best for her. And now in two days Callum had dragged her into conspiracies and made her
question everything around her.

But as for his single-minded oath of vengeance,
he'd already veered a little off the trail. "Why did you
kiss me?"

The barouche rolled to a halt, and he stood to unlatch
the door and step to the street. "Because I'd been imagining doing it for ten years, and I wanted to know someaught," he returned, holding out his hand.

Trying not to show her hesitation, she clasped his

warm fingers and stepped out of the vehicle. When he offered his arm, she wrapped her hand around it. "You wanted to know what?" she prompted, though every ounce of her shrieked at her not to ask the question. If he'd been imagining kissing her for ten years, she did *not* want to know why. Except that she did.

"If ye were as curious about me."

"Well, I wasn't."

The slight smile that curved his mouth this time was genuine, a remnant of the high-spirited, adventurous boy he'd once been. "Aye, ye were. And ye are. As for what that means, I reckon I'll find out."

"You're mistaken, Call—"

"At the risk of losing five quid, lass," he interrupted, "I'm willing to accuse ye of lying. Now smile and tell me all about the local gossip while we eat. I still have some catching up to do."

Rebecca wasn't so certain about that. All of this might have caught him by surprise, and he'd had all of five weeks, most of them on a ship, to decipher as much as he had, but Callum MacCreath already seemed well ahead of her in discerning not only what he meant to accomplish, but what, precisely, he thought of her. And if she couldn't catch up, or better yet change his mind, they would all be in a great deal of trouble.

"M'laird," Dennis Kimes said, making another note on his third sheet of paper, "I cannae decipher all this in one morning. I do recognize some of the names, but I've nae way of knowing who else does business with them, or who the owners might be."

Callum shifted a stack of books and crossed his booted ankles atop them. "What do ye require, then?"

"Honestly?"

"Do I look as though I want lies from ye, Kimes?"

The younger man paled a little. "Nae, m'laird. Honestly, then, I require a week, some assistance, and ye nae staring at me like the devil himself."

In his own opinion he'd been doing more glaring than staring, but it likely amounted to the same thing. "I'll do ye two better," he returned, standing carefully in the clerk's tiny paper-and-book-strewn office. "I'll give ye a week, an assistant, access to whichever papers I have still at MacCreath House, another lad to keep a watch over ye in case ye uncover someaught . . . interesting, and I'll ride out to Geiry Hall to collect whatever books might still be there."

Kimes looked up, the pen in his hand dripping ink as his fingers abruptly shivered. "To keep watch over me?" he repeated. "Is this going to get me murdered, m'laird?"

"Nae," Callum returned firmly. "It willnae. If there's danger about, I mean to see that it's aimed directly at me. That extra lad will remain by yer side, though, just to be certain." That had to be a rule. No one else was allowed to be harmed either by Dunncraigh or by his own investigation into Ian's death. And the more he considered it, the more he did want to know the exact details, exactly whom he owed a death, and why it had suddenly needed to go this far after ten years of apparent harmony.

That made several other paths clear, as well. He did need to go to Geiry; he wanted to go, to see where Ian had driven that phaeton, where his brother had spent his last hours and days. But he couldn't go alone. Not with the Maxwells here in Inverness.

"If ye need me, send word by messenger. I'll be but two hours away, and I'll be back as quick as I can," he stated, as he and Waya picked their way into the main part of the Crosby and Hallifax offices. "Make certain Mr. Crosby kens what ye're about."

"Aye," Dennis returned, following him out. "Will ye have someone watching out for him, as well?"

"I'll give ye a trio of lads from my warehouse here," Callum decided. "Ye use them how and where ye see fit." He turned around, taking a step back toward the shorter man. "And ye're nae to trust anyone but those who already have yer confidence. Ye ken?"

The clerk nodded. "Aye. And thank ye for having trust in me, m'laird."

Pushing back at his own impatience for answers, Callum inclined his head. "I've nae found a shilling missing in eight years, Dennis. The lot of ye have given me every reason to trust ye. Keep me informed."

With that he returned to the busy dockside streets. Waya at his side, he walked down to the water, taking in the sight of half a hundred ships loading cargo, unloading it, or jockeying for position in the harbor. The wealth to be had was almost tangible; no wonder Dunncraigh had dug in his claws the moment he saw a chance to grab some of it.

What had it been, though, that had pushed the Maxwell to murder Ian? What opportunity had come along that the duke simply couldn't share, couldn't allow anyone else to partake of? *That* was what Callum needed Dennis Kimes to discover; without a reason, proving that a duke had committed a murder would be impossible.

Of course in truth he only needed to satisfy himself. Once he knew for certain who'd done what and why, he would act, and everything else be damned. Callum rolled his shoulders, shaking off the sensation that fate waited in the wings. A good quarter of the ships in the harbor flew the small white and green flag of George Sanderson's fleet—or rather, of Rebecca Sanderson-MacCreath's. A portion of the profits of every voyage those ships made went into her coffers now. Even deducting the pay of the captain and crew, insurance, the ships themselves and their upkeep, she was worth a fortune.

He frowned. Did she realize that? Had it occurred to her yet just how valuable a commodity she'd become? Because he would have been willing to wager everything he now owned that that fact hadn't escaped Dunncraigh or his dear eldest son, Donnach Maxwell.

Waya uttered a soft, low growl beside him. Stiffening, his hand instinctively going to the knife tucked into the back of his trousers, Callum turned around. Half a dozen men rode toward him, the one in the lead mounted on a muscular gray charger. They spread out as they approached, enclosing him in a half-circle with the harbor at his back.

They could attempt to pen him in if they wished; the moment he recognized the stiff posture and lifted chin of the lead rider, flight became the last thing on his mind. He'd wondered when the Duke of Dunncraigh would deign to acknowledge his presence in Inverness, and it seemed he'd just found the answer to that question.

It also meant the duke had someone keeping an eye on him, or they'd never have found him in the tangle of people and wagons about the harbor. That didn't surprise him in the least, but he would have to take it into account from now on. He stood where he was, one hand on the knife handle, and let Waya move a step or two in front of him. And then he waited for them to finish closing in, as if that rendered Dunncraigh any safer from him.

"Callum MacCreath," the duke finally uttered. "I nae thought to see ye back on Scottish soil, lad."

"I nae thought to be here," he returned. "But ye

didnae have to come looking for me. I'd have gone to find ye, soon enough."

Deep-set green eyes assessed him. How much of that last conversation did Dunncraigh even remember? Callum doubted it had crossed the duke's mind since, except perhaps when he'd felt the need to tell Ian he had all the friends and family he needed here, and he was lucky he'd run off that drunken brother of his before any harm could come of his association with the wastrel.

"I didnae see any reason to delay," the duke commented. "We are partners now, after all. Join me now for luncheon at the Olde Club, and we can discuss our business." He glanced down at Waya. "I dunnae recommend ye bring that beast with ye, though."

The Olde Club, at the time he'd lived here, at least, had been the stiffest, most prestigious gentlemen's club in Inverness. He'd set foot there once, in Ian's company, and had detested every overstuffed moment of it. But this wasn't about a pleasant luncheon, or the company he might find there. This was about information, and power. "Nae," he returned easily. "I'd sooner set my own kilt on fire than sit at a table with the likes of ye, Dunncraigh."

A muscle in the older man's cheek jumped, but otherwise his expression remained unchanged. "That's nae wise, lad. We *are* partners, and it's to yer own benefit to know yer business. At least I assume ye've nae idea of what yer dear brother had planned for the family Mac-Creath. But he confided in me, and it behooves me to help ye figure out all the twists and turns."

Every time Dunncraigh uttered the word "lad," Callum wanted to punch him—which was likely what the duke intended. "I reckon ye can wait until I'm ready to meet with ye," he retorted. "If ye care for a word, send a note. I dunnae recommend ye come calling at my home." He smiled. "Nae doubt Stapp can testify to that."

"We left off poorly, lad," the duke pursued. "Ten years is a long time to carry a grudge for someaught ye did to yerself. Let's begin again, shall we?"

"I reckoned that was what we were doing," Callum said. "Ye brought yer wolves," he went on, gesturing at the men surrounding him, "and I brought mine. I'd call the playing field level. Dunnae ye fret though, old man. I'll be seeing ye again. Soon."

With that he walked off down the pier, eyeing the rider who blocked his path until the man backed his horse out of the way, then whistling Waya to heel. Dunncraigh had likely seen what he expected—the "lad" who drank too much and spoke too freely about whatever tickled his mind. Good. The less worry the duke had, the more likely he would be careless. Arrogant. Unmindful of any consequences for his actions. Especially the ones that he'd taken a year or so ago. Even if he wasn't, Callum would find the chinks in the Maxwell's armor.

What concerned him at the moment was whether Rebecca had begun to find the chinks in his own, and what he meant to do about that. And about her.

Chapter Seven

The moment the coach stopped, Margaret flung open the door and nearly fell on her face to the ground. Before Rebecca could even gasp a warning, Callum grabbed the girl by the back of the gown and hauled her back inside the carriage. "What's yer hurry, Mags?" he asked, setting her onto her feet.

Of course he'd adopted the nickname the Scottish servants called Margaret—Mags would never do in London, for it sounded much more like the name of a shepherd's daughter than that of an earl's—but of course Maggie had now begun to refuse to acknowledge any other version of her name.

Rebecca hadn't realized how much her daughter craved having a father about, because other than a slowly lessening recitation of where Ian had gone and the acknowledgment that he wasn't coming back, Margaret had never attempted to replace him with Pogue or any of the other male servants, or even with Donnach or His Grace the duke. But however . . . confused she felt about Callum herself, Margaret clearly adored him.

"I want to show you my bedchamber," the little one returned. "And I forgot to wait for the steps."

As she spoke, the butler hurried out of the house and flipped down the coach steps himself. "My lady," Duffy exclaimed. "And Lady Mags. I'd nae idea ye were . . ." He trailed off, his narrow face going gray, as Callum emerged from the coach. "Sweet, merciful Saint Andrew," he intoned.

Callum offered his hand. "Hello, Duffy. I didnae think to send word ahead, so ye can blame me for the surprise."

"M . . . Master Callum? I mean to say, Laird Geiry." The butler shook his proffered hand vigorously. "I, that is, *we,* thought ye—"

"Aye. I'm aware." He turned around, offering that same hand to help Rebecca down from the coach.

She should have been insulted, she supposed, that he treated a servant with the same deference he offered her, but that just seemed petty. She'd heard that Americans treated everyone equally, with no use for kings or lords, so perhaps he'd simply become accustomed to this greater familiarity. It suited him, actually. This new version of him, anyway.

"My lady?" he prompted, wiggling his fingers.

Shaking herself free of the thought of him in one of those raccoonskin hats and wearing a bear's coat over his shoulders, she took his hand and allowed him to help her to the crushed-oyster drive. "Please see my things moved to the south corner room, Duffy," she instructed, to save herself from being ordered to remove from yet another master bedchamber.

"Aye, my lady. I'll have it aired oot at once." Gesturing, the butler took his new master's bags himself while more footmen scrambled out of the house to collect her luggage and Margaret's small trunk, and to aid the second coach, which carried Mary, her lady's maid, and Agnes, the nanny. Callum didn't have a valet, and she wondered if she should recommend Wallace, Ian's former man.

". . . introduce Waya to my Daffodil, so I can go riding with you," Margaret was saying, as she took hold of Callum's big hand and began tugging him toward the house.

"Daffodil is yer pony, then?"

"Yes, of course. Mama doesn't let me ride her in town, because Daffodil is very little and would be frightened."

Callum glanced over his shoulder at Rebecca. "That seems wise," he offered, a slight, attractive grin touching his mouth.

She remembered that he could be charming, but in this instance she knew he'd only brought Margaret along so he could keep an eye on his ward. As for herself, at least she'd been invited along instead of having to chase the coach down the road.

Reginald leaped down from the second coach and ran to the front door, the wolf loping up a moment later. She'd trotted beside them for a good two hours as they traveled south from Inverness, and from the look of her she could have carried on for another hour or more.

"Do ye mean to stand on the drive all day?" Callum asked, appearing beside her.

Rebecca started. "I'm merely taking a last look," she improvised. "Geiry Hall is yours now, after all."

"Aye." He looked up at the pretty gray-stoned mansion and its wide, well-windowed front. "Dunncraigh ran across me this morning," he went on conversationally. "He invited me to luncheon and pointed out that he and I are partners."

"Goodness. And you didn't throw him through a window?"

"Nae. There werenae any handy. When I left he'd

agreed to rent his pier to yer da'. I wouldnae call that a partnership."

"The business kept growing," she said, wondering why she was attempting to word her explanation diplomatically. Of course she didn't want a fight erupting between Callum and the Maxwell simply because of a ten-year-old disagreement. Neither, though, did she want to say something unintentionally suspicious to the man looking everywhere for conspiracies. Whatever he found, he would have to look for on his own. Because what he suggested about Ian's death was ridiculous in light of what she knew of Donnach and his father, and she had no intention of feeding his . . . fury. "Larger investments meant larger returns. It was sound reasoning."

"And I wager in the past few months Dunncraigh's been kindly taking on more than his share of the work, aye?"

"There hasn't been anyone else to see to it," she stated. "I've been attempting to learn the nuances of my father's investments, but without His Grace I would have given up by now."

Callum nodded, setting off back toward the front door. "Well, I imagine he'll have it in fine shape by the time ye wed Donnach and they take over ownership," he commented.

"At least Donnach was here," she returned, clenching her jaw.

His shoulders squared, but he didn't stop his retreat. "We'll stay here at Geiry for a few days, I reckon. And to avoid any misunderstandings later, dear Donnach's nae welcome in this house, either. Neither is Dunncraigh."

And there he went, making declarations again just to remind her that he had control of . . . of everything. Rebecca stomped her foot. "I hope you realize that if there was a conspiracy and that if I was a part of it, or being urged to be a part of it, your high-handedness would not be encouraging me to take your side."

At that he *did* turn around. "And I hope *ye* realize that ye flayed me alive once, and that I'm nae likely to trust ye again until I ken exactly what's afoot. I warned Ian, and came back to find that exactly what I feared came to pass. So mayhap it's ye," he went on, pointing a finger at her, "who needs to earn *my* trust."

If she hadn't been a lady, if she'd been fourteen or fifteen years old again, Rebecca would have yelled back at him something about how he was not allowed to stomp back into her life after ten years and upturn every applecart in the countryside. *Damnation!* She had things figured out again, finally. She had her future—and Margaret's—figured out. Some cousin of Ian's would inherit the Geiry title and properties, she would marry Donnach Maxwell, and he and clan Maxwell would see that she and Margaret were comfortable and safe and that Margaret would have a fine future as a stepgranddaughter of the Duke of Dunncraigh.

With a barely stifled growl Rebecca gathered her skirts and tromped around the house to the vast garden at its rear. She'd spent a great deal of time amid the roses and lavender, beneath the haphazard shade of the tall birch trees. Today she didn't seek solace as much as she did a solution to the turmoil caused by Callum Mac-Creath. Because while her first thought might have been simply to press for a swift engagement and wedding with Donnach—which would at least see her away from the house and somewhere safe and protected—that would also mean leaving Margaret behind. And that, she couldn't do.

Even before Callum's return she'd had the nagging thought that, among the trio of businessmen with whom she'd found herself over the past ten years, two of them were dead. And the son of the one who remained would control two-thirds of the enterprise if she married into his family.

She'd heard other things about the Duke of Dunncraigh over the past two or three years, completely aside from the venom Callum spewed at him. Things about people who disappeared if they displeased him, and threats to his own clansmen if they disagreed with his policies.

Two years ago he'd turned his back on a thousand cotters of his own clan, giving their care over to the English Duke of Lattimer for no other reason than that the folk had declined to side against Lattimer, their own landlord, when Dunncraigh had demanded they do so. It had been in the newspapers, but Donnach had only commented about it to tell Ian not to ever mention Lattimer in the duke's presence.

Last year, within a few weeks of Ian's death, she'd heard some rumors about a near kidnapping of an English duke's sister because Dunncraigh disliked her brother. Not much news had penetrated the fog around her then, and she'd absorbed even less of what she actually heard, but she remembered thinking that the brother, the English duke, had more than likely been Lattimer, as well. She wondered if Callum knew any of these things. If not, she certainly didn't want to be the one to tell him. He didn't need more firewood for his conspiracies.

And then there was Callum, himself. He'd been such an attractive young man, constantly tempting her into the sin of showing off her ankles, swimming in his company while wearing nothing but a shift, and he'd made her feel as wild and exhilarated by life as he seemed to be. Angry as he'd been prone to get, that Callum had been her friend and confidant until his brother had approached her with an offer of marriage that she couldn't—and didn't wish to—refuse.

This Callum, the one who'd reappeared three days ago, had all the soft edges ground away. He was strong, determined, and evidently willing to charge at one of the most powerful men in Scotland because of a self-made belief that Dunncraigh had done wrong. Ian had bent with the wind, making the best of any situation, seeking diplomacy and logic over any sense of personal affront he might have had. Not so, Callum. After only three days she already knew it—he would not bend. And part of her, the part that had once wished he would see her as more than his adventuring friend, worried that he would break. Or rather, that the much more experienced and patient Duke of Dunncraigh would break him rather than wait for whatever damage he feared Callum might do to their joint business.

She stayed in the garden all afternoon, brushing away Duffy's attempts to lead her in for luncheon and Mary's offering of a heavier shawl to protect her against the wind. In truth, today was lovely, with fat, unhurried clouds breaking up the sky's deep blue, and a breeze just strong enough to keep the birch leaves dancing.

Clarity continued to elude her, and so she finally made her way through the back entrance of the house to find Duffy ordering the dining room to be opened and the table set for dinner. "My lady," he said, bowing. "May I have some tea brought for ye?"

"No, no. Thank you. Where is Margaret?"

"Lady Mags is in the library with Agnes, where they're searching for books about wolves, I believe."

"Oh, dear. Nothing horribly bloodthirsty, I hope."

He smiled. "I did see Agnes hiding someaught behind the geography books."

"Excellent. A bit of curiosity is healthy, but I certainly

don't want her to have nightmares. And . . . Lord Geiry?"

"He went oot to the church nae more than ten minutes ago, m'lady." The butler's expression sobered again. "I reckon he wanted to see his *bràthair.*"

"Of course." The St. Andrews parish church lay on the grounds of the Geiry estate, less than a quarter mile from the house. She and Ian had married there, and uncounted generations of MacCreath lords lay beneath the stately oaks on the east side of the old stone building.

For weeks after the funeral she hadn't been able to go back there herself, despite the urging of her father and Margaret's obvious curiosity. It seemed so . . . final. Irreversible. Then when she'd laid her father to rest at the Inverness Cathedral, she'd felt surrounded by inevitability, and intentionally going to view it had made things even worse. But doing so alone . . . She took a quick breath.

"Excuse me, then. I shan't keep you from your duties."

"Of course, m'lady. Lord Geiry requested dinner to be served at seven o'clock."

"Thank you."

She wandered off in the direction of the stairs until Duffy exited the hallway. Then, still breathing harder than she liked, Rebecca slipped out the front door and hurried down the road toward the quaint church. However angry she might be at him, and he at her, Callum shouldn't have to go see Ian alone.

At the low stone wall that divided the cemetery from the meadow beyond, she stopped. Some of the old MacCreaths lay beneath grand, angel- or lion-draped monoliths, but for Ian she'd had a plain marble slab commissioned, one that only spoke of him as a husband and father and of his honorable nature. Had it been enough? It had seemed fitting at the time, but it should have been his successor who approved the design. Callum, of course, had been in America, while cousin James Sturgeon hadn't felt comfortable taking on the duty when he hadn't yet been declared the heir.

Well, Callum could commission another one if he didn't approve. Squaring her shoulders, she stepped through the low, wooden gate. Close by the wall on one side she spied him, and she stopped to lean against the trunk of one of the ancient oaks. She was here to offer any comfort if needed, she reminded herself. If he didn't appear to need any, she could just slip away and he would never know she'd intruded.

"Ye damned fool," Callum said quietly, and it took a second or two for her to realize he was speaking to Ian, rather than to her. "I warned ye. I *warned* ye about tangling yerself up with that devil. But ye have to think the best of everyone ye meet. Except for me, of course." Picking up a small rock, he threw it at the headstone. It smacked dead center, then ricocheted off into the bushes beneath the church's closest window.

"I dunnae ken why ye wrote me, or what ye wanted of me," Callum went on, squatting at the foot of the stone-covered grave, "but I'm here now. I mean to make him pay for what he did to ye and yer lass and yer bairn. I gave my word. As for what comes after that, I reckon that's up to me." He straightened. "If ye have any objection, ye'd best let me know it now, Ian. I'm nae likely to ask ye again later."

For a long moment he stood there, as if waiting. All Rebecca could hear was the birds, and the light breeze ruffling the leaves. Down in the village beyond the church the blacksmith was working, the clang of his hammer sharp despite the distance.

"Well then," Callum finally said, inclining his head. "I'll take that as ye being in agreement with me. Ye rest now. I'm nae certain we'll meet again, but know that I'll do what needs to be done. Whatever the cost. I'll nae disappoint ye again. I swear it."

Rebecca ducked behind the tree as he turned and walked past her through the gate and up the path leading back to Geiry Hall. That had been close. As for what Callum had been referring to, what he'd thought Ian might object to, she didn't know, though after that kiss the other day she could hazard a guess. *Heavens.*

"Ye shouldnae be out here alone, lass," he called after a moment, not slowing his pace. "It'll be dark soon."

Oh, blast it all. Belatedly she straightened, brushing bark and dirt from her shawl. "I only wanted to make certain you weren't in distress," she returned, trying not to rush her steps and not managing it well. "I wasn't eavesdropping."

"I'm in distress that my brother died when he didnae have to," he said, finally relenting enough to slow his ground-eating pace. "And I ken that ye reckon I'm being emotional because I only learned about this six weeks ago. That's only partly true, Rebecca, because in all honesty I'm nae surprised it happened. I mostly hoped I'd turn out to be wrong about all this."

"You still m—"

"Aye, I still could be wrong," he broke in, finishing her thought as she drew even with him. "Come with me to the loch tomorrow morning. Show me where it happened. Do ye still have the phaeton?"

"It's behind the stable. I didn't want to sell it, or to have anyone else use it."

He nodded, then offered his arm. He did remember how to be a gentleman, then; he simply chose not to be one for the majority of the time. "I'll take a gander at it, as well."

"You know that won't be enough to convince me of

anything." She tensed, waiting for him to counter with the statement that she was the one who needed to convince him of Dunncraigh's and Donnach's innocence. "What if I said I didn't want to be any part of this?"

He moved his arm, tugging her in a little closer against his side. "Then I'd reckon ye had someaught to hide from me, and I wouldnae be nearly as friendly as I have been."

" 'Friendly'?" she repeated, lifting an eyebrow. "Is that what you've been?"

Belatedly it occurred to her that she shouldn't bait him, but he only sent her an unreadable sideways glance. "Ye've nae idea, lass. Now. Has anyone been into Ian's papers or his office since he passed?" he asked.

"My father came to collect an account book, and there was a schedule His Grace needed, and I started to straighten things up, but nothing else. And that was only the first fortnight or so. Only the maids and perhaps Duffy have been in there since."

"Who collected the schedule?" he pursued, his voice hardening as she mentioned Dunncraigh.

"Donnach. They were all in business together. That doesn't signify anything nefarious."

"Nae to ye, perhaps. *I'm* nae that naïve."

Naïve. No one had called her that in a very long time. They walked past an oak tree with one down-hanging branch, an old swing with frayed rope still hanging above the grass. She'd swung in that tree, when she and her father came down from Inverness to stay at Geiry Hall with the MacCreaths. It seemed like another lifetime ago, but she could still remember the wind rushing past her, and her happy shrieks as Callum pushed her far higher than she should have allowed herself to go.

But she wasn't that girl, any longer. She was eight-and-twenty, for goodness' sake, with a six-year-old daughter and a third of an empire to manage—at least for the moment. She'd never forgotten her responsibilities before now, but just walking beside Callum caused all sorts of odd, uncomfortable, heady thoughts to surface. She didn't like it. He didn't fit with any of her plans.

"I should have asked," she made herself say, "do you have a family? Children? A wife?"

He glanced up toward the house. "Nae. I sold my horse here to buy passage to America, and sold everything else I owned to purchase some land in Kentucky. From there I bartered for what I needed, did some fur trapping and scouting until I could put together enough blunt to begin distilling whisky. That's nae a life for a woman, or a bairn."

"But you said you were wealthy even without your inheritance."

"Aye. I am now. And I live in a fort surrounded by trees and a million acres of wildlands, filled with bear, wolves, Indians, panthers, and winters that would put the Highlands to shame. I'm a powerful man there, because I damned well earned it with my own two hands. I've nae been celibate, mind ye, but I dunnae live a life that's fit to share."

"You *didn't* live a life fit to share," she corrected, trying to ignore both his comment about celibacy and the nonsensical flash of . . . jealousy, she could almost call it, that made the fingers of her free hand coil. That made no sense. Almost the entire time she'd known him before his flight from Scotland, he'd had one young lass or another pining after him. He'd *never* been one for celibacy. But seeing how magnificent he looked now, how single-minded and . . . centered he'd become, could easily be mesmerizing.

"This isn't a fort surrounded by Indians and wilderness," she continued, trying to find the reasonable tone she'd meant to adopt. "You're Lord Geiry, now. You have villagers and businesses here that require your attention." She stopped, trying to pull him to a halt beside her. He likely could have kept going without pause while she dragged behind him in the mud, but instead he faced her. "You do mean to stay here, don't you? In Scotland?"

"I've nae decided that yet," he said, glancing over her head back toward the church. "I reckon that depends on whether I have to drag Dunncraigh to hell, or I can shove him into the pit."

Her breath caught. "You truly mean you would sacrifice yourself for some . . . vengeance that you don't even know is merited? Callum, that's horrific." And if for a brief moment she'd allowed herself to panic at the thought of being left alone again, he didn't need to know that.

To her surprise, he gave a short laugh. "I'd have thought ye'd be happy to be rid of me." He resumed walking, his firm grip over her hand keeping her moving with him. "Or am I wrong about that?"

"I suppose my answer depends on your plans," she returned, wishing this odd . . . ease at being back in his company would go bury itself back in the graveyard where it belonged. No, not ease, precisely, because he continued to unsettle her. Trust, perhaps. She'd been injured in his company, but never more than scrapes and bruises. Looking to him for protection, though—logically it made no sense. For goodness' sake, she had a safe, predictable, kind beau for that. "I want to be happy you've returned. But the last time you were here, you were chaos personified. You can't deny that."

"Nae. I cannae."

"I'm not so certain that's changed."

Callum nodded, unexpectedly veering them off the path and heading them toward the stable. Did he want to look at the phaeton now? She would have preferred that he examine the vehicle by himself; personally she didn't like being anywhere near it.

At the side of the stable, the one farthest from the house, he stopped and dropped his arm, loosing her grip on his sleeve. His gaze holding hers in a way that made her heart skitter a little, he dug into one of his pockets and produced a five-pound note. Wordlessly he took her hand and placed the paper in it, curling her fingers over the money.

"What are you—"

"I dunnae want to be nice right now," he murmured.

Callum put his hands on her shoulders and pushed her back against the stable's exterior wall, then leaned down and took her mouth in a hard, warm kiss. Heat speared through her, putting the lie to whatever she wanted to tell herself about how wrong this was and how much she didn't want it. Want him.

With a low moan he tilted her head up, plundering her mouth. Rebecca grabbed onto his lapels, holding on both to keep her balance and because she had the mad desire to climb inside him, to be so close that no space existed between them. His tongue invaded her mouth, tangling with hers, his breath hard against her cheek.

When he tugged her gown up past her knees, his big hand splayed along her bare thigh, she groaned. God, she could feel him, feel his arousal pressed against her through his trousers and her muslin skirts. And she wanted him. For a year she'd slept alone, and even before that except on the occasions Ian visited her bed, and abruptly it felt like decades. Eons.

Thank goodness she knew better than to fall for him. Rebecca kissed him back, hot and openmouthed, wondering if he had any idea that if he'd kissed her ten years ago as he was doing now, she likely would have thrown caution, logic, and self-preservation to the wind and gone with him anywhere he wished.

A good portion of her still wanted to do so, still felt the pull of him against her better judgment. But she was a woman grown now, and one with a child and responsibilities and employees and all of those futures resting on her shoulders. And he . . . He wanted revenge, and had openly declared that he didn't care if he lived past the moment he found it.

Gathering up all her willpower, all the anger and frustration she'd ever felt in his presence, she doubled her hands into fists and shoved. It felt like trying to push over the Rock of Gibraltar, or so she imagined, but he backed off by an inch or two. "What?" he murmured, nibbling at her lower lip.

She knew he could feel her shaking. "No," she managed.

He stilled. "Nae because of Ian, or nae because of me?" he asked, keeping his tone level and his voice very quiet.

Rebecca knew what he meant. Did she cherish the thought and memory of Ian so greatly that the thought of being touched by his brother filled her with dismay? Or was it simply Callum who gave her pause? If she answered with the former, he wouldn't touch her again. She knew that, without either of them having to say another word. He would leave her be, find his vengeance, and then she'd likely never speak another word to him unless it involved Margaret. But then she might never feel this wanton, this wanted, this . . . alive, ever again.

"It's not Ian," she whispered.

Callum touched his forehead against hers, very softly. Then he backed away, nodding. "I reckon I can work with that," he said, and turned on his heel.

Chapter Eight

Lighting a second candle against the one guttering in the lamp, Callum pushed it into the soft wax of its predecessor. Beyond the closed door of Ian's office—*his* office, now—the house lay silent and dark. Even the servants wouldn't be stirring for another hour or two.

At his feet Waya lay stretched out on one side, her legs kicking a little as she no doubt ran down an imaginary deer. A few feet beyond her the well-groomed mop, Reginald, snored softly, his nose pointed toward the wolf as if he needed to keep an eye on her even while he slumbered.

Rolling his shoulders, Callum turned to the last page of the ledger. These accounts were all in regard to Geiry Hall; evidently his brother kept separate books for each property and business, and then an additional ledger combining his entire income and expense. To Callum it seemed like intentionally sending himself to hell, but Ian had always liked organization.

Once again, though, he found nothing. Yes, money coming from and going out to Dunncraigh for various ventures, and the business ties between the MacCreaths and the Maxwell and George Sanderson growing more tangled over time, but as much as he wanted to find something that shouted murder or deceit, nothing of the kind caught his attention.

As long as a single book remained for him to search in the office he wasn't about to admit defeat, but if his brother had suspected anything—*anything*—he would have left a clue about it. Callum knew that, with every bone in his body.

Why the devil hadn't anyone else been suspicious? Why hadn't Rebecca kept Stapp, at the least, from rummaging through drawers and taking whatever he pleased? After ten years of doing business together, the damned marquis probably knew just where to find whatever it was he'd wanted for himself. He'd probably known about the hidden panel at the bottom of the left drawer, as well. At any rate, it was empty. Still, Callum couldn't be certain whether anything had been there to be removed or not. But finding nothing didn't meant that nothing existed.

Sitting back, he ran a hand through his hair. Searching at three o'clock in the morning likely didn't help anything either, but it had felt more useful than the previous two hours he'd spent pacing in his new bedchamber, unable to sleep.

For the devil's sake, he wanted Rebecca. And it didn't matter whether he could trust her or not, or that she'd been married to his own brother. Traditional Highlands law actually encouraged a man to marry his brother's widow, to keep clan and property intact. This . . . need wasn't about the law, though, or about his plans for Dunncraigh and whoever had helped him.

Every time he looked at her, he felt like that idiotic boy he'd been—all spleen and no wit. And why hadn't he touched her all those years ago? He couldn't explain it, not really, except to admit that perhaps she'd been more significant to him than all the other lasses with whom he'd dallied. She'd been a friend, and a lass with some damned sense in her head. In treating her with his version of respect, though, he'd lost her to his logic-minded brother, who saw her for the monetary prize that she was.

And she'd hurt him because she'd been more decisive and more mature than he had been. It had taken another man removing her from the chessboard for him to realize that firstly he wanted her about, and secondly that he'd done nothing to earn her loyalty or respect but drag her from one scrape to the next. Just the opposite, from what she'd said to him. And as drunk as he'd been, as drunk as he'd gotten at the Seven Fathoms after he'd packed a single bag and left the house in Inverness, he remembered every single thing she said. He might as well have tattooed her words across his chest, because they'd burned themselves onto the inside of his ribs, anyway, exactly where his heart had been before she'd clubbed it to death.

Callum shoved to his feet, growling as he stalked to the office's small window. Behind him Waya rose, padding over to rear up against the windowsill beside him and gaze out into the darkness beyond. No doubt she sensed his aggravation, and had put it to a possible attack by Indians or Irishmen.

He scratched her behind the ears. "Ye reckon we should have stayed in Kentucky, do ye, lass? I'm nearly ready to agree with ye. Cousin James would've made a fine Earl Geiry. Hell, he might end up as the earl, anyway." Callum sighed. "There's the young lass, though. Does she smell like me to ye, Waya? Ye took to Mags quickly enough, and that's for damned certain."

The wolf gave a slow wag of her tail, though he didn't know if that was to acknowledge his speech or because she'd heard Margaret's name. He knew enough by now, though, to be able to tell when Waya accepted another member into her pack, and Margaret had been accepted nearly from the moment the wolf had set eyes—or nose—on her.

With a last glance at the dark, moonless sky, he returned to snuff the candle out, leaving the room full of silent black shadows, the half glass of whisky still standing where he'd poured it three hours earlier. When he opened the door to leave the room Waya moved out ahead of him, and then he nearly tripped over the white mop as Reginald wheezed to his feet. He and the Skye terrier looked at each other for a long moment, before Callum inclined his head. "If Waya says ye're acceptable, I'll nae argue," he muttered, "though I dunnae quite see the attraction, myself."

Upstairs in the master bedchamber the wolf leaped up to sleep in the deep windowsill, while the mop settled into a ball down beneath her on the floor. Callum shed his clothes and slid naked beneath the cool sheets of the bed. He had three hours until dawn, when he could go take a look over the scene of the accident and the phaeton. *That* should have been the only thing that mattered, the only thing occupying his mind at all. The fact that it wasn't, he could only blame on himself—and the mesmerizing blond lass a few doors down from him and likely sleeping with the bliss of a wee bairn.

The next morning he'd just finished slathering his chin and cheeks with shaving soap when a knock sounded at his door. "Aye?" he called, opening the razor and lifting it.

"It's me, Mags," his niece's young voice returned. "I'm looking for Reginald, but Mama says I cannot enter a gentleman's private rooms."

"I'm nae a gentleman; I'm yer uncle. Come on in, lass."

Tail wagging furiously, the mop scrambled to meet the door as Margaret opened it. With a happy squawk she plunked herself down on the floor and pulled the terrier onto her lap. "There you are, you silly dog!"

"He asked to spend the night with Waya," Callum explained. "And I didnae want him scratching at yer door all night."

Waya hopped down from the window and padded over to lick the bairn's ear, making her squeak again. "Good morning, Waya," she said, giggling. "I wanted to bring you some roast chicken this morning, but Mama said you would eat my hand off to get to it."

"She wouldnae," he countered, stroking the bare blade of the razor down one cheek. What an odd gathering they were. The wolf, aye, but now he was keeping company with a spoiled lapdog and a wee girl child. And it felt . . . comfortable. "A wolf pack always looks after its bairns. Ye're a bairn of her pack. She'd die for ye, lass. But she'd nae ever harm ye."

"How did you come to find her?" Mags asked, giving her four-legged, long-fanged nanny a hug.

"I was hunting deer about three years ago. Someone had set a bear trap, and I found a she-wolf caught in it, dead. She looked like she'd been nursing, so I looked about for the pups. I found the den, but a coyote had gotten there first. Waya was the only one left alive, black as pitch and too wee to even open her eyes. I should've left her, I reckon, but I tucked her into my coat and took her home."

Margaret's eyes were wide, her expression one of fascinated horror. "What's a coyote?" she whispered, checking the shadows in the corners of the room.

"It looks a bit like a fox, only bigger and lighter colored," he said. "Mostly they scavenge, and the pups were likely too easy a meal to pass by."

"Are there any coyotes here?"

"Nae. I reckon Waya's the fiercest beast in all of Scotland, other than me."

The lass grinned again, laughing. "And the both of you are my pack."

"Aye, that we are. And nae a speck of harm will come to ye while we're about." He glanced past his reflection in the mirror as Rebecca stepped into the doorway. She'd donned a pretty gray muslin gown, no doubt to point out to anyone who might see them at the loch today that while she wasn't still officially in mourning, she continued to honor her husband's memory. Or perhaps it was for his benefit, alone.

"If she was so wee, how did you feed her?" Margaret wanted to know, standing to wander over and seat herself in his vacated dressing chair as he stood at the mirror.

"I cut the tip of a finger off my best pair of leather gloves and had one of my men bring me half a pitcher of fresh, warm cow's milk every two hours for the next fortnight, and I convinced her that I was her mama."

"That's marvelous!" she exclaimed, picking one of his new gloves off the table to examine it, no doubt for holes in the fingers.

"My men thought it was a bit mad, actually, and I had to purchase another cow for my trouble," he commented. As he recalled it, "mad" hadn't been the term they'd used, but "fucking nodcock" didn't seem like the kind of dialogue he should be sharing. "But there she is, and I've nae had a finer hunting companion. Aside from that, just having her by my side saved me at least twice from being murdered by the Cherokee when some other fool broke a treaty with them."

"Do you think I'll ever find a wolf cub?" Mags

asked, contorting her face to match his as he shaved his upper lip.

"Young ladies do not have wolves as pets," her mother finally interjected, straightening in the doorway before she strolled into the depths of the room.

"Waya's not a pet, Mama," the lass returned. "She's part of our pack."

"Ah. My mistake, then." She glanced at him in the mirror, her light blue eyes more amused than he'd seen since he'd returned. "Am I part of this pack? Or is it just for wolves and young girls and uncles?"

"Oh, no," her daughter said, shaking her head. "It's also for you and for Reginald."

"Well, I'm pleased both your dog and I are included, then."

"Yer mama once found a wee kitten out in the woods," Callum put in, watching to see whether the reminder would annoy or embarrass Rebecca.

"She did?" Mags faced her mother. "You did? Was it precious?"

Callum snorted. "It was the cub of a wildcat, turns out. That she-devil chased us until we had to jump in the loch to escape."

"The lesson being," Rebecca added, putting out a hand to fix one of the lass's dark curls, "don't go about picking up wild babies."

"Unless we know they're orphaned," Mags amended.

"Unless you have permission. Will you lead your pack downstairs for breakfast?"

Margaret bounced to her feet. "Of course. Come along, pack."

The mop trotted after her, but Waya stayed where she was in the middle of the floor. "Mags, tap yer thigh and say, 'Waya, close,'" he instructed, demonstrating. The wolf rose and approached to stand directly beside him, her head tilted as if she couldn't figure why he needed her there by the dressing table.

When the lass did as he said, he patted Waya on the rump to release her, and the wolf padded over to join the mop. Then the trio trotted for the stairs, one of them singing loudly about a girl and her wolf pack.

Abruptly aware of just how close Rebecca stood behind him, Callum finished shaving and shoved a towel over his face to clean off the excess soap. He'd learned over the years to guard himself, to refrain from saying or acting on whatever came into his skull, but even so it took some effort not to turn around and grab hold of her. Not to drag her to the bed and lift her pretty gray skirts and take her for himself.

"It was your idea to pick up that kitten," she pointed out.

"Aye, but ye did it. I had nae idea ye could run so fast."

A brief smile touched her mouth before it fled again. "When do you want to go down to the loch?" she asked.

He lowered the towel again. "After breakfast. How far is it from here to where the phaeton went in?"

"About half a mile. Walking distance, if that's what you're asking."

"It's just beyond shouting distance, which is what I was asking. Even if he called for help, none of ye here would've heard him. And we'll ride, I reckon. I had Jupiter brought down. And I saw ye still have Peaches." The chestnut mare would be nearly thirteen, still serviceable for a lady's mount, and it had felt . . . comforting when the old girl had nickered at him from her stall. At least someone didn't have bad memories of him from his last days in Scotland.

"You should take that down," she said abruptly.

"I beg yer pardon?" He turned around to look where she gazed. "Oh, that. Nae, I like it where it is."

The portrait had to have been painted shortly after Rebecca and Ian had married, for the young lady seated in the garden still had the angles and hopeful blue eyes of a young lass. And she smiled, as she used to smile at Callum—a look he'd seen but once since he returned. He liked her smile.

"It's a portrait your brother commissioned of his wife. It's not appropriate for you to have it in your bedchamber."

"I dunnae give a damn if it's appropriate or nae. I once carried a torch for that lass. I like it. It stays." He faced her. "Now, do ye want to find someaught else to argue about, or do ye wish to go down for breakfast?"

For a long moment her light blue eyes held his gaze. "If you carried a torch, it didn't burn very brightly," she finally said. "Not until after you noticed that someone else also carried one."

He could debate whether Ian had carried a torch or an abacus, because he would have been willing to wager that his brother had written more calculations than poetry over the merits of the match, but he kept his mouth shut about that. It was done and over with, except for the pieces he needed to gather and sweep into something that made sense. "It may nae have burned bright," he returned, "but it burned so hot and deep it's nae gone out yet."

"You came back for revenge. Not for me."

That stopped him. He'd become more comfortable with lying—or "diplomacy," as Rory Boyd had termed it—but lying to Rebecca was another animal entirely. "Ye broke my heart, lass. For ten years I looked for reason to hate ye, because I couldnae forget ye. When I read about Ian, I decided ye must have had someaught to do with it, because that fit the tale I'd built around ye."

"So you hate me."

"Ye were there for that kiss yesterday, aye?" he asked dryly.

"You *tried* to hate me, then," she amended, still looking annoyed. "I only spoke the truth that night, you know."

Callum swallowed back his immediate retort. "Aye. I ken. I was a drunken boy. I also told ye—every one of ye—the absolute truth. Only where I listened to *ye,* ye never listened to *me.* So aye, I came here for revenge, and I thought to sweep ye up with the rest of the devils who killed Ian. But firstly ye've a daughter who looks like him," he said, clearing his throat as his voice broke. "Secondly, I'm fairly convinced that while ye likely encouraged Ian to tangle himself up with Dunncraigh, ye didnae have anything to do with killing him."

She gazed at him in silence for a moment. "And the kiss?"

He began to feel like he was leaving his belly exposed to a knife blade, and that she held the weapon. Picking up his gloves, he moved around her for the door. If he knew anything about Rebecca, though, she would hound him until she had an answer to her question. Drawing a breath, he left the bedchamber for the hallway. "Mayhap it wasnae hate I felt," he muttered, and descended the stairs for the breakfast room and the welcome interruption of Mags and her pack.

Rebecca stood back on the road, the reins of both horses in her hands, as Callum made his way down the shallow bank to the edge of Loch Brenan. The broken ruts in the road where the phaeton's wheels had turned were softer-edged now, almost invisible after a year of weathering, but she knew they'd found the right place.

"It was raining that night, ye said?" he called up,

wading into the water as if he didn't care that he wore expensive Hessian boots, not to mention a fine linen shirt and buckskin trousers. At least he'd taken off his jacket and waistcoat, but that was likely for reasons of buoyancy rather than concern over his garb.

"Yes. It had been, all that day. The weather didn't clear until the next afternoon."

"How far out was the phaeton?" he asked, continuing forward until the water rose to his chest.

On the shore, the black wolf paced back and forth, whining and clearly trying to summon the courage to jump in to join her master. "Only the top of the seat showed above the water," she returned. "Another five or six feet beyond you."

With a nod he faced forward again and continued into the loch. She had no idea what he might be looking for; Loch Brenan hadn't caused the accident. It had only been there when the carriage ran off the road. But he was after a conspiracy that didn't exist anyway, so the idea that this needed to make sense to her had flown away with the geese.

"About here?" he called again.

"Yes. I believe you're standing right where the left front wheel would have been."

"And where was Ian?"

She looked away up the road. "Why are you doing this to yourself? To me? Do you think I'm enjoying this?"

"Nae, I dunnae. Where was Ian found?"

Curling the fist holding the reins, she pointed her other hand toward the reeds just to the left of where he waited. "In there. Facedown, with a large purple bruise and a cut over his right temple." She shifted, pointing to the stand of trees on the far side of the road. "And the horses were over there, with the remains of their tack."

"What did they find with him?"

Rebecca frowned. "What do you mean? They found the phaeton and the horses."

"In his pockets."

"Callum, this is ridiculous. Get out of the water before you catch your death. They found nothing in his pockets but what he usually carried: money, his pocket watch, some calling cards, and one of Margaret's hair ribbons." She stopped, covering her eyes with one hand so he wouldn't see her crying and accuse her of being weak-kneed or something equally ridiculous. "You're an awful man, to make me remember all this."

"Rebecca, look at me," he urged instead.

Stomping one foot, she complied. "What?"

"I'm standing."

"I can see that."

"Nae, ye cannae. I'm *standing*. I'm nae swimming or treading water. How does a man drown in five feet of water when he can swim like a fish, and when he could just stand up?"

"I told you he had a horrible bump on his head. He was unconscious."

"And what did he bump his head on, then? The bank here is smooth, and the road's fairly straight. Even if the horses spooked and bucked the traces, the carriage had to turn nearly eighty degrees left, roll down the bank, and keep him in the seat until it came to a stop in five feet of water, at which time he . . . floated away on his face?"

"That's what happened, Callum. Precisely. So yes, that's what I'm telling you."

He waded back toward her, water making his white shirt cling to his skin, the ribbons of muscle beneath making her abruptly wonder whether she needed to take a cold dip in the loch herself. The wolf shoved her head beneath his hand, and he gave her a scratch before he walked back up to the road. "I dunnae see it," he said.

"Only because you don't want to see it," she countered.

That merited her a sideways glance. "I want to look at the phaeton now."

Before she could lead Peaches over to a likely looking boulder, he took her around the waist and lifted her into the sidesaddle. *Good heavens.* The sensation of breathlessness lingered even after he released her to swing up on Jupiter, and Rebecca shook herself. Yes, he was strong. That fact didn't make him less aggravating.

The wolf loped in a wide circle around them, making Peaches give a nervous sidestep. Glad of the distraction, Rebecca pulled the chestnut mare back under control and nudged her into a trot behind the big stallion. "Did you have to bring the wolf with you?" she asked.

"Waya watches my backside for me. And if she doesnae get a good run every other day or so, she gets irritable." He glanced over his shoulder at her. "Mayhap ye could use a good run, yerself."

Oh, that was enough of that. With a sniff she urged Peaches into a canter, passing by Callum and Jupiter. Half a dozen heartbeats later the pair drew even with her. Unless she wanted to gallop she would have to tolerate him, she supposed, but at least a canter would see them back home sooner. Not home, though, she corrected herself. Not *her* home. Not any longer.

Back at the stable yard he kicked out of the stirrups and jumped to the ground before Jupiter could come to a complete halt, then strode over to take her around the waist before the groom, Thomas, could reach her. "Stop grabbing me," she muttered, putting her hands over his as he lifted her to the ground.

"Ye didnae used to complain about it," he returned in the same tone, letting her go again.

"I'm not eighteen any longer." Smoothing her skirt,

she headed around to the back of the stable, listening until he fell in behind her.

"Nae, ye arenae," he agreed. "Ye're . . . curvier now. Softer. Nae all skin and bone and sharp elbows in my ribs. I like it."

That made her blush, when it likely should have made her turn around and slap him. "It is not appropriate to talk to me like that in front of this . . . thing," she stated instead, and kicked the rear wheel of the phaeton. The fancy vehicle had always seemed frivolous, unlike her logical husband, and since the accident it had become almost a living embodiment of everything she hated about what had happened.

Callum didn't reply to that, but sent her a sideways glance as he pulled the heavy canvas covering off the phaeton, walked around to the front of the vehicle and then, to her surprise, stepped on the front wheel and pulled himself up onto the water- and weather-worn seat. Shifting a little, he held out his hands as if he was holding the reins, then bent forward and back again, twisting from side to side.

"What in the world are you doing?"

"What did he hit his head on, do ye reckon?" he asked, having to fold over nearly double to lower his forehead near to the low dash rail above where his feet were braced.

"The phaeton no doubt bounced down the bank quite a bit. It could have been anything," she retorted.

"Nae. I'm serious, Rebecca. Come and look. What do ye see that might have caused that blow to his head?"

Reluctantly she stepped up to the front of the carriage. "He was driving through the wind and rain, Callum. A tree branch might have hit him. Perhaps that's what spooked the horses." It made sense; something had caused this, after all.

"And did ye find any downed trees by the loch? Any broken branches?"

"No, but—"

"Answer me this, then. Where was he going in the dark and the wind and the rain in a phaeton? Why did-nae he have himself driven in the closed coach?"

"I have no idea. He didn't tell me. Perhaps he was in a hurry to meet my father."

"Did he receive a note from yer father?"

She dug her fingers into the hard metal of the dash rail as she glared up at him. "No. At least Papa said he hadn't sent anything to Ian that day. Perhaps he needed a new contract signed, or to go over some figures."

"But he didnae have anything in his pockets, ye said. Did he leave with anything in his hands?"

"I'm going to begin throwing things at you," she snapped. "Stop it. There isn't anything to find. You're looking for trouble to justify hating Dunncraigh, and there just isn't any."

Callum held her gaze. "Did he have anything in his hands when he left the house?" he repeated evenly. "Or did he drive out into the middle of the night for nae reason at all?"

Rebecca shut her eyes, trying to remember. It had been just any other night, up until the point that it hadn't been. Yes, he'd been quiet, and a little short with his words, and he'd snapped at Margaret when she'd scam-pered into his office begging for him to read to her. Then he'd gone striding about, back and forth, opening and slamming his desk drawers, and then he'd shoved some papers into a leather pouch and—

"Yes," she said aloud, opening her eyes again, to find Callum watching her intently. "He had a leather pouch with some papers in it. I didn't see what they were, but he was . . . annoyed—upset—about something, to the point that he snatched Margaret's favorite book away from her when she asked him to read it to her, when he did so regularly. That . . . surprised me. He put the pouch in his inside breast pocket. On the left."

"And it wasnae with him when he was found the next morning."

A chill, slow and dark, trailed down her spine. "I don't recall anyone with it. The farmers, Mr. Landry and Mr. MacKendrik, were the ones who found the phaeton. They pulled him from the water."

"I know them," he returned. "Or I did. Good men, both of them." He hopped down to the grass again.

"The papers might have simply floated away and sunk somewhere," she proffered. "And he frequently found bits of his business annoying. You haven't proven anything."

"Nae. But it's a start. I'll find more. Enough to prove it to ye."

"And to a court."

Callum sent her another glance before he strode around to reclaim Jupiter, no doubt so he could call on Mr. Landry and Mr. MacKendrick. Rebecca felt another chill. She knew why he hadn't replied to her. Because once he'd proven to her and to himself that Ian had been murdered, he didn't mean to take his accusations to court.

Men had, on occasion, attempted to kill the Duke of Dunncraigh. He kept kinsmen about him at all times for just that reason; a man who burned out his own cotters had enemies. But none of those enemies had been Callum MacCreath. And she was very soon going to have to decide on whose side she wanted to stand.

Chapter Nine

Callum closed his satchel and fastened it, then did the same with the portmanteau he'd liberated from the attic. His luggage had doubled in a matter of ten days, despite his best efforts. He'd forgotten how many clothes being in Society required; Kentucky had been much simpler.

And here, at Geiry Hall, was simpler than Inverness. A good portion of him wanted to stay, to spend his days riding his land, watching his niece grow up, and figuring out what the devil lay between him and Rebecca. Something remained; he felt it every time she entered the room. And he wanted to know how far it went, where it might lead. All that, without knowing for certain he could trust her.

He felt that he could. Waya didn't sense anything nefarious about his former sister-in-law. He couldn't explain how she did it, but the wolf could smell a liar—and evidently they stank, because Waya didn't like them anywhere near her.

Or perhaps he *wanted* to trust her, because he wanted her so badly he even dreamed about her at night, now. And he hadn't done that in years. The—-

"Uncle Callum," Margaret said from the doorway, "I'm willing to return to MacCreath House, but I think Daffodil should come with us. I didn't even have a chance to go riding more than two times, and that makes her very sad."

"Yer mama told ye nae, I wager, and ye're here now to twist me about yer wee finger," he returned, grinning.

The lass pranced forward, flinging her arms about his waist and tilting her head back to give him a hopeful smile. "Please?"

"Good God, ye're shameless." And she was already the reason they'd stayed for three days longer than strictly necessary. Callum tapped the end of her nose with his forefinger. "Nae. But I'll go riding with ye every morning the next time we come down here. And that'll be soon. I swear it on Waya."

"You aren't supposed to swear, but very well. Can Waya at least sleep in my bedchamber with me at Mac-Creath House?"

Looking down at her upturned face, he envied her. Even with her father gone, the lass had every confidence in the world. She knew for a fact, in her mind, at least, that she ruled her world, that she would always have enough food to eat, friends with whom to chat and play, pretty gowns to wear, and a wolf at her feet. And by God, he meant to make certain all of that remained true. Taking her around the waist, he lifted her into the air so she could look down on him. "Aye, as long as ye leave yer door open. Wolves sometimes need to roam at night. Agreed?"

"Aye," she returned, giggling.

"And lasses do *nae* roam at night. Aye?"

"Aye," she repeated stoutly.

Outside, the coaches clattered up the drive from the stable, and he set Margaret down again. "Go fetch

Agnes," he said, naming the six-year-old's nanny as he nudged her toward the door. "Tell her we're leaving in ten minutes."

"Aye," she called again, galloping up the hallway.

Hefting both bags, he left the room as well, Waya falling in behind him. When Jamie, one of the two footmen he remembered from his previous residency, left the corner room with four bags clutched in his arms, Callum appropriated one of those, as well.

"M'laird, ye shouldnae be carrying yer own bags, much less her ladyship's," the servant exclaimed, rebalancing his load.

"It's nae trouble," he returned, heading down the stairs and leaving the footman with no option but to follow. "They're lighter than barrels, which is what I'm accustomed to hauling about."

"Is it true ye own the Kentucky Hills Distillery, then? If ye dunnae mind me asking."

"Aye. I do own it. Ye've heard of it?"

"Down at the Bonny Bruce they call it the finest whisky nae made in the Highlands."

Callum chuckled. "I'm nae certain that's a compliment."

"From Highlanders? Aye, it's a compliment."

His sales numbers said likewise, but he settled for nodding. In the Highlands, nothing was permitted to be superior to what was made here—at least not anything admitted to publicly. The very fact that the Bonny Bruce, a small tavern with naught but locals patronizing it, stocked his whisky spoke volumes all on its own.

"So it's back to MacCreath House, then?" Rebecca asked, as she joined them on the front drive.

"Aye. And I'd like yer permission to go through yer da's office at Edgley House."

"So now you think my father had something to do

with Ian's death?" she retorted, lowering her voice as the servants loaded the coaches.

"Nae. I think yer father's death had someaught to do with Ian's."

He watched her expression, waiting for her to absorb the fact that he considered both Ian's and George Sanderson's deaths to be anything but accidental. In his narrative it all made sense; he only needed to find the threads that connected the entire mess together.

Her eyes widened, and she grabbed his arm to drag him down the drive. It would take a man a good bit bigger than she was to move him, but he acquiesced, walking away from the house and the general chatter behind them.

"Stop this," she hissed, facing him. "I understand you feel somewhat . . . responsible, and you want to make amends for not being here. But it's beginning to sound mad. For heaven's sake, Callum. Let the dead rest, and look to your own future."

He tilted his head. "I'm looking to *yer* future, Rebecca. And Margaret's." Seeing her skin darken and anticipating another browbeating, he took a breath. "I'll make ye a bargain. Let me look. If I dunnae find anything, if there's nae a pencil mark out of place, I'll stop. Agreed?"

That was all a lie; he *knew* something lay just beyond his reach, and he'd die before he let it go. But she nodded, which was what he required. Without her permission he would have to break into Edgley House, and that could get complicated.

"I'm going with you," she stated, the clench of her jaw enough to tell him that it wouldn't do any good to argue.

He nodded. "Good. And if I find someaught, ye're going to stop telling me I'm mad, and ye'll listen to what I've been telling ye."

"Agreed. Because you won't find anything."

For the devil's sake, she was a stubborn lass. But then she'd had better than a year to reconcile losing the two men closest to her. He needed to be respectful of that. Aye, six weeks ago he'd been ready to doom her with the rest of the rats. But the past few days had convinced him that she was just as much a victim as Ian—she merely didn't know it yet.

It was well past nightfall when they drew up in front of MacCreath House, to find another coach there before them and blocking half the street. The crest on the door, a lion standing on a wolf, made his jaw clench—and not simply because of the metaphor. *Dunncraigh.*

He grabbed for the handle of his own coach, barely slowing when Rebecca snatched at his sleeve. "Don't, lass," he growled.

"You're his partner," she whispered after him. "This is business."

"I'm nae his partner."

"Your accountant would say otherwise."

Shrugging free, he kicked out the step and descended to the ground. Seeing Pogue approach from the house, he gestured at the pair of vehicles behind him. "See to the lasses," he ordered, stalking up to the Maxwell's heavy coach.

The door opened as he reached it, and Dunncraigh himself stepped to the ground. "Good evening, Lord Geiry."

"Ye're in my way," Callum grunted. "Get out of it."

"I wanted a word with ye, lad," the Maxwell returned, his words smooth despite the hard set to his eyes. "We've another business, one located in Knightsbridge down in London, that wants to do its shipping with Lady Geiry's fleet, but there's a matter of a signature or two still required."

"And so ye came and sat in yer coach all day long and waited for me?" Callum returned. "The bloody Maxwell, himself? Or was it that ye had the road watched, so ye knew I was headed back into town?"

"Or is it that Donnach and I've come by for the past few days, hoping to catch ye without having to darken yer door?" the duke countered. "This is business. We dunnae have to be friends for business."

"Whose signature do you need, Your Grace?" Rebecca asked from close behind him.

"A month ago yers would have sufficed, my dear," the duke returned with a warm smile that made every muscle in Callum's body go taut. "But Callum here has been recognized by the courts, I hear, so it must be all three of us." He put an arm on her shoulder, and Callum nearly flattened him. "Will ye give me a moment with the lad, Rebecca?"

"Certainly." She stepped away, leaning toward Callum as she did so. "Behave," she breathed.

"Nae," he returned in the same tone.

"Now. Walk with me, will ye?"

"I thought we went through this already. I'm nae walking with ye."

Beneath the street's lamplight Dunncraigh's smile faltered a little before he resumed it again. "I dunnae think ye want either of the lasses to hear what I mean to say to ye, lad. Walk with me."

Margaret stood in the doorway, chatting to Pogue about wolf packs, while Rebecca had returned to wait behind her, one hand on her daughter's shoulder. Scowling, Callum turned back to the duke. "Waya, guard Margaret," he ordered. With a low growl the wolf sent a look at Dunncraigh, then walked away, tail down. "The wolf doesnae like ye, either, Dunncraigh," he said, and began stalking up the street. "She can smell carrion."

"Ye've picked up an interesting companion. I'll give ye that." The duke matched his pace as they continued away from the house. "I hear ye began a brewery in America. The only way for ye to slake yer thirst these days, aye?"

"If that's how we're beginning, I foresee ye taking a swim in the river by the end of this conversation," Callum returned, rather than answering. Let the Maxwell think what he wished. There were other men who'd found that underestimating him could be fatal, as well.

"Ye're a strapping lad, now. I'll grant ye that. But I ken who ye are, Callum. Ye're a man who craves adventure, nae wanting to rest yer head in the same place twice. I can make that possible for ye."

Abruptly interested in more than just trading threats and insults, Callum slowed his pace. "And how is it ye reckon ye know me?"

"I heard ye, the night ye left. And yer brother told tales of ye all the time, how ye wished to visit China and Africa and cross the Atlantic to see the southern Americas. I can give ye that."

He could have it now if he wished it, but that wasn't the point of this conversation, clearly. "I'm the earl now. I have duties."

"If ye hadnae made an appearance within the next few weeks the title would've gone to yer cousin James, as I reckon ye've been told. A fine, bright lad, by the way. With a good head for business. I very much doubt the courts would fight ye if ye decided ye could-nae accept the responsibility and ye handed it over to him."

"Aside from the fact that James has the smarts of a mushroom and ye know it, that plan of yers sounds like it would make me considerably less wealthy."

Dunncraigh folded his hands behind his back, re-

minding Callum of nothing so much as a vulture waiting for its dinner to die. "I'll be honest with ye. Ye've a
large share in a business where I've sunk a great deal
of my money and my time. And the idea of a reckless
lad with a penchant for too much drink having that much
control over my future doesnae sit well with me. So
I'm asking ye to sign over yer share of Sanderson's fleet
to me, and I'll definitely be generous with yer compen-
sation."

"How generous?"

"I'll give ye thirty thousand quid for it, lad. That's
more than it's worth, but it'll see ye well gone from here
and in considerable style. Ye could purchase a kingdom
in China with that amount of blunt. In fact, ye dunnae
have to sell it to me. Just go away and leave the running
of it to me or to yer cousin. The thirty thousand'll still
be yers."

For a moment Callum considered that the idiot he'd
been ten years ago would have jumped at the offer. Taking responsibility off his shoulders and paying him for
the privilege? Leaving him free to drink and whore on
every continent and island between here and Australia
and back again?

Now, though, he had more important things to pon-
der. Had that been it? Had Dunncraigh resented Ian and
George having the reins to the shipping business? Had
Ian protested against his increased involvement or some
new commerce the duke favored? Dunncraigh had as
much as said he didn't like anyone else steering his
ship. Was that reason enough for a murder? Two murders, even?

Callum gave a slow nod. "I've a counterproposal for
ye, Yer Grace. I'll take my third of the shipping business and run it as I goddamned see fit. Ye'll take yer arse
off my street and go fuck yerself. I know what ye did.

And I know what ye're trying to do by having Stapp court Rebecca."

The duke's face darkened. "I—"

"Shut yer gobber. I'm talking," Callum cut him off. "Him marrying her would give ye two-thirds ownership. Then all ye'd need to do would be to buy off my gullible cousin with some blunt and flattery, and it'd be all yers. Or ye could pay him to leave the running of the business to ye, and ye'd have nearly the same outcome. Ye're nae fooling me. Ye ken shipping is where the new money's to be made, and ye dunnae want to share. Just as ye didnae want to settle for the profits of renting a pier to Sanderson's."

"Whoever ye think ye are, MacCreath, ye're clan Maxwell," the duke retorted, his green eyes narrowed. "I'm *the* Maxwell. I'll nae abide ye ever speaking to me that way again. Take what I offer ye and go away."

"I'm nae going anywhere, Dunncraig. By my way of thinking a man who murders for greed sells his soul to the devil. I mean to help Auld Clootie collect yers. And I dunnae think we should make him wait much longer."

"Och," the duke retorted. "I've seen yer sort before, lad. Ye're a disappointment to yer family, looking for proof of someaught that didnae happen just so ye can hold up yer head again. Ye cannae act without that proof, or the world'll nae view ye as anything but what ye are—a failure. Give up. There's nae a thing here for ye."

The duke couldn't have been more in error. Callum had nothing to prove to the world. In fact, the knife tucked into his boot would already have kissed the duke's throat except that he'd promised one person proof before he acted. One person stood between Dunncraig and the grave. And at that moment Callum remained motionless, debating whether he would be willing to give up a chance for anything with Rebecca in exchange for immediate, final revenge.

"Is there anything ye require, m'laird?" Pogue asked, the butler abruptly appearing, a lantern in his hand, from the direction of the house. He trailed behind a trio of Dunncraigh's men, Callum noticed belatedly, the hounds no doubt attracted by the commotion.

He shook himself free of his bloodlust. Whatever he wanted to do, meant to do, Rebecca still trusted the Duke of Dunncraigh and his son. Callum had to prove them unworthy of her trust and her compassion before he acted. And that was purely for her sake. Not for theirs. Not for himself, because he already knew. The bloody butler had just earned an increase in his salary for giving him a moment to find that clarity. "Some tea and biscuits would be grand, aye," he said aloud.

The duke forced a laugh that wouldn't have fooled a bairn. "We're finished chatting." Dunncraigh took a half-step closer. "Ye rant all ye like, Geiry. It'll make ye sound more like a fool than ye already are, and however loud ye bellow, ye'll nae prove a word of any wrongdoing in court."

"What makes ye think I'll take this to the law?" Callum murmured, holding the duke's gaze for a hard quartet of heartbeats before he turned on his heel.

"Callum?" Rebecca said quietly as he passed her and stalked into the house.

"Get inside and stay there," he snapped, and headed for Ian's—his—office.

Oh, dear. She'd seen this before, countless times. Ian and Callum would argue about something, usually Callum's recklessness, and then Callum would stomp off somewhere and get drunk and make things even worse. It had been frustrating and predictable back then. Now, it could be dangerous. He wasn't twenty years old with no power and no responsibilities. And while she could flee if necessary, Margaret could not—which meant neither of them could do so.

"Maggie, please take Agnes and your wolf pack upstairs," she said calmly, stepping into the foyer as their luggage passed them by. "It's nearly your bedtime."

"I don't want to be Maggie," her daughter said, frowning.

"No?" With some difficulty Rebecca tore her attention from the closed door at the end of the hall. "Who do you want to be, then? I already told you that 'the Splendid Princess Margaret of the Faerie Realms' is too long to remember."

"You just remembered it," the girl pointed out. "But I want to be Mags. That's what Highlanders call me, and I'm half Highlander. And Uncle Callum calls me Mags."

She'd known this was coming, blast it all. "Mags is very informal," she countered. "In London they will say you're being too familiar."

"I'm nae in London."

Rebecca shut her eyes for a moment. "You're *not* in London."

"And that's why I can be Mags."

Agnes gave a quiet snort, covering it with a cough. *Outmaneuvered by a six-year-old.* "Very well. Here, you may be Mags." Catching the nanny's dark-eyed gaze over Margaret's head, she angled her chin toward the stairs. "Remember to leave the door open for the wolf. I'll be up in a moment to say good night."

"Of course. Wolves sometimes need to roam."

Yes, they did. And that was what worried her about the other wolf in the pack. Once Margaret and the rest of them vanished upstairs, she moved quietly down the hallway until she reached the office. Nothing she'd ever said or done ten years ago had prevented his drinking, and more than likely she should simply turn in for the night and leave him to destroy himself as he chose. Having him gone would return her life to normal—or what had become normal over the past year, anyway.

She lifted her hand to knock, but paused again. The last time she'd been alone in his company he'd nearly kissed all her clothes off, his passion raw and addictive. And then, he'd been sober. Taking a breath, she knocked. Perhaps she'd become addicted.

"What?" he said, from somewhere beyond the door.

"It's Rebecca."

"Go away. I dunnae want to hear why ye think I'm wrong. Nae now."

Mentally crossing her fingers, Rebecca lowered the handle and pushed open the door anyway. Callum stood glaring out the dark window, his fists on his hips. A half-full glass of whisky sat on the desk, with no sign of the decanter or bottle.

"What in heaven's name did you say to His Grace?" she demanded.

He whipped around to catch her gaze. "Go ask him, if ye're so curious," he snapped.

"Perhaps I will, then," she retorted. "He's been far kinder to me than you've been. In fact, I'd be foolish to have any empathy for you at all."

"Aye, ye would be." Lowering his arms, he strode up to her. "I've a question for ye, Becca. The man offered me thirty thousand quid to go away. I didnae even have to hand over my shares of Sanderson's. Just leave. Why do ye reckon he'd be willing to part with that kind of blunt and nae have control of the business?"

"Because you don't simply make trouble. You *are* trouble. I would imagine he thinks that you'd counter anything he proposed to aid or increase profits, just because you don't like him."

His shoulders lowered. "Ye need to develop a better instinct for self-preservation, lass," he muttered. "Do ye truly nae see it?"

"See what? That I have money and a fleet that will go to whomever I marry? Of course it will."

"Aye. And if yer da' had died before Ian, all that property of yers would be mine, now. I—or Ian—would have two-thirds ownership. Do ye honestly think Donnach Maxwell would still be courting ye if that were so?"

Rebecca opened and closed her mouth again, her thoughts bouncing between affront and horror. "Bad things happen, Callum. And perhaps Donnach is courting me because we've been acquainted for ten years, and he cares for me." As for the order of deaths, it felt like he was only looking for ways to make a horrible set of circumstances even worse. Tragedy didn't require a conspiracy. It made sense as she thought it, so she decided to say it aloud. "Tragedy does not require a conspiracy."

Callum, though, had tilted his head again in the way that made her think him vulnerable, despite the fact that she knew him too well to be fooled. "He cares for ye, ye say," he took up, clearly not even hearing the last thing she'd uttered. "Do ye care for him, then?"

Was he jealous? "First of all, that's none of your affair," she retorted. "Second of all, no one's feelings but yours seem to matter, so don't expect me to expose mine to your ridicule."

"Have yer secrets then, Rebecca," he said more quietly. "I dunnae think ye had a thing to do with this, and so whether ye want me about or nae, I mean to keep ye safe. Ye and Margaret. Ye dunnae have to like what I do, but know that as much as I mean to end Dunncraigh, I'll see to it that ye and the lass are protected." He took a slow step closer, bending down a little to reach for her hand. "I do recommend ye nae pin yer hopes on Stapp.

And if he *does* have yer heart, then I suppose I apologize to ye in advance for what I mean to do to him."

God, he was so blasted stubborn! "If you're apologizing to me," she returned, refusing to back away when he continued directly up to her, "don't stop with my injured heart. You've always been a wildfire, without aim or direction. Your . . . antics have singed me before. So however safe you think to make Margaret and me, we're still directly in the middle of this. And if you begin murdering people left and right, people connected to *me,* at the best I will face censure. I might face arrest. How will you protect Mags when you and I are both shipped off to Australia?"

He scowled, a muscle in his jaw jumping. "I said ye'll be safe. Ye will be. If ye dunnae get asked to a soiree over it, well, aye, I reckon I'm willing to apologize for that, too." He tightened his fingers around hers. "If being singed a little is what truly troubles ye, it's likely just as well ye decided nae to join me ten years ago when I asked ye to." Callum placed her palm against his chest, and she could feel the hard beat of his heart beneath her fingers. "I mean to burn them down to ashes, aye. *Them.* But that isnae what troubles ye, is it?"

"Callum, you don't know for certain if anything untoward happened at all. I don't wish to see you hurt because you can't forget ten-year-old wounds."

"I could forget *those* wounds, lass. I don't give a damn about Dunncraig or Stapp. I earned my embarrassment and exile. They didnae do it to me. If they had naught to do with Ian dying, they'd nae enter my thoughts again."

"It's me you haven't forgiven, then? Is that what you're saying? Because those kisses didn't feel like anger or revenge. They felt like—"

He bent his head and kissed her before she could

finish her thought. "Felt like what?" he murmured against her mouth.

Sin. Lust. Need. All the things she thought she didn't want from him, but nevertheless seemed to crave. She kissed him back, breathing in his heady scent of leather and shaving soap. Sliding her arms up over his shoulders, she sank into the heat of him, into the heady sensation of being wanted.

Leather and shaving soap. Rebecca pulled back a little, looking up at him from inches away. "You haven't been drinking," she breathed, studying his two-colored gaze.

"What?"

"I know you," she persisted. "You get angry about something, and you go get drunk. But you haven't had anything to drink today."

Callum grimaced. "I keep trying to tell ye, ye *knew* me, Rebecca. The idiot boy who realized how stupid he was just a wee bit late and who by his own actions made certain he lost everything. I dunnae drink. Nae any longer."

"But there's a glass there on the desk."

"I like to be reminded how close I am to disaster."

"You own a distillery. How can you—"

This time his mouth curved into a rueful smile. "I've a particularly good sense of smell. And I'll take a swallow when necessary. One swallow. My men have orders to club me over the head if I try for more than that." He blew out his breath. "I've nae been clubbed but once. That was after I got the first letter from Ian, after five years of nae a word."

"The letter you burned."

"I burned them all, but aye."

He took her mouth again, and she closed her eyes, sinking into the sensation of him wrapped around her.

A Devil in Scotland   147

She'd been desired before, of course; she'd spent nine years as a married woman, after all. But Ian had approached her differently. He saw her value as an entire being—the inheritance she would bring into his control once her father passed, the additional power that wealth would bring to the MacCreath family. When Donnach had begun to express more than friendship she'd realized the same thing. He wanted what she brought to the table, the power and wealth she carried with her, wrapped around her like a cloak.

Callum looked at her differently. In his eyes, in his arms, she felt like a woman. A woman of flesh and bone desired by a man of flesh and bone. No numbers, no logic between them. Her money, her business ownership, fell to a very distant second, if it even mattered to him at all.

Unless that was just her, wishing for all that. But when he touched her, when he kissed her like this, as if he simply couldn't keep his distance no matter what he might have preferred, she felt it. He wanted *her*.

Tangling her fingers into the back of his dark hair, she opened her mouth to his, seeking and tasting him as he tasted her. With her back pressed against the wall she could feel his strength. She could feel his power, how self-confident he'd become, how driven. Callum still burned, but he had a firm grip on that fire now. He'd set his gaze on Dunncraigh, but for this moment he looked at her. Perhaps she could save him, save both of them, if she gave in to what she wanted anyway, if she let herself fall for him as much as her heart ached to do so already.

The door bumped against her back. "Mama, I found my book. Come read to me."

Swallowing and out of breath, Rebecca leaned her forehead against Callum's. If she couldn't stay away from this man, she would need to explain some things to Margaret *before* her daughter saw the two of them together.

"I'll read to ye tonight, Mags," he said, before she could gather her wits together enough to speak. "Will that do?"

"Oh, aye," Margaret returned. "Yes, please!"

"Go upstairs and wait for me, lass."

"Aye, Uncle Callum. Good night, Mama."

"Good night, Mags." Once the sound of Margaret's footsteps retreated, Rebecca slipped out of Callum's arms. "Are you certain you want to read to her? She'll demand it every night if you begin it."

"Ye said Ian read to her. I reckon I can manage."

Rebecca searched his face. When he'd first arrived she'd thought him the devil himself. Perhaps he still was. But this devil seemed to genuinely adore his niece. And if the least of the conspiracies he claimed happened to be true, she couldn't imagine a better protector for Margaret. Or for her, for that matter.

That all teetered on what would happen to him if his suspicions were correct. And what would become of him if his suspicions were wrong.

Chapter Ten

Callum dragged a chair over beside the pillow-heaped four-poster bed where his niece nested like a baby bird in an overlarge nest.

"No, no," she said, lifting her head up over the edge of the pillow canyon. "You must sit here." She pointed toward the far side of the bed.

"If I'd realized ye were going to be so strict, I'd have run away," he commented, leaving the chair behind and moving around to sink down onto the bed beside her nest.

She handed a large, worn book over the top of the pillows. "No you wouldn't," she returned. "You're wrapped around my little finger. You said so yourself."

"Aye, that I did." He turned the book over in his hands. Charles Perrault's *Tales of Mother Goose*. "I remember this book."

"It used to be Papa's, he said," she returned, yawning. "I saw that someone squished a bug in one of the pages, and that's when he told me about you."

Callum smiled. "Aye, that was me." He cleared his throat. "Which tale do ye wish tonight, my wee bug?"

Mags giggled. "I want 'The Sleeping Beauty.' It has ogres."

Still running his fingers along the worn bindings, Callum flipped pages until he found "The Sleeping Beauty in the Wood." He could imagine Ian sitting here, reading tales to Margaret with the wind whispering outside beyond the green and yellow curtains. What the devil had happened, for him to risk losing all this? Why hadn't he, a man who thrived on thought and caution, been more cautious that night?

"Uncle Callum?"

He shook himself. "Aye. Are ye certain this will-nae give ye nightmares?"

"The bad people get what's coming to them. I like that."

Out of the mouths of babes. "So do I, bug." He lifted the book. " 'Once upon a time there lived a king and queen who were grieved, more grieved than words can tell, because they had nae children. They tried—' "

His thumb went through the binding. "Damnation."

Her face appeared over the pillows again. "There's no swearing in this fairy tale."

"I ken. Give me a moment."

"Papa had to repair the binding all the time," she chimed in. "Keep reading, if you please. You're not even close to the ogre part, yet."

Callum pulled his thumb free, opening the book to the back to try to push the binding back in place. Right at the edge, a small *CM* written in black ink caught his attention. *CM.* For Callum MacCreath? It seemed far-fetched, especially if his brother had aimed it at him. Kentucky was nowhere near Inverness. And yet if Ian had repaired this book frequently . . . Glancing up at the sleepy face of his niece, he picked at the corner of the binding. It lifted easily, revealing a small, folded piece of paper pressed against the leather cover.

God. Trying to stop the shaking of his fingers, he freed it and set the book onto the bed. "What is it?" Mags asked, clambering closer over the mountain of fluff.

"I dunnae have any idea," he returned. "Did ye and yer da' read any other books together?"

She shook her head, her loose, dark hair covering her blue eye. "No. I don't think so. We always read *Mother Goose*. Sometimes Mama read it with me, and Agnes once in a while, but mostly Papa." Yawning again, she brushed her hair from her face.

And he was stalling. Shutting his eyes for a heartbeat, he opened them again and unfolded the missive. "Callum," he read to himself, and his heart stammered again. "Callum, I hope if you're reading this it's because you're here in Scotland and I showed it to you. If not, then I'm sorry. I should have listened to you. It began so slowly I didn't even notice it, Dunncraigh tangling himself into the enterprise George and I began. Then I thought he was being helpful, or interested, or at worst, ambitious.

"Tonight I finally unraveled it. He's been making large investments in our names, siphoning off profits to fund his own ventures. And now he's hired solicitors—I'm not certain why, but I imagine it's so he can wrench majority control from George. I have a ledger book, in the bottom drawer of my desk, where I noted several discrepancies. Find it, if you don't already have custody. George and I need to meet and stop this.

"I hope again this is all old news to you, and we've already resolved it and are sharing a bottle of your Kentucky Hills whisky as I show this to you. I fear, though, that is not so and the trouble's been dumped in your lap. Keep my lasses safe, whatever comes. I know you will. And forgive me. Ian."

"You don't look very well," Margaret said into the silence, startling him. "Are you going to be ill?"

"I might be," he returned, standing. "Will ye go fetch Agnes and ask her to read with ye tonight, bug? I need a word with yer mama."

"This is not how I like things, but very well," the six-year-old said, and rolled off the bed. "Come along, pack."

Armed with the half-disassembled book and with Waya and Reginald trotting behind her, she headed downstairs for the servants' quarters. Pacing, Callum read the note again. He'd already searched the desk; no such ledger was there. The words swirled around him, accusations and apologies and worry and frustration. What if he'd read those letters Ian had sent him? Would he have known what his brother faced? Would he have had time to return home and prevent this disaster?

Growling, he left the room and strode up the hallway to the bedchamber Rebecca had taken for herself after he'd removed her from the master suite. Not bothering to knock, he shoved the door open and walked in, shutting it soundly behind him and turning the key which rested in the lock.

She sat up in bed, her blond hair disheveled and a sleeve of her night rail falling down one shoulder. "Callum? What—"

"I found it," he interrupted, reminding himself that he needed to watch her—not because she looked lovely, but because if she had known any of this, he would see it in her face when she read the note. He held it out to her as he reached the side of the bed.

"You found what?" she asked, taking it. "Light a lamp, if you please."

He did so, turning back in time to see her face drain of all color. Any guilt he felt at not preparing her for the note, though, he would keep to himself. It was more important—to him, and for Margaret—that he know for certain whether she'd had anything at all to do with Ian's death. He more than suspected she hadn't, but half of that was just as likely lust. He *wanted* her to be innocent, because he wanted *her*.

"No," she whispered, reading the missive. "No. It was an accident." She looked up at him, tears in her eyes. "It was an accident! They were so kind to me, after . . ." She hurled the paper away from her, but it floated down to land on the foot of the bed. "It was an accident, Callum!"

Without thinking he sat on the bed, pulling her into his arms as she sobbed. He should have been kinder, gentler. For God's sake, she'd fainted when he'd first walked into the house. If he hadn't been so certain that because she'd broken his heart, she must have helped kill his brother, he would have seen that the losses of the past year had left her more fragile than he'd ever seen her.

"I'm sorry, lass," he whispered into her hair. "I've forgotten how to be kind."

"No you haven't," she hiccuped between sobs. "You kept trying to tell me, and I wouldn't listen. Where did you find this?"

"In the binding of that *Mother Goose* book of Margaret's. I found my initials in one corner and picked at it."

She slumped against his chest. "Good heavens. He took that book from Margaret, just before he left."

"Aye. So ye told me."

"He knew it was her favorite. She would never part from it. When she left it behind earlier this week, I thought I would have to send someone back for it, until Waya distracted her."

"It was still a risky thing," he commented, feeling her shoulders easing a little. "I reckon he wanted to keep ye safe, but needed to let someone else know."

"He needed to let *you* know. Even after everything, he still trusted you. I should have, as well."

"Becca, I didnae earn any trust. I should have read his damned letters. I might have—"

She straightened, putting a hand over his mouth. "Don't do that to yourself, Callum. If you do, I'll have to blame myself for being glad you were gone."

Wiping a tear from her cheek with his thumb, Callum shook his head. "Of course ye were glad I left," he said, moving her hand from his mouth and placing it over his heart. "I made trouble everywhere I went. And ye ken I still do."

"I was glad you left because then I wouldn't be . . . tempted."

That stopped him. "Ye'll need to explain that, lass."

"I can't. Not tonight." She plucked at the collar of his shirt. "Because I did love him. I did. But you were wild, and Ian was kind and safe. For a young lady of eighteen, the head knows one thing, and the heart, another."

Callum kissed her. She'd been angry that night, but she hadn't hated him. She hadn't found him repulsive. Whatever else he'd just confirmed, just learned, *that* seemed the most significant. And he had no intention of watching another moment of possibilities pass him by. He'd learned that much, at least.

Bending her backward against the headboard, he kissed everywhere he could reach—her throat, her eyes, her soft, soft mouth. Moaning, she dug his shirt out of his trousers and slid her hands up his chest, the heat of her burning away the chill of the night, of what Ian had just confirmed from beyond his grave.

Boots should not go on the bed. Wherever that thought came from, it did seem polite to remove them. Freeing one hand he did so, letting them drop to the floor and glad he'd had the foresight to lock her bed-chamber door. Then he shrugged out of his shirt and tossed it aside, as well. His skin needed to be against hers. He needed to touch her, to feel her heat, to be inside her. For ten years, more than ten years, she'd haunted his dreams more than anyone else. For ten years he'd called himself a fool for being unable to forget her, for being unable to find some other lass to share his life. But she was the only one he'd ever wanted. And tonight, nothing was going to keep her from him.

Lifting her onto her knees, he grabbed the bottom hem of her night rail and pulled it up over her head, casting it into the pile. Generous breasts, a soft curve to her hips—he noted her in general, then nudged her back onto the bed again. He could admire her specifically later.

Callum moved over her, taking a breast into his mouth and flicking the nipple with his tongue. When she groaned again, he thought his cock would split right out of his trousers. Her hands at the fastenings only made it worse, but he liked that she wanted to undress him. Lifting up a little, he made room for her hands as he shifted his attention to her mouth again.

When she finally opened the last button of his trousers he kicked out of them one leg at a time, every muscle taut with need. Keeping his mouth hungrily on Rebecca's, he lifted her legs and pulled them around his hips, impaling her on his shaft.

She dug her fingers into his back, breathless need on her face as he sank deeper inside her. *Finally.* She was no damned virgin, and he didn't want to be gentle or slow. The need, the urge to claim her, overwhelmed everything. Planting his hands at her shoulders, he pushed into her again and again as she locked her ankles around his arse and dug her fingers into his back and held on.

Her light blue eyes, darkened to purest sapphire in the candlelight, held his gaze as she moaned and panted in time with his thrusts. Neither of them spoke; he for one didn't want her coming to her senses and asking him to stop. Perhaps she had the same concern about him. Regardless, the room was quiet except for the crack of the fire, her breathy groaning, and the rhythmic creak of the bed.

Her breathing came more quickly, and then she tilted her head back as she spasmed around him. Good God. Clenching his own jaw, Callum sped his pace, digging his fingers into the sheets as he climaxed, emptying himself into her.

When he'd finished he rolled onto his back, panting and sweaty. More. He wanted her again already, but his damned body needed a few minutes. When she turned and curled against his side, he wrapped his arm around her shoulders and finally relaxed a little. She hadn't tried to escape, at least.

"I'm generally more composed than that," he finally murmured.

She kissed his chest. "I honestly didn't mind," she returned, trying to keep the amusement from her voice and not quite succeeding. Good heavens. One moment she'd been weeping over Ian, and the next . . . "Good heavens," she said aloud.

"It might've been wiser to show ye I've a slow, patient side," he commented. "Ye said ye already knew the wild one."

"The wild one has its merits." In nine years of married life she'd never experienced an encounter quite so invigorating. The fire in the hearth snapped, and she lifted her head—and caught sight of Ian's note still on the foot of her bed. A touch of guilt chilled her fingers. "What are we going to do? This is—"

"Dunnae say it's wrong," he broke in, his accent deepening. "It's nae wrong, Rebecca."

"Would Ian think that?"

"I already reminded ye about levirate marriage. Highlands men end up dead more often than ye'd think. If a lad couldnae marry his brother's widow, wealth and property and clan would end up fractured and broken all about the countryside." His arm tightened around her. "And I'm nae finished with ye yet."

That started a low shiver deep in her belly. And abruptly it seemed like a great deal longer than fourteen months since she'd had a man in her bed. Ian had told her that he'd forgiven Callum, and that he'd written to tell him so. At the time it had made her angry—or so she'd told herself. The last thing she wanted was Callum back in her life to complicate everything. But Ian's death had jumbled and wrecked any plans she'd had for her future. And now here Callum was, in her bed.

"That ledger Ian mentioned isnae in the desk," he said into the silence. "Might yer da' have taken it? To protect ye or himself?"

"I don't remember him taking anything, but several of my recollections from then are . . . fuzzy."

"Understandable. I need to take a look."

"You still need more proof?"

He cocked his head, looking down at her. "I'd have been content to gut Dunncraigh the moment I set foot on land. But ye wanted proof, and now I want to know *why* they did it. I dunnae ken that it matters, all in all, but the part of me that cannae conceive of that level of greed wants to hear him confess. At the least I want to understand why he decided Ian needed to die. Do ye nae want me to look into what happened to yer da'?"

The magnitude of what she'd begun to realize tonight continued to stun her. A week or two ago she'd been considering whether an autumn wedding with Donnach Maxwell would raise any eyebrows, or if they should wait until the following spring, when not even the most stiff-backed of matrons could mutter that she hadn't finished with her mourning duties.

"If ye dunnae want to know whether George passed on or was pushed to it, I ken," he went on. "I willnae tell ye if ye prefer. I mean to find the answer, though."

"I would prefer that he was still here," she countered. "He said he would take on everything he could of Ian's duties, and I was so relieved. And then I had his affairs *and* Ian's to wade through." That was when Donnach had stepped forward, and she'd been grateful. *Grateful*.

"Then come with me in the morning, and we'll take a look at George's papers."

This was all leading somewhere she wasn't certain she had the courage to go. "There's a difference between knowing that Ian suspected something and someone actually taking his life because of some investments."

"So ye'd rather I sit on my arse and let things go on as they are? I cannae do that, Rebecca. I willnae."

This would end up with him dead. Abruptly she knew it, as well as she knew anything. "I want to see proof," she said, keeping her voice as level as she could. "I want something we could, if we needed to, present to the magistrate."

"The magistrate," he snarled. "Dunncraigh owns the courts."

"No he doesn't. Two years ago he was forced to pay

reparations to the Duke of Lattimer for attempting to devalue the Lattimer property. Through sabotage, according to the newspaper. Dunncraigh said that he'd decided not to contest the decision because it would only cost him more time and money, but as I consider it now, he seems to want things that other people own on a fairly regular basis."

"Rebecca, if ye're trying to make me change my course ye're doing a poor job of it."

"I'm trying to tell you that he doesn't own the courts. And that he's annoyed enough of his own people that some of them might be willing to listen to you."

"The courts. Giving him over to someone else to judge doesnae sit well with me. I gave my word that I'd end him. Nae that I'd see he gets a fair trial and a chance to squirm out from under his actions."

Of course it didn't sit well with him. He saw and then he acted—which *was* a change from his youth, when he hadn't bothered to find a reason or an explanation before he set his course. This Callum, well, of course he disliked the idea of courts and trials, but at least he hadn't told her no. "I said I would help you once you convinced me. You've convinced me. His Grace—Dunncraigh—hurt . . . oh, heavens, killed, my husband." She took a breath. "And yes. I also would like to know why he would do this. And I'd truly like to look him in the eye while he tells me."

His grim smile unsettled her even further. "I'd wager I can arrange that for ye." He turned onto his side, facing her. "But ye leave this to me. Ye've Margaret relying on ye. Stay well away from Stapp and Dunncraigh."

Touching his cheek with her palm, she smiled. "I said I would help you, Callum. I've sat behind my walls and let the world go by as it chose for far too long."

"Ye had every reason to do so, lass."

She wanted to ask him what came next for them, what he thought tonight meant. For her it had been a release, the answer to a question she'd asked back before she'd truly known what her desire to be constantly around him meant. Since then she'd learned the futility of wishes, but she couldn't help but make one more: she wanted Callum MacCreath to remain in her life.

How much of a life did he have remaining, though, if he went after Dunncraigh? Even if he succeeded in killing the bastard, the Maxwell headed a very large clan. How long would it be until some nephew or cousin decided that murdering the man who'd murdered their chief would elevate his own position? How long until she found herself alone again?

"Ye look very serious," he murmured, sliding closer and kissing her again.

Flinging her arms around him, she kissed him back. Worry could wait until morning.

Chapter Eleven

Y e're certain of this?" Callum asked, knocking on the roof of the coach.

"I'm certain," Rebecca answered, straightening her spine. "And stop asking me as if you think I'll turn tail and flee."

A delicious grin danced across his mouth. "I reckon I know ye better than that. But it did take three tries to get ye into that fine dress."

She glanced down at the soft gray and black muslin. "Because you kept taking it off me."

"Aye, and I'd do it again if the ride was longer."

With a deep breath that trembled a little at the end, she pushed open the coach's door herself when they rolled to a halt. If not for the nerves beating like bats in her chest, she would almost have thought herself still dreaming. Last night—and this morning—had been . . . a revelation. An exhausting, eye-opening, shivery revelation.

Once the driver flipped down the steps she emerged, fixing her black bonnet against the stiff morning breeze. How could the world feel so different today? The only circumstance that had truly altered was her own knowledge. And now she'd agreed to help prove that the men on whom she'd most closely relied for the past horrid year were very likely the ones who'd put her in that situation in the first place.

All that left her thoughts again as Callum stepped to the ground. Two of her circumstances had altered since yesterday. And this one was . . . magnificent. He rolled his shoulders as if the coach had been too small to contain him, then offered his arm. Across the street Lord and Lady Hannick emerged from a shop, both of them stopping to ogle. Well, good. They wanted witnesses.

"Is that Molly MacKenzie?" Callum muttered.

Wrapping her hand around his forearm, she nodded. "Countess Hannick, now." A thought occurred to her, and she hid an abrupt frown. "Did you know her?"

"I recall feathers, but that could be one of several things," he returned. "I'm a wee bit hazy about most of that time."

It was very likely he was lying, but she appreciated that he'd gone to the trouble of doing so. "Mm-hm."

He lifted an eyebrow. "I cannae change who I was a decade ago. Believe me, I've wished otherwise. But I'm nae that pup any longer. Now lead the way. My knees are getting cold."

She started off in the direction of Edgley House. The coach might have driven them right up to the front door, but she understood why Callum had had them stop four streets away. He wanted them to be seen. He wanted Dunncraigh to know where they went. Thinking about that, though, only made her more nervous, and she had something she'd much rather contemplate at the moment.

"You're the one who chose to wear your tartan," she pointed out, glancing down at his kilt.

"I'm a Highlander, am I nae? Buckskins served me

better in Kentucky, but I dunnae want to be seen as an outsider here. Nae if I'm to convince a magistrate of any of this."

She could hear the distaste in his voice as he spoke the last bit, but hopefully he would keep to that plan until he actually began to believe it would be better than charging headlong into the fray. And hopefully he wasn't just saying the words so she would stop arguing with him.

Ahead of them Mrs. Ketchum and her lady's maid approached from the direction of the bakery, the stout woman nearly falling over her own shoes as she caught sight of them. "Good morning, Mrs. Ketchum," Rebecca called, smiling, before anyone could duck into hiding.

"Lady Geiry," the older woman greeted her, inclining her head, her wide-eyed gaze on Callum.

"Oh, do forgive me," Rebecca went on. "Callum, Mrs. Ketchum. Morag, my brother-in-law, Callum Mac-Creath. Lord Geiry."

"Ye're the one with the devil wolf," the maid exclaimed, covering her mouth when her employer hit her with a reticule.

"Aye," Callum returned. "I am."

"So ye're back in Inverness, m'laird?" Mrs. Ketchum took up, her voice pitched a little high. "From America, wasn't it?"

He nodded. "From Kentucky. Aye."

"Do ye mean to stay, then?"

"I reckon I will. For a time, anyway. I've my duties here to attend to, now."

"Oh." The matron visibly shook herself. "Oh. Well, that's bonny, then. If ye'll excuse me, I've some biscuits to purchase." Shoving her maid ahead of her, the woman reversed course and dove through the bakery door with not an ounce of subtlety. It was rather marvelous, really, seeing people flummoxed by someone other than her.

"That's the most polite I've heard you be since you returned," Rebecca noted with a smile, continuing up the street toward the harbor.

"I was worried she'd have an apoplexy if I scowled."

The woman likely would have. "I'm not complaining," she went on. "It's . . . nice not to have the first question on everyone's lips be an inquiry as to my health or how I'm managing. Especially when they don't care and are only looking for fodder to gossip over."

He looked sideways at her. "Is that how it's been?"

"I had to stay indoors for most of the first six months, but since then, yes. I suppose they're just being polite—I mean, I wouldn't know what to say, either—but even a chat about the weather would have been better than simply staring."

"Ye should have climbed a tree. That would have 'em wagging their tongues about someaught else."

A laugh escaped from her chest. "Yes, about how I'd gone mad and needed to be sent straight to Bedlam."

"I never thought ye mad. I thought ye daring."

She had been much more daring before she turned fifteen or sixteen, though that might just as easily have been ignorance on her part. Raised by a too indulgent father and allowed to run free while he attempted to make business connections in a new town, she'd relished Callum's swift friendship and his unconventional ways.

"Why are ye staring at me?" he asked, pulling her a breath closer to his side.

Rebecca shrugged. "For some reason it struck me last night that I used to enjoy your company."

"Aye, back when I put worms on hooks so ye wouldnae have to touch 'em." A grimace pulled at his mouth. "We had some fine adventures. When we were bairns."

She frowned right back at him. "You mean to discount everything in the past, then? Yes, we were naïve, and we're both different now, but we *were* those bairns. I used to love chatting with you. And adventuring with you."

"Nae, I'm nae discounting who we were. I also spent ten years to nae be that idiot any longer. I stopped being naïve."

"But young Callum did have his moments," she pointed out. "We're both here now because we were friends back then, because we liked similar things."

"When I thought about ye, I didnae contemplate the times we went fishing, Rebecca. I thought about how yer shift would cling to ye when ye came out of the loch, about how ye'd tuck yer hair behind yer ear before ye did someaught that scared ye. About how blue yer eyes looked in the morning."

Her skin warmed. "I thought you hated me for what I said to you. For what I did."

"I did," he said matter-of-factly. "Ye gave all that to another man."

And there it was again. "You didn't think about me that way *until* I accepted Ian's proposal, and don't you dare pretend otherwise."

He snorted, not at all the reaction she'd expected, and yet more evidence that he'd . . . matured, that he'd become more self-aware or controlled. "I didnae think of marrying ye before Ian proposed to ye. I'll agree about that." He tilted his head a little. "Likely because I just . . . It didnae ever occur to me that we wouldnae be together. If ye dunnae think I looked at ye from time to time, well, ye werenae paying attention."

Rebecca swallowed. Perhaps she had noticed. That

didn't make her any more willing to admit that from time to time back then she'd had some very interesting dreams about him where her imagination had filled in the blank spaces made by her lack of actual experience. Or that last night he'd put her imagination to shame.

"If ye keep looking at me like that, I may just forget myself and kiss ye right here in the open," he murmured, his arm muscles flexing beneath her fingers.

By his way of thinking that would probably serve to make Donnach and his father panic over the idea of losing her. Of losing Sanderson's, that was, and cause them to reveal all their evil deeds. "You would have to marry me to save me from the resulting scandal," she pointed out, sending another acquaintance a nod. "I may be a widow, but there are still rules."

"It would be that simple?" he asked, stopping so quickly she nearly turned into him.

"What?"

"To make ye marry me," he pressed. "It would be as simple as kissing ye in public?"

Her heart fluttered. "Don't you dare, Callum," she whispered tightly, reflecting that a few days ago she would have taken that as a threat. They didn't seem to be enemies any longer, thank goodness, but "complicated" didn't even begin to describe . . . this. Them. The whatever it was that lay between them. "Last night was . . . a release," she offered. "I've felt alone for a very long time. At the same time I haven't forgotten why you came back here. Or that some of your plans, such as they are, seem more than dangerous. 'Danger' is not on my list of requirements for a husband. Nor is 'careening toward getting yourself killed.' "

"Hm."

She scowled up at his profile. "What is that supposed to mean?"

"Exactly what it sounds like, lass. Naught's decided. Dunnae think that means I'll keep my hands off ye in the meantime."

Rebecca snorted, not at all averse to that. "You're a madman."

"I'll take that as a compliment."

At the front steps of Edgley House he let her move ahead of him, standing back as Williams the butler greeted her and held the door. She appreciated his deference. This, more than anywhere else in the world, was her domain. It was the one substantial item that would remain hers once she remarried. In addition, for the moment she owned a large portion of a shipping company and a small house in fashionable Knightsbridge in London. Everyone, herself included, saw this ownership as temporary, as part of an obscenely large dowry that would go to the man of her choosing.

Perhaps that was the true measure of her power. She could choose to whom she gave her wealth. A few weeks ago she'd decided to give it to Donnach Maxwell, the Marquis of Stapp. That made sense, in her world as she'd known it then.

And now everything had upended. Not only because of what Callum had suspected and now begun to prove, but because of the man himself. Ian had married her on the expectation of inheriting her inheritance. He'd died a fortnight before that could happen. At the time she'd thought it ironic. Now, though, because of Callum, she had to wonder if Dunncraigh had taken steps to see that the fleet remained under her control, so she could bequeath it to his son through marriage.

"There was no reason for anyone to murder my father," she announced, keeping her voice below the butler's hearing as they reached George Sanderson's old office and she let them inside. "Once I remarried, my husband would inherit my father's share, just as Ian would have."

"They killed Ian to stop him from talking about something, or from taking action about something he'd discovered," he returned in the same low voice. "I reckon either they didnae want to risk George figuring out what happened, or they didnae want to wait for him to die in his own good time."

"That's awful."

"Aye, it is."

"I don't like being a pawn," she said more loudly, bending down to unlock her father's desk with the key she'd brought.

"Then dunnae be one." Callum sat in the chair and began pulling open drawers, setting the contents onto the smooth mahogany desktop.

She didn't know what she expected from him—more reverence, an acknowledgment that he was digging through a man's life—but of course he had other goals in mind. Still, acknowledging that a good man—a man he'd known for a decade and one he knew she'd adored—had died wouldn't have taken much effort. Only a little compassion. It angered her, as did his flippant response to a dilemma that had been weighing on her for better than a year.

"Of course. That's the answer," she snapped, taking a stack of papers and setting them in her lap as she plunked down in the chair facing the desk. "I'll magically change my sex so I may keep what I own. I'll have Maggie—Mags—do the same so she may inherit my riches."

Williams cleared his throat from the doorway. "May I fetch you some tea, my lady? A glass of whisky, my lord?"

"Tea will do for me," Callum returned. "I'll nae answer for the lass, or she'll punch me."

"Tea is fine, Williams. Thank you," she said stiffly. "And I may punch you on principle."

"My lady?" the butler squeaked.

"Not you, Williams, of course. Him." She jabbed a finger in Callum's direction, not looking at him as she turned another page in the stack she'd selected.

"Ah. Very good, then."

Once the butler had left, she did glance up. Across the desk Callum gazed at her, his two-colored eyes at once so similar to and so different from Ian's. She'd never spoken to her husband as she just had to him, but then she'd never bothered to mince words with Callum—just as he never had with her. Of course no one had ever aggravated her as much as Callum had, either. Evidently some things didn't change, after all. "What is it?"

"Ye ken what's at stake now, who wants what from ye. And ye can make yer moves accordingly. That makes ye a queen. Nae a pawn."

"Is that so? And what would you have to give up if you wished to marry, Lord Geiry?"

"Revenge," he said coolly, and returned to the ledger he'd pulled from the pile.

After that, she couldn't concentrate. He knew he was likely to die because of this pursuit of his. They'd both spoken about it. But earlier when they'd jested about marriage, for him it had been nothing but that. A jest. Because he wanted revenge, and nothing else mattered as much to him. Why was it worth so much? Rebecca studied him as he carefully went through each page, looking for clues of Dunncraigh's duplicity. Because he still blamed himself, she realized. It had to be that. Nothing else made sense.

Perhaps, though, he hadn't considered every possibility before him. "Why didn't you simply march off the ship and shoot Dunncraigh between the eyes?" she asked, setting aside the part of the stack she'd perused.

She felt his gaze on the top of her head. "I wanted to," he returned. "I didnae know who else might be involved."

"Meaning me," she said, glancing up at him.

"Aye."

"But now you know I had nothing to do with it."

"Aye." He paused. "Ye're aiming at someaught. Tell me what it is, Rebecca."

He actually wanted her opinion, her thoughts. If a man had ever asked her such a question before, she couldn't recall it. Another way in which he differed from his older brother. "I've been thinking," she said, feeling out a path for her words as she spoke. "I know you said you'd look for evidence that could see him arrested and prosecuted, and that you don't like that idea."

"Nae, I dunnae like it," he agreed readily.

"Yes. And your way, killing him and Donnach, *would* get you your revenge. Our revenge. But you know it wouldn't end there. You would be immediately arrested, or killed in return."

"I ken. But ye and Mags would be safe."

"Are you certain of that? At the least we would have to move to London, because we're outsiders enough here as it is. I don't know *anyone* there. What if—"

"Ye decided to marry again?" he finished for her. "Ye're worried ye'd nae know whom to trust."

"Of course I wouldn't know whom to trust. And if I don't remarry, then Margaret would become the target of fortune hunters the moment she came of age, because she'll inherit after me."

"And in this imaginary land, how do ye reckon me nae killing the Maxwell will alter yer circumstances?"

At least he still listened. "I told you what happened with the Duke of Lattimer. He's not the only one who's bested Dunncraigh over the past year or two. The world grows more modern. A clan chief who looks after his own interests before those of his clan finds that his people have elsewhere to go, other, more sympathetic ears to listen and to help."

"Ye want me to join forces with the lordlings who dared to snarl at His Grace? I willnae. Snarling at him or making him pay a fine is nae stopping him. This is my fight. My way."

"Of course it is." Though an outside opinion or two might prove very helpful, she hadn't expected that would interest him. This was far too personal for that. "What I'm trying to say is that if he condemns himself, shows his true colors and in so doing shames himself in full view of clan Maxwell, then haven't you won? The legal approach can work. It will work. But I want everyone else to know what a . . . a damned rat he is."

Callum ran his fingers through his dark hair. Pushing to his feet, his steaming cup of tea in one hand, he walked to the nearest window. "Ye're suggesting I trade killing him for embarrassing him? They dunnae sound like equal punishments to me."

Rebecca took a breath and held it, sending up a silent prayer at the same time. "Then go now and kill him. End this searching-for-clues nonsense, and do what you came here to do."

The teacup shattered in his hand, china and hot liquid splashing over his hand and to the floor. Evidently he'd been able to stifle his old volatility, but not extinguish it completely. "I think about it," he muttered, not moving. "Walking straight up to him and gutting the bastard. Every time he strolls up to me and offers his sympathies or to buy me out, he has no idea how close he is to dying. And I havenae stopped myself because I was afraid, or because I lost my will."

"Then why?"

Finally he faced her, his face a blank mask except for the utter fury in his eyes. "Because it would be too easy."

" 'Easy'?" she repeated, steadying her legs beneath her in case she needed to move quickly.

"Nae for me, because aye, it would be nice and simple. One slice, and he'd be gone. But it would've been too easy on *him*."

"You want him to feel your pain."

"I want him to feel my pain, yer pain, Margaret's pain that she'll nae have a da' to help her learn to dance, or walk her into church for her wedding." He clenched his fist, blood from cut fingers dripping to the floor. "Before, it would have been enough to drop him in his tracks. Before I knew wee Mags. Before I knew that he'd hurt ye, as well as me."

"Then let's hurt him back," she said, with far more courage than she felt. Once she agreed to go along with this, there would be no stopping. Callum Mac-Creath wouldn't turn aside for anything—even her. "Court, yes, but not just that. Making certain everyone knows he's a damned dog, whatever it takes to see him gone and you . . . not dead. So you can continue to protect us." That would appeal to him, she knew. Not his survival, but his ability to continue to protect Margaret and her. This Callum would want that, she hoped. She believed.

He looked at her, the sound of the clock ticking in the hallway and dim outside noises of Inverness loud in the silence between them. If he realized she was trying to keep him safe, that keeping him alive and close to her mattered much more than what happened to Dunncraigh, she would lose. Abruptly, though, he nodded. "Aye. Let's hurt him."

As a twenty-year-old, Callum had spoken his mind, and not having hold of all the facts hadn't slowed him down an ounce. He'd also been furious when his elders—namely Ian—had declined to listen to him, much less follow his advice. In the boldness of youth he'd felt utterly secure in the fact that he was a Mac-Creath, a man, unconquerable, and the only one who knew the answers.

The idea that he wouldn't inherit the Geiry title, wealth, and estates hadn't overly troubled him. He would have enough blunt to be comfortable, and anything he did with that money would belong to him. Therefore, when he'd left Scotland for Kentucky to make his own way, he'd still felt like he had his feet under him, even if his pride and his heart had been blasted into oblivion.

He looked to his right, where Rebecca sat dining on a beefsteak with oyster sauce. Margaret did the same to his left, with one wolf and one white mop keeping a close eye on her from below. The formality of meals had been the most jarring reminder that he'd left the wilds for an aristocratic household, but given that it had been ten years since he'd had a decent oyster sauce, he was willing to wear a fresh cravat and jacket for the occasion.

His mind returned to the fact that had been troubling him all day; Rebecca had never had any prospect of being independent. Aye, as she said, she could have avoided marriage altogether. That would have made her a wealthy spinster, but with no one to pass on her father's holdings to in turn, all of her wealth would have eventually gone to partners or other investors, or at worst the

Crown. Now that she had a daughter, if she didn't remarry then Margaret would be the recipient of her
wealth—which the bug could only hold on to as long as
she remained unwed.

Rebecca, though, had wanted to marry. She'd therefore chosen a steady, kind man, a man her father liked
and trusted, and one with whom she would be comfortable and content. And then it had all fallen apart, anyway.
Because her husband had died before her father, she
was the one who inherited the fleet and associated business interests, but as far as she knew that had been accidental. She still had some leverage, a chance to find
another kind, steady husband, because she still had
monetary value.

He'd never been steady, nor particularly kind. At least
never in the time she'd known him. Bellowing that he'd
changed rang hollow, too, since he'd stomped into her
house, thrown water at her, and then announced that he
meant to kill anyone who'd had a hand in harming Ian.
Even to his ears that didn't sound like a man she'd want
for more than an evening or two.

In truth, when he'd arrived it hadn't been with the
idea of surviving much past killing Dunncraigh, anyway. Two things had begun to alter that—meeting
Margaret, and setting eyes on Rebecca again. And what
the devil he meant to do about that, he had no idea.

"Why are you mad at your dinner?" Margaret asked.

He shook himself. "I'm nae mad at my dinner. It's
bonny."

"But you're frowning at it." She wrinkled her own
face up, imitating him.

"Good God, I'm terrifying," he commented, sprin-
kling more salt atop the beefsteak.

"No, *I'm* terrifying. But I didn't forget; you're mad at
something."

"I've just been thinking about how brave ye and yer mama have been over the past year or so." He leaned closer to her, putting his chin near the top of the table. "Did she have gentleman callers telling ye to call them 'uncle,' bug?"

She giggled. "Only Uncle Donnach. But yes, she had gentleman callers. And so, so many yellow and white roses. I could smell them everywhere." Margaret made an expansive gesture, taking in the whole house.

His good humor squeezed into anger at her comment. *Uncle Donnach.* Rebecca had been trying to survive, he reminded himself forcefully. And Stapp had of course been extremely helpful and understanding about her situation—because the marquis wanted her fleet.

"Margaret, why don't you—"

Callum lifted a finger at Rebecca before she could hurry the wee one away. He kept his gaze on Mags. "I need ye to listen to someaught, lass," he said quietly, reaching over and taking her free hand. Her fingers looked so small and delicate in his; it seemed a miracle that she could exist in this place with conspiracies and dangers all around. "Ye've but one uncle in this world, and that's me. So call Donnach Maxwell anything else ye like, but please dunnae call him yer uncle."

She nodded, her two-colored gaze meeting his. "Very well. May I call him Stapp, like you do?"

"Aye."

"And you'll always be my uncle? Because I didn't know you for a very long time."

A smile touched his mouth, and his battered old heart. "I will always be yer uncle. And ye'll always have me wrapped about yer wee little finger."

Margaret stuck out her pinkie. "Good. Then I have another question for you."

"I'm listening."

"May I wear a kilt?"

On his other side Rebecca burst out laughing. "No, you may not wear a kilt, Lady Mags. Kilts are for Highlands men. And ladies do not show their knees or their ankles."

The six-year-old sighed. "Is Grandmama spinning in her grave again?"

"Very likely."

Sweet Saint Christopher, she was a delight. If he could somehow forget everything else, the oath that had brought him back to Scotland, the devils circling around them, he would have been content to chat with his niece, sit for her tea parties, and go walking in the park with her and her mama. The three of them, for the rest of his life.

Was that why he'd agreed with Rebecca that hurting and disgracing Dunncraigh would be preferable to killing him? When he'd thought she was involved he'd wanted nothing more than to end all of them, whatever the consequences to himself. Callum sent her a sideways glance. Was that why she'd suggested this twistier path? Did that mean she wanted him about? God knew he wanted to be here, however much it upended the life he'd carved out for himself.

"Does Waya get to stay here with me tonight?" Margaret asked, not even attempting to hide the bites of beefsteak she dropped for the mop and the wolf.

"Aye," he returned. "Much as I'd enjoy the stir she caused, I dunnae think Laird and Lady Braehaudin want to risk their other guests getting devoured."

Margaret laughed again. "That would be funny."

"People getting devoured is never amusing, Mags," her mother put in. "And I know this is the first evening in some time that I've been out late, but you will listen to Agnes and go to bed when she tells you to do so."

The lass wrinkled her nose. "Very well. Are you and Uncle Callum going to dance?"

"I reckon so," he put in, before Rebecca could say otherwise. "I didnae get dressed up in my best tartan to stand alone in the corner."

Nor had Rebecca. Against her own better judgment, or so she'd claimed, she'd donned a deep blue silk gown with black beading throughout the bodice and down the short, puffy sleeves. Together with the black lace gloves sitting by her left elbow, she looked lovely, sophisticated, and very, very desirable. And despite the black, not at all like a widow just coming out of mourning.

"M'laird, ye asked me to tell ye when the clock struck nine o'clock," Pogue said, as two of the footmen cleared dinner from the table.

"Aye. Thank ye, Pogue. Have the coach brought 'round, will ye?" Rising from the table, he called Waya to the foyer while Rebecca's maid retrieved her reticule and heavy black wrap. "Waya," he said, squatting in front of the wolf, "guard Margaret."

With a soft *whumph* she rubbed her side against his thigh, nearly shoving his kilt up to his hip, then padded back into the dining room, only to appear again as Rebecca and the lass emerged. "Is Waya guarding me now?" Mags asked, skipping forward to put her arms around his neck.

He kissed her on the cheek, lifting her in the air as he straightened again. "Aye."

She twisted around to kiss her mother, and smoothed her skirt as he set her down again, a miniature image of propriety—temporary or not. "Have a pleasant evening, then," she chirped, and went traipsing up the stairs with her pack as Agnes appeared on the landing.

"We could stay in," Rebecca commented, looking after her daughter.

"Nae." He took her in from head to toe again. "But dunnae think I'm nae tempted." So tempted, in fact, that he was beginning to think the kilt might have been a poor choice of attire.

With a fine color touching her cheeks, Rebecca led the way out the front door. He handed her into the waiting coach himself, though, mainly because he wanted to touch her. Because she was his sister-in-law and he was the patriarch of the household they didn't require a chaperone, which, considering Scottish law, seemed rather questionable. On the other hand, he didn't want a damned maid traveling everywhere with the two of them. Especially not after last night.

"You know people will talk when they see me wearing this," she commented again once the coach rumbled onto the street.

"Aye. Ye look like a woman and nae a widow."

"A widow is a woman."

"A widow's a lass ye feel sympathy for, nae desire for." He moved from the opposite seat to the place beside her. "I want Stapp and Dunncraigh to see that ye're nae some weepy lass they can pretend to rescue. Ye're a woman that other men desire, and they're nae the only men in the hunt."

"Donnach has a legitimate reason to want to marry me, though. Whether or not he . . . cares for me, he and his father have a great deal of money invested in Sanderson's. If he can acquire a much larger share through marriage, why shouldn't he make the attempt?"

"I've nae argument with that," he returned, though just the idea of Donnach Maxwell laying hands and mouth on Rebecca made his jaw clench. "They murdered two men in order to acquire Sanderson's. That's nae a plan they'll be willing to abandon." He took her hand, curving his fingers around hers. "If I'm correct, which I reckon I am, the second they see ye dancing with other men, and in particular with the man who owns the other large portion of Sanderson's, they'll crawl out of the shadows to push ye into marrying Stapp. And ye'll have to be ready to push back."

"I know."

"Are ye ready? I very much doubt it'll be pleasant, lass. Especially if ye resist."

The look she gave him physically hurt his heart. Sad, angry, hopeful, and resolved all at the same time, it made him wonder if *her* heart had room left for him in it. She'd been through hell over the past fourteen months, and he'd arrived to make things worse, to put more of a burden on her.

"I've been thinking," she said quietly, and he pretended not to be holding his breath as she leaned against his shoulder. "In your scenario, they killed Ian because he was on the verge of exposing the way they'd begun taking money and making agreements without his or my father's knowledge."

"Aye," he agreed, knowing she hadn't yet reached the point.

"And they deliberately killed him first, because if they'd killed my father first the business would have gone immediately to me and thereby to my husband. This way, Ian died, keeping my inheritance out of Mac-Creath hands. And then the other partner who'd begun to suspect wrongdoing could be killed, giving me said inheritance. In their thinking I become available, and I own what they want. They killed my husband and my father in order to get . . . me."

"In order to get their hands on yer father's share of Sanderson's," he amended, displeased by the bleak tone in her voice. She did understand it all. That was good for him, he supposed, but it couldn't possibly be comforting to her. "I dunnae reckon they gave a damn about ye otherwise."

"They will," she stated, straightening again. "Whatever you have planned, Callum, I'm with you."

He nodded. A few days ago the idea of having her as a willing participant, ready to use herself as bait to snare the monsters, would have seemed a boon. Now, though, he didn't want to see her put in danger, despite the fact that she had as much reason to want vengeance as he did. Perhaps more. But when she declared that she was with him, it wasn't revenge that came to mind. It was long, sweaty nights, and days filled with laughter. And suddenly he didn't as much want to get *to* vengeance as he wanted to get *through* it.

Chapter Twelve

Rebecca smoothed her skirt. Standing just outside the ballroom doors, her arm over Callum's, she tried to convince herself that it wasn't fear tickling at her spine, but anticipation. Whatever happened inside that noisy, warm room, he would protect her. She knew that as well as she knew her own name.

But she would have to chat with Donnach Maxwell, and very likely the Duke of Dunncraigh. She'd known them for better than ten years, and had considered herself friends with the Marquis of Stapp. For heaven's sake, she'd come a hairsbreadth from agreeing to marry him.

Another chill crept up her spine. What if she'd done it? What if Callum had decided to wash his hands of the lot of them and stay in Kentucky? When she signed the marriage registry, giving Stapp her property, she might well have been signing away her own life. And Margaret's.

"Dig yer fingers in if ye need to, Rebecca," Callum murmured from beside her. "I'll nae let ye out of my sight. Ye have my word."

She lifted her shoulders. Dunncraigh and Stapp would be the same men she'd known for the past years, but she was no longer the same woman. She *knew*. Yes, the only proof they owned at the moment was a short letter from a dead man and Callum's declarations, but those were enough. Everything Callum had said, all his suspicions back before he'd left Scotland and now that he'd returned, carried a strong logic. Yes, she'd tried to attribute his anger and his warnings to jealousy and pride, but she saw the truth now.

All the kind, considerate offers to help her keep Sanderson's profitable and growing, arranging for the "improvements" they'd known her father had been pursuing, the amended documents saying that majority approval and not unanimous approval was all that was necessary to make changes in the business. They'd been taking over little by little, and she'd been grateful for it. *Grateful.* Well, she wasn't grateful any longer.

"Are ye growling now?" Callum whispered. "That might scare 'em a bit."

That made her smile despite her nerves. "I'm not growling. I'm just . . . I'm tired of their smugness and false friendship," she whispered back. "And I'm angry about what they've taken from me while they smiled and offered sympathy."

"I ken. Dunnae seem too disdainful, though. They thought they had ye all wrapped up with a wee bow. Now they'll have to run with the rest of the hounds if they want to win ye. We need them to make a mistake. Someaught we can use against them."

"I know. I won't forget."

"And ye look like a goddess," he continued. "As soon as we're done here I aim to take ye out of that gown and have my way with ye."

This time a completely different kind of shiver went through her. After better than a year without a man in her bed she craved him, but she couldn't blame it purely on loneliness. Donnach had several times offered to—how had he phrased it?—keep her company through the long evenings. No, this was about Callum, and how she felt in his arms. How she wanted to feel that again.

For heaven's sake, she was eight-and-twenty, nine years married, and with a young daughter. She knew better than to be smitten. She certainly knew better than to be smitten with Callum MacCreath. Perhaps it was just that she trusted him. She always had, really. The answer didn't quite suffice, but it would do for now.

The couple in front of them vanished into the ballroom, and a moment later the butler took her invitation. "Lady Geiry and . . ." The servant looked from the handwritten amendment she'd made to the card to the tall, broad-shouldered man standing beside her. "And Lord Geiry," he continued.

Holding her breath, she let Callum guide them into the noisy, bright, far-too-warm room. Three blazing chandeliers hung across the high ceiling, while more dozens of candles stood along walls and tables and the two mantelpieces. Most of the heat came from the blazing fires in the pair of fireplaces and of course the two hundred guests wandering through the ballroom and the adjoining drawing room and informal sitting room.

Rebecca had no idea why the room's lighting had so much significance, but the flames gave her something on which to focus while she mentally readied herself for all the sideways glances and behind-the-hand whispers.

Over the past month or so she'd been to a few luncheons, a recital, and that one evening at the theater. Many of these people she knew fairly well, but hadn't seen since she'd left Society to go into mourning. And now she'd reappeared—on the arm of the brother of the man she'd buried.

In London that would have been horribly scandalous,

and might even have seen her given the cut direct. Here, of course, the rules were different. She squared her shoulders.

As far as *any* of them knew, Callum was here as the Earl of Geiry first, her brother-in-law second, and nothing at all third. But she had to at least imply that there was a third thing, however much it might dent her reputation with the handful of London residents present. Donnach needed to have a reason to feel pressured to act, and she meant to give him one.

While Callum hadn't disagreed with the fact that she'd been cut out of the Sanderson family and the MacCreath families with the skill of a woodcarver, laid out vulnerable for a Maxwell feast, neither had he pointed out what would likely have happened if he hadn't returned. But it was those thoughts that had her waking up startled, and very glad not to find herself alone in the bedchamber she and Ian had once shared. The moment she married Donnach she would have become a liability. They couldn't have her becoming suspicious about Ian's and her father's deaths once she saw the full scope of what they'd done with the company.

And then there was the secondary, more awful bucket of possibilities. If she had decided to refuse Donnach, they would have to do her in before she could marry anyone else—thereby handing her shares of Sanderson's over to her husband and his family. With her gone, her part of the company would go to Margaret. A spirited, naïve poppet surrounded by hungry, murdering hyenas.

"Smile, lass," Callum said, leaning closer to her. "We're three steps ahead of the Maxwell now. We need to keep it that way."

"I suddenly have the urge to punch Donnach," she returned, forcing a smile that hopefully didn't look as ghastly as it felt.

"If he kens ye hate him, he'll stay clear of ye until they can figure out another way to get what ye own."

"I know that. I won't put Mags in danger."

A muscle in his forearm jumped beneath her fingers. "Nae," he said, his voice a low growl. "Neither of them would live long enough to set eyes on her."

Of course he'd already followed all the trails Dunncraigh could take. And the flat, hard tone of his voice made it clear that he absolutely meant what he said. As bloodthirsty as it sounded, the statement actually left her a little more steady. While Callum had breath in his body, no harm would come to Margaret. This was not a pride-pricked, blustery boy making boasts. He'd become a man—and a very dangerous one.

"I will hold you to that," she returned.

"That, ye may do." She felt him shake off his anger. "Now. Introduce me about. I've been gone a time. And ye must take invitations to dance." He pulled her a breath closer. "After ye give me two of them. I'll let ye choose which ones."

"Do they waltz in Kentucky?" she asked, glad to be thinking about something else for a moment.

"Nae. But there are two of those, aye? I'll watch the first and take the second one."

She nearly pointed out that the waltz was far too complicated to be mastered after watching it once, but she kept her thoughts to herself. If he didn't want to risk embarrassment, she would be more than willing to sit out the dance with him, after all. Pulling the dance card she'd been given from her reticule, she marked his name next to a country dance and the evening's second waltz. And whether this was to stir Donnach to action or not, she liked the idea of dancing with Callum, nearly as much as she liked what he'd said about stripping her out of her sapphire-colored gown later.

Rebecca held on to that thought. It didn't worry or frighten her like the prospect of all the "what ifs"; it made her feel strong and desired and safe—something that for a time she'd never expected to feel again. This was for her and for Margaret and for their future. And even if she didn't put much . . . hope into hope these days, to herself she could admit that perhaps her future had a spot for one more person. And his wolf, of course.

"Rebecca, my dear," an older woman with the honey-eyed, sophisticated tones of London in her voice called, gesturing them closer to the fire. "I was hoping you would attend tonight."

"Emma," she returned, guiding Callum through a flock of young debutantes who began chattering like excited geese as he passed. "Lady Caldwell, my brother-in-law, Lord Geiry. Callum, the Countess of Caldwell."

He inclined his head. "My lady."

The countess looked him up and down with a thoroughness that made Rebecca clench her jaw. "My lord. You're the one from America, are you not? They do grow them large, there. You're a very striking young man. If I were ten years younger, I'd be after you, myself."

"I grew up here," he returned, his brogue deepening a little. She wondered if that was deliberate. "They added some grit and muscle in Kentucky, I reckon. And I might have let ye catch me."

It went like that for the next twenty minutes, introducing Callum to the current Inverness aristocracy. Even the ones who remembered him from before were polite and complimentary, though she didn't think the pleasantries fooled him for a moment. He was an unknown quantity, a curiosity, a half-familiar foreigner with the physique they were more accustomed to seeing on a blacksmith than an earl. Many of them mentioned the wolf, and while he admitted to having one, he declined to explain her.

"They're afraid of you," she whispered, as they finished their circuit of the room.

"If they have any sense they are, aye."

"You want them to be."

He glanced sideways at her. "They all ken how and why I left here ten years ago. Even the ones I've nae met before today. Half of them came here ready to laugh behind their hands at the sad, lucky drunk who managed to stay alive long enough to claim his brother's fortune and title. I reckon nae a one of them's laughing now."

"No, but you do seem to have several ladies ready to swoon at your feet," she countered, attempting to sound amused and fairly certain she'd failed.

"They can swoon wherever they like. Dunnae expect me to go about catching them. I'm where I want to be, and with whom I want to be."

That sent warmth from her toes to her fingers, and everywhere in between. How was it that with Ian and the preparation for marriage she'd been more concerned that everything looked perfect, that all the correct guests received invitations, than with how she'd felt about it all? Certainly she'd been excited, but now she wondered if that had been in part because her father was excited that the Sandersons, self-made merchants, were poised to join the aristocracy. The things she felt now—naughty, improper, and certainly unwise—felt foreign, reserved for daydreams that she'd ceased having the moment she walked into the church to say her vows.

"Be ready, lass," Callum breathed abruptly, his arm jumping beneath hers. "The weasel and the rat are headed this way."

She didn't know which of the Maxwells was the weasel and which the rat, but then that didn't particularly matter. Instead she concentrated on the advice Callum had given her—make them concerned that he'd snared her interest, and make them worried enough to make mistakes to get her back.

"Ye're nae going to punch anyone are ye, Geiry?" Lord Stapp commented, as he stopped before them and inclined his head in her direction. His father beside him settled his gaze on Callum and left it there.

An uneasy shiver went through her. "I'm glad to see you recovered, Donnach," she said, making herself smile.

He touched a long scratch on one cheek. "More or less," he returned. "The cut on my arm took a few stitches."

"A shame it wasn't on yer neck, then," Callum put in easily.

"We're all civil here, lad," the duke countered. "Nae need to begin a brawl. I see ye still wear the Maxwell tartan, whatever bellowing ye do about us."

"I've nae a thing against clan Maxwell. Only its chief and his firstborn."

Donnach grimaced. "Rebecca, for the sake of our mutual investments, I do hope ye can convince yer brother-in-law that dear Ian's death was a horrible accident. I fear he cannae blame himself for being gone, so he chooses to blame those who witnessed his disgrace."

If she hadn't seen Ian's note, that would have made sense. Now, it made her want to spit in Donnach's face. That, though, would never do. Jealous. She needed to make him jealous, not suspicious that she believed Callum's claims about what he and his father had done. "Whatever happened back then," she said, tilting her head toward the man whose arm she still held, "Callum has changed. Margaret simply adores him."

"Aye, he's changed," Donnach took up. "He's gained a few inches and some muscle. So now he's nae just a squawking boy; he's a squawking man."

The music for the country dance began. Thank goodness; she wasn't good at either spite or coyness, however motivated she felt. "If you'll excuse us, my lord, Your Grace, we must take our places for the dance."

She turned, trying to pull Callum with her. He held back, though, pinning Dunncraigh with a grin that chilled her to the bone. "Levirate," he said, and turned his back on the pair.

"I thought we were supposed to be subtle about this," she hissed, releasing his hand and stopping opposite him.

"For me, that *was* subtle."

"No it wasn't." She curtsied as he bowed, and then took his left hand in her right as they stepped down the line behind the other pairs of dancers. "However much you want to punish them, you agreed to go this route. I will not have you or anyone else drawing weapons in a ballroom."

His mouth twitched as they circled around again, turned, and clapped once before joining hands again. "Look at 'em," he returned. "Stapp looks like his head's about to pop off."

When she could do so without being too obvious, she snuck a look in the direction of the Maxwell and his son. They had moved away from the dance floor and were clearly in deep conversation about something. And yes, Donnach's face was so red he might be mistaken for a summer tomato.

As she looked back at Callum, his calm, amused expression unsettled her even more. Then it occurred to her. "You did that on purpose."

"Of course I did. My mouth moved, and words came out."

"No. You meant to set them after *you*. You lied to me, Callum."

"Nae, I didnae. But if ye think I'd set them after *ye* when *I'd* do just as well, ye're mad."

"Callum, y—"

"Ye needed to show interest in me, or they'd nae believe whatever I said about anything. So I didnae lie, Becca. And if I choose to have them look to me as the threat rather than ye as the prize, well, I reckon that's my right. It's my duty, my privilege, and my honor to keep ye safe."

Men. "That's very chivalrous of you, then," she sent back at him after they separated and joined up again at the end of the line, "but you might have told me. I've been kept ignorant of far too many things for far, far too long."

He didn't speak at all for their next turn about the room. That should have annoyed and troubled her, no doubt, but it didn't. For nearly a decade long ago, she and Callum had been the best of friends. And as different as he was now, she recognized his thoughtful face, the one he donned when he'd been an idiot and she'd reminded him of that fact. He would consider, grumble, and then apologize.

As the dance ended he looped her hand over his arm again. Her next partner, Mr. Basingstoke, approached for the evening's first waltz, and she glanced up at Callum. "Well?" she prompted.

"Well, what?"

"Aren't you going to apologize for keeping your plan from me?"

"Nae. Ye were on yer own before, and now ye arenae. Ye play yer part, and I reckon I'll play mine. Now go dance while I watch ye."

"You'd best watch the men, or you'll be learning the waltz backward."

He shook his head, his two-colored eyes glinting. "I'll be watching ye," he repeated, lowering his voice still further, "imagining ye naked out there with naught but me in the room."

Well, that wouldn't make this any easier. Before she could point that out to him, Mr. Basingstoke held out his hand to her. "If you'd do me the honor, my lady," he intoned. "I haven't waltzed with you in over a year. I do not think I can wait any longer."

Callum tilted his head, watching her make her way to the center of the ballroom. If he'd been her, he would have pointed out to Basingstoke that she hadn't danced because she'd been mourning her husband, but Rebecca was far too composed and polite to say any such thing.

Despite what he'd said, he did know something of the waltz. The last time he'd been in Boston a few of the more daring lasses had demonstrated it at some soiree or other. He'd never attempted it, himself, but he'd be damned if he missed the chance to have Rebecca in his arms in front of everyone.

Aye, he could claim that was part of his plan, but that would be another lie. Dunncraigh and Stapp saw her as a means to an end—an end they wanted badly enough to kill for. When he'd seen them looking at her, he'd realized just how perilous her circumstances were. Whatever the cost, he needed the Maxwell looking elsewhere—looking at him—as the largest obstacle to his plans.

"That's yer plan then, is it?" Stapp asked from just behind him. "Marry yer brother's own widow? Ye always did want her for yerself, I recall. Hardly seems fair to her, though, to be saddled with a sot who'd rather drink and shoot bears in America than be a landowner here."

"Ye ken a great deal about me for someone I've nae spoken more than two or three sentences to at a time," Callum returned, keeping his gaze on the lithe, golden-haired, azure-draped goddess swirling before him.

"I ken who ye are. A younger brother desperate to be half the man his older brother was. So desperate ye'd even take his widow for yerself."

"I see throwing ye out my window didnae knock any sense into ye. Care to try again on the balcony?" He gestured toward the open doors to one side of the room, the only place where he'd noticed a breath of cool air and the scent of damp evening.

"My father offered ye a very generous price for whatever claim ye have on Sanderson's fleet, Geiry. Take it. The next offer willnae be as generous."

Taking a last look at Rebeca, Callum faced the Marquis of Stapp. "Ye're interrupting a mighty pleasant view here, so I'll ask ye plain—what will that next offer be, exactly? Because I did turn down the first one."

Donnach's brow furrowed for a heartbeat before it smoothed out again. "More than likely it'd be beating ye half to death and throwing ye on the next ship back to America."

"That doesnae sound very gentlemanly. And how do ye mean to explain two Earls of Geiry vacating the title within eighteen months?"

"Ye can keep the title. In Kentucky, or wherever ye were hiding." Stapp took a half step closer, and Callum edged his fingers toward the *sgian-dubh* sheathed against his right calf.

Hiding. Had they looked for him? Ian had known where he was. If his brother had trusted the Maxwell so much, why hadn't he said anything? Or had they not told Ian they were looking?

Hm. It would have made sense to remove him even before killing Ian. Then the title would have gone to his softheaded cousin, who would have wet himself at the idea of being noticed by a duke and the head of their clan. And then, with Donnach's marriage to Rebecca, Dunncraigh would have owned Sanderson's entirely.

Callum clenched his jaw. Damn him for being too stubborn to read Ian's letters. The last one, at least, though he hadn't known at the time that there would be no more. It might have told him what was afoot, that they were all in danger. It might have convinced him to return home in time to save the lot of them.

"Interested, aye?" Donnach asked, misinterpreting his silence for consideration. "I'll convince the duke to grant ye a boon for going away. It might nae be what he offered ye before, but I reckon it'll be enough. More than enough."

"More than enough for what?"

"To compensate ye for nae marrying a lass who nae wanted ye, anyway. I was there, if ye'll recall. I heard what she called ye. And I saw her choose yer brother. I even heard the conversation after ye left the house like a scalded cat." The marquis chuckled. "I'd wager yer ears were burning, because it was fairly unpleasant."

Ah, the bit where Stapp tried to turn him against Rebecca so the marquis could move back into the "almost betrothed" position. "Back to Kentucky," he mused, wishing he hadn't allowed Rebecca to convince him that shooting both Maxwells was too easy. He knew it, too, but damnation, it was tempting. "Have ye ever seen a man scalped?"

Stapp blinked. "What?"

"Scalped. I've seen it. Lost three of my men back when I first began my business. They strayed where they shouldnae have, and paid for it. My point, though, is that once ye've seen a man scalped, still alive and begging to be killed, being threatened with a beating doesnae much signify."

"Ye'll nae win her, Geiry. Ye cannae be trusted, and ye cannae be relied on. I'm the one who's been here for the lass when she lost her husband and her father. Ye were somewhere off seeing men getting scalped until ye got word ye'd inherited a title and blunt."

"Dunnae fu—"

The Duke of Dunncraigh stepped between the two of them before Callum could jab a finger into the marquis's chest, grab hold of his jacket, and drag him out to the balcony.

"Away with ye, Donnach," his father said.

With a curt nod the marquis turned on his heel and walked into the crowd. Given how close he was to losing his temper, Callum was surprised to see that no one else seemed to have noticed the confrontation. But then Stapp was much more accustomed to navigating Inverness soirees than he.

As for Dunncraigh, well, Callum had insults aplenty for both the marquis and his father. After holding them in for a decade, it felt good to let them fly. Especially since it wasn't just for his own satisfaction. He had two lasses to keep safe. "Rebecca may think ye're some kindly grandfather to her," he said aloud, gazing at the duke levelly, "but I know ye killed my brother, and I know ye killed George Sanderson."

"That's a dangerous thing for a lad with yer reputation to say to a man with mine," the duke returned, not looking even a wee bit surprised at the accusation.

And both the duke and his son continued to pick at the man he used to be, the one they thought he still was. Callum curved his mouth in a slow smile. "Just because ye couldnae find me in America doesnae mean Ian couldnae. And just because he was a bit late in moving against ye doesnae mean he didnae tell me what he knew—and how he planned to fight ye." He inclined his head. "Good evening to ye, ye old goat. I look forward to seeing ye again. Soon." Turning, he walked away.

"Ye've said that before, and ye've insulted me before. I still seem to be . . . unharmed."

Callum stopped. The man made a good point. Slowly he turned around and returned to stand in front of the duke. Bending his head a little to reach the man's ear, he whispered, "Ye're unharmed because this is *my* kingdom now, ye pile of shite. Ye'll live for as long as I say ye will, and nae a breath longer. I warned ye that I'd end ye. I keep my word. But nae on yer schedule. Because if there's one thing worse than being scalped, it's waiting for the blade to touch ye. Think on that while ye lie in yer soft bed tonight."

With that he did walk away, but only to the far side of the ballroom. He might have set the Maxwell's gaze on him, but the easiest path to what the duke and his son wanted was still Rebecca. For God's sake, he should just marry her now, and cut them off at the knees.

The thought tempted him. More than tempted him. He wanted her, and he had no intention of letting her go. Ever. But she wanted justice with a taste of ridicule, and he craved revenge. Stapp and Dunncraigh needed a taste of hope, or they might well cut bait and run—or rather, shut themselves behind locked doors where he couldn't get at them, and where a single letter from a dead man wouldn't sway a judge to action.

Still . . . He gazed at her, swirling and smiling halfway across the room, candlelight glinting along the silver clips in her golden hair. When she and her gangly partner came to an abrupt stop, he actually felt unbalanced for a moment. When he saw what—who—had stopped them, though, he pushed through the soft haze and started forward. *Stapp.*

As he reached the outermost dancers, Rebecca waved her fingers at him, though her gaze remained on the marquis. She knew the game they'd chosen to play, and while he might not have told her all of the twists and turns, she damned well had spleen. With a nervous half bow Mr. Basingstoke relinquished her to the marquis, and Donnach Maxwell put his hand on her waist, took her hand, and turned into the waltz with her.

Callum didn't like it. At all. Whatever else that man had done to their family, he'd gone after Rebecca's hand in marriage. Hell, he was still in pursuit, as far as he knew. *Fuck.*

They would have danced at some point during the evening; both he and Rebecca had realized that. She had to be swayable, for their plan to work. But not the damned waltz. Not a dance where the marquis held her in his arms.

He made himself watch, anyway. Aside from his vow to protect her, the sight of the two of them served to remind him of just how close he'd come to missing the chance to save her, and to have her. To know her again, and to realize all the ways in which he'd been an idiot ten years ago.

If she could knowingly dance in the arms of the man who had a hand in killing her husband, then he could watch her do it. But tonight, after they returned to Mac-Creath House, she would be his. Part of him wanted to think, to imagine, in much longer terms than that, but he stopped himself. The deeper they played this game, the more likely it became that he would die protecting her. And he couldn't—wouldn't—promise her a future he couldn't deliver. No matter how much he'd begun to desire it.

Chapter Thirteen

"What did ye chat about?" Callum asked, appearing at her elbow as if out of thin air.

Rebecca took his arm, grateful for the solid warmth of his presence. "Air, if you please," she said, trying not to look behind her to see if Donnach followed, ready to pounce on her again.

Without another word he guided her to the double doors that opened out onto the balcony. An iron railing ran along the front except for the section closest to the wall of the house, where shallow steps curved down into the pretty, walled-off garden.

A half-dozen guests stood about on the balcony already, and without pause Callum headed the two of them down the steps and into the torch-lit garden. Once amid the trees and flowers he led the way off the stone path and up to the back wall, beside a small stone birdbath ornamented with stone cherubs and a stone sparrow.

"Don't trample the bluebells, or Lady Braehaudin will have you clapped in irons," she cautioned, releasing her tight grip on his sleeve.

"I'll keep that in mind. What did Stapp say to ye?"

Of course he wanted to know how his plan was progressing. Rebecca took a short breath. For a moment she'd thought he might have wanted her out here amid the shrubbery for something else, and she felt disappointed for and annoyed with herself all at the same time for wishing it. "He reminded me how volatile you are, and how you'd only bothered to reappear when you had an inheritance to claim. And how he and I have been friends for a decade, and confidants for fourteen months."

His eyes glittered reddish in the reflected torchlight. "And ye said?"

"I agreed with him. He wasn't lying, after all. Not about that."

He nodded, a muscle along his jaw flexing. "And he thinks ye can still be swayed to his side, then?"

"Of course he does. That's what we agreed on, isn't it?"

"Aye." Turning half away, he seemed abruptly interested in the birdbath. "Considering ye fainted dead away when ye set eyes on *me,* I wasnae certain ye had it in ye to smile at him. But ye did."

That snapped her spine straight. "Don't you dare try to turn this on me," she hissed as loudly as she dared. "Yes, I smiled at him. You asked me to." She dug her forefinger into his shoulder. "You wanted me to dance with him."

"Nae a waltz."

"Well, that wasn't up to me, was it? Should I have refused? Told him, 'no, I'll only tolerate you for a quadrille'?"

He swung around so quickly she lost her balance. Callum caught her by the shoulders and shoved her backward against the stone wall, then claimed her mouth in a breath-stealing, openmouthed kiss. "Every lass," he growled nearly soundlessly, his lean, hard body pressed along hers, "every lass for ten years was ye. Every damned one. There were times I almost wished Ian dead so I could have ye. I want ye for myself. I dunnae want to share an ounce of ye, even for justice. Or for vengeance."

Heated, delighted shivers began between her legs. She would never, ever admit that on occasional, brief moments she'd closed her eyes and tried to imagine Ian was his brother, but Callum was here now, and real. Sliding her arms around his shoulders, she sank against him, relishing in his touch.

Callum pulled at her skirt, lifting it along her thighs. Rebecca opened her eyes wide, looking beyond his shoulder to see if anyone might be watching. Of course he'd chosen the most secluded spot in the entire garden—he was a born wilderness hunter, after all.

Holding her against the wall, he hiked her skirt up to her waist, lifted the front of his kilt, and drew her legs around his hips. As he slid inside her she gasped, covering the sound with her mouth against his shoulder. The distant realization that Ian would never have dared be so reckless and bold blasted into pieces as she locked her legs around his hips and he thrust into her again and again, hard and fast and desperate. She came, muffling her ecstasy against his mouth, not caring if he was scratching up her gown with bumping her up and down the hard wall at her back.

While she clung to him he released his grip on her thighs, holding on to the top of the wall on either side of her, shoving in hard as with a grunt he climaxed. He held her pinned there, a blue-garbed, half-naked butterfly splayed on a card, as he spilled himself into her. She could feel the hard breathing that matched her own, the taut center of him focused entirely on her.

She spasmed again, abruptly and violently, as he gazed into her eyes.

At the other end of the garden someone laughed. Had they heard? "Put me down," she whispered, still panting.

"Nae."

"The longer we're here the more likely someone will see us. For Margaret's sake, put me down."

Scowling, he released the wall and put his hands around her waist. Her legs a little unsteady, she lowered them to the ground again, brushing her skirt back into position as he took a step away.

"I ken," he murmured, resettling his kilt. "I pushed ye to come here tonight. It's on me that ye had to dance with Stapp, that ye had to smile at him and Dunncraigh. I reckon I have 'em aimed at me, now. I'll nae put ye into the middle of this again."

"Brush the leaves off my back," she countered, and turned around. Once she felt his hands on her back and tickling deliciously through her hair, she squared her shoulders. "I've noticed," she said, picking and choosing her words, "that when I'm not about, you take more chances. I saw you talking with His Grace. And I saw your expression. That was not the least bit subtle or polite."

"I r—"

"I know you were trying to make them see you as the largest threat to their plans, you big brute. My point is, I have as much to risk as you do. Perhaps more. And I've been wronged by them, to a greater degree than you. So no, you are not going to set me aside and go lay waste to clan Maxwell on your own. We shall do it together."

It was more than the wish to be near him, to chat and jest with him as she used to do. Now that he'd returned, now that she'd met this new, much-improved version of

Callum MacCreath, the idea of watching him leave again, or of allowing harm to come to him, made her physically ache. And if she allowed him to view her as some delicate hothouse flower no matter how ill-prepared she felt for this task, then that old relationship she'd enjoyed so much, when they'd been equal, if wild, partners, would disappear.

"Together, aye," he commented, as music began for a quadrille. "With me standing between ye and the vermin."

That wasn't much of an answer, but he hadn't argued with her, either. "I have to go back. I'm to dance with Lord Braehaudin."

"And I've his wife for a partner." She started back to the pathway, but he took her hand. "I ken that ye're nae the lass I pined after ten years ago. Ye're an entirely different lass—a lady. And ye—you, standing right there—fascinate me. I've nae wish for harm to come to ye, but aye, I could use yer help. Just for God's sake, be careful."

Rebecca put a hand on his chest. "I'll be careful if you're careful. You used to be a man I liked despite my better judgment. You're different now, in ways I can't even describe."

"Good ways, or bad ways?" he asked, lifting an eyebrow.

Tightening her grip on his fingers, she towed him in the direction of the steps and the balcony. "Good ways, mostly."

"I'll see if I can do someaught about that."

In truth, over the past fortnight she'd probably had more conversation with him than she had with Ian in the last six months they'd been married. Yes, they'd chatted about the weather, and meals, and Margaret, but clearly he hadn't thought to confide in her about his growing suspicions of his partners. And she saw now that that had begun to consume him. He'd worked hard to improve the profitability of Sanderson's, but she didn't know if owning part of a shipping company had been his dream—or if he had dreams. And he'd never, *ever,* had sex with her in someone else's garden, as if he couldn't stand the idea of not having her for another minute.

Back inside the ballroom Callum relinquished her to their host, the Marquis of Braehaudin, while he partnered with the marchioness. She tried to keep her attention on what she was doing; stepping on toes wouldn't impress, and it had been quite a while since she'd danced with anyone. Even so, her mind kept wandering back to the garden, to the man who'd so unexpectedly stormed back into her life.

For heaven's sake, more than once she'd actually prayed that he was dead, so she would never have to wonder what if. That was when she'd imagined him as he had been—a quick-tempered, easily offended rake in pursuit of any of a dozen different women at any given time. The man he'd become—a protective, hard, clever warrior—felt much easier on her conscience, but at the same time much harder on her heart.

As the quadrille ended, Donnach Maxwell came forward to collect her for the next country dance. She was beginning to feel like a tennis ball, batted back and forth and not even knowing on which side of the court she found herself. And she still managed to smile as he led her back onto the well-polished dance floor.

Callum wasn't dancing, which should have pleased her. Instead, though, every unmarried female with whom he'd been previously acquainted seemed to have picked this moment to stroll by in front of him, accidentally notice his presence, and stop for a chat. As if they could have avoided noticing such an Adonis in their presence until now.

"I wondered," Donnach said, as they bowed and curtsied, then hopped forward in one of the sillier dances she'd learned as a young lady, "if ye would consider meeting me for a stroll tomorrow." He hopped beside her, keeping pace. "I'm nae to call on ye at MacCreath House, but surely ye dunnae mean to allow him to keep ye from seeing yer own friends."

She tried not to linger on that word, because her definition and his seemed to vary wildly and she needed to remain cordial. In her dictionary a friend did not murder husbands and fathers to gain control of a business. But then she wasn't supposed to know about that. Or if she did, she wasn't supposed to believe it. Even now, even reading Ian's letter, she could still find room for doubt. It was so mad, after all. Could anyone commit two murders and then smile and pretend perfect innocence to the degree that Donnach and his father apparently had?

Every word he said needed now to be examined for a hidden, second meaning, every compliment for a secret threat. It was dizzying, and after her interlude in the garden she already felt off balance. "I'm residing in Callum's house," she said, keeping a smile on her face. "I shall honor his rules. But no, he didn't say I couldn't go walking with you. Where shall we meet?"

"Along the river walk in front of the cathedral," he said promptly. "We'll take a stroll south to the Ness Islands for a picnic luncheon."

"You have it already planned, don't you?" she asked, just barely refraining from sending a glance in Callum's direction. He didn't want her to risk her safety, but at the same time, all they had by way of proof was Ian's note and Callum's unwavering conviction.

"I've missed ye, Rebecca. We had plans, ye and I. Am I wrong to think we still do?"

If she hadn't known, if Callum hadn't insisted that she listen to his mad accusations and then provided Ian's letter as proof, she would have been touched by Donnach's pleading tone. She would have worried that he stood at risk of genuine heartache. If Callum had never returned at all, she would have been tempted to tell Donnach that wooing wasn't necessary, and she would of course marry him.

But Callum had returned, and whatever lay between them was like lightning, bright and dangerous and mesmerizing. She craved it. Whether this was just her clinging to an old memory, an unfulfilled desire, or something that had a future, the idea of anything pulling her away from it—from him—before she'd had a chance to figure it out made her angry and almost . . . frantic.

This flirting with Lord Stapp was for a cause, though. It didn't mean anything. Not any longer. It wasn't real, and it would more than likely help. More importantly, by spending a day with Donnach Maxwell, she might discover enough information to save Callum's life. All it would take from her was some courage.

She waited until they'd danced separately down the lines then rejoined again at the end of the row. "You are not wrong, Donnach," she said, following that with another unfelt smile. "I have missed our chats."

"I renew my offer to settle ye in at Samhradh House with me. Or at Edgley House, if ye prefer. Ye dunnae need to remain under Geiry's roof."

"I do," she returned. "He is Margaret's guardian. I won't leave my daughter behind."

"Well, I see that as a problem," Donnach said. "Because he'll be her guardian until she's eighteen, at least. I cannae adopt her without his permission. How can I marry ye, Rebecca, if ye willnae come be with me?"

A perfectly logical question. And it still made dread crawl down her spine. "Running away to hide and marrying are two different things," she countered, feeling her way as she spoke. "He won't harm her, but I can't leave her there without a very good reason."

To her relief the dance ended before he could question why she'd very nearly just contradicted her own logic. She joined in the applause, but kept clapping longer than she should have when Donnach offered her an arm. Blast it all, she had no talent for subterfuge. Hiding a scowl, she put her hand over his forearm.

"For the past year, lass, ye've been able to rely on me to help ye," he murmured, guiding her toward the open balcony doors. "I've nae a reason to stop helping ye, now. None of us wants that drunk here interfering. So ye may continue to rely on me. All I ask in return is that ye dunnae listen to his nonsense. He's a madman who's been carrying a grudge for ten years over someaught he did to himself. He needs to nae be here."

What did that mean? Had he just offered to kill Callum? Had she inadvertently encouraged him to do so? *Oh, no.* This couldn't—

"The next dance is mine," Callum said from directly behind them.

Donnach stopped them just short of the balcony. "Go away, Geiry. Ye're nae wanted here. Ye're barely tolerated. Do everyone a favor and go spend the rest of the evening at one of yer taverns. The Seven Fathoms managed to survive without yer blunt, but I reckon they'd weep with joy to see ye back again."

"Aye? Well, I reckon I can break yer nose before ye can make a fist. Care to wager on that?"

Rebecca pulled her fingers free and turned around. "There's no need for stamping and shoving," she stated, meeting Callum's narrowed gaze. "I've promised this waltz to my brother-in-law, and I'm a lady of my word."

Without waiting for anyone to respond to that, she took Callum by the elbow and, using all her strength, turned him an inch toward the dance floor. Abruptly he relented, and she nearly fell on her face as he gave way. Moving with whip-quick grace, he caught her beneath the arm and pulled her against his side.

"What were ye thinking," he murmured, "going out to the balcony with that snake?"

"I was trying to keep up with his conversation," she retorted. "I have no idea where my feet were going."

A low rumble sounded in his chest. She looked up at him sideways, belatedly realizing that whatever she'd said had amused him. Well, at least one of them was enjoying the evening, then—though in truth she'd enjoyed it very much up until that last dance.

"And with whom were *you* dancing?" she asked stiffly.

"Morag MacKenzie," he replied, taking her right hand in his left and sliding his right hand around her waist.

A little breathless at being touched by him in public, she put her free hand on his shoulder. "Morag . . . Wasn't she one of the women with whom you spent your evenings when you were last here?" She hadn't liked it then, but now she had the sudden urge to hit the pretty redhead in the nose. The jaw-clenching dislike punching through her felt unlike anything she'd ever experienced, but she knew precisely what it was—jealousy. She didn't want any other woman touching him as she touched him now.

"Was she?" he returned, gazing down at her face. "I

thought perhaps, but they're all a wee bit fuzzy in my mind. I dunnae recall spending much time sober back then."

He was in all likelihood lying, but she actually appreciated it. Neither of them was the same person they'd been ten years ago. Not even close. "Was I a fuzzy memory, then?"

"Nae. Ye were the siren calling me back from a very long time at sea, my lass."

That sounded lovely, but too many men seemed to be attempting to sway her with pretty words, lately. "Don't those who listen to sirens find themselves dashed upon the rocks? Am I deadly, then?"

The orchestra sounded the first note, but instead of straightening, he leaned his head closer to hers. "Aye. I'd die for ye, Rebecca."

With that they were off. It took several turns for her to realize that he'd evidently been studying that first waltz very closely, because he knew the steps. He'd always been graceful, but for a few moments she had the distinct sensation that she was flying, floating a few inches above the ground as she twirled in his arms.

He'd likely meant to sound romantic. In light of his original plans and what Donnach had just said, though, she had the sinking feeling that he was being prophetic. How could she give her heart to a man who seemed determined to pay for his transgressions—or what he perceived to be his transgressions—with his life? How could she go through that again, especially knowing the pain that lay ahead?

"I would rather you lived for me," she said quietly, but didn't think he heard.

Chapter Fourteen

The rooftops of Inverness didn't much resemble the wilderness of Kentucky in appearance, but climbing from a thatched roof to one of crumbling stone to another of hard tiles did seem somewhat familiar.

Callum paused on the roof of the Inverness cathedral, squatting in the shadow of the highest steeple to look out over the pathway along the river. The Marquis of Stapp stood there; from what he could tell, damned Donnach had arrived a good twenty minutes before the time of his designated rendezvous with Rebecca.

Thank Lucifer she'd told him about today, even though it had left him tempted to tie her to the bedpost this morning. His cock twitched at the mental image. Perhaps he should do that, anyway. She'd said Stapp wouldn't attempt anything but honey-coated words and then had asked him to give his word that he wouldn't interfere.

Well, he wasn't interfering. He was watching. If that bastard laid a hand—or worse, a mouth—on her, though, "watching" could go fuck itself. She'd left first, taking his curricle to the cathedral, while he'd waited and then galloped off on the waiting Jupiter. He'd left the stallion at a tavern three streets back from the river Ness, then approached via the rooftops. No sense in alerting any of Stapp's men who might be watching.

Back at MacCreath House, Waya had taken up her now-usual position at the head of the stairs to watch over Mags, and he'd begun to think the she-wolf didn't miss running down boars and deer all that much—not when the exchange was table scraps and raw beefsteaks. She'd even chosen a nap first thing this morning over joining him on his ride. But she'd keep Mags safe, and that left him free to clamber about on rooftops.

South of the cathedral along the walking path Stapp had chosen, the buildings trailed off into tangles of brush, then trees and pretty glades with scattered thatched-roof houses and an old ruin or two breaking up the wilderness. It was damned pretty, and he wished he'd thought to take Rebecca walking there himself. Now she would only see it as him aping the ape.

It would also make following the two of them much simpler for him, and increase the temptation for him to put a ball between Donnach Maxwell's shoulder blades. Callum rolled his own shoulders. He'd become accustomed to a certain lack of civility, to using brute force without hesitation when the occasion called for it. That had been for stakes of life and food and land. This, revenge, was both cleaner and more . . . messy. Especially when one particular lass continued to tempt him toward peace and domesticity.

Still, it had taken courage last night for her to agree to picnic with Stapp, and even more to tell *him* about the rendezvous. She had a backbone, and resolve. How far would she be willing to go, though, to avenge a man who'd been dead for fourteen months, and another who'd been gone for just short of that? No, he corrected himself. She didn't want to avenge anyone. She wanted the

Maxwell and Stapp to stand before a judge and be weighed for their crimes, and to accept whatever punishment or lack thereof some stranger decided they merited.

His curricle stopped just short of the cathedral. Before the groomsman could jump down to help Rebecca to the ground, Stapp stepped forward to see to it himself. When he took her hand, Callum clenched his fist.

The drizzle of the morning had ended, and blue sky crept closer along the western horizon. The grass would be wet, but given the trio of footmen who fell in a dozen or so feet behind Rebecca and Stapp, the marquis had planned for that. Among them the lads carried a small table, a pair of chairs, a blanket, and a large picnic basket. Callum was glad to see them present, loyal to the Maxwell or not. At least Stapp wouldn't be attempting to remove Rebecca's clothes in front of his footmen—or so he hoped.

There were several ways to convince a lass to marry a lad, after all. So far the marquis had tried faux protectiveness and flattery of her weak, feminine heart. That didn't mean he wouldn't tire of being patient and move on to threats or ruination. Of course that would also be the last thing Donnach Maxwell attempted.

Keeping to his crouch, Callum returned to the back of the roof and walked out along an overhanging, adjoining oak branch, then clambered to the ground. He'd worn his old Kentucky buckskins today; bold red and green and black plaid didn't blend well into the greenery growing along the Ness. And he didn't think for a moment that the three footmen were the only Maxwell men wandering about along the river walk today.

Rebecca carried an umbrella of green oiled silk, and used it presently as a walking cane. She'd dressed in a matching green walking dress, simple and half covered by a black pelisse. Whether she'd worn black to continue to honor Ian or to send Stapp a reminder that she was freshly out of mourning, Callum approved. He approved the umbrella, as well—anything she could use as a weapon if need be.

Using trees and low-growing greenery for cover, he kept thirty or forty feet behind and to one side of the strollers. Her dark colors hadn't kept *him* away, but then he and Ian had always had a complicated relationship. Ian's death had made this, today, possible with Rebecca. But at the same time he'd adored his brother. With a low growl, Callum shoved the thoughts aside. Not even Saint Michael could reconcile gratitude for the new possibility of a life with Becca against fury over Ian's death. They didn't fit. But there he was anyway, in the middle of it.

The sound of Rebecca's sweet laugh drifted out to him, shaking him out of his idiotic thoughts. His only duty today was to see that she remained safe. Anything else, he could tolerate, including the anticipated insults to himself and his character. Hell, he'd spent too much time mulling those in his own mind to be hurt when someone else spoke them.

After a mile or so they turned off the trail for a small, tree-edged clearing. While Rebecca and Stapp stood arm in arm chuckling over something, the footmen set up the table and chairs, laid out plates and utensils and glasses, poured Madeira, and served stewed partridge and Jerusalem artichokes in a white sauce. Heavy for a luncheon, but no doubt Stapp meant to impress. It smelled good, per the rumble in his own stomach.

While the two of them sat to dine, he crept closer, settling in behind a cluster of young cherry trees. A half-dozen men seemed to have found interesting bits of ground all about the glade, because they all stood in separate, silent contemplation in a rough circle surrounding the luncheon. Of course Stapp would want men to guard his precious backside—and likely to keep Rebecca from leaving if she'd felt so inclined. Callum had stalked panthers on occasion, however, and avoiding the view of a few Highlanders wasn't much of a challenge.

". . . comfortable profit," Stapp was saying around a mouthful of partridge. "Even before ye wed me, we'll keep ye and Margaret safe and earning a fine income nae matter what nonsense yer brother-in-law gets into. Together we own two-thirds of Sanderson's business. He cannae stand against that, even if he tries to wreck us out of spite or someaught."

"Do you think he would attempt such a thing?" Rebecca countered. "He does seem to look kindly on Margaret, and he's been pleasant to me."

"Lass, he's threatened to murder my father on the three occasions they've crossed paths since he crawled back to the Highlands. He threw me through a damned— pardon me, blasted—window. That's why I dunnae like the idea of ye staying beneath his roof. If he blames us for Ian drowning, he likely blames ye, as well. I couldnae guess what he might try, especially when he's been drinking."

"Callum would never harm Margaret or me," she returned. "I'm certain of that."

"And yet he willnae let Margaret leave his household. Doesnae that hurt ye, Rebecca? He might as well be keeping ye prisoner. Ye said so, yerself."

Callum gazed at her through the filter of damp bark and leaves. She lowered her gaze to her plate, her sunrise-blue eyes thoughtful and, in his opinion, wary. Her golden-blond hair coiled at the top of her head caught the weak sunlight, an angel's halo for a lass who'd gone through far more sorrow in her twenty-eight years than she deserved. This lass deserved laughter and warmth and a far distance from plots and deaths and hidden enemies wearing the faces of friends.

Had he made things worse for her? Callum scowled. Stapp would say so. The marquis would say that his anger and accusations had caused her—were causing her—nothing but more worry and frustration that she should have been spared. But then Stapp and Dunncraigh had begun this war in the first place. And if stopping it meant another share of worry, then he would take as much of it as he could from her, and then see that it ended. Permanently.

"Callum and I were friends before you and I met, Donnach," she said. "I knew him well. Or I knew who he used to be. He does seem to have changed."

"Dunnae tell me ye're carrying a torch for him, Rebecca." Stapp picked up his knife, then set it down with a clatter. "Fer God's sake. The man's a devil. Ye cannae deny he wants nae a thing more than to destroy everything Ian ever touched."

Callum touched his fingers to the ground, ready to launch into the open and take down the marquis. With surprise on his side, he had no doubt he would reach Stapp before any of his men had a chance to move. One flick of the blade in his boot, and Rebecca would be safe, damn the consequences.

"Have you and your father made an attempt to reason with him?" she asked. "He is your partner—and mine—now, after all. Perhaps your expectations of him have colored your own views."

"Mayhap it's jealousy that's colored my views. Ye could stop all this feuding if ye'd agree to marry me. We could do it today. With yer part of the business added to mine, we could buy him out. Or force him out."

"I thought we were becoming friends, Donnach.

More than friends. Are you saying I'm a . . . monetary decision?"

Good lass. Anything they could make him say, any way they could draw him out, would help, whether they decided to go to the authorities or hang him by his own belt.

The marquis leaned forward, laughing. "That didnae sound even a wee bit romantic, did it?" he asked, no amusement in his voice. "Of course we're friends, Rebecca. We have been for nearly a decade. I'm . . . frustrated. The bastard's been back for less than a month, and he's managed to step between us. Is it so odd that I want to move past him?"

She smiled. "Of course it isn't. I have some things to consider. Please give me a day or two to do that. In the meantime, might we discuss something less serious? Tell me our next step in expanding Sanderson's."

"I dunnae know if that's less serious, but I do like talking about making money."

From there he spoke about wanting to expand the fleet, open a second office in London and a third one in New York. He even envisioned one in India, which wouldn't make the East India Company very happy. Callum could hear the Duke of Dunncraigh in the plans, though, his thirst for power and importance. Being the chief of clan Maxwell didn't satisfy that, apparently. Looking after his own, keeping them fed and safe in a land where sheep were worth more than a human life—there clearly wasn't enough glory in that.

The Maxwells had big plans. Long-term plans. The sort of plans that wouldn't stand for interference from a cautious man whose heart would always remain with the Highlands and her people. The sort of plans that went beyond what a wealthy, self-made English merchant needed to see his daughter and granddaughter safe and comfortable.

Rebecca encouraged Stapp to prattle on for nearly an hour before she set aside her napkin and declared that the day had been refreshing. Callum would have termed it enlightening, but then he hadn't eaten any of that fine-smelling fare. Once the footmen had packed up the remains of the picnic half the men in the glade began wandering along the path back toward the cathedral, while the other half waited until Stapp and Rebecca headed in that direction so they could fall in behind.

As if it had been waiting for the picnic to end, the drizzle began again. Rebecca opened her green parasol, and Stapp moved closer to her to share in the cover. Callum could repeat to himself that he didn't need to be jealous, that whatever happened to him Rebecca wouldn't ever agree to wed the marquis now. But she'd come close to doing just that, and as far as Stapp knew, he still had a very good chance of winning her hand.

"Touch her and lose yer arm," he muttered, slipping past trees as he trailed them. "Try it, Stapp. I dare ye."

Whether Stapp heard the warning or decided he'd be wiser not to press his luck today, he didn't move any closer. As they reached the cathedral he continued on with Rebecca to the waiting curricle and helped her up to the seat. He said something to her that Callum couldn't hear, then backed away as the curricle turned into the street.

Once she was safely away Callum sprinted behind the cathedral and through two alleys to reach Jupiter and the lad he'd left watching the stallion. He flipped a coin to the boy and swung into the saddle, heading them toward the bridge at a gallop.

He hoped Rebecca would tell him about her conversation with Stapp; he hadn't followed them to eavesdrop but he hadn't made any attempt to give them privacy, either. He'd followed to make certain she returned home safely and without incident. She might be a "friend" of Donnach and Dunncraigh, but Ian and George Sanderson had been "friends," as well.

Thudding across the river Ness just before the curricle reached it, he sent the big bay pounding up the narrow streets, past the rows of opulent, well-kept mansions, and up the short, gated drive of MacCreath House. Swinging down, he tossed the reins to Johns and dove into the house just as Pogue pulled open the front door.

"Is everything well, m'laird?" the butler asked, stepping back hurriedly.

"Aye. I've been here all day, in the office."

"Very good—ye've a visitor in there now. Ye said he could have the run of the house. Mr. Kimes."

Damnation. "Bring me a dry coat," he shot, and headed down the hallway.

The clerk sat behind the large desk at the back of the room, three ledgers open before him and a much scribbled on set of papers on top of that. When Callum walked in the lad stood, nearly dumping the entire mess onto the floor. "M'laird. I—"

"Sit," Callum said, shutting the door behind him and taking one of the chairs facing the desk. "I apologize for being late."

"There's nae nee—"

"As far as ye're concerned, we've been in here together for two hours," he continued.

"Um. Aye. Certainly."

"Good. What did ye find?" Callum shrugged out of his wet coat and tossed it at a footman when a dry one arrived at the door. He couldn't do anything about his buckskins at the moment, but hopefully Rebecca wouldn't notice.

"Well, to begin with," the clerk said, pulling still more papers from a satchel, "I'm nae certain what ye may already ken about Dunncraigh. Some of it's common knowledge, after all."

"Assume I dunnae ken anything that's happened within the last ten years. I've heard a few things, but the more ye can tell me, the better."

"Aye. Just over two years ago, then, he tried to purchase Lattimer Park. It's a grand estate south and west of here, used to be the property of Malcolm MacKittrick before he was hanged for being a Jacobite. King George gave it to one of his Sassenach cronies, and it was last owned by one Ronald Leeds. He'd more or less abandoned it, but when he died the Crown found an English soldier to be his heir. Gabriel Forrester. This new Lattimer didnae want to sell, and Dunncraigh bought off the estate's gamekeeper to sabotage the property. Lattimer found him out and took him to court over it. Dunncraigh lost nearly a thousand clansmen and five thousand pounds in damages over the mess."

Dennis handed over a set of newspaper clippings that seemed to detail the story, but Callum set them aside for later. "Lost his clansmen to what?"

"To Lattimer. His cotters declared him the reincarnation of MacKittrick, and themselves MacKittrick's clan. He's doing well by them, from what I've heard."

"They turned their backs on Dunncraigh? A thousand of them?" The Dunncraigh he knew would never have let that stand. Especially not when it elevated someone else's standing in the Highlands.

"There's only rumors about that, but it seems His Grace said they could either leave Lattimer's land or leave clan Maxwell. All but a dozen or so stayed with Lattimer."

"Serves the bastard right," Callum muttered. Dunncraigh had been burning out cotters for years, sending them scattering to make room for his profitable Cheviot sheep. Eventually clan Maxwell would have had enough of the abuse. Or a thousand of them had, anyway.

"That's nae for me to say, of course," Dennis Kimes returned, glancing up from his papers. "The next incident that ended in the newspapers was six months later, when the Duke of Lattimer's sister ended up married to Laird Maxton, one of Dunncraigh's chieftains. Then another of his chieftains, Sir Hamish Paulk, had the sudden urge to pursue business in America. Ye didn't know him, did ye?"

"America's fairly large," Callum returned. "Nae, I didnae meet him. I did know a Graeme Maxton, eldest boy of Brian, Laird Maxton. He'd be my age. That lad could drink."

"Aye. That's him. He married the English lass a bit over a year ago." Dennis looked up. "He has three younger brothers under his wing, and a new bairn of his own. A good man, from what I hear."

So someone with his own background hadn't needed to be banished from home and take ten years to decide what sort of man he wanted to be. He didn't know whether to be pleased for Graeme, Viscount Maxton, or annoyed with him.

"From there all I have is rumors and conjecture," the clerk went on. "Business deals refused then agreed to with worse terms, things burning mysteriously, a lad here or there gone missing without explanation. But it's the Highlands, so . . ." He shrugged.

"A great many things seem to burn in the Highlands, even with all the rain," Callum observed. As his brother hadn't gone missing, he could only speculate how many other lads had met with unfortunate "accidents" if they attempted to defy the Maxwell, with no one ever thinking anything suspicious. One thing became ever clearer, though—someone needed to stop him. Permanently.

Down the hall Rebecca's voice answered Pogue's, and he brushed at his wet trousers again. "Ye have a list of his other investments?"

Kimes handed a paper across the desk. "Some of them. I also took the liberty of looking into purchases made by His Grace over the past few years. They're in the second column."

"Ye're a good lad, Dennis."

The clerk smiled. "Ye're a large client, m'laird." He began stacking papers and ledgers again. "Incidentally, Mr. Bartholomew Harvey, Esquire, came about the office yesterday, seeking employment."

Callum scowled. "I dunnae want him anywhere near my business. As far as I ken, he gave every bit of information he knew about my brother to Dunncraigh."

"It seemed suspicious, him coming to Crosby and Hallifax after ye let him go right in front of us. Mr. Crosby told him nae. I thought ye should be aware, though."

"Thank ye again. The—"

A knock sounded at the office door, and it inched open. "Callum?"

"Come in, Rebecca," he returned, standing. "Ye've met Mr. Kimes, aye?"

"I have," she said, inclining her head as Dennis stood and sketched an impressive bow. She turned back to Callum. "Do you have a moment?"

"Aye. We're finished here. Have some tea if ye like, Dennis. And I'll meet ye tomorrow morning at the warehouse."

"Thank ye, m'laird."

The hem of Rebecca's gown had darkened with wet, a strand or two of grass sticking to the soft-looking green muslin. He gestured her to the library, opposite, hoping she paid less attention to his trousers and boots than he did to her dress. Perhaps not wanting to tell her that he'd followed her was silly; perhaps she would realize that he had been there to protect her, and not because he didn't trust her or because he was jealous.

"How did ye find Stapp?" he asked, shutting the door and leaning back against it.

"Much as we expected," she returned, perching on the back of the couch, one hand draped behind her. Coy, almost. Not what he expected from someone who'd just spent luncheon with a killer.

"Aye?"

"Mm-hm. Full of reasons why I should put as much distance between myself and you as possible, and why marrying him immediately would be to everyone's benefit." She tilted her head down, gazing up at him through her thick eyelashes. "But you know that, don't you?"

"It's nae a surprise," he returned, mentally scrambling. Was she simply flirting? Or did she suspect he'd been close by? "Did he say someaught we could use against him?"

"Well, given how determined my father was to keep Sanderson's manageable from one office—you know how much he enjoyed overseeing every aspect of his business—hearing Donnach's plans to add additional offices and more ships could certainly indicate that he and his father didn't approve of my father's decisions."

Perhaps he'd been overthinking. He could track a bear to its den with it being none the wiser, after all. Callum relaxed his shoulders a little. "We're getting closer to the proof ye wanted, I reckon."

"The proof *I* wanted. Yes. Because you wanted to walk up and shoot them, and damn the consequences to yourself and those who rely on you."

"I do recall that conversation, Becca."

"Then why were you following me?"

Damnation. Time for a change of tactics, then, because he wasn't about to lie. "Because I didnae want to see ye grabbed by Stapp and dragged off to the altar before ye could call for help."

Her shoulders lifted. "Do you think for a moment that I would allow such a thing?"

"Did ye see all those men strolling about the park? They werenae there for the scenery, lass. And I ken ye're a strong-willed woman. He's a killer. And his lads likely are, as well. I reckon he could do someaught to convince ye."

While the mantel clock ticked away, she stared at him. "I would have to give my consent for a marriage to be valid."

"Ye'd have to consent, aye. Ye'd nae have to be happy about it." Pushing away from the door, he walked up to sit below her on the couch, twisting half around to face her. "Ye went with him because ye wanted to come to yer own conclusions. I went because I wanted ye to return here safely with all of those conclusions."

"So you weren't there simply to eavesdrop?"

"Ask me what ye really want to know," he countered.

"And what is that?"

"Ask me."

Slowly she leaned her face down around behind him to his right ear. "Were you jealous?" she whispered.

He looked at her sideways, her face just a few inches from his. "I'm jealous of ten years of conversations ye had with him and nae with me. I'm jealous that he made ye feel safe and protected, whether ye truly were or nae, when ye needed someone for that. I've lost ten years, Rebecca. I dunnae want to lose any more than that."

Turning further, he pulled her around across his thighs, digging his fingers into the golden hair at her temples as he kissed her. If not for the electricity crackling through him as they touched, he could almost believe he was dreaming again, that none of this was real, that she and Ian were married and far away while he sat alone in a cabin in Kentucky.

"Marry me, Rebecca," he murmured, kissing her again. "Keep Donnach's hands off yer business. Ye'll nae be a target once ye're wed. Ye'll be safe."

Somewhere in the middle of that she'd stopped kissing him back. Lifting his head, he caught her narrowed gaze. "You came here to murder people, Callum."

"What does that have to do with anything? I agreed that we'd find ye proof first, and we have, I reckon."

"After Ian died it took me nearly six months to leave the house again," she said.

"Decide what yer disagreement is, will ye? Ye're making my head spin." He didn't try to hide his scowl. He'd just proposed, for the devil's sake. It was a new experience, aye, but it didn't seem the time for her to recall pain.

"Then just listen for a damned minute," she snapped back at him.

Callum lifted both eyebrows. "I'm listening, then, ye foulmouthed minx."

She batted him in the shoulder with a closed fist. "You're the one who taught me how to curse." Rebecca rubbed her fingers across the spot she'd hit. "You can't propose to me when you're still not certain if you intend to live through this or not. I know what you said, but I caught sight of you when Donnach was gesturing with his stupid knife. You would have killed him, and all those men in the park would have killed you. And you would have died satisfied, because you got your vengeance."

"I'd die to save ye. I'll nae apologize for that."

"I know that. But I also see it as a problem. I don't want you to die for me, Callum. I want you to live for me. I want you to look forward to something past this. *I* have to look past this. I have a daughter. If I were to marry you and you got yourself killed, then your cousin James would inherit our two portions of Sanderson's. I would have the house here in Inverness. Everything else would have gone to Ian, because my father adored him and trusted him. I own it only while I'm unmarried. So Mr. Sturgeon would inherit everything. And he would become Margaret's guardian."

He didn't like that, the idea that his amiable, easily swayed cousin would have charge of the wee lass's future. "I'd see to it that ye had someaught, Becca. Enough to be comfortable."

"And that's what I get in exchange for a marriage? A promise that I'll have enough money to buy dresses? I have that now. I want something more." She cupped her hands against his cheeks, gazing deep into his eyes. "I will not be a widow again. If something happened to you now I would . . ." She swallowed. "I'm not certain how I would manage," she finished. "If I gave you my future, my heart, my soul, my hopes, my child, Callum, and then you threw your own life away even for my supposed benefit, how would I survive that?"

She made some damned fine points, little as he wanted to admit it. "It's ye or my revenge, then?" he asked. "That simple?"

"Yes." Rebecca kissed him soft as the touch of a feather. "It's that simple. It has to be."

Chapter Fifteen

Rebecca opened her eyes. The fire in the hearth to her right side had become nothing but a dim red glow of embers, and from the dark curtains she could deduce that the moon had set. At this time of year the sun rose by five o'clock, so she put the time at somewhere just before that.

Soft, warm breath touched her bare shoulder in slow, steady rhythm. One strong, sinewy forearm lay draped over her waist, her relaxed fingers twined with his. She pressed her back closer against his hard chest, relishing his solid warmth. When Callum slept beside her like this it felt almost like she'd managed to tame a wild beast just long enough to enjoy his company, and that when he woke again he would resume his dangerous hunt.

He'd wanted her to agree to marry him. That would ease many of his worries, and part of her longed for just that, for a way to ensure that he would stay with her. But until he could prove to her that he valued something more than his revenge, she couldn't afford to risk entangling herself with him further. This . . . closeness between them was bad enough, and losing him would kill her inside. Even that, though, was better than giving him all her power and options and losing him then.

Ten, twelve years ago she'd dreamed about him, but those had been a girl's dreams, full of adventure and tortured affairs and tears. In retrospect, the tears would have been the most likely outcome—especially once she married Ian. Callum would have brooded and wanted what he couldn't have, and tempted her at every turn. It would have been torture, even knowing that he was absolutely wrong and ruinous for her.

That Callum, though, had died the moment he'd left Scotland. Yes, parts of him remained—that deadly anger certainly. But it felt more . . . focused now, aimed at one, or rather two, specific targets. And he'd become infinitely more patient, willing to wait for the perfect moment rather than lashing out at everyone and everything between him and his prey.

He'd listened to her when she insisted that walking up to Dunncraigh or Lord Stapp and shooting them would be a horrid mistake—for him. Not for them. Now that she'd seen Ian's letter, heard the two Maxwell men speaking with her new knowledge in mind, revisited old conversations through the same filter, she knew. Not the details, perhaps, but she knew they'd somehow killed Ian and her father.

She wanted them to answer for that. But Callum needed to survive it. *They* needed to survive it. Her father and her husband hadn't told her of their suspicions, presumably in an attempt to protect her delicate sensibilities. That decision had left her feeling lonely even with both of them present, and it had made her vulnerable to the machinations of Dunncraigh and Donnach because she'd had no reason to mistrust them.

Callum not only looked at her, he *saw* her. He included her in his thinking, now that he trusted she hadn't been a party to any of this subterfuge. He'd listened to her when she'd advised caution. And he clearly desired her. That could have been mere manipulation or flattery, a way to gain her cooperation, except that he'd proposed.

He'd proposed. Even if he'd only made the offer because he wanted to protect her, it meant she could have him, forever, if they could find a way around this. And now she would never sleep. Rebecca carefully untangled herself from him, slipping from his bed and pulling her night rail on over her head. She'd left a heavy shawl over the back of the chair before the hearth, and she wrapped herself in it, missing his warmth.

Padding quietly in her bare feet, she opened the door of the master bedchamber and slipped into the dark hallway, the single lamp at one end barely enough to allow her to avoid the furniture. Margaret's bedchamber lay across the hallway and down a bit, the door cracked open a few inches. She pushed against it—only to have it blocked by something solid.

Frowning, she pushed again. A low growl directly on the far side of the door answered her. *Good heavens.* "It's me, Waya," she whispered, noting that despite her alarm, she couldn't name any one thing more likely to dissuade any housebreakers from entering Margaret's room, door partway open or not, than a full-grown wolf.

The barricade shifted, and she opened the door wide enough that she could slip into the room. Yellow-reflecting eyes caught the dim light, staring at her as she tiptoed over to the bed. Evidently she'd been approved, though, because the wolf didn't attempt to eat her.

Quietly she sat on the edge of the bed. Margaret lay in a tangle of blankets and pillows and wild dark hair, secure in her self-made nest. Reginald at the foot of the bed, out of reach of restless feet and elbows, lifted his head, blinked at her, then went back to sleep.

If Callum hadn't returned, if the Geiry title had passed to James Sturgeon as she'd thought she preferred . . . Back when she'd trusted Donnach and even thought to marry him . . .

Rebecca shivered. She couldn't imagine what might have happened to her if she'd married Donnach. He wouldn't need her, after all, once her property passed to him through marriage. And then Margaret would have had no value, no place, in this world of backstabbing, greedy men.

But Callum had come, and the first thing he'd done was place Margaret under his protection. At the time she'd thought it underhanded and cruel. Now she knew otherwise. And if for no other reason, Rebecca loved him now because of that.

She loved him. Her heart pounded hard in response, an affirmation to what it had known for days now, despite her mind's refusal to acknowledge such a basic, vital thing. She loved him. He'd upended everything in her life, made her look all over again at things of which she might have preferred to remain ignorant. He argued with her, unsettled her, threw ice-cold water on her ideas of safety and comfort. And she'd never felt as alive as she did in his company.

A soft *whumph* from the wolf at the door made her look up. Callum stood in the doorway, naked but for the kilt knotted at his hips. Waya rubbed against his thigh, and he reached a hand down to scratch behind the wolf's ears.

Rebecca held out a hand in his direction and he stepped forward, silent on the hardwood floor, to take her fingers in his. Tightening her grip she stood, drawing his arm around her so she could lean back against his chest. Standing there in her daughter's room, Callum's arms around her, the abrupt sensation of contentment, of peace and comfort and calm, surprised her with its soft warmth. After Ian's death, she'd never thought to feel it again.

"Did someaught fright ye?" he breathed into her hair.

"I just want to check on Mags," she returned in the same quiet tone.

"She's either asleep or twirling about like a pinwheel. There's naught in between."

With a soft chuckle, Rebecca stepped out of his arms to lead the way to the door. "She's always been very confident, but now that she has a pack, I don't think she can be stopped." Now that she had a father again, Rebecca almost said, but stopped herself. Callum didn't get to be a father unless he proved himself able and willing to remain with them.

In the hallway Callum tugged her back against him. If they weren't careful the servants would notice and begin talking, and then she would have to figure out what to tell Margaret—which would be supremely difficult when she didn't even know what to tell herself.

"I wish ye could go about with yer hair down," he said, pulling a long strand of the blond stuff over the front of her shoulder and twining it around his finger.

"I'm not a maiden, or a hoyden, so I can't. Not outside the house, anyway." She leaned up and kissed him. "I didn't mean to wake you."

"I'm glad ye did. I'm discovering there arenae enough hours in the day, any longer."

"Not for vengeance and a family, you mean?" she asked, before she could stop herself. "Perhaps you need to choose one and let the other go."

"Let it go? Ye mean let *them* go. Let them get away with two murders. How can I do that, lass?"

She looked up at his face. Even in the dark both of his eyes looked light, though if she hadn't known she wouldn't have been able to tell which was green and which one, blue. "I can't answer that. But I've been looking for solutions, and I can't seem to find one that includes both."

He lowered his arms, their absence leaving her cold. "Then ye dunnae know me very well, Becca." Turning around, he walked back up the hallway past the open master bedchamber door, and toward the stairs.

"I know *them*," she said to the empty hallway, and turned for her own bedchamber. "And that's what frightens me."

Callum shoved the close-written notes Dennis had left him aside and stood, stretching. The muscles across his back had spent so much time being knotted up with frustration and anger he was going to become a hunchback if he wasn't careful.

As he sifted through the growing pile of evidence that Rebecca had insisted he compile, he found himself wishing he could talk to Ian. His brother had always been proficient at separating wheat from chaff where information and rumor were concerned. Callum knew himself well enough to realize that he wanted to pile every bit of news he found, reliable or not, onto the pyre he'd built for burning Dunncraigh at the proverbial stake.

He'd returned to Scotland to do one thing. And the other things that kept coming between him and that goal, things and people he'd begun to view as astonishingly vital to him, kept twisting him about and making him hesitate—which he'd never expected.

Leaving the office, he sent a quick whistle toward the stairs, then continued into the foyer. "Is Jupiter saddled?"

he asked, shrugging into the caped greatcoat Pogue handed him.

"Aye. It's a wee bit windy out there today, m'laird," the butler supplied. "And the rain's nae falling straight down."

Callum grinned. "It feels like the Highlands, ye mean." Waya trotted down the stairs, shoved her nose into his knee, then pawed at the closed front door. "Ye smell it too, aye, lass? Wild and rain." When Pogue hesitated to push the wolf out of the way so he could open the door, Callum did it himself, and Waya slipped outside in front of him.

"Ye might consider taking one of the lads with ye, m'laird," the butler commented. "Or waiting until this afternoon, to see if the weather clears."

"I'll risk it. We'll be back in an hour or so. Nae visitors and nae a man—or woman—leaves while I'm away."

"Aye. We'll keep watch."

The white mop galloped down the stairs, but skidded to a halt in the doorway. Evidently Reginald didn't like rain weighing him down. Stepping over the black-eared terrier, he hunched his shoulders against the biting rain and collected Jupiter from the waiting groom.

"Let's go, Waya," he said, swinging into the saddle as the wolf set off at a gallop down the drive.

The rain didn't bother the wolf, and it didn't trouble him, either. He needed to clear his head. Vengeance had been much easier when he didn't care about anything else. Before he'd known Margaret existed. Before he'd realized that Rebecca was another victim of Dunncraigh's, and not an adversary of his.

This morning in looking through Dennis Kimes's notes he'd found the list of seven properties Dunncraigh had acquired over the past decade. The more significant ones he'd purchased over the past eighteen months or so. A small building just off the port at Dover, another in Southampton. Property just south of Dover along the water—for a dock, perhaps? To someone looking for it, it said that Dunncraig wanted offices in every major port, private docks for Sanderson ships out of sight of the harbormasters . . . Power without the mess of having anyone regulating it.

Of course Ian and George would never have stood for it. While to him it said—screamed—motive, though, it was all he had. A note from his brother, and some property purchased in the company's name. He couldn't prove the purchases had been made without the permission or knowledge or approval of the duke's other partners. He couldn't prove much of anything at all.

If he couldn't go at them directly, though, he needed to do it as Rebecca had suggested—via the courts. The damned Maxwell had covered his tracks well, but the duke had only known he had someone moving against him for the past few weeks. Before that he'd removed Ian, and then he'd removed George. The problem, or so Dunncraig had thought, was ended. All he needed was to bring Rebecca into his clutches, buy off James Sturgeon, and he would have control of what would, under his ownership, become the second-largest shipping conglomerate in the world. Second only to the East India Company.

He'd taken Ian's ledger, and more than likely whatever notes George had made. Had he destroyed them, though? Or kept them in case some legal tangle appeared and he needed them? Dunncraig would have no reason to do away with them, because he'd done away with their owners. *Hm.*

Of course that had changed now that he'd arrived from Kentucky and made his threats. Callum angled

Jupiter back toward the harbor as he considered. He needed to pay Maxwell Hall a visit. And he needed to make certain Dunncraigh wouldn't be there to greet him when he went calling.

A heavy splinter flew off the bakery sign beside his head. He ducked instinctively as the hollow sound of a rifle firing cracked into the street, half muffled by the rain.

Callum whipped around, counting off seconds in his head as he searched rooftops and alleys. Waya had circled back close behind him, no doubt sensing trouble. With the rain pushing scent out of the air she would have trouble finding a single shooter in a large town full of men, and he didn't want to linger long enough to give the would-be assassin another chance.

As he reached twelve he kicked Jupiter in the ribs, sending the stallion pounding up the street the way they'd come. With Waya on his heels he retreated to the nearest alley, then jumped down from the bay. Tying off the reins on a piece of fence, he squatted down beside the wolf. "Hunt, Waya. Let's see who shot at me, aye?"

Her head went down, shoulders up, in classic stalking pose. They'd hunted people before, though rarely and never in a town of thousands. As she glided soundlessly around the corner he reckoned the odds were equal that she'd find the shooter or a rat. Setting one foot into Jupiter's stirrup, he stood on the saddle then jumped up to grip the nearest eave. Pulling himself onto the roof, he crouched, making his way toward the corner where he'd come into the shooter's view.

The buildings here were close enough together to touch in places, and moving from one roof to the next was more a matter of keeping an eye out for loose shingles than anything else. Once he had a view of the street he settled lower, trying to figure where the shot had originated. Below people walked to and fro, huddled against the rain and utterly oblivious to the fact that a murder had nearly occurred just five minutes earlier.

Spying the bakery sign, he shifted one rooftop over. The shot had to have come from within a foot or two of where he crouched. Turning, he found a spot on the roof just turning dark from rain—as if someone had been lying there, waiting. "Damnation," he muttered, taking a last look for anything left behind before he dropped to the eave and then down to the street.

"Good heavens," a thin lass said, backing away as he landed in front of her. "What the devil?"

"Aye, the devil," he returned darkly, as Waya padded back to join him.

The girl gasped, grabbing for her companion's arm as Callum and the wolf returned to the alley where he'd left Jupiter. In a sense, this was the best thing he could have expected. He'd annoyed or worried one or the other of the Maxwells to the point that they wanted him dead. They'd tried bribery, twice, some more direct suggestions that he go back to Kentucky, and now they'd moved on to a more permanent solution to their troubles.

He'd wanted them too worried about him to try anything else with Rebecca, but it seemed more likely that the best he could hope for was to make them reckless. Having someone shoot at him in the middle of Inverness in broad daylight definitely fit his definition of reckless—but it also seemed rather . . . chancy. How had they known he would be riding there today? Aye, he rode most mornings, but he didn't always take the same path. That bored him.

Or did they have possible assassins lurking throughout the city? As the Maxwell, Dunncraigh certainly wielded enough power with his clan to convince a few of his men to kill. Even if their intended target was part of clan Maxwell, himself.

The other possibility, of course, was that this had been a distraction, something to keep him away from MacCreath House. That idea shot dread down his spine, and he sent Jupiter into a dead run back across the bridge, Waya sprinting behind them.

He skidded to a halt, jumping down from the bay and striding for the house. "Any callers?" he demanded, as Pogue pulled open the door.

"Nae, m'laird. It's been quiet. Yer coat?"

The butler reached for it, but Callum ignored him as he pounded up the stairs. "Rebecca? Mags?" he called out, shoving doors open as he went.

"We're in the nursery," Rebecca's voice came from the end of the hallway, and he let out the breath he'd been holding. She emerged as he reached the door, and he couldn't stop himself from pulling her into a tight embrace.

"Thank God," he muttered, lowering his face into her hair.

"What in the world's happened?" she asked.

"Someone took a shot at me." Reaching around her, he pulled the nursery door closed. "I wanted to be certain it wasnae a distraction while Stapp dragged ye out to a church or someaught."

Her face grayed. "Someone shot at you?" Seizing his arms, she held him away from her, searching his front— evidently for holes.

"They missed." He shook himself free. "And I'm getting ye all wet. My apologies."

"We need to go to the authorities, Callum," she said quietly, grabbing his sleeve again. "Before you *do* get shot."

"We havenae a damned thing to give them." Tilting

his head, he wondered what she would say if he suggested they hand over Sanderson's to Dunncraigh and simply flee to Kentucky. That would never do, though; she'd made a life for herself in Scotland, but Rebecca was no adventurer. Her steadiness helped anchor him, and given the way his life had gone, he needed her to be logical and forthright. He simply . . . needed her.

"Then what do we need to do so we can stop this before I lose you, too?" A tear ran down her cheek.

He brushed it away with his fingers. "We need yer da's ledger, and Ian's. So I need *ye* to find out for me when Dunncraigh's most likely to be away from Maxwell Hall. Can ye do that without putting yerself in harm's way?"

Her eyes lost focus for a moment as she considered. "Yes, I believe so. I'll invite Her Grace to luncheon. We're still friends, as far as anyone knows. Give me a day or two."

Callum leaned in and kissed her sweet mouth. "I'll give ye a day or two, Becca." He'd give her a thousand thousand days, if only he could figure out how to end this with both of them alive and well.

"Uncle Callum, why are you kissing my mama?"

Margaret stood in the open door of the nursery, the mop on one side of her and Waya on the other, her nanny Agnes standing behind the pack with her hands over her mouth. "Friends kiss each other," he stated, belatedly lowering his own hands from Rebecca's waist.

"I don't think so," the wee lass countered, shaking her head. "Not like that." She stuck out her tongue, mouth open, to demonstrate.

"Oh, for . . ." Rebecca knelt beside her daughter. "Uncle Callum thought I'd gone out into the rain and gotten hurt," she explained, taking her daughter's hand. "He was very relieved to see that I was well. That's all."

"Well, I'm never going to kiss anyone like that." She made a face. "Yuck."

"I should hope nae, bug," Callum commented. "Now if ye'll excuse me, I need to find some house plans." As he passed, he helped Rebecca to her feet. "I hope my face doesnae look like that when I kiss ye," he murmured. "I'm like to have nightmares, now."

"We're going to have to tell her something sooner or later," caught him as he headed for the stairs.

Aye, they were. Not until he could be certain he wasn't going anywhere, though. Not to prison, and not to the devil. Because he wasn't about to offer the bairn another chance at a father and then take it from her again. Or let anyone else take it from her.

Chapter Sixteen

The two days Rebecca asked for turned into five. She was ready to storm Maxwell Hall all on her own and demand the return of any stolen property, or at the least risk looking desperate by sending another note to the Duchess of Dunncraigh asking to go to luncheon. Just as she sat down to write it, though, the reply arrived via special messenger and Pogue brought it to her in the morning room.

"Oh, thank goodness," she said, relieved that she hadn't somehow single-handedly ruined their—her—plans for a more peaceful resolution, until she recalled that if Eithne Stewart Maxwell, the Duchess of Dunncraigh, accepted her luncheon invitation then Callum would immediately put himself in more danger.

Then again, Callum had just that morning declared that he was finished with patience and meant to visit Maxwell Hall before sunrise tomorrow, regardless of who might be in residence. Now, at least the duchess would be away.

Standing, she broke the wax seal and unfolded the note. "Oh." As she read the half-dozen lines her relief dropped into a tight, twisting dread. Rebecca closed her eyes. Callum would like it as little as she did, but she could do it. She would do it, because this would actually make things easier for him.

"Where's Lord Geiry?" she asked, preceding the butler to the doorway.

"In his office, my lady. With that skinny ginger man, again."

"That skinny ginger man is Dennis Kimes," she informed him, "as you know. He is Callum's . . . business adviser." Actually she didn't think Mr. Kimes had a title, but Callum clearly trusted him—which made him at least half an ally, as far as she was concerned.

"Och, he's a new face. New faces are naught but trouble, if ye ask me, my lady."

"Old faces can be trouble, as well." Lifting an eyebrow at the servant, she curled her fingers and rapped on the closed office door.

"Enter," Callum said, and she pushed down on the handle and stepped inside.

He stood behind his desk, the ginger-haired accounting clerk beside him, both of them looking over what appeared to be building plans. Hopefully it wasn't Maxwell Hall—since including a "new face," as Pogue termed Mr. Kimes, in something that Callum tended to call "vengeance" or "revenge" seemed exceedingly risky.

"I have a note," she said as he looked up at her.

His mouth curved in a grim half smile. "Do ye now? Might I have a look at it?"

Mr. Kimes cleared his throat. "I'll have a breath of air, I reckon," he said, and bowing like a frightened bird, brushed past her out the door.

"He seems terrified of me," she noted, nudging the door closed with her hip. "What in the world did you tell him?"

Callum shrugged. "I said he could disagree with me about whatever he chose, unless it was someaught involving seeing ye and the bug kept safe and comfortable. And that the last lad to threaten yer safety got tossed out my window."

"Ah. I'm flattered then, I suppose. But I'm hardly that delicate."

He took the note from her outstretched fingers. "Ye're precious to me." In his mind that seemed to answer everything, because without another word he unfolded the missive and read through it. Abruptly he looked up again, his brows diving together in a deep frown. "Nae."

"It's perfect, Callum. You will very nearly have the run of Maxwell Hall."

Moving around the desk, he stopped so close to her she had to tilt her chin up to look him in the eyes. "Do ye think for a minute that I'll allow ye to go to a luncheon with the duchess *and* Dunncraigh? Nae. Ye write 'em back and tell 'em I forbid it."

"I seem to recall that your concern was for Margaret, and that I could do as I liked."

"Ye mean to hold me to that? That was nearly a month ago, when I'd nae sorted things out." He caught hold of her arm, not gently. "Ye may have spent time with the Maxwell and his bonny wife before I came back here, but I'm here now. Ye cannae." He turned around to swear vehemently at the papers on his desk, as if they'd personally offended him. "Nae, Rebecca. It's too dangerous."

She resisted the urge to rub her arm, and instead put her palm on his back. "I *have* dined with them before. No, I don't like the idea of sitting across a table from that . . . man. But this is our plan. Isn't it? Let them have enough hope to continue, and see to it they're worried enough that they rush their plans and make mistakes?

Set them off balance and give us time to find what we need? That's precisely what they've done. They've just given you time and opportunity to break into their blasted house and find those ledgers."

"Ye—"

"Don't you dare tell me what I'm not permitted to do, Callum MacCreath. I won't stand for it. I was naïve. I was never stupid. We will have luncheon at Alba Gàrradh, a respectable restaurant, in front of other people. I will take my own carriage there and back again. And I will bring a driver and a groom with me to watch the doors and make certain I won't be going anywhere against my will."

His jaw clenched, he stalked away from her. She had no doubt in the world that he could physically prevent her from doing any of the things she'd just said. If she admitted to thinking that by taking more of a risk herself, she would enable him to take a little less, he'd likely lock her in her bedchamber. At this moment, before the Maxwell realized she would not be convinced to marry Lord Stapp, she had a certain immunity. Dunncraigh wouldn't murder her, not while she literally owned the keys to his kingdom.

"I dunnae like it."

"I know you don't. I don't like it, either. But it's necessary."

Callum walked back up to her. She opened her mouth, ready to protest that she wasn't a child and would not be locked away like one, but he took her hand and placed her palm over his chest. Beneath her fingers his heart beat hard and fast. "I should be the one taking risks. It shouldnae be ye."

"I think I've left plenty of risks for you, Callum. I'm eating a meal. You're breaking into the home of the chief of clan Maxwell."

From his short breath, he wasn't convinced. "If ye hear anything—*anything*—that makes ye nervous, ye're to stand up and go to the maître d' and tell him ye need some air. Is that clear?"

"What's the maître d' to do about that?"

"Considering that the moment we finish here I'm riding out to the Alba Gàrradh and paying him two hundred quid to see ye kept safe, I imagine he can do a great deal."

Goodness. He'd agreed. Attempting to hide her surprise, she leaned up and kissed him on the cheek. "I'll be fine. I'm much more worried about you."

Covering her hand with his, he kissed her back on the mouth. "Stubborn woman. Dunnae try to get them to admit to someaught, and for the devil's sake, dunnae agree to anything. It's just a luncheon, and ye're looking for advice because ye dunnae want to be parted from Mags."

So now he thought she would suddenly become an idiot and end up married over tea. Rebecca tried to tug her hand free, but he held her there with his. "I know what it is," she stated.

"Are ye angry?"

"Yes, I am."

"Good. Ye hold on to that." With that he let her go and left the office.

Yes, parts of the man resembled the boy she'd known ten years ago, but not many of them. She did recall how angry he could make her, but that had generally been because he was drunk or just back from bedding some silly young thing who thought she could tame him. Now he'd done it to give her strength. The boy no longer existed. The man knew what he wanted and went after it.

The man still remained fierce and stubborn, but at least he listened. And he'd just proven that he could bend. As for taming him, she rather enjoyed the wildness in his soul. It made her feel warm and protected and wanted. After fourteen months of being alone, and nine years of . . . not coldness, but moderation, she supposed it was, the heat of Callum MacCreath intoxicated her.

If she'd gone away with him ten years ago, he likely would have destroyed her along with himself. She wouldn't have been strong enough, wise enough, to stand against him. They'd both learned a great deal since then. And painful as the lessons had been for both of them, without those experiences they would never have been able to find this moment.

Wandering over to the desk, she looked down at the papers spread across the surface. They were floor plans, but not of Maxwell Hall. One of them looked like the warehouse Callum was constructing down by the port, a place to house the barrels of whisky coming in from Kentucky while they finished aging. She picked up the other paper. This one was more complicated. A distillery?

A shiver ran down her spine. Was he building here? Did he mean, then, to stay? Had he begun looking to the future as she'd urged? But why not say anything? Of course not an ounce of Kentucky Hills Distillery belonged to her, but if they were going to be together, he should have said something about it. That was how Dunncraigh and Donnach had worked, seeing to all aspects of Sanderson's because she was, well, a woman. Making it seem as if they were being kind by not troubling her with a business of which she owned a third.

"Och, my lady," Mr. Kimes said, leaning into the room. "Have ye seen Laird Geiry?"

She jumped. "He went out for a moment." She tapped her finger against the floor plans. "A distillery?"

"Aye. He's been looking at property that might suit." He sent her a cautious smile. "It seems he wants to stay in the Highlands."

"So it does." And if it hurt a little because he'd chosen to show that by moving his business rather than by simply telling her that she'd been correct and that he needed to look for ways to live rather than to die, she supposed it didn't signify. Except that it did. He'd begun with his business, and not with her.

The rain had held off today, but it still looked like a close thing as Callum stood in the shadows of a stand of birch trees at the end of the street. Just down the way the Duke of Dunncraigh emerged from his large, rectangular house and stepped into his coach, the red coat of arms emblazoned on the door panel. The duchess appeared a moment later, looking even more skeletal than she had the last time he'd seen her.

She climbed in, as well, and the coach rolled into the street toward the less fashionable houses and more fashionable eateries closer to the water. From her appearance anyone would think Her Grace a kindly old lass, but on the half a dozen occasions he'd spoken with her, he'd found her to be hard and claws-deep into anything that affected clan Maxwell. If she hadn't had a hand in the deaths of Ian and George, she'd at least known about them. And she'd still pretended to be a surrogate mama to Rebecca, a shoulder to cry on all the while her husband and son went about finding a way to take everything Becca owned.

He waited another five minutes or so, giving the duke and duchess time to realize they'd forgotten a parasol or a coat, then made his way past the usual strings of orange girls, rag-and-bone men, milk peddlers, and everyone else out walking for the afternoon. When a cart of cabbage spilled, he took advantage of the momentary chaos and hopped the fence that circled Maxwell Hall.

With the lord and lady gone, the servants would likely all be headed below stairs for luncheon themselves. Even so, he moved around to the back of the house. Some of the upper-floor windows stood open, taking in the day's cool breeze. Hopefully some of the ground-floor windows would be unlatched, as well. Days without rain were rare enough that they had to be utilized.

Crouching, he made his way to the glass double doors of the orangery and pushed down on the handle. The door opened, and with a grim smile he slipped inside. Potted citrus trees too delicate for Highlands winters stood scattered on the tile floor, birdcages and benches among them. The duke evidently liked his oranges, because he'd sacrificed part of his garden to make the glass-enclosed room.

Gripping the door handle to the main part of the house, Callum pushed it down slowly, allowing the door to open an inch or so as he peeked through. A maid hurried through the room, and he held still as she continued on in the direction of the servants' stairs. Once she'd gone he moved into the back of the house, pausing just short of each doorway to listen.

Rebecca had said that the duchess rarely left home these days, so the servants would likely be giddy with the idea of having a long luncheon to themselves. They'd linger, hopefully, and give him enough time to find what he needed.

He'd been here once, when Dunncraigh and the duchess had held a soiree. He remembered it mostly because he'd found a very fine decanter of brandy in the duke's office and liberated it for his own use. Callum grinned again as he swept through a downstairs sitting room to the door at one side. The idea that his misspent youth would ever come in handy would never have occurred to him, but he knew where Dunncraigh's office was because of precisely that.

The handle didn't give; of course Dunncraigh locked his private office. He glanced over his shoulder again. Picking the lock would take time, but he could manage it. On the other hand, breaking it down would be much simpler. If he broke open the door, though, the duke would know someone had been inside.

Rebecca wanted evidence, a chance for justice rather than revenge. She knew he wanted something more immediate. And yet she'd trusted him to come here alone and do as they'd agreed, while she encouraged the Maxwells to keep up their pursuit of her. Well, perhaps he could do a little flustering and still keep his word to her. *Hm.* "In for a penny," he muttered under his breath. Holding his shoulder close against the door, he shoved. Hard.

With a muffled crack the door frame splintered, and he half fell into the room. There. A little deliberate destruction to make him feel better—and to let Dunncraigh know someone had broken into his private sanctuary even with all his servants in the house.

Righting himself, he pushed the door shut, but it wouldn't stay closed. A lead horse statue propped against the door held it in place, and he moved on to the desk. The window behind him overlooked the back of the stable yard and part of the small garden, but he wasn't interested in the view. He sat in the duke's chair behind the desk, feeling distinctly smug as he did so. Lucifer knew the damned Duke of Dunncraigh didn't deserve a fine seat in a fine house. Not when it had been built on murder and the burned-out homes of his own clansmen and cotters.

The three drawers on the right were locked, an ornate, scrolled bar holding them all shut. The shallow one across the top was open, but all he found there was pages of blank writing paper, additional quill tips, a half-eaten biscuit hard enough that it had been there for months, and a cheroot.

Pulling the knife from his boot, he dug into the expensive mahogany on the face of the top locked drawer. A minute later he pried off the catch and drew the metal bar from its posts. Every bit of destruction felt . . . good, but he didn't want to be reckless about it. He didn't want Dunncraigh thinking his office had been ransacked by some random hoodlum.

He'd practically been one of those, a decade ago. Only a titled brother and his choice to self-destruct kept him apart from the common law-breaking rabble. No wonder Rebecca had turned down his proposal for marriage. And thank God she had. However much it had hurt, she'd had a good life without him there. If Dunncraigh hadn't acted against Ian, he likely would never have returned to the Highlands.

As he pulled several ledger books, more paper, two journals, a bottle of whisky, and a short stack of signed contracts from the drawers, he paused. He would never have chosen for Ian to die. His brother's absence from the world left a hole in him that he didn't think would ever heal. A very odd series of events had led him to where he now sat, and while he hated most of them, for a select few he was exceedingly grateful.

He wanted Rebecca in his life, for the rest of his life. He'd had ten years to decipher where she fit, what he'd thought he'd lost forever before he'd even opened his eyes to it. Now that his world had shifted to include her in it again, he refused to let her go. Ever. And that was how he would continue to think of it—an awful thing had happened, and he'd found her again. Reconciling it any other way was simply . . . impossible, and so he didn't make the attempt.

None of that would matter, though, if he couldn't find a way to put a stop to Dunncraigh. Shaking himself, he opened the first of the ledgers. Ten years ago he'd had only the dimmest idea of how accounts worked; Ian had been the earl, and those duties had fallen to him. Once he'd begun Kentucky Hills, though, he'd had to learn, and he'd become proficient at it. And what he saw in Dunncraigh's accounts was a great deal more money going out than coming in.

Aside from the expected purchases—sheep, drovers, household repairs, servants' salaries, and the like—the duke had purchased the land and properties he'd already learned about from Kimes's research. There was even more to it than that, though. Seven ships, built in Southampton and presently on their way up to Inverness, ships for which the company had paid—and about which his partners clearly hadn't been informed, and whose profits would no doubt go straight into Dunncraigh's pockets. Shares purchased in Caribbean tobacco farms, which would explain the additional ships.

Balancing all the purchases were taxes he collected from cotters on his land, and the tithes paid him by his chieftains, the fee for the Maxwell keeping his clan safe and protected. Except none of the incoming funds had gone back into the clan. They'd gone to Domhnall Maxwell's private plan to make himself even more wealthy.

How would the clans' fifteen chieftains feel about that? Callum found a satchel beneath the desk and shoved the accounts book into it. The contracts were mostly for the properties about which he already knew, but they were additional proof in case someone thought he'd altered the ledgers. They went into the satchel, as well. Then, trying to keep his heart steady and remember the time, he mentally sent up a prayer and opened the first of the journals.

It had been written by Dunncraigh, and after four pages of spitting about the Duke of MacLawry and his ludicrous progressive ways, the journal ended. With a curse Callum flipped through it, but the rest of the pages were blank. He dropped it back into a drawer and grabbed the second one. Dunncraigh making business deals without the knowledge of his partners was one thing, and evidence that he'd defrauded his clan was another. But neither of them were proof that the duke had either murdered Ian and George, or that he'd ordered it done.

The second journal was much older, with the initials of Dunncraigh's late father embossed on the hard leather cover. Pulling out his pocket watch and deciding he still had plenty of time, Callum checked through it. Other than a great deal of ranting about the Sassenach in Scotland and the Jacobites ruining the Highlands, he couldn't find anything of interest. That one went back into the drawer, as well.

"Damnation," he murmured, standing to go through the bookcase on the opposite wall. Shakespeare, Robert Burns, Walter Scott, and a first edition of *Robinson Crusoe* by Defoe made him wonder whether Dunncraigh read or simply wanted to give that impression. The rest of the tomes were almanacs, treatises on the different breeds of sheep, grain supplies during the Peninsular War, and a few others where even the title made him sleepy. He shook them out just to be certain, but found nothing.

Where, then, would a duke keep information he didn't want anyone else to have? He wouldn't have given a ledger or journal to Stapp, because he would have wanted to control them. The items could be back at Dunncraigh, he supposed, the duke's fifteen-thousand-acre estate just north and west of Fort William, but they'd been taken from Inverness. It didn't make sense that he would transport them.

Aye, he might have burned them, but as he took over the business shares of two men who'd been involved for longer than he had, Dunncraigh might have found a use for accounts and private thoughts, completely aside from anything incriminating.

Where would they be, though? The office would be the most protected spot, but also the most obvious. The master bedchamber? Servants would have the run of most of it. Still, though, he wouldn't get another chance to look.

Hefting the satchel, he shifted the horse statue and slipped back out into the hallway, reaching back in to lean the equine against the door so it would fall over and leave it shut. He wanted Dunncraigh to know someone had been inside, but he didn't relish being found out by some footman while he was still upstairs.

Someone coughed close by, and he ducked into the shadows beneath the main staircase as the butler passed through, collected a tray from the hall table, and continued on his way. After tracking down deer in thick brush, moving silently up the stairs felt fairly simple, and he reached the top before the butler returned to take his station in the foyer.

Well, he wouldn't be leaving that way, then. Callum had never been upstairs in Maxwell Hall, and it took trying five doors before he found what had to be the master bedchamber. Two large stag heads faced each other across the room, the larger one with its antlers reaching nearly to the ceiling directly over the large bed, and the other over the fireplace on the opposite wall.

More striking was the large brown and gray bear head above the door. If the animal had come from Scotland it would have to be over four hundred years old, so it seemed more likely Dunncraigh had purchased the trophy from someone who'd been to America. Either way, he hadn't killed the beastie.

The head above the far window, though, made him pause. A white wolf, lips curled back to show sharp fangs, yellow glass eyes snarling at him.

Like the bear, wolves had long ago been killed off in Scotland, though there remained rumors from time to time that some drover or shepherd had seen one high up in the Cairngorms. This specimen had likely come from the same place as the bear, but the fact that Dunncraigh had of all things a wolf up on his wall, seemed . . . prophetic.

Hell, he'd killed wolves himself when they'd gone after the cows in their compound's small herd, but he'd never made a fucking trophy out of an animal. And he'd damned well never display an animal he hadn't even killed. But that was Dunncraigh, he supposed, taking credit where he'd earned none.

The complete masculinity of the room surprised him a little, perhaps because it made him realize that his own bedchamber looked nothing like this one. The lighter curtains and wallpaper, paintings of heather and thistle, the carved wooden rabbits and foxes on the shelves—that had to have been Rebecca's influence, because he couldn't imagine Ian bothering with any of it. Clearly the Duchess of Dunncraigh held no sway in this room. He was rather glad to say that Rebecca's touch was everywhere in his.

Pulling his mind back to his task, Callum rifled through the single bed stand and then the trunk at the foot of the bed. Nothing. The short bookcase beside the fireplace held nothing of interest, either. These were all places, though, the servants could reach. Someone as cautious as Dunncraigh wouldn't put anything possibly damaging where anyone else could see it.

He made his way into the dressing room, filled mostly with hats and boots, and drawers with fresh cravats, shirts, and kilts. The valet would likely know more about the room than the duke, but he rifled through everything, anyway. After this, Dunncraigh would likely have men stationed every ten feet inside the house and around its perimeter. Callum wouldn't be getting in here again.

And still, nothing. Swearing, he shoved the drawer holding the kilts closed, ready to slam the large wardrobe doors closed over it, but something shifted. Opening it again, he pulled everything out. Just heavy wool in the black, green, and red of Maxwell. Frowning, he pushed the drawer hard again. Something distinctly slid from back to front, but the velvet-lined box was empty.

Pulling the drawer out completely, he put it on the floor and crouched in front of it. As he looked at it from the side, the inside seemed more shallow than it should have been, but only by an inch or so. Unless he was imagining it because he wanted it to be so.

With a deep breath he pushed his forefinger down on the front right corner of the bottom piece. Nothing. The same with the back right corner. Then he pushed down on the front left corner, and it gave. The opposite corner lifted. He dug his fingers into the small space, caught hold of the bottom piece, and pulled it up.

An accounts ledger and a smaller journal lay side by side in the shallow, velvet-lined space beneath. For a half-dozen heartbeats Callum simply stared at them. Then he scooped them up, opened the ledger to see Ian's neat handwriting, and shoved them both into the satchel. "I've got ye now, ye bastard," he growled. "We've got ye."

Moving quickly, he left the master bedchamber for the back of the house, looking for one of those open windows and a convenient trellis. He might have what he wanted from here, but Dunncraigh still had Rebecca far too close to him. And however much he'd paid the maître d', he trusted himself more. He might not be able to perform a rescue without her punching him or chewing his ear off, but he could damned well watch over her until she was home safe.

And then he—they had some plans to make.

Chapter Seventeen

When Callum paid the maître d' at Alba Gàrradh to watch over her, Rebecca decided he should have added a few more pounds to ask for discretion. She put her hand over her glass as the man leaned over to refill it with Madeira for the fourth time. "No, thank you," she said.

"Did ye find the pheasant to yer taste, milady?" the tall fellow pursued. "That was a prime one. Hung for five days."

"It was very fine, thank you," she returned, wishing she could motion him to go away. She could certainly find him if needed. He'd barely moved more than ten feet from the table over the past hour.

"If ye'd like," the man pursued, "I can show ye where we hang the game bir—"

"Go away," the Duke of Dunncraigh said. "If we need ye, we'll summon ye."

The man swallowed and bobbed his head. "Of course, Yer Grace. I didnae mean to disturb y—"

"Now."

Ignoring the exchange, the duchess reached out and put her hand over Rebecca's. In the past she'd found the gesture comforting, a signal that she wasn't alone, that people in the Highlands cared for her even if she was an Englishwoman by birth. Now, however, Rebecca had to wonder if Eithne knew what her husband and son had done, and even if she'd approved of the venture. And she made herself smile, anyway.

"I wish ye wouldnae be so stubborn, Rebecca," the duchess said in her soft voice. "Ye could come stay with us, and nae even the worst gossip in Inverness could so much as raise an eyebrow at ye."

"I'm staying in a house with my brother-in-law and my daughter," she countered. "I can't leave Margaret, and Callum won't allow her to go elsewhere."

The older woman glanced at her husband. "We do have some influence, ye ken. Perhaps we could persuade the court that the new Lord Geiry isnae fit to be anyone's guardian. And when ye wed Donnach, he'd be pleased to adopt the bairn. Then her upbringing would be his responsibility, and we could all tell MacCreath to go to the devil."

"I'm flattered you're willing to take such drastic steps on my account," Rebecca returned, wishing she could tell them exactly what she thought of them and their "charity" toward her and Margaret. "It's something to think about, but I would need to be absolutely certain that Margaret could remain with me before I took any action. He—Callum—is very fond of her," she went on. *Make them worry a little,* she reminded herself. That had been part of the plan. "And he . . . he and I were friends for a very long time before he left Scotland."

"Before he was chased out of the Highlands for being a disgrace, ye mean," Dunncraigh amended. "He wanted ye to run away with him, after ye'd agreed to wed Ian. That wasnae done with yer best interests in mind."

Abruptly glad some Madeira remained in her glass, Rebecca took a drink. "Yes, I recall. It was a terrible night."

"Aye. And now here he is again, still panting after ye. I cannae even imagine what Ian would make of all this." He sat forward, covering her other hand so that she felt pinned to the table like an insect.

"Now, now, husband, dunnae be so hard on our lass," the duchess countered, though her gaze remained on Rebecca. "She's had enough turmoil. Give her some peace."

"I know I cannae replace yer father, lass," Dunncraigh went on, nodding, "but I've tried to give ye my shoulder and my advice over the past year. And I find Callum MacCreath to be a poor excuse for a man, and an even worse one of a potential husband for ye. Ye called him what he was, and what he still is—a drunken boy. That's nae a man to raise Margaret. That's nae a man to have anywhere near ye." He sat back again. "That's a man who begins fights he cannae win, and ends up dying over pride."

With her hand free, she took another drink. Where had she found herself, when she couldn't be certain whether her luncheon companion had just threatened the man she loved, or if he'd acknowledged that they'd already tried to shoot him? And personally, she didn't think Ian would be at all offended to see the man his brother had become, or the way he and she had chosen to respond to Dunncraigh's betrayal.

"You make some very good points, Your Grace," she said aloud. "And Donnach has of course been a steadfast friend."

The duchess patted her hand rather firmly and released her. "My lad doesnae want to be yer friend, Rebecca. He wants to be yer husband. And he wouldnae give ye a moment's worry, which is more than ye can say about that MacCreath."

Yes, she'd never have a moment's worry until the second he pushed her down the stairs or put poison in her tea. Rebecca nodded. "Your advice has always been invaluable to me. And believe me, I am listening to it."

"Good." Dunncraigh pushed to his feet. "I'd like to leave here before that damned fool offers to chew my food for me," he said.

More than ready to flee herself, Rebecca stood, as well. "Thank you so much for joining me today. It seems like it's been ages since we've had time for chatting."

They walked out to the street, and the two coaches rolled up to meet them. Rebecca thanked them again, but before she could step into her own vehicle, the duke took her arm. "Allow me, lass," he said, helping her inside.

When he stayed in the doorway, a hand against each side of the opening, she took a breath. "I will consider everything you've said, Your Grace," she said, figuring he was looking for assurance. "I promise you that."

"A few weeks ago ye told Mr. Bartholomew Harvey to find someaught to get ye out from under Callum Mac-Creath's paws," he said, his voice low. "I can see Margaret freed from him. But I need to know that I can trust ye to cooperate and to keep yer silence about anything that might seem . . . irregular to anyone on the outside looking in. Are ye willing to do that?"

She had a very good idea how he meant to "free" Margaret. It would be the same way he'd freed her from Ian. *Good heavens.* "I would like Callum to relinquish his guardianship," she returned slowly. Callum would likely want her to agree to whatever Dunncraigh said, but giving her permission for him to be killed? *Never.* Not even to help his plans. "Perhaps even to go back to his business in Kentucky. But he is Margaret's uncle, her only close family on Ian's side."

"Ye cannae have yer daughter back as long as he's anywhere about, Rebecca. Do ye want to lose her to a drunken madman? He's brought a damned wolf into yer home! He's become naught but a common brewer, for the devil's sake. He needs to not be here."

" 'Not be here,' " she repeated. "You mean . . . dead?"

Hard green eyes studied her face. She didn't know what she showed him; as hard as she tried to look stoic and hopeful of finding a way out of her predicament, the bile rising in her throat threatened to give away precisely what she thought of him and his suggestion.

"I've known ye for a long time, lass," he said. "Long enough that ye owe me some truth."

Nothing in the world could have prevented her from flinching at that. "I don't understand," she ventured, anyway. "When have I not told you the truth about something? You just proposed killing someone. Would you prefer if I didn't hesitate?"

He cocked his head, the gesture much less enticing and vulnerable than when Callum did the same thing. "I want yer word that ye'll marry Donnach. My lad's been courting ye for a year. Until a month ago, ye were ready to plan the wedding. Why has MacCreath changed any of that? And dunnae say it's because of young Margaret."

"It *is* because of Margaret. I told you, I won't leave her. With Callum here, she isn't going to be allowed out of his care. Not in favor of Donnach." She grimaced. "You know he and Donnach have never gotten along."

"I'm aware. Are *ye* aware that Donnach will be duke in my place one day? That ye'd be the Duchess of Dunncraigh, wife to the chief of clan Maxwell? Here in the Highlands, I've more power than the King.

Donnach'll give ye sons, lass. Sons to be kings. Ye said MacCreath likes young Mags. Let him have her, then. Ye'll have more."

This was him. The man who'd killed Ian, and her father, because he thought himself better than they were. Because he wanted what they had, and felt he deserved it. And he continued staring at her. "I . . . You've given me a great deal to think about," she said, unable to stop her voice from shaking a little. "Too much for me to give you an answer at this moment."

He drew a slow breath. "And yet ye did just give me an answer, I reckon. I'm disappointed, Rebecca."

"Give me a day or two to decide, Your Grace. Please."

"Aye. Ye take a day or two. Ye decide how the rest of us are to proceed. What good clan chief wouldnae allow a Sassenach female to make the rules we're all to follow? Good day to ye, lass." He backed out and closed the coach door.

Rebecca put her hands over her mouth as the coach rumbled up the street. The worst part of this had been the way she'd had to look again at every conversation she'd ever had with Dunncraigh and Donnach, searching for clues about who they truly were, what they'd truly done. For ten years she'd called them friends. For the past year she'd thought of them as family. *Family*—when they'd actually taken her true family away from her.

The coach rocked hard sideways. Gasping, she grabbed onto one of the rope handles and hung on, listening to muffled conversation above her. Before she could ask what in the world had happened, the door nearest her swung open.

She gasped again, clutching her reticule like a club as Callum swung his head down from above into the doorway. "Dunnae kill me, lass," he grunted, flipping down and pulling himself inside the coach. He hooked the door with his fingers and shut it before he took the seat opposite her. "I said I wouldnae eavesdrop, nae that I wouldnae drop from the eaves."

Rebecca threw herself at him, wrapping her hands into his coat and pulling herself as tightly against him as she could. Callum made a low sound deep in his chest that might have been a growl, and put his arms hard around her shoulders.

"I'm here, lass," he murmured into her hair. "They cannae hurt ye any more."

But they could hurt her. They could hurt her by harming him. "Maybe we should just leave," she said into his collar. "You and me and Margaret. Let them do whatever they wish, as long as they can't touch us."

"I agreed with ye about going to the magistrate, to the courts, Becca," he returned, still using the same soothing tone. "I cannae let them go entirely. It's nae in me to do that."

She pushed away from him a little, looking up at his face. "What if I asked you to, Callum? If I asked you to take us to Kentucky with you and never come back?"

His two-colored gaze searched hers. "First I reckon ye'd have to tell me what he said to ye that scared ye so much."

And if she told him that, he would likely alter his plans back to murder. "Suffice it to say that he knows I have no intention of marrying Donnach. The way he worded it . . . I tried to go along with everything, to sound willing but a little hesitant, but— For heaven's sake, he suggested I let you have Mags, because Donnach and I will have other children."

"Hm. That sounds like someaught that would get ye angry, nae frightened. Did he tell ye I've nae much of a future? Did he threaten ye with someaught, yerself? Tell me, lass, or I'm likely to imagine the worst, anyway."

She grumbled a curse under her breath. He *did* make a point—Callum had never required much in the way of proof to set him against the Duke of Dunncraigh. "It was just . . . Yes, he suggested some things, including that he could see I kept Margaret if I was willing to co-operate and be silent about whatever they planned on doing. The idea that this was something acceptable to him, that he would simply trample whatever happened to get in his way, whether what he wanted actually belonged to him or not . . . It made me angry. And I realized I was very unprepared to see him like that, even knowing in principle what he's done, when I thought for a long time we were friends and allies."

"Aye. If it makes a difference, at the very beginning ye likely *were* allies. Every time he dug an ounce deeper into the business, though, he likely figured he needed yer da' and Ian a little bit less."

"And their shares a little bit more." She nodded, belatedly shaking herself. "What are you doing here, though? Did you find anything? Or could you not get into the house?"

He loosened his grip from around her shoulders and pulled a small book from one pocket. "I found someaught."

Her father's journal. The old, cracked leather cover had been part of her everyday life for decades, so much so that she couldn't believe she hadn't realized it wasn't among his things. But then her father hadn't been among his things, and that had set everything at Edgley House off balance. She took it with shaking fingers, lifting it to her face to smell it.

After a year it didn't carry the scent of her father or his cologne any longer, but it still had the faint musty smell of old leather clinging to its pages. "Thank you," she breathed, pinning it to her chest. "Did you look through it?"

"Nae. I grabbed what I could find and trotted down here to look in on ye."

"Is this it, then?"

"Nae. There's a satchel up with Wicker," he said, naming the coachman. "I sent Johns back for Jupiter."

"And?" she prompted.

"Ian's ledger, contracts showing the dates Dunncraigh purchased ships and land and buildings—some of it paid for by Sanderson's—to expand the fleet, and his ledger showing how he's been using his clan's tithing money, and yer money, for himself."

She stared into his eyes. He'd found . . . everything. "Do we go to the authorities now? Heavens, I don't even know for whom we should be asking."

"I want a closer look, first. I didnae make things neat and tidy when I left Maxwell Hall, either, so he'll know someone took his papers. He'll reckon it was me. I'm a bit curious to see what he does about that."

"'A bit curious,' you say," she commented, her heart thumping. "I do think you're a madman, sometimes."

He smiled. "Sometimes, I reckon I am." Callum kissed her lightly on the forehead, protective rather than romantic. "I came back here to kill two men. I didnae expect to find anything else. If keeping what I *have* found requires me to go after justice and nae revenge, I reckon I'll live with that. As for who we should seek out, he's the Maxwell. If I went to a parish constable, Dunncraigh would know about it before I'd finished my first sentence. I hate to say it, but I reckon we need the Crown. I'll have to ride down to Fort William, or dispatch someone to the House of Lords in London. That'll take time, lass."

"I don't like either suggestion," she returned. A trip
to Fort William would take him two days, plus another
two days to return. And sending someone all the way
to London and waiting for a response could take weeks.
"What about the clan Maxwell chieftains?"

"And ye said *I* was mad, lass. If half of them werenae in his pocket, I suppose they could take the leader-
ship of the clan from him. They couldnae see him
arrested or tried for his crimes." He took a deep breath.
"I'll send for Kimes, and have him find me a judge he
can trust. I'll nae sleep until Dunncraigh and Stapp
have iron bars between ye and them."

"Do you really think they would attempt to drag me
off by my hair and force me to marry Donnach?" Rebecca retorted, glad to feel some anger replacing the
dread of the past hours. "I would be screaming the entire way. I'm more worried about you." She tapped her
forefinger against his chest.

"I wish they would come after me, straight at me this
time," he said in a soft, low voice that made her shiver.
"I'm nae a trusting man, to be struck from behind or
poisoned." Unexpectedly he took both of her hands in
his, holding them tightly. "Ye know I would trade places
with Ian if I could, aye? That I'd spare ye from the pain
ye've had if it was in my power to do it?"

Hearing that rocked her to her soul. "No," she said,
her voice a barely audible rasp as she shook her hands
loose and cupped his face in her fingers. "Something
evil happened," she whispered, willing him with all her
heart to listen. "I refuse to feel guilt because I—we—
have found something new and unexpected. I would
never wish anything bad for Ian, and I know you
wouldn't, either. I had nothing to do with what did happen, and neither did you. Everything after that . . . It's
good, what we found. I wouldn't trade it, or you, for any-

thing. 'What if' has no place in our lives. We only have 'now' remaining. And you are not to sacrifice yourself out of some misplaced sense of loyalty. Do you understand that?"

"I understand I'm nae accustomed to having a lass dictate terms to me," he murmured. "And aye, I ken. But ye're wrong about one thing, Becca."

"And what might that be?"

"It's nae only now we have to think on. Ye left out tomorrow, and all the tomorrows after that."

Oh, she wanted to tell him that she loved him, that part of her always had, but it seemed like something he needed to say first, if and when he felt ready to do that. She understood it, of course. He was feeling his way through this just as much as she was. Claiming something—claiming *her,* desiring her, as he clearly did—was one thing. Saying the rest meant having to reconcile a very difficult relationship with his brother first.

As long as he continued to look at her the way he was now, as if he found her rare and precious, she could be patient. And she could be very happy with the way things were, if not for two very large problems—the Duke of Dunncraigh and his son. They weren't finished with this, and neither were she and Callum.

"This one has the date of signing on it."

They made for an unlikely group, Callum decided, shoving another of the contracts across the cleared breakfast table. Michael Crosby, of Crosby and Hallifax, let out a breath in order to extricate himself enough from the chair to reach the pages. The way he'd wedged himself in there, Callum doubted the piece of furniture would survive his removal.

Dennis Kimes sat beside his employer, making notes

and filling the large man's cup of tea every few minutes. He himself sat at the head of the table, his interest snagged by Ian's ledger and the story it told about his dealings with Sanderson's, while at his right elbow Rebecca read her father's journal.

Another tear slid down her cheek, and she whisked it away with a handkerchief as if such a motion had become second nature to her, never even pausing in her reading. He hoped that wasn't true, that she hadn't been so deep in sorrow and acceptance of broken dreams that she expected it around every turn. Lately she'd laughed more often in his company, and in bed she came at him with a voraciousness that thrilled him, so hopefully reading about sad memories and missed opportunities would anger her rather than lower her spirits again.

Waya had joined them as well, sprawled out in a patch of sunlight beneath the nearest window. She'd declined to go for a run again this morning, which he put to a certain young lass feeding the wolf far too much ham at breakfast, until the mop bounced into the room, licked Waya's nose, and settled atop her front paws for a snore. The sleek, midnight-black wolf resting her head on the much smaller fluffy, white-haired terrier's back looked . . . quaint, he supposed, frowning, except for the ramifications of their abrupt affection.

Was that him, now? A wild soul lured into domesticity by a pretty face and promises of large breakfasts? He sent Rebecca another glance. In between tears she'd been making notes on a separate page as well, a litany of accusations against Dunncraigh and Stapp for which they needed the contracts and ledgers to prove culpability. Except that he'd known for weeks that they were fucking guilty.

But she'd smiled and kissed him and told him that she wanted him about, and that seeing them tried for murder and theft would be just as satisfying as seeing them bleeding in the street—and had the additional bonus of leaving him alive and not in jail or transported for killing them.

The oddest part of it had been the realization that she was correct. When he'd first arrived he'd had nothing to lose, nothing precious to protect or to keep him bound to life. On that first day in Scotland he'd discovered Mags, a lithe, hilarious translation of her staid, unimaginative father, and keeping her safe and happy had become his everything. Or so he'd thought.

His everything had expanded to include one more being in the days and weeks that followed. He thought he'd convinced himself that she was a sister to him, until the night Ian had claimed her, taken her away from him. She'd called him a foolish boy, and by God she'd been correct.

For the next ten years her words, her face, her voice, had haunted him, even when he'd thought himself free of her. Everything he did had been in part to prove her wrong, to prove to himself that she'd been wrong about him. The man he'd become between his twentieth and his thirtieth years had learned a great deal from his mistakes. In returning and attempting to prove to her how wrong she was, he'd merely proved that she'd been utterly correct in throwing him aside. And he'd never been more proud to realize that he'd finally met her expectations, even if it had taken a figurative trip through the desert of his soul for him to do so.

"What are you looking at?" she asked quietly, lifting her face to meet his gaze.

His mouth curved. "A summer's day. A winter's night, and all the times in between."

She smiled back at him, the expression lighting her blue eyes. "Oh, good. I thought I had ink on my nose."

He damned well hadn't expected to laugh today, but amusement burst from his chest. It felt like hope, light and bubbling and warm. She felt like hope. "Ye have a way of cutting to the heart of a matter, lass."

Crosby cleared his throat. "We need to bring in a solicitor, m'laird. I can make note of what appears to be irregular, of numbers that dunnae balance and purchases that werenae approved by Mr. Sanderson or the previous Lord Geiry, or by Lady Geiry or yerself. I can show how those purchases are tied to profits—and potential profits—larger than those to which he's supposed to be entitled. But a solicitor could tell ye what laws are being broken and what charges ye could bring against him."

"My brother's wife's da' is a judge," Dennis said. "A 'right honorable.' "

Callum didn't want to bring anyone else into their circle. Another mouth that could spill secrets and carry tales to Dunncraigh. "What clan is he?"

"Clan MacDonald. But dunnae hold that against him. He's a good man, I reckon."

Frowning, fighting to balance risk against expediency, Callum took a deep breath. "Send for him then, if ye would." They needed someone; none of them in the breakfast room had ever brought charges against a duke or a marquis, and they had evidence against both.

"Aye. I'll be discreet on paper, just on the chance someone comes across my note."

"Ye do that." Closing Ian's meticulous ledger, he pushed it down the table to Mr. Crosby. "I'm going for a breath of air."

"I wish ye would," the accountant said with a grimace. "Ye make me nervous, glowering over there."

"Well, we cannae have that." Callum nodded at Rebecca as he stood and left the room. Waya barely bothered opening one eye before she went back to her nap. He wanted a run; missing the one with Waya and Jupiter this morning had left him restless and irritable to begin with. But he also knew better than to go roaming today without the wolf by his side. Dunncraigh or Stapp, or both of them, had already tried to have him shot once that he knew of.

Instead he headed for MacCreath House's small garden, blooming with summer roses, Scottish primroses, and the deep red royal helleborine. Some of the flowers seemed almost exotic now; he'd grown more accustomed to seeing the larkspur and columbine and Virginia bluebells in the hills of Kentucky. He squatted down, running his hand through a patch of lavender and breathing in the scent.

"I know this frustrates you," Rebecca said from the pathway.

Still on his haunches, he turned his head to look over at her. "Nae. Ye had the right of it, Becca. Justice, and nae vengeance. Ian would approve of that. I reckon yer da' would, as well."

She walked over to kneel beside him, straightening her pretty blue and gray muslim about her. "They would," she agreed. "They would be surprised, and proud of you. Especially Ian."

Sinking onto his backside next to her, he reached out for her fingers. "After this is over with, I want ye to know I mean to ask ye again to marry me," he said, hoping he wasn't tempting fate by planning for something beyond stopping Dunncraigh. "I made a disgraceful, thoughtless plan for my life one evening, and had it pulled out from under me because of my own stupidity. I spent the next ten years making certain I didnae ever repeat my mistakes. I love ye, Rebecca. There's a hole in my heart that's only filled when I'm around ye. I want ye to know that."

She twined her fingers with his. "I thought my entire book had been written," she said quietly, leaning her shoulder against his. "You were an early chapter of regret and disappointment and questions." Rebecca kissed the frown on his brow. "Now I think perhaps you were the prologue, and my next set of chapters is just beginning." This time she kissed his mouth, so softly it made him ache.

"I hope I'm in all the rest of the chapters," he commented, putting his arms around her and pulling her onto his lap.

"So do I. You . . . excite me, Callum. I was content before, but you excite me and arouse me and fill me with joy. I love *you*. I want *you* to know that."

If she'd asked him at that moment, he would have agreed to take her and Margaret away with him to Kentucky—or anywhere else she wanted to go. If she asked, he would turn his back on everything Dunncraigh and Stapp had done, whatever the cost to his soul. He had . . . everything, the most improbable occurrence in the world considering he'd never expected any such thing.

"I'm trying to earn that honor, Becca," he murmured, wishing he could sit there in the garden and gaze at her forever.

"You did," she returned, lowering her head to his shoulder. "You have."

Chapter Eighteen

"Ye cannae expect me to believe that this ledger fell from the sky, m'laird," the right honorable Liam MacMurchie of clan MacDonald argued, gesturing at Dunncraigh's accounts ledger.

"When someaught that useful arrives on a man's doorstep, Yer Honor," Callum returned, keeping a hard hold on his temper, "a man would be a fool to ignore it."

Light brown eyes continued to eye him suspiciously, though the straight fringes of gray hair peeking from beneath the white, curling wig on the man's head rendered him a tad ridiculous rather than awe-inspiring, at least as far as Callum was concerned. "And how would ye answer that question under oath, Laird Geiry?"

"That I found it on my doorstep," Callum stated. He'd put it there and picked it up himself to be certain he wouldn't be lying. As for where it had been before that, he doubted Dunncraigh would press the issue. Otherwise Callum would be obligated to explain that previous to his front step he'd found Ian MacCreath's and George Sanderson's private ledger and journal, respectively, hidden in His Grace's bedchamber.

Silence. "Very well, then." The judge let out a hard sigh. "Give me what ye have, and I'll present it to my fellows within the next fortnight. I'll nae send out a writ for an arrest against a duke without more voices than my own saying it's to be done." He pointed at the top of his head. "I reckon I'm fond of wearing this."

"Nae."

MacMurchie blinked. "I beg yer pardon?"

Evidently the judge wasn't accustomed to anyone arguing with him. "Ye'll nae remove those items from this house, and I'll nae have ye showing what we found to yer cronies. Ye either see what we see in these pages, or ye dunnae. And if ye dunnae, then I reckon ye're already in Dunncraigh's pocket."

The judge's color deepened to crimson across his cheeks and nose. "I didnae travel across town to be insulted, m'laird."

"Then dunnae insult *me*. My brother is dead, Lady Geiry's father is dead, and someone shot at me last week. Every moment Dunncraigh and Stapp are left to roam about, Rebecca faces danger. That's nae acceptable."

Even if they hadn't been lovers he would have spent every minute of the past nights in her company, just to be certain Stapp didn't attempt a kidnapping and forced marriage, after all. They couldn't continue like this, where he needed to protect her perfectly and Dunncraigh only needed one lucky moment to turn all this to disaster. The odds didn't favor him, and they grew worse with each passing day.

"I do ken what yer concerns are, Lord Geiry. But ye have to understand that I, too, have a reputation, and that I only set eyes on this conspiracy two hours ago. I need more time."

He did understand that, damn it all. "Take the notes we all wrote out, then. They summarize what we found.

If ye need the exact words or figures, ye can call here and look at them." He looked from the judge to the two accountants to Rebecca. "Two days, Yer Honor. I'll give ye two days."

Every bone and muscle and sinew screamed at him that Dunncraigh would be using every minute of that time to counter his moves. The duke had known for better than a day now that the stolen things and his own ledgers and contracts were missing. He wasn't a stupid man. Since Callum hadn't come for him, he would reckon that the law would be doing so.

Being civilized was a fucking nuisance. But the prize it carried with it happened to appeal to him more than what he gained from defying it, so he would wait. For a very short time. Evidently reading the barely restrained fury in Callum's gaze, Liam MacMurchie took a step backward, then nodded. "Two days. Under the circumstances, I agree. I ken this isnae an easy thing, m'laird, Lady Geiry. It makes me wish I'd nae set eyes on young Dennis, myself." He sent a sideways glare at his son-in-law's brother.

Callum nodded. "Thank ye. I sent for some of my men, and I mean to have three of them keeping an eye on ye and yer home for the next two days." He faced Michael Crosby and Dennis Kimes. "The two of ye, as well. I'm adding to the lads already watching over ye."

Dennis, at least, looked relieved. "Thank ye. I've seen naught yet, but I sleep a wee bit better at night knowing they're about."

"And send off those letters I wrote as soon as ye leave here. They should arrive with Dunncraigh's chieftains about the same time the duke finds himself in irons." That part was a gamble, but with the information they'd included about where the clans' tithes were going, even the most loyal of them wouldn't be happy. With any luck the clan Maxwell chieftains would withdraw all support from their chief and leave him to the courts without the might of the clan at his back. And with more luck no Maxwell clansman would be motivated to stab *him* in the back to avenge his clan chief. A letter to the Duke of Lattimer would leave with Dennis as well, under the old banner of enemies of enemies being friends. Hopefully.

"Ye're nae a lad afraid to make a ruckus, are ye?" the judge asked, shaking his head. "Fetch my watchdogs, then. I've work to do."

The construction of the warehouse had more or less ground to a halt with all the builders employed as guards to his allies, but protecting those who helped him had to come first. He sent one of the footmen to the morning room where he'd had a dozen of his men waiting, and divided them among his compatriots. It didn't seem enough, but he couldn't be at every house himself. Not when he had MacCreath House and its occupants to watch over.

When Pogue closed the door on the last of his guests, Callum took the butler aside, as well. "Nae a man or woman is to go anywhere by themselves, Douglas. Keep at least four or five footmen walking the floor all night, in shifts so they stay awake. Use the lads from the stable if ye feel the need to do so."

Pogue nodded, his stern face even more lined than Callum had become accustomed to seeing. "Nae a soul will set foot inside this house without my permission, m'laird. Ye have my word on that." The butler cleared his throat, then reached out to put a hand on his employer's shoulder. "I swear it."

"Ye're a good man, Pogue."

Ian had actually surrounded himself with good people—with two notable exceptions. Or three, if he counted the Sassenach Bartholomew Harvey, Esquire. But at least the solicitor had thought enough of his own reputation to send that last letter seeking him in Kentucky. Thank the devil for that—even if, as he'd begun to suspect, it had been done at Dunncraigh's behest in an attempt to verify Callum's location in Kentucky. And he wondered if the next letter from Rory Boyd at Kentucky Hills would make mention of any armed strangers who'd come calling, looking for Callum MaCreath.

He turned as Margaret galloped down the stairs, Agnes clucking behind her. "Where's my pack?"

"They're sleeping in the breakfast room, bug," he returned, scooping her into his arms. "Tell me, have ye witnessed any odd play between yer Reginald and Waya?"

"Well, sometimes Reginald tries to ride Waya, and his pipe sticks out when he does it."

In the doorway behind him Rebecca made a choking sound. "His pipe?" she asked faintly.

"That's what Pogue says it's called. A pipe and bags. Like a bagpipe. All boys have them."

"So they do," Callum agreed.

"Why did you want to know if they were playing?"

"Because I think Waya's going to have wee, mop-shaped pups," he answered, still deeply ashamed for his wolf companion. He thought she had more dignity than that. But then again, nae a soul could predict where love would strike.

Margaret put her little hands on his cheeks, pulling his face around to hers. "Puppies?" she exclaimed, looking deeply into his eyes with her own mismatched pair. "You're not jesting with me, are you, Uncle Callum? Because this is very important."

"I'm nae entirely certain, because this is late in the

year for a wolf to pup, but she did spend four weeks on a ship crossing the ocean, and she's nae in the wild. But I'd be willing to wager on it."

"Put me down, please. I must go see to her."

He complied, setting the little bug back on the floor. "Dunnae go poking her while she's asleep."

"Oh, I know that," Margaret declared over her shoulder as she bounced into the breakfast room. "I'll wake her, first."

Fingers twined with his as he looked after the six-year-old. "How did Reginald even manage such a thing?" Rebecca whispered. "Waya's three or four times his size."

"I reckon he stood on a chair," he returned with a half grin. "Or his pipe's more mighty than he is."

She cuffed him on the shoulder with her free hand. "That's an image I'll never scrub from my mind, now," she said, laughter in her voice.

He faced her. "Ye heard what I told Pogue, aye?"

"Yes, I did. You don't think Dunncraigh would actually attempt to break into the house."

"They need ye, lass. Or yer hand in marriage, anyway. I'd remind ye that if ye married me this second, they'd lose all their plans, but I ken why ye want to hold on to yer choices until this is settled." The protector in him didn't want to see the logic of it, that she would want the ownership of a third of Sanderson's to remain with her and not pass on to him—or to his heir should he get shot in the head over the next few days. But he did understand it. She had to think not only of her own future, but of Margaret's. And charming as the wee bairn was, and whatever he might put in his own will, he couldn't guarantee that his cousin would find her as precious and vital as he did. And as for Rebecca, after what had happened over the past year, he wouldn't blame her if she chose never to remarry.

"I'm a prisoner here, then?" she murmured, pulling him in the direction of the stairs.

"Aye. And while I'm amenable to ye trying to persuade me otherwise, I'll nae be giving in to ye. Nae about that."

The smile that touched her mouth made him hard. "Let's just begin with persuasion then, shall we?"

Being a prisoner in MacCreath House wasn't as intolerable as she might otherwise have expected, Rebecca decided. Unbuttoning the trio of fastenings holding Callum's trousers closed, she slid a hand down his hard chest and abdomen, following the dark trail of hair that narrowed to a line before widening again at his . . . pipe and bags.

"Fer God's sake, woman, dunnae start laughing when ye're exposing a man's nether parts," he stated, pulling the remaining half-dozen pins from her long hair.

He didn't sound horribly offended, but then he had no reason to be insecure about his nether parts. They were magnificent, if she said so herself. "I was thinking about what Pogue told Mags," she explained, curling her fingers around his half-erect cock.

"Mm-hm. I'm nae a self-important Skye terrier." Taking her by the shoulders he twisted, putting her breathlessly onto her back on his soft bed. "And I dunnae have need of a chair."

With a laugh she reached up to shove his trousers down past his hips, and he kicked out of them. He'd already undone the trio of buttons between her shoulders, and when he yanked down the front of her gold and brown muslin gown to lick her left breast, she could only gasp and tangle her fingers into his dark, lanky hair.

She loved this, when he couldn't seem to take his eyes off her, when she had every ounce of his attention and his passion. That was one of the most striking changes to his character—he'd been angry and quick to take offense before, but about everything. Now the man presently drawing her dress past her hips as she wriggled to aid him had a calmness to his center, a focus that made him a deadly opponent and an exceptional partner.

Flinging her gown behind him, he sank down on the bed and lowered his head between her thighs. As his fingers and tongue teased at her most intimate place, Rebecca twisted her hands into the bedçovers and moaned. However this had happened, however the two of them had managed to overcome years of imagined animosity—a heated dislike that she had begun to realize had more to do with loss and disappointment than actual hatred—she wouldn't have traded these moments.

As she'd told him, the past couldn't be reconciled, and so she didn't attempt to do so. Perhaps her life now wasn't so much a new chapter as it was a new book. Volume the Second in the life of Rebecca Sanderson-MacCreath. Bad, terrible things had marked the end of the first book, but the second one, barring something unforeseen from the villain, looked to proceed much more happily. And she hoped it would be a very long book, full of boring passages about long walks and warm evenings and laughter.

And this, of course. Spasming in ecstasy, she arched her back and tried not to crush his head between her thighs. "Stop teasing me, Callum," she ordered, when she regained the ability to speak again.

He lifted his head, looking up along her body at her. "Are ye in a hurry, then?" he murmured, a delicious grin on his lean face. As he lifted an eyebrow, his fingers slipped inside her again.

Oh, she tried never to compare, but Ian had never done . . . that to her. Rebecca pounded a fist against the mattress as his wicked, wicked tongue dipped into her once more. "Callum," she ground out, unable to stifle a very unladylike squeal of shaky laughter. "Now!"

His chuckle warm against her thighs, he lifted up, wrapping his hands around her ankles and pulling her down the bed toward him. Arranging her legs around his hips, he went down onto all fours, hands on either side of her shoulders. "I could nae refuse ye, Rebecca," he murmured.

When he slid inside her, she shut her eyes, reveling in the filling sensation, the weight of him across her hips. Opening her eyes again, she swept her hands along the hard, taut muscles of his shoulders and back. He was beautiful, a man accustomed to hard work and with the body to show for it. Fit and lean and large, he dominated every room he entered just by walking in. And since he'd returned, he'd had eyes for no one but her. She'd seen him walk right past lasses with whom he'd dallied as a nineteen- and twenty-year-old and not even blink. Ten years had changed them both, but he bore time's marks both inside and out.

The headboard thumped against the wall with every deep thrust he made inside her, her back arched to take him in more fully. She pulled his face down and kissed him, every inch of her alive and aroused and excited by him.

He changed his pace, practically lifting her from the bed as he stroked into her faster and faster, then slowed again. The shivering light inside her stretched and drew tighter until she shattered, moaning helplessly as she clung to him.

As she finished he sped his pace again, rocking deeply into her until with a low, groaning growl he came, spilling his seed inside her. Panting, Rebecca loosed her legs, tilting her chin up as he kissed beneath her ear and worked his way around to her mouth.

"Ye undo me, lass," he said, rolling onto his back and pulling her over on top of him.

She rested her head on his chest, feeling the fast beat of his heart beneath her cheek. Her own heart matched it, the two of them in perfect harmony—for the moment, at least. He'd acquiesced to her request that they see to Dunncraigh legally, but she could see his impatience in every motion he made, every word he spoke.

"I saw the plans on your desk," she commented, goose bumps lifting on her arms as he twined her long hair around his fingers. "The warehouse and what looked like a distillery."

"Aye. It seems I've a talent for brewing that I nae had for drinking," he returned.

"You're beginning an empire of your own," she pressed, still not certain why that annoyed her, except that men seemed to have the maddening ability to completely separate business from domesticity, and she was damned tired of being treated as part of one but not the other. Especially by a man who'd seen her as a partner when they'd both been children together. "You'll have two empires, if everything works out as you plan."

"Only until the bug turns eighteen, if ye reckon that's old enough. I've nae decided precisely, but it's what I put down for now. I'm nae partial to ill luck, but it happens. I wanted to sign someaught."

Frowning, she lifted her head to look at his face. "What are you talking about?"

"Kentucky Hills belongs to me, nae to the Geiry inheritance. Do ye reckon that eighteen is too young to give it over to Mags? Mayhap one-and-twenty would be wiser." He shifted a little, putting his free hand beneath his head. "And I dunnae care who might be courting her or promising to wed her, I'm making damned certain that it stays with her. I'll nae see the lass marrying for any other reason but that she loves the lad." He sighed. "I admired yer da', but he put ye in a mess when he didnae allow ye to keep Sanderson's once ye were wed."

She continued staring at him, at his relaxed expression and the growing amusement in his two-colored eyes. "You're giving Kentucky Hills Distillery—both distilleries, your warehouses, everything—to Margaret?"

"Aye. I have been listening to ye, Becca. I cannae change yer inheritance, but I can see to it that Mags doesnae lose what she owns. Ever. I'm willing to manage it unless—until—she wants to take it over."

"What . . . What if you have children of your own?"

"If *we*," he returned, emphasizing the word, "have children together, the first lad will have Geiry. The rest can have a share of Kentucky Hills, unless I conjure another brilliant business idea in the meantime."

She couldn't have stopped her smile if her life depended on it. " 'The rest,' " she repeated. "How many children are we having? Not that I've accepted your proposal."

"I reckon four," he said, stretching deliciously beneath her. "Including Mags."

Oh, my. "I was married for nine years and managed to have only one, you know," she commented.

"Then one will do for me," he returned promptly, moving again to wrap both arms around her. "Dunnae expect me nae to attempt to give ye more. What do ye reckon, once a day? Twice a day?"

She snorted. "That might do it, I reckon," she said, mimicking his accent. In truth she and Ian hadn't attempted anything close to that—especially as he became more distracted by what he saw happening to Sanderson's, she realized now. "It's very generous of you to think of Margaret that way."

"I'd have to be a damned fool nae to be wrapped around her wee pinkie. She's the grand lass; I'm just happy to be part of her pack."

Rebecca chuckled again. He made the future sound so grand, and so achievable. All they needed to do, then, was see that he—and she—survived the next few days. She wanted more than a daydream. She wanted the past finished, dealt with so she would never have to worry about anyone attempting to take her present and her future away from her again. And she wanted . . . him.

As for four children, including Margaret, that sounded divine. Their pack, as he would say. Rebecca sank onto his chest again, twirling her fingers idly against his skin. From the amount of time they'd spent in his bed over the past fortnight or so, she could well be pregnant, now. While part of her would be delighted beyond words, the part of her that recognized the look in Callum's eyes—the one that said he remained ready to turn justice back into vengeance if the wind blew southerly—didn't feel ready to face anything so overwhelming while what felt like the entire world kept trying to pull them to pieces and stomp on the remaining bits.

"That's nae a happy expression there, lass," he commented, raising his head to eye her.

And now she had to weigh what she wanted to say very carefully, so he wouldn't go charging off to slay her dragons. "It's . . . wonderful to think of a future," she said, picking each word. "I don't want to get too far ahead of the present, though."

"I ken." One of his hands slid down her back to cup her bottom. "I reckon ye need some more distracting."

"Callum, you are a wicked—"

A shot rang out, freezing the words in her throat. Half a heartbeat later a young scream answered it. Before Rebecca could do more than gasp, Callum had slid out from under her, grabbed his kilt in one hand, and was out the bedchamber door. *What now?* she wondered frantically, yanking on her gown. *Dear God, what now?*

Chapter Nineteen

W here's Margaret?" Callum bellowed as he flew downstairs.

One of the footmen paused in the foyer. "In the garden, m'l—"

"Go put yer eyes on Rebecca and dunnae take them off her. Now!" Yanking tight the knot he'd put in his kilt, Callum ran for the rear of the house. He didn't have a gun with him, but he yanked a claymore free of a suit of some ancestor's armor as he tore past it.

He shoved through the garden door, his heart beating loudly enough that he could hear it in his own ears. If not for the scream he would have thought the gunshot a ruse, something to get him away from Rebecca. But men, armed men, remained in the house. She was safe. "Margaret?" he bellowed.

"Here, my lord."

Agnes, Margaret's nanny. A thousand curses pushing about in his chest, he found the woman, seated in the grass with Reginald in her lap. Waya lay a few feet away. With her black fur it took him a moment to see the splatters of blood around her.

Callum swallowed. "Where's Margaret?" he asked.

"Five men took her," the nanny managed around sobs, as she held on to the wriggling terrier. "One of them hit Andrew across the head, and then Waya—she was very fierce—she bit the man, nearly tore off his arm, and another of them shot her. I couldn't—"

Spying Andrew lying halfway inside a hedge, Callum tossed aside the sword and pulled him free. The footman had a knot the size of a shilling on the back of his head, but he opened his eyes and groaned when Callum shook him by the shoulder. "Are ye alive?" he asked.

"Aye." Andrew started to rub the back of his head, then flinched and changed his mind. "Where's Lady Mags?"

"Gone!" Agnes sobbed again, burying her face in the mop's fur.

"They wore Maxwell tartans," the footman groaned, putting his head in his hands.

Callum ignored that. He already knew. Instead he walked back to where Waya lay, silent and still. Taking a hard breath, holding tightly onto the fury biting into him, he squatted down beside her. "Good lass," he whispered, putting a hand gently on her head.

The wolf twitched. Jolting back into motion, he scooped the animal up in his arms and made for the house. "Water and light," he snarled, heading down to the kitchen.

He laid her on the table there, grabbing up a lamp and trying to part her fur with his free fingers. Someone took the light from him, and he went to work with both hands, cursing as he followed the trail of the ball. It had dug into her chest, lodging into her shoulder. The force must have knocked the wind out of her, but she was whining now.

"Pogue, send for a doctor and get Waya and Andrew

looked at," he said, straightening as he pressed a cloth against the oozing wound. "And have Jupiter saddled."

"Aye, m'laird."

"Get out of my way, and stop following me!"

Rebecca shoved into the room, a collection of armed grooms and footmen dogging her. She stopped as she saw Waya, her hands going to her chest. With her loose blond hair and gray tone she looked more like a banshee of legend than a flesh-and-blood woman.

"Where's Margaret?" she asked, her voice breaking.

"They've got her."

" 'They?' You mean Dunncraigh?"

It had to be Dunncraigh. No one else would dare. "Aye. He couldnae get close enough to ye to convince ye to cooperate, so he found something else that would. They wore tartans so there wouldnae be any question over who did it."

A tear ran down her face as she clutched at his arms. "What do we do, Callum?"

He shrugged out of her grip, moving for the servants' door. "I go back to my first plan," he snapped, pulling open the door and heading for the stable.

"You can't," she protested, running after him. "If you kill Dunncraigh, I'll never see her again. And I'll never see you again. I know it!"

He heard her. He understood her frantic tone, and her worry. To him, though, one thing mattered at that moment—getting Margaret back. He'd wagered everything that the target would be Rebecca, and he'd been wrong. And Mags had paid for his mistake. Waya and Andrew had paid for it, the wolf perhaps with her life.

"I will fetch her for ye," he snarled.

A horse trotted toward him, but it wasn't Jupiter, and it already had a rider. Narrowing his eyes, he noted the shovel leaning against the side of the stable as he looked up. A young man, his expression a mix of haughtiness and nerves, danced a gray gelding toward him. He wore Maxwell plaid as well, Callum noted peripherally.

"I've a message, Geiry," the lad called, keeping out of arm's reach.

"Then deliver it." Holding out his left hand, he flexed the right, ready to grab the shovel and swing.

"It's nae in writing. We're nae fools."

"Ye took the bairn. Ye're dead fools."

The horse fidgeted beneath its rider before the young man brought it back under control. "We'll give her back to ye. Bring the things ye took—all of 'em—and the lass to Maxwell Hall tonight at eight o'clock." He pointed at Rebecca, close behind Callum. "And the lass has but to say one word. I'm to tell ye it's 'aye.'"

Dunncraigh's home, Dunncraigh's men. "Nae," Callum countered. "I'll meet ye out in the open, where ye willnae be able to put a ball through me and bury me in the garden. On the dock. Sanderson's dock. If the wee lass has so much as a scratch on her, I'll murder the lot of ye. Ye'll nae see me coming. But I'll start with *ye*." Callum gazed at the man levelly, daring him to retort.

Instead the lad nodded. "She'll nae be harmed. But ye might want to put some more clothes on before ye meet with yer betters, Geiry."

Callum didn't move. "Eight o'clock. Sanderson's dock. They'd best be there, boy."

"They will be." With that the lad wheeled the gray and galloped down the drive again.

The groom led Jupiter out of the stable. With every muscle and bone in his body Callum wanted to seize the stallion and ride Dunncraigh's man down, beat him until he told them precisely where they'd taken Margaret. This lad would be a cousin at best, though, someone the duke didn't value too highly. No one with any sense sent a potential hostage to negotiate a hostage exchange.

Even so, he took a long step forward, until a muffled sob behind him stopped him cold. "Rebecca," he said, turning around and pulling her into his arms.

She sagged against him. "They took her. They took Margaret."

Wrapping his arms close around her, he lowered his face to her long, loose hair. His anger he could manage. Hell, he'd been coiled with it for ten years. She'd lost a husband and a father over the last fourteen months. Now the same bastards had snatched her daughter. He couldn't even imagine her pain. "They'll nae harm her, lass. Without her, they've nae leverage against ye."

"What do I do? I can't—"

"Nae out here." Callum swept her up into his arms and carried her back into the house. The last thing they needed was someone overhearing them and reporting the conversation to Dunncraigh or Stapp. He set her down on one of the chairs they'd dragged away from the kitchen table. Waya lifted her head to look at him woefully, then dropped it again.

Most of the servants had gathered in the large kitchen, and from the sniffling and hand-wringing and quiet cursing going on around him, each and every one of them had given young Mags a piece of his or her heart. He wasn't the least bit surprised. She owned a good half of his.

The other half of his heart sat rocking in a hard wooden chair, refusing all offers of tea or water or a blanket or whatever else they could think to give her. He took a hard breath, pushing back at his fury. Fury didn't allow him to think. And he needed to think.

Then he knelt at her feet, taking both her hands in his, becoming conscious again of the fact that he was shirtless and barefoot, with nothing between him and the weather but a knotted kilt. "Lass, listen to me. I've a plan. But I need ye to help me with it. Can ye do that?"

"I don't want a plan. I want my daughter back."

With his mind still spinning through possible twists and turns and figuring the odds for their success—and by the devil, the odds needed to be a one hundred percent certainty—he nodded. "Margaret and ye safe is all I care about. I reckon ye know that. But I need ye to trust me."

The glazed look cleared a little from her eyes. "I trust you. And I know how angry you are. We can't—"

"We'll meet them on that pier, and ye'll agree to whatever they ask. That's all I need ye to do. Nae a lie or a trick, or any subterfuge. The truth."

Blue eyes studied his. "You'd let them win? You'd have me marry Donnach?"

"Nae." His scowl would have proven any other response a lie. "But that's *my* part. I know the bastards. I know their finances, their dreams, and their nightmares."

She grabbed his shoulder. "Do not attempt anything that might get Margaret hurt." Her voice broke. "Promise me."

He felt her pain all the way to his bones. "I would die first," he whispered.

Abruptly she released him. "Then go do what you need to do. I'll be here."

Straightening, he leaned in and kissed her. "I'll be gone two hours. Three at the most. Keep lads with ye every moment."

"Ye'll nae be going anywhere alone either, m'laird," Pogue spoke up, his low voice rough.

He wanted to; the day he couldn't see to himself . . . Callum stopped the thought before he finished it. He wouldn't have Waya with him. And without him, Margaret and Rebecca would both be lost. With a curt nod he headed for the side door. "I'll take Malcolm and Johns," he agreed, naming the two grooms.

Outside he ordered two more mounts saddled. He had several stops to make, beginning with Crosby and Hallifax and ending with Judge MacMurchie, and a few more visits in between. No matter the cost, nothing was permitted to harm his two lasses. Aye, he had plans, but none of them would be what damned Dunncraigh expected.

If she'd ever had a doubt about who now commanded the household, the two footmen still dogging her heels despite nearly three hours of demanding they give her room to breathe would have answered that question. Rebecca almost appreciated her growing annoyance, though—it gave her something to think about aside from Margaret and how frightened her daughter must be. And how angry and murderous Callum must be feeling.

He'd given his word not to do anything to endanger Mags, and that was the *only* reason she'd meant it when she'd said she trusted him. Because she could otherwise quite easily imagine him charging through the Maxwell Hall front door and shooting the first person who challenged him. If there'd been a way to be certain they could secure Margaret, she might well have urged him to do just that.

The nerve of these men. Business she could understand, but firstly they'd seized on her father's good fortune and murdered to make it their own. His hard work, his dream, his trust in Ian MacCreath, and they'd stolen it and taken advantage and then killed when they didn't like the percentage they'd earned. And now . . .

Now they'd taken a six-year-old girl, willing to threaten her, to trade her for their own blasted greed. She hated them.

And if Callum hadn't returned from Kentucky, she would have been marrying one of them, fooled, lulled into thinking them friends who had her and Margaret's best interests at heart. But she knew better now. Once he had her hand in marriage and her property in his name, Donnach wouldn't have needed her any longer. Would he have been willing to risk her eventually discovering what he'd done to her father and previous husband? Or would she have died of some mysterious ailment as soon as he could be rid of her without causing undo suspicion? And then what would have happened to Margaret?

She shuddered, wrapping the shawl she'd finally donned more tightly around her shoulders. Just the idea of that spirited little girl alone in the world with no one to look after her but Stapp and Dunncraigh made her ill. And she was with them now.

But in this instance Margaret wasn't alone. As Callum had said, Dunncraigh needed to keep her safe, because at this moment Mags was the only thing between the Maxwells and a bloodbath. And by his words to Dunncraigh's messenger, he'd made certain they knew it.

She heard the front door open, and rushed to the balcony that overlooked the foyer. Callum stood in the entryway, his shirt collar open beneath the heavy black coat he'd donned, and his kilt . . . He wore different colors, she realized abruptly. The Maxwell green and black and red was altered to show more red and thicker bands of black, the green reduced to thin lines and darkened. That was the MacCreath tartan, from before the time they'd joined clan Maxwell. She'd seen it in some of the oldest portraits at Geiry Hall, but she hadn't known any examples of the pattern still existed.

He looked up at her, all sign of humor or anything at all but anger and worry gone from his two-colored eyes. "Are ye well?"

"No, I'm not. Did you do what you needed to do?"

"Aye. How's Waya?"

She tried to be angry that he would ask after his wolf in the middle of much larger worries, but for heaven's sake, Waya had tried to protect Margaret. "Better," she returned, squaring her shoulders as she descended the stairs. "Are you going to tell me what you were off doing?"

He tilted his head at her. "Come to the kitchen with me."

Without waiting for her reply, he headed toward the servants' area at the rear of the house. Her two footmen guards in tow, she followed him. Yes, anger seared through her, anger and frustration at what had happened and at not knowing what to do about it. Blaming him for stirring up this mess might make her feel better for the moment, but logic demanded that she acknowledge how much more dire her—and Margaret's—predicament would have been without his presence.

They'd moved the big wolf to a corner, cushioned by pillows and covered with blankets, a bowl of water and a plate of raw beef on the floor directly in front of her. The uneaten meat didn't seem a good sign, but she opened her yellow eyes as Callum squatted down in front of her.

"The doctor was scared he'd be mauled if he tried to dig out the bullet," Pogue said from beside the big stove, "so we all held her down and I saw to it, myself."

For the first time she looked over at him, to see his

right hand swathed in bandages. "She bit you?" Rebecca asked, more guilt digging at her.

"More like she tried to eat me whole," the butler said, a grim smile touching his mouth. "But we got the damned thing out, and poured yer best whisky on the wound. She lapped up a glass of it, too, and I reckon that quieted her down some."

"I'm sorry I wasnae here to help," Callum said, scratching behind her big black ears.

"Nae. Ye had to see to getting the bairn back," the butler returned stoutly. "And as I wasnae outside to look after her myself, I reckon a bite or two is nae more than I deserved."

Rebecca strode up to the butler. Despite his startled expression she gave him a sound embrace. "Do not blame yourself because evil men do things we could not fathom," she stated.

"Aye," Callum agreed, straightening. "Rebecca has the right of it. The lot of ye give us a moment, will ye?"

With a nod Pogue extricated himself from Rebecca's hug and motioned the other half-dozen servants present to vacate the kitchen. In a moment the two of them were alone but for the wolf and the low whistle of a boiling kettle of water.

"It's nearly time, lass," he said, gazing at her as he offered Waya a small piece of meat.

The wolf sniffed it, looked up at Callum, then delicately took it from his fingers. The same wolf that had nearly cost two men their arms today. And the Maxwell still thought him a drunken boy. They had no idea what they'd done. The thought comforted Rebecca a little. They had no idea who Callum MacCreath was.

"I'd be obliged," he went on, "if ye'd dress in something light-colored. White, or yellow. I ken ye dunnae like doing that yet, but it would—"

"Why the devil do you care what I wear to meet the men who stole my daughter?" she broke in. "I certainly don't."

"Because the rest of us, the men, will likely be wearing dark colors. I want ye to stand out."

She studied his face closely as he straightened. "So I don't get shot by accident," she said slowly.

Silence. "Aye."

Rebecca strode up and dug a finger into his chest. "You promised me that you wouldn't do anything—*anything*—to put Margaret at risk! Do not—"

He grabbed her hand. "Do ye think I mean for the two of us to walk onto that pier with nae a soul to see what happens? Of course I'll have men about. So will Dunncraigh. And if someaught happens, I'll nae see ye shot by accident. Put on a damned light-colored gown."

If it hadn't been her daughter, if the stakes hadn't been so very high, she likely would have run to do as he bade. Instead she yanked her fingers free and put her fists on her hips and lifted her chin. "Not until you tell me what you've planned."

Callum continued to look at her, something very like admiration crossing his lean face. "So ye're nae the lass who'll do as she's told any longer, are ye?"

"No, I am not."

"Good." He pulled several folded sheets of paper from an inside pocket of his black coat. "Then I'll ask ye to sign this."

That wasn't at all what she'd expected. "What is it?"

"Yer shares of Sanderson's. I need ye to sell them to me."

Her heart thudded. With the subsequent ringing in her ears she couldn't be certain she'd actually heard what she thought she'd heard, but even as she tried to fathom why in the world he would bother with that when she meant to marry him and he could have it as her dowry, she understood. He was trying to take her out of the equation again, to remove her from danger.

"Tell me why."

"Lass, ye—"

"I trust you," she stated, over whatever he'd been saying. "I trust you to have mine and Margaret's best interests in mind. What I do not trust is for you to have your *own* best interests in mind. Tell me why you want me to sign my company over to you. Other than to redirect Dunncraigh's attention to you, and to force his hand."

He lifted an eyebrow. "Isnae that enough?"

This was who Callum MacCreath was, she realized. A man who would always put himself, his own safety and well-being, behind that of her, Margaret, and everyone else who'd earned a place in his heart. His mind, his being, simply didn't function any other way. Taking the papers from his hand, she went to the small table in the corner of the kitchen, found a quill and ink, and signed her name to the bottom of the last page. Turning, she handed it back to him. "I would risk everything for you," she said, trying to keep her voice steady. "I can't fault you for feeling the same way about me. *That* is why I signed this."

With a swift kiss he took her hand again and pulled her toward the main part of the house. "Then let's get ye dressed and see this finished."

Chapter Twenty

Callum stepped down from the coach first, slung over his shoulder the satchel containing Ian's ledger, George's journal, and the Duke of Dunncraigh's ledgers and contracts, and put out a hand to help Rebecca to the cobblestones.

A light mist dampened his face, putting a small halo around the lamps lining the street and reducing the harbor to a gray shadow of occasional masts and bobbing ship lights. Men could be anywhere and everywhere, both his and the duke's. Good. The more, the merrier.

Rebecca thought she knew what he meant to do, and he left it at that. He'd pushed Dunncraigh to this point, and he would answer for that. Tonight he had two goals: retrieve Margaret and keep Rebecca out of Stapp's fat hands. And above all, make certain they would remain safe from this point on. Nothing else mattered.

He offered his left arm to her, keeping his right close by the pistol that bumped against his hip with every step. That small gun in his coat pocket and the knife in his boot were his only weapons, and this time, on the one occasion he would have found her most helpful, he didn't have Waya at his side. It felt almost like being short a limb, but she'd done her part. He would do his.

Two additional lamps flared at the head of the pier. Five figures, one less than half the size of the others. His heart began beating again. If they hadn't brought Margaret . . . Callum rolled his shoulders. He didn't have another plan for that contingency. But she stood there, Dunncraigh with a hand on her shoulder keeping her still and directly in front of him, the bastard. In his right hand he held a pistol, pointed down for the moment, at least. The threat, though, was clear enough.

"It didnae have to come to this," the duke said.

"I agree with that," Callum returned, slowing some twenty feet in front of the quartet of men and young Mags. "This is on yer head, Domhnall. Every bit of it."

If the duke didn't like being called by his Christian name, he didn't show it. Instead he gestured at the satchel on Callum's shoulder. "Toss that to Donnach. And it had better hold *every* piece of parchment ye stole from my home."

Callum tossed it into the marquis's waiting hands. "Aye. Even the parchment ye stole from Ian and George Sanderson, first."

"Uncle Callum, I want to go home," Margaret said, her voice quavering.

"Hush," Dunncraigh said, shaking her a little. "I told ye to be silent."

Rebecca's grip tightened on his arm. Resisting his own temptation to comfort the wee lass, Callum kept his gaze and his attention on the duke. "Nae one hair harmed," he said. "That's our agreement. And dunnae bother saying ye wouldnae hurt a bairn. Ye already did, when ye made her half an orphan."

"It's all here, da'," Stapp said, closing the satchel and

handing it to one of the other men. "Now ye send Rebecca over here, Geiry."

He shook his head. "Nàe. Ye give me Margaret, first."

Dunncraigh pulled the lass harder against his legs, the pistol in his other hand twitching. "This isnae a trade, MacCreath. This is ye give me what I want, and when I'm satisfied, I'll give ye what *ye* want."

"Callum," Rebecca breathed.

"I'm nae about to give ye both lasses *and* every bit of paper that proves ye a murderer," he returned, wet running down his face from the mist.

"Ye dunnae have any other choice, lad." Dunncraigh offered a half smile that looked smug even in the fitful lantern light. "Ye thought to outsmart me. *Me.* Donnach, burn the ledger and the journal. And Rebecca, come over here before yer daughter trips and falls into the harbor."

Rebecca gasped.

"Aye, the lass told me she cannae swim. A shame. I recall the tales about ye and Ian and Callum there swimming all about Loch Brenan." He tilted his head a little. "A shame Ian couldnae swim the night he drowned."

"But how many of ye did it take to hold him down after ye beat him senseless?" Callum shot back, watching as Stapp pulled Ian's ledger from the satchel and walked over to the nearer of the lanterns. "And all for what? Some ships?"

"The fact that ye dunnae ken the importance of Sanderson's tells me ye dunnae deserve to profit from it," Dunncraigh returned. "Rebecca. Now. Once she signs the matrimony register and says 'aye' in church, we'll give ye the bairn."

"We seem to be at an impasse, then," Callum said, clenching his free hand. "I've another offer."

"And what might that be?"

With a muffled boom, one of the ships in the harbor blazed into view, yellow and orange and blue light enveloping it halfway up the main mast. Everyone on the pier flinched away from the light, except Callum. He freed his arm from Rebecca and took a long step closer to Dunncraigh. "That's the *Sunrise Star,*" he commented, having to raise his voice a little over the roar of the burning ship. "Part of yer new fleet, I believe."

Dunncraigh whipped back around to stare at him. "Are ye a madman? I've the bairn, right here."

"I wanted to make certain I had yer undivided attention." Moving slowly, Callum drew two bundles of paper from inside his coat. "Yer other six ships out there, the ones ye purchased without getting approval from the two other people who own the company, the ones ye havenae yet finished paying for, are also loaded with thirty kegs each of Kentucky Hills whisky."

"Ye son of a b—"

"Here, in my hands, are agreements handing over my shares in Sanderson's, and Rebecca's shares. To ye." He lifted the papers. "They're signed, approved, and witnessed by a judge and a magistrate. They're yers. All I need from ye is Margaret, and yer agreement to leave the lot of us alone, in peace. The other six ships out there, the entire company. Yers."

He could practically feel Rebecca's shock running cold up his spine. Of course she didn't approve, but since Ian and her father had died she'd clung to Sanderson's as her only security. He didn't approve, either. But it made sense, if Dunncraigh agreed.

"Ye expect me to believe that?" the duke retorted, flinching as the ship exploded again. "Ye'd hand me everything, when for weeks ye've been swearing to kill me. To 'end' me, ye said, and that was ten years ago."

"Killing ye willnae bring my brother back to life. I

reckon if giving ye what ye want will convince ye to leave us be, I can live with that."

The duke looked from him to Rebecca. "Ye want her for yerself. Ye always did, I reckon."

"Take the papers and we'll be done with this," Callum urged, moving another step closer. If the duke had any idea how contrary even making the offer was to his sense of honor and justice and decency, the man would grab the agreements and run for it. "And give Margaret back to me."

Dunncraigh continued to glare at him, white hair painted orange in the reflected firelight. "I am the chief of clan Maxwell," he bit out. "Ye dunnae dictate to me."

"I'm nae—"

"Ye think just because I allowed the Duke of Lattimer to take some useless cotters off my hands that I can be placated? That I've gone soft? I could've had Lattimer's own sister killed, and I decided to be magnanimous. Me. I'm the Maxwell. I'll nae be made a fool of."

All the tales had been true, then, about the duke having to surrender a good thousand clansmen to Lattimer when the cotters decided an English duke cared more for them than did their own clan chief. As for Lattimer's sister, that would be Lady Maxton, Graeme Maxton's bride.

Callum shook himself. Domhnall Maxwell's ravings didn't matter, as long as the duke took the logical route here. "I didnae say ye werenae the Maxwell. I'm giving ye a company, Dunncraigh."

"So ye can go about saying I kidnapped a wee bairn to make ye do it? So ye can tell every man ye come across that I had Ian MacCreath and George Sanderson murdered? So my own clan thinks they can stand up to me and get away with it? Nae. I'll keep the girl, and I'll take the lass. With them both in my household, I reckon ye'll keep yer damned gobber shut."

Lowering the papers, Callum took a deep breath. The man in front of him was clearly coming loose at the seams. An offer of everything he'd been after for ten years had done nothing but anger him. Well, he had another tack to try, but he'd given his word.

"I've been away for ten years, Yer Grace," he said, keeping his voice even. "I dunnae ken what ye might be talking about. All I have to give ye is these papers. And all I ask ye in return is to give me the lass and to leave Rebecca be."

"Da'," Stapp said, still clutching Ian's ledger. "At least let me take a look at the p—"

"Shut yer mouth," Dunncraigh snapped. "Ye should have taken her the second she came out of mourning. I told ye how it should go. But nae, ye had to woo her, as if I give a damn what she thinks. As if she and this little bit of muslin matter."

That hadn't been a confession, but it felt damned close to one. The momentary elation Callum felt, though, strangled into silence when the duke lifted the pistol to point it at Margaret. *No, no, no,* he shouted silently, keeping himself still.

"Ye dunnae like my offer, then," he said aloud, trying to turn the duke's attention back to him. "Listen to this, ye old rat. If I say but one word, yer other six ships burn. And then I'll raze Maxwell Hall. I've a judge already writing up the papers to bring formal charges against ye, and I've sent to Fort William for soldiers. I've sent for yer chieftains to have ye run off from the clan. How much are ye prepared to lose? Because I'll take it all. Ye refused my offer. The only two choices ye have now, Dunncraigh, are to go to prison, or to leave Scotland tonight with naught but the clothes ye have on yer back. Just like I did. Ye're done. Give me the lass. *Now*."

"Donnach, shoot him!" his father bellowed, and lifted the pistol to Margaret's head.

In one fluid motion Callum pulled the pistol from his pocket, aimed, and fired. He'd brought down bucks galloping full tilt through tree-choked ravines, axe-wielding Cherokee warriors running at him with death in their eyes. The Duke of Dunncraigh's head snapped back. A heartbeat later he dropped bonelessly to the pier, then slid into the harbor with a splash muffled by the rain and the fire out on the water.

With a roar Stapp charged at him. Callum dropped the pistol and pulled his knife.

"Stop!"

The roar came out of the rain, followed by the sound of weapons being brought to the ready. The marquis skidded to a halt, but it took Callum a moment longer to decide. But he'd given his word. Justice, not vengeance.

"I reckon ye can pay for yer father's greed," he snarled, shoving the knife back into his boot as Dennis Kimes charged into view, a handful of well-armed Highlanders on his heels.

They might well be there for him, as well—he'd just killed a duke, the chief of his own clan. He'd done what he could to prevent that from happening, but not a damned ounce of him regretted it. That bastard wouldn't be taking anyone else's husband or daughter away from them.

Callum turned his back on the approaching group, instead walking forward to where Margaret stood, her arms straight down at her sides and her eyes screwed shut. He knelt in front of her, the sight of her shaking making him wish he could kill the duke all over again. "Bug," he said quietly. "Ye're rescued."

Her eyes flew open, the right one blue and the left one green, just like his own. Then she flung her arms around his shoulders. "I knew you'd rescue me," she sobbed. "They killed Waya!"

"Nae, they didnae," he answered, scooping her into his arms and standing as Rebecca reached them. "She's bloodied, but I reckon she and the pups will be dandy as daisies."

The bairn grabbed her mother, pulling the three of them together on the pier. "I'm so glad!" she wailed. "And I'm glad you didn't have to marry Lord Stapp, Mama. He was very mean to me!"

"Oh, was he, then?"

Rebecca put her free arm around Callum's shoulders before he could turn around. "It's over," she breathed shakily, kissing her daughter's cheek.

"I kept my word," he said, holding both his lasses tight.

"You did. Thank you, Callum. Thank you a hundred, thousand times."

"I'd do anything for ye, lass. Ye know that."

Callum tried not to see the irony as the nearest tavern was cleared out to make room for him, Rebecca, Margaret, Stapp, all the witnesses, magistrates, local soldiers, and the four clan Maxwell chieftains and one additional guest Dennis Kimes had managed to drag to Inverness, but the Seven Fathoms remained full of old, uncomfortable memories. And it still smelled of beer and piss, even after ten years away.

From the arguing going on at the front of the main room, the captain of the guard wanted him taken into custody, if only for the sake of appearance and to prevent the locals from rioting at the news that a clan chief had been murdered.

"Not murdered," one of the men, a tall, dark-haired one with an English accent, retorted. "I witnessed it, myself, and I'll swear before anyone you please that by his actions Lord Geiry saved his niece's life."

Ah. That would be the Duke of Lattimer, then. "I dunnae ken if ye'd be considered an impartial witness, Yer Grace," the captain returned, confirming Callum's suspicion. The tall lad had smarts enough to look uncomfortable, at least.

"I'm a clan Maxwell chieftain," the second, much more familiar-looking man said. "Do ye consider me impartial? Because if Geiry hadnae taken the shot, I would have."

"Lord Maxton, once again, I ken that this is very emotional for everyone. But we must be certain the letter of the law is being followed here."

"Then put Stapp in irons and march him down to Fort William," Graeme, Lord Maxton returned. "I took a gander at those ledgers, the same as everyone else here. I saw theft, and a damned fine reason for him and Dunncraigh to murder two people, just as Geiry says."

"But Lord Stapp is now the Duke of Dunncraigh." The captain took off his hat and ran a hand through his damp hair. "This isnae what I had planned for my evening."

"What are they fighting about?" Margaret asked, sipping a very watered-down rum and looking sleepy despite the excitement of the past day.

"About whether to arrest your uncle or Donnach," Rebecca replied, her arm still close around her daughter's shoulders.

"Arrest him!" the bairn yelled, pointing a finger at

where Stapp—the new Dunncraigh—sat, surrounded by soldiers. "He kitnapped me, and he shot my wolf!"

"Kidnapped," her mother corrected calmly, and reached across the table for Callum's hand. "I remember this tavern. Do you?"

"Aye. Never thought to set foot here again, though."

Light blue eyes assessed him. "You would have given him all our rights to Sanderson's."

"Aye. I told ye I'd get Margaret back safe, whatever the cost. I would've told ye, but I wasnae certain what I'd need to use."

"I was about to shout at him to just take the stupid fleet, that if he'd given any of us the choice last year we all would have done what you offered." She looked at their entwined fingers. "He won't hurt anyone else. Ever again."

"My laird?" The captain of the guard stopped at the foot of the table.

"Aye?"

"In my opinion ye should take Lady Geiry and the wee lass home. I've talked to every witness, and nae a man but His Grace over there," and he gestured at Stapp, "says ye could have done anything but what ye did."

"And Stapp? Dunncraigh, I mean?" Callum returned. Because while Domhnall Maxwell had been stopped, he couldn't yet say the same for his eldest son.

"Yer man says ye sent for soldiers from Fort William. I reckon we'll hold him at the garrison until the Sassenachs arrive, and they can decide what to do with him. I hear the Old Bailey in London is for lairds going to prison, aye?"

"That's what I hear," Callum agreed. "Thank ye, Captain."

Inclining his head, the officer walked over to where

Stapp and his men waited. Donnach immediately began protesting, but a man used to naught but ordering others about was no match for a half-dozen strapping Highlands soldiers.

Turning to face Rebecca again, Callum squeezed her fingers. "Would ye say I've kept my word to ye, then? I know I kept my word to Dunncraigh."

"Yes. You've more than kept your word, Callum."

He smiled. "Good. Because while this is the last place in the world I'd care to do this, I have to know this damned minute: Will ye marry me now, Rebecca Sanderson-MacCreath?"

A tear ran down her cheek. "Yes. I will marry you, Callum MacCreath. Very, very, happily."

He leaned across the table and kissed her, ignoring the subsequent stir around them. They would have to become accustomed to it. And there was a damned precedent for a marriage to the widow of a man's brother, anyway, at least in the Highlands. And this was the Highlands.

"What is going on?" Margaret demanded, sloshing her drink against the table.

"Your uncle and I are getting married, Mags," Rebecca said, touching his cheek with her hand.

"But are you my uncle or my papa? I'm very confused."

Callum grinned at her. "I'm yer uncle. I'll be standing in for yer papa as best I can, though. Can ye make do with that, bug?"

"The puppies will be mine, though?"

"They'll be a part of the pack, with the rest of us."

Margaret sighed. "Aye. I can make do with that. But I would like at least one of them to be called mine, anyway."

"But ye dunnae mind me marrying yer mama?" he pressed, ignoring Rebecca's chuckle.

"No," she returned, taking another sip of weak rum. "I think you make each other happy, and we're all in the same pack, anyway. Though I also think I may be three sheets to the wind." Setting the mug aside, she rested her head against the table.

Standing, Callum moved around the table and picked her up. She laid her head against his shoulder, her arms and legs tucked against his chest. For a bairn with such a mighty heart she weighed barely more than a feather, and it struck him again how delicate she was, and how close he'd come to losing both her and her mother tonight.

Rebecca slid her arm around his waist. "I love you," she murmured, "and I love that you love her."

Leaning sideways, he kissed her as the rest of the men present moved out of their way. "Thank ye," he said to the Duke of Lattimer, and nodded at Maxton.

"I'm glad I was here to witness it," the duke said crisply, and Callum remembered that he'd been a soldier before he'd inherited the dukedom. "The man ruined far more lives than he protected."

"Aye," Viscount Maxton said, nodding. "I'll sleep better, knowing he's nae about any longer. Ye've done us all a favor, ye ken."

Callum looked over at Rebecca. "I didnae do it for pleasure, and I didnae do it for ye. I did it to protect my own, and because I'd nae other choice. And if this is the end of clan Maxwell, well, he brought it on himself."

"I dunnae think it's the end of the clan," Graeme Maxton commented. "We've all been looking after our own for years, while Dunncraig was busy lining his pockets. Lattimer here's got over a thousand Maxwells masquerading as MacKittricks. Mayhap they'll rejoin us, now."

Lattimer pulled open the Seven Fathoms front door so Callum could pass through it. "Whatever your motives, Geiry, you've taken a stand for a great many people who could never do so themselves. Don't think that'll go unnoticed."

Callum nodded, though at the moment he didn't give a hang who noticed what. All he noticed, all he cared about, was that his two lasses were safe, and that he would never have to leave them. Settling Margaret in one of the coach's seats, he handed Rebecca into the other and sat beside her.

"What did they mean by that?" she whispered, tucking the coach blanket more closely around Margaret as they started back for MacCreath House. "This won't go unnoticed?"

He shrugged, pulling her against his shoulder. "Politics and arguing, I would guess. They can do as they like. I'm figuring Donnach will be needing to sell his third of Sanderson's now, so we'll have a fleet to manage, plus two distilleries and four bairns."

"And wolf mop puppies," she added, twisting to kiss him.

Relishing in her touch, in the quiet intimacy after the evening's chaos, he kissed her back. "I love ye, lass. With every ounce of me."

Rebecca sighed against his cheek. "You made us more than a pack, Callum. We're a family."

Aye, they were. In ways he'd never expected, but now couldn't do without. A pack, a family, their own wee clan—whatever they chose to call themselves, this was precisely what he required in his life. She was what he needed, just to make his heart keep beating. Now and forever.

Epilogue

Three months later . . .

"I dunnae ken why ye've settled on me," Callum said, flinging a rock into Loch Brenan and watching it skip a half-dozen times. "I'm nae a chieftain, and I've nae more than a hundred cotters on my property."

Graeme, Lord Maxton, leaned back against a pine tree and crossed one ankle over the other. "Exactly. Ye've nae potatoes in the pot. That's why."

"If that's what qualifies me, I've a niece with nae a potato in the pot, either," Callum retorted, then pointed at the third man, standing midway between himself and Maxton. "And why is Lattimer here? He's the chief of clan MacKittrick."

Tall Gabriel Forrester, Duke of Lattimer, squatted down as a wee bairn ran up and grabbed the back of his leg. "I'm not a clan chief. I'm a Sassenach landlord whose cotters gave him a nickname." He straightened again, holding the toddler against one hip. "Where's your mama, Kieran?"

"Puppies," the boy returned, laughing and shaking his hands in clear excitement.

"Ah."

"We already voted on it, Callum," Graeme continued, pushing upright as the three of them headed back toward the blankets and tables set out beneath the shade of the pine trees. "All the clan chieftains. We couldnae agree on much of anything but that even his own relations did-nae want any of Dunncraigh's sons, nephews, brothers, or cousins to be clan chief. And we agreed that what ye did was right, and that ye were more fair than ye had to be."

"I'm nae made to be a clan chief." For God's sake, he had a pack, and that kept him busy enough.

Rebecca approached, one of the white, long-furred, long-nosed puppies in her arms.

"They want you to be chief of clan Maxwell, Fiona and Ree say," she commented, looking at him intently.

"Aye. Because I'm nae interested in the task, appar-ently." He glared at Maxton. "Dunnae ye think this'll have all the Sassenachs looking sideways at us, if the man who kills a clan chief gets to become the clan chief? And it's nae a precedent I want to set, considering that I'd be the next one to get a ball through my head."

"We all have our own concerns, our own groups of cotters and industries and cattle and sheep. Ye do, as well, but ye've been gone. Ye've nae had the chance to dig in and ignore the rest of us in favor of yer own."

Marjorie, Lady Maxton, joined her husband, their four-month-old daughter in her arms. "I suggested that since you have an English wife, you'll be more open to having better relations with the Crown," she said, her own tones English and well educated.

Her brother, Lattimer, nodded. "And yet you're a Highlander, and one who's demonstrated the willing-ness and ability to protect his own." He handed the two-year-old bairn off to the slender, redheaded woman who joined them. "Kieran tried to shove me into the loch."

Fiona, the Duchess of Lattimer, laughed. "Och, ye didnae try very hard, did ye, my lad?" she said, lifting the boy up into the air.

Callum looked over the meadow, at the half-dozen puppies of varying blacks and whites jumping about in the flowers as Waya and the mop, along with Mags and Graeme's youngest brother, Connell, rolled around with them and shrieked with laughter. Peace, love, and warmth fell about them like blossoms.

"Give me a damned minute to talk it over with my wife, will ye?" he demanded, and she handed the puppy to Graeme as Callum held out his hand to her.

Together they walked back to the water. He'd chosen this place for the picnic because this was where they'd swum as children, and because it was halfway around the loch from where Ian had fallen. He didn't want to remind her of that, any more than he wanted to continue thinking about it. They'd put a great deal behind them, and he remained uncertain that he wanted more responsibility piled back onto his shoulders.

"You employ half a hundred men from clan Maxwell in the distillery already," Rebecca pointed out, wrapping her hands around his arm and leaning against his shoulder.

"Nae only clan Maxwell, though," he returned. "The warehouses, the ones in America, are full of Highlanders, aye, but from all the clans."

"Precisely," she said.

He sent her a sideways glance. "All the barking's made me a bit deaf, lass," he said. "Could ye explain yerself?"

She chuckled. "For a decade you've brought together Highlanders from all over Scotland, and found a way for them to work together. Doing so within clan Maxwell would be much simpler than that. And you even have the means to help the poorest of them find employment. You own a fleet of ships, two distilleries, three warehouses, and—"

"*We* own all that," he corrected, blowing out his breath. "I'm actually more surprised than anything. I would think I'd be their last choice, nae their first."

"Why? You learned how to survive using your own two hands. I know you never expected to inherit the title. Everything you've done, everything you've learned over the past ten years, makes you the best choice I can think of."

He faced her. "So ye wouldnae mind me having to ride about the Highlands bellowing orders and pretending I'm a king?"

"Stop that. That was Dunncraigh's idea of a clan chief. I know it's not yours. And I think the one question you need to answer is if this is something you want to do? Because it's forever, if you take it on." She leaned up along him, going up on her tiptoes to kiss him softly. "And you can ride about the Highlands all you want. Just don't expect me to stay behind while you're doing it."

"Graeme last knew me ten years ago. He couldnae have seen anything then to give him confidence about me." Callum glanced back toward the viscount, currently muttering about something with his English brother-in-law. Two damned conspirators.

"They saw you at the harbor. And they've seen you since then. They know who you've become." She put her warm palm against his cheek. "I know who you've become."

He grinned. "A couple of months ago ye thought I was the devil."

Rebecca chuckled. "You're *a* devil," she commented,

kissing him again as he wrapped his hands about her hips. "*My* devil. And now you're also the chief of clan Maxwell. And the leader of our little pack. And my husband. And my love."

"When ye put it all like that," he returned, kissing her back, "I reckon it sounds like I can manage it. I do like surprises."

"Do you?" She leaned against his chest, looking up at him with her light blue eyes. "Good. Because I have another one for you. You'll have to wait about six months to open it, though."

He froze. The world slowed around him as what she'd said sank into him, through his skin and his bones and into his heart. "I love ye, Rebecca," he murmured and, grinning, lifted her into the air. "One bairn, two, or four. But ye ken we'll have to stop calling our pack wee."

She laughed, holding on to his shoulders as they twirled slowly. "Call us whatever you like, as long as you keep saying 'ours.'"

He started to answer, but Waya and her pups galloped over to leap around them, followed by Mags and Connell, Reginald, and wee toddling Kieran Forrester. "I can do that," he said, raising his voice to be heard over the cacophony. "Aye, lass! Aye."